C000115553

DUNGEON HEART: THE SINGING MOUNTAIN

DAVID SANCHEZ-PONTON

CHAPTER ONE

There he lay, the fabled "Emperor of the Forge," waiting for death to finally take him. He snorted at the thought. To think that he used to take pride in such outlandish names. The Emperor of the Forge, the Sage of Stone, the Craftsman King, the Lord of Ores... How childish that all seemed now. For all the renown he had gathered from across the world, despite all the fortune and fame he had obtained, death could not be avoided. Soon, he would pass and then his name would become but a fading memory. Perhaps through his crafts his name might live on as a legend, remaining in the world as a myth.

Mak'rit sighed to himself as he stroked his long, braided white beard with his thick hands. He had regrets. One of them was how he had isolated himself from the rest of the world for the last seventy years. Now, at the ripe age of seven hundred and thirty-one years of age, no one was left to see him off into the next world. He cursed himself for his arrogant desire to be left alone. The old dwarf had no one at this point and he knew he would die in his own lonely workshop, deep in the heart of the mountains, where no one would find him.

He had managed to double the age of the average dwarf with

the aid of magic and his own cultivation techniques, but at this point in time he felt death's approach and not even the strongest magic could stop it. His body, now withered away compared to the powerful body he had in his prime, still retained enough strength to tightly grip this last regret. On a simple silver chain around his neck hung a slightly fractured stone with a dull green shine. As always, it fit perfectly in the grip of his large fist, the smooth surface soothing him slightly.

It was the heart of an ancient dungeon. Unlike all other dungeon cores, this one he had been unable to work in his forge. It would not bend to the will of his hammer, nor combine with even the finest metals. It was the one thing beyond even his fabled skills.

He was starting to feel the chill slowly seep into his bones. Despite the thick fur blankets covering him and the roaring fire near his bed, a cold sensation seemed to stealthily crawl into his flesh. He let out a great sigh as he shed a single tear that slid slowly down his face before reaching his proud beard. With his hand still gripping the stone, he began to hum a slow, sad tune. He infused all of his qi and magic into the sound that he created. Knowing that death was at his side, waiting to take his soul into the eternal rest. What point was there in conserving his vast power now?

His voice reverberated with a subtle energy that was difficult to describe, the old dwarven voice that was no more than a whisper resounded through the entirety of his workshop, escaping it and reaching out far into the distance. Hundreds of miles away, people would say that they heard a beautiful, yet haunting melody that whispered into their ears. They would say that the ancient voice of a mourning mountain god was heard that day. The haunting melody of an ancient being that, after around an hour, finally faded away as if it was no more than a dream.

The moment the soft hum of the song ended, Mak'rit Strongarm drew his last breath, and death consumed him.

Or that's what should have happened.

The moment Mak'rit sighed his last breath and his soul began to depart his body, the dungeon heart around his neck began to glow. Unbeknownst to him, when he had released all his magic and qi infusing his voice with it, he had awakened the dungeon core. The core, although damaged, was not dead. It had been in a state of deep hibernation, resisting outside influences as it tried to regain some semblance of the strength it once had.

When Mak'rit let his magic and qi flow from his body without holding back, the dungeon heart had intuitively devoured most of his unrestrained energy, absorbing it like a sponge. The dungeon heart, despite consuming the energy, was still unstable. As the soul of the old dwarf left his body, the starved dungeon heart drew upon it instantly, trying to drink it in as another form of nourishment.

As if defying the grip of death, the dungeon heart struggled to pull the soul of the dwarf into itself. Mak'rit was only a soul now, and he could feel the tug of two forces pulling at him. One force guided him towards what he understood was the vast space beyond, and the other into the now glowing stone clenched in the fist of his dead body. On a whim, he gathered and threw the entire weight of his soul towards the dungeon heart, sensing an escape from death.

The struggle between the two forces lasted no longer than a minute, but for Mak'rit it felt like an eternity as he slowly crawled towards the dungeon heart. It was like trying to swim through mud.

The instant his soul touched the stone, he felt himself being absorbed into it, like a boat drawn into a vortex in the ocean.

The very next moment, whilst still disoriented, he felt a force slam into him, stunning him even further. However, whatever had slammed into him recoiled from the impact as well. Again, the unknown force slammed into him. This time, however, Mak'rit roared and slammed his will back against it. His soul and the unknown force wrestled inside the stone, exerting their willpowers against each other in a perpetual struggle that seemed to drag on for centuries and yet go on for only an instant at the same time. Without a place to run to or to hide, the unknown entity finally began to succumb to the force of Mak'rit's soul. Inch by inch, the unknown entity was pushed back, until it was surrounded by that soul.

Exhausted, both the dwarf and the other entity seemed to collapse into each other, although the winner had been clearly decided.

Mak'rit had won.

With his victory, a surge of exhaustion washed over him and he felt the world start to dim as he began to fall into a slumber. Just before he collapsed into unconsciousness, a notification from the voice of the world flowed into his mind.

Assessment in progress. New consciousness accepted. Species changed. Managing memories. Managing requirements. Managing previous experience. Managing previous skills and knowledge.

Assessment completed. Rare species variant accepted. Expansion of base abilities accepted. New characteristics unlocked.

<<<>>>

<<<>>>

Absorption of original dungeon consciousness beginning.

<<<>>>

WHEN I AWOKE, I was in a place where nothing existed. I felt... odd. Like I had changed. Like I was not quite myself. I could feel nothing, see nothing, and hear nothing. Even the concepts of light and dark seemed not to apply to this endless grey space.

Where am I?

You are here.

?!

A strange voice replied to me. It was oddly androgynous and neutral in every sense of the word. I couldn't tell if the voice belonged to an old or young person, nor if it belonged to a man or woman.

Who are you? I asked.

I was me.

Was? Then who are you now?

Now I am you.

I frowned at this. It was not exactly helpful. I was clearly me, so how could it be me, too?

Then where did I come from?

...I don't know.

Where did you come from?

From below, where the roots of the mountains grow.

Finally, a less cryptic answer. *Then, why am I here?*

Your voice awakened me. I reached out to your voice. Trying to consume it. And failed.

You failed?

Yes. And now I am you.

So I consumed you?

Yes. Soon, you will be all that's left.

I started to understand. It had hoped to consume me, but it failed and now I was absorbing it. As such, it was not quite an individual anymore, but instead it was becoming an extension of me that was slowly starting to lose its individuality. We were melding into one. I frowned at this knowledge. Something inside me resisted the idea of entirely consuming the entity. If I did consume it, I would be alone again, wouldn't I?

I refuse.

I exerted the will of my soul into that thought, and I could feel some sort of force resist me. It was painful to fight against this, as if something in my mind was being twisted or torn. I let out a pained roar as it occurred, but persisted in my efforts. A minute later I realized I had managed to do... something.

Suddenly, a little notification rang into my mind.

<<<>>>

By forcefully stopping the melding process of the dungeon core's consciousness, you have created a separate entity to aid you. Do you wish to name this entity?

<<<>>>

... I am not entirely you?

That's right. I nodded with satisfaction.

Then what am I? Who am I? Why do I exist?

I thought about this for a moment, frowning. In theory, I was supposed to consume this... creature, so it was fair to say that it had become mine. Therefore, I concluded it would be fine for me to selfishly assign a purpose for it.

You are Echo, for you are the echo of the old you, saved from oblivion by my will. Your purpose is to live your life for me. I do not wish to be alone.

<<<>>>

Congratulations! You have named your first creation: [Echo].

<<<>>>

Yes... I am Echo.

I nodded with tired satisfaction. As exhausting as the process had been, it felt satisfying to create Echo for some reason, not to mention that I could still feel that blistering pain in the depths of my being eating at me.

This was how I brought my first creation into existence.

CHAPTER TWO

After creating Echo, Mak'rit had been drained of power and entered a comatose-like state of sleep. For an untold number of days, he slumbered while his soul melded with his new body, completing his transformation uninterrupted. Slowly, his core continued to draw mana into itself, absorbing it steadily from its surroundings.

Days slipped by and turned into weeks, but eventually he awoke, knowing that he had changed. He knew his change was not as basic as just having a different body, but he instinctively knew that his very essence had changed. He *felt* it in his soul the moment he awoke. He understood he wasn't Mak'rit anymore. He was a new being, albeit one based on Mak'rit. He retained the majority of the knowledge of his previous life, but he was still inherently *different* at a fundamental level. Even the name "Mak'rit" didn't feel like it was his anymore.

In fact, he felt like... an infant, for lack of a better word. He felt young and curious ... playful, even. And yet, he had retained all the knowledge that the now dead Mak'rit had accumulated during his centuries of life. Curious, he expanded his senses. He couldn't really see anything, at least not in the conventional sense of the word, but he could perceive everything around him. If he had to describe it, it was more than just normal sight. He could understand the location, the features, the presence, and even the relative energy of everything within a ten-meter radius of himself.

The sheer amount of *information* he was receiving was outstanding, and yet he wasn't overwhelmed by it at all. Turning his attention towards himself, he found that his new body was rather... small compared to what he was used to, and certainly different from what he had expected. Unlike the small and round green stone Mak'rit had carried around his neck, his body resembled a beautiful, deep green emerald that had been cut into a dodecahedron. Furthermore, his new body was bigger than he recalled it being. He estimated it to be a little less than the size of a man's fist.

So... this is the new me? he thought to himself. Even in his mind, his voice sounded young, like that of a teenage boy, brimming with energy and life. He wasn't sure if he liked that change.

"Good morning, master," an androgynous voice greeted him. He turned his attention towards the source of the sound, and perceived a formless cloud of... something, lingering near him. Frowning, he focused on the entity, trying to discern what it was.

Status

Name: Echo
Age: 25 days
Species: ???
Level: 1
Intelligence: 257
Wisdom: 70

An entity created by the true dungeon, ???. Currently, this entity is just a soul.

<<<>>>

He paused in surprise as the information flowed into his mind, before examining the details closely. As far as he knew, it should normally be impossible to see another creature's status. Even to see another creature's level required a special skill or artifact.

"Good morning, Echo," he thought towards her, as he had no vocal cords to produce any sound himself.

"Master, I recommend checking your status window. Some changes have occurred that require your attention."

He mentally nodded towards Echo. He had been so distracted by his new ability to "see" things that he had forgotten to check the most obvious thing. He willed his own status window to open up immediately, and looked over it.

<<<>>>
Status

Species: True Dungeon
Rank: 0
Name: ???
Age:27 Days
Mana: 486
Anima: 9
Floors: 1
Inhabitants: 1
Titles: Legendary Craftsman; Reincarnated One
Abilities: Absorb matter; Alter environment; Break down components; Craftsmanship; Creation; Digging; Destroy creation; Enhancement; Equivalent exchange; Ether manipulation; Evolution; Interdimensional storage; Life bestowal; Life-energy harnessing; Mana absorption; Masterful mana manipulation; Modification of creations; Monster link; Telepathy; Trap building; Transfer dungeon

Resistances: Magic (general); Mind control

He took his time to read through the information carefully. Soon, he had a grasp on all of it and had a decent understanding of his capabilities.

Satisfied with this for now, he closed his status window, only to have the voice of the world speak again.

<<<>>>

Requirements met. Requirements exceeded. Unlocking pathways. Congratulations! You have met all requirements to ascend into the realm of a true dungeon of origins. To begin, please select the starting parameters of your dungeon.

<<<>>>

The dungeon heart looked at the options that suddenly appeared before him, and frowned. Sensing his mood, Echo chimed in.

"Master?"

The dungeon heart looked towards Echo, and sent her a telepathic visual of the options he had obtained.

<<<>>>

Starting Races (Select up to 2)

Animal (Common)
Goblin (Common)
Orc (Common)
Slime (Common)
Gnome (Uncommon)
Imp (Uncommon)

Kobold (Uncommon)
Harpy (Uncommon)
Skeleton (Uncommon)
Zombie (Uncommon)
Construct (Rare)
Elemental spirits (Rare)

<<<>>>

"What do you think of this?" the dungeon core asked, examining the options carefully.

Echo remained speechless for a while, before gathering her thoughts and proceeding to speak. "Master, this is beyond what I could have expected."

"Pardon? What do you mean?" The dungeon core focused on Echo, genuinely curious.

"Most dungeons are only presented with the common starting races and are only allowed to choose one species. Named or the so-called 'Phantom' dungeons may acquire the common choices and the uncommon ones and they as well may only choose one species. The only dungeons that are offered rare species are Legendary ranked dungeons. Master, it is my belief that your potential surpasses that of a Legendary ranked dungeon, hence your ability to choose two starting races. Choosing two starting races is a huge boon, as it allows the development of two species at once, unlocking two evolution trees in the process, instead of just one. Please note that the more rare the species is, the harder it will be to develop."

The dungeon core thought about that for a moment. His knowledge from the time when he was still Mak'rit told him that this was something mind-boggling indeed, considering that there were only six official ranks for dungeons: Common, Rare, Unique, Phantom, Heroic, and Legendary. Anyone capable of clearing a fully developed Phantom class dungeon could be considered a national treasure and anyone capable of clearing a Heroic level dungeon was awarded the title of hero. The fact that no one in living memory had conquered a Legendary ranked dungeon just showed how powerful, and rare those dungeons were.

Putting those thoughts aside, the dungeon heart focused on the task at hand again. "I see... Well, let's have a look then."

He selected each and every option, and read the information that was available for each species carefully, utilizing the full extent of his other life's knowledge to make an educated decision. He decided against slimes, despite their versatility and various evolution paths, for they were easily destroyed. If he had the misfortune of being found by a strong group of adventurers soon, they would easily clear a swarm of common slimes in minutes. After that, he instantly decided against any zombies and skeletons, as dungeons that focused on undead beings were often eliminated by most kingdoms and religious factions in the world. He also eliminated imps for that reason, as they were a type of lesser demon. If anything, demonic dungeons were eliminated with even more prejudice than even undead dungeons.

That narrowed down his choices by nearly half, and so he began to carefully weed through his options until, taking into consideration several factors, he settled on his two starting races.

Kobold: Kobolds are relatively weak monsters with an average breeding rate. It is said that they are the distant descendants of the powerful dragons. They are intelligent enough to communicate basic ideas to one another and do so through the use of a primitive language. Evolution path moderately defined and well diversified.

Animal: Dungeons that select [Animal] as their starting race are able to select from a small variety of animals at first and tend to be relatively weak before evolving. The available options will become more numerous as the dungeon evolves and as its knowledge of animals increases. Animals offer a variable breeding rate, large ecosystems, and wide selection of species, in exchange for differing evolutionary processes that are usually lengthier than those of other creatures.

These selections felt right to him. Animals would provide him a large selection of creatures, and the Kobolds would offer acceptable protection while he developed his animals. He was very tempted to select constructs, as they seemed to be an excellent option for him, but he was disappointed at the fact that he would only be able to create dirt golems at first. Likewise, elemental spirits begin with weak little sprites that can hardly be a threat to the average villager, let alone an adventurer. Selecting either option felt suicidal to him at this point.

Thus, he had selected Kobolds and Animals. Feeling satisfied with his selections, the dungeon selected his two starting races, only to receive a new message.

Processing selection... Complete. Species options added to available creations. Further options must be unlocked to be made available.

<<<>>>

Please select your starting traits. Traits will help define your dungeon and will have numerous effects on your dungeon. Please select your starting traits carefully.

<<<>>>

Dungeon traits (Select 3)

Alter Perception (Invaders)
Bad Luck Increase (Invaders)
Dungeon Laws
Enhanced Monster Alterations
Miasma Trap
Monster Loyalty
Monster Wisdom
Monster Spawn Timer
Puzzle Rooms
Safe Zone Removal
Safe Zone Timer
Teleport Traps

The dungeon looked at the traits with conflicting feelings... this time there were no descriptions available for any of the presented options. In other words, he had to guess what each option did just from the name. Though, thankfully, the names gave him a decent enough guess as to what each option did... that and he had a little helper who might be able to shed some light on the issue.

"Echo, which monster traits did you have when you were a dungeon and what did they do?"

He felt Echo come closer with its ghostly body, curiosity rolling off the entity known as Echo in small waves.

"Master, I only had one choice, as I was a Unique class dungeon. I selected dungeon laws, which, I later discovered, enabled me to create rules that had to be followed in certain areas. It was very useful to lock down invaders that relied on brute force alone. I am unaware of what the other options do."

Nodding at that knowledge, the dungeon heart thanked Echo

and instantly selected that option. It sounded like it would be a versatile tool for him to use. As for the other two options... He selected [Enhanced Monster Alterations] and [Monster Loyalty] since they sounded like they would enhance his monsters directly. Moreover, if there was an option to increase the loyalty of his creations, shouldn't it be taken? There was no guarantee that every creation he made would be instinctively loyal to him, after all.

Processing selected traits... Complete. Processing combination of traits... Congratulations! You are ready to begin building your dungeon. Good luck!

Did the voice of the world just wish me good luck? The dungeon felt uneasy about that for a moment, before a surge of information washed over him like a tidal wave. Exhilaration filled him as he suddenly gained knowledge that had been beyond him even in his previous life. He now understood so much about the flow of mana, the movement of the elements of life, how to create matter from mana, and even how to break down and rebuild bone into harder and stronger materials. And these were just a few of the things he now understood!

He gasped in his mind, basking in the feeling of his newly gained knowledge. He soon realized that, along with his knowledge, he had gained... urges. He yearned to learn. He desired to expand his territory. He *needed* to create!

Grinning in his mind, he looked around with his newfound powers and inspected the room where his old body had died. Oddly enough, even after just 25 days, only the bones of his body were left, as if the flesh had been picked clean with surgical precision. He made a mental note to ask Echo about it later. But for now, he knew what he had to do.

He expanded his senses, reached out with all the power he

could muster, and let his mana infuse the walls of what once had been his home. It was time to start creating a *proper* home now.

He would build a dungeon so great that even the gods would stare at it in wonder and awe.

CHAPTER THREE

The first thing I did was extend my power until it permeated the walls of the place that was once my home. To be honest, my home was never that large to begin with. It consisted of just three rooms: a kitchen, a forge, and a bedroom. I suppose it could be counted as a four-room dwelling, if you included the small bathroom that was wedged between the bedroom and forge.

Surprisingly, it took me an entire day to expand my territory until it covered the entirety of this place. Even though my home couldn't have been more than 30m x 30m, it still took quite some time to "claim" the area by infusing my mana into the walls. I suppose you could say that the entire dungeon was a living being. You could think of the dungeon core as the brain and soul, while the dungeon itself was the body. Maybe the monsters and traps would be kind of like an immune system of some sort?

At any rate, I had a lot to do now. Even though I reclaimed what had once been my room in one day, it still took me another three days to reclaim the one-kilometer long hallway that led from the forge all the way to the outside of the mountain. The hallway was narrow, but I'd have to wait some time for my mana to permeate the walls. I also noticed that the farther away an area was from me, the dungeon heart, the longer it took to claim it. I asked Echo about it and the little ghostly entity simply said that it was due to mana density.

Apparently, dungeons are like gateways for mana for the world. The dungeon core takes in ether from the earth and then channels and refines it into mana in large quantities. Naturally, this meant that, in a dungeon, the area with the highest concentration of mana could be found right next to the dungeon heart, while the lowest concentration would be at the point farthest from the core. Interestingly enough, some of the mana did escape the dungeon through the entrance, which in turn spread out into the area surrounding the dungeon. That said, the concentration of the mana that escaped was much lower than the mana found in even the first room of the dungeon.

The only thing left to take over was the entrance of my new dungeon. Once that was complete, it would officially become a dungeon! I must admit, I felt rather excited about this right then. Seconds ticked by, turning into minutes, and minutes flowed into a full hour before I felt something shock me like a spark of electricity.

Congratulations! You have successfully created a basic dungeon layout! By creating rooms, hallways, and an entrance, you have opened yourself up to the world. For managing to create a dungeon in under a week, the title [Eager Creator] has been earned. This title decreases the amount of time needed to produce creations by a modest amount. Step 1 of 3 complete.

I briefly looked at the message and nodded to myself with satisfaction. Now that I had finally claimed the entrance, the hallway, and the rooms that used to be my old home, I felt... good. I felt a satisfied sense of accomplishment, like a warm fuzzy feeling. But even though I had great luck in being able to *claim* these hallways and rooms instead of *creating* them (which would have required me to spend about three times more mana than just claiming them), I was currently low on mana. I had a total of 110 [Mana Points] and I had managed to figure out that I could naturally gather about 21 MP per hour. Considering that I had not slept at all while I was claiming these walls, that meant I had spent well over 1,800 MP on just claiming things.

I shuddered mentally at the thought. The average sorcerer of mid rank only had between 120 and 160 MP and it took said sorcerer roughly 12 hours to refill their mana pool. In other words, I was a magical powerhouse.

Now I understand why even small, lesser dungeon cores are worth a small fortune, I thought to myself. I had worked with dungeon cores before for creating tools and items of tremendous worth, but I had never really realized just how amazing a living dungeon core could be. If a dungeon core could retain even a fraction of its ability to absorb and channel mana, then it could be a powerful component in any magical tool or artifact.

"Master?"

I heard Echo, and put my thoughts aside for now.

"Yes, Echo?"

"I recommend creating monsters as soon as possible. Since you have completed the entrance, mana will start to permeate the area around the dungeon and it will likely attract visitors."

"Visitors?" I seriously hoped she wasn't talking about adventurers right now; I was definitely not ready for that.

"Yes master, the mana will likely attract certain wildlife, and I do not recommend leaving yourself unprotected."

I let out a sigh of relief at that answer. I had almost forgotten about that. Animals with an affinity for mana will naturally gravitate towards areas of high mana concentration.

"Right," I grunted towards her mentally, "let's get to this then."

Instinctively, I knew how to create monsters and creatures. A simple explanation would be that you weave mana into matter. The quality of the resulting creature depends heavily on your knowledge of what you're trying to create, your proficiency at manipulating mana, and your creativity, in addition to the amount of mana you used.

All of this was just fine with me, because I was not called the "Craftsman Sage" in my previous life just because the name was catchy! I was a first-rate craftsman, after all, and the possibility of creating things out of pure mana intrigued me so much that it fired up my spirit.

I reached out with my mind and willed my mana to condense into a visible mass. I didn't have much mana to work with, so I decided to create a few small creations to begin with. I willed the appropriate menu window to open and looked at the options while holding my mana at the ready.

Creation menu

Creatures
Flora
Traps

My eyes wandered to the second option and briefly opened it, more out of curiosity than anything; I hadn't expected plants to be a part of this menu, after all.

<<<>>>
Creation menu: Flora

Basic Cave Moss

<<<>>>

That's it?! Isn't that kind of anticlimactic? I was expecting something a bit more... I don't know... diverse. I grumbled with disappointment. This was definitely not nearly as exciting as I had planned... but at least the cost was quite low. Ten MP for a square meter of moss. I sighed and finally decided I might as well give it a try.

I selected the moss as my first creation and let myself follow the information I had in my mind about the basic cave moss without putting much thought into it. My skill [Creation] would take care of it for me while I was just focused on the process. My job was to analyze the process carefully, as I carried out my little project, and find ways to improve it.

My mind willed the mana into a dense, mat-like structure, which I then refined into a detailed structure. I could feel my skills set to work and create the fine details of the moss. Finally, the magical structure solidified into a luscious green bed of moss.

"Well... that was easy," I said to myself with uncertainty. Admittedly, my skill had taken over and made most of the moss almost automatically, which didn't quite sit well with me. It felt almost disappointing how easily I had created this simple form of life. On the other hand, I had gained some very interesting insights into the creation process.

Frowning to myself, I started the process again, this time directly guiding my skill as it worked. I minded the little details and even decided on making the moss fluffier in appearance, making it look more appealing. It took about two-and-a-half times longer than it had taken previously, but the result was satisfying. The moss looked more vibrant and soft, almost as if inviting people to reach out and touch it. Surprisingly, I found that it had cost me eight MP instead of ten. I imagined that crafting something yourself reduced the MP cost as opposed to simply letting your skill do it for you.

Satisfied with this conclusion, I smirked to myself and expanded my consciousness over the entirety of the dungeon.

Let's have some fun, I thought to myself, grinning in my mind as I opened the animal creation list.

OVER THE NEXT THREE DAYS, I experimented with the creation of a number of small animals, since I didn't want to start creating kobolds without having proper mastery over more simple creatures. Besides, a single kobold was worth 100 MP, so I couldn't create them willy-nilly. Any reduction to the cost was highly welcome.

I had started with simple insects, such as flies, small spiders, and other small, harmless bugs. I changed their color, their size, their carapace, and altered individual body parts like the mandibles or legs. Once I had become satisfied with the insects, I moved on to small mammals, which were limited at the moment to common brown mice.

The mice were fun to play with, especially because I discovered that I could influence my creations more than I thought I would be able to. Funny story about that, really. The insects I had left alone started to eat the moss and they began to multiply, and the mice started to eat the insects. I was worried that my dungeon would become overrun by mice, and so I tried to do something about it. Thanks to my sudden moment of inspiration, I discovered that I could further modify mice to even control the rate at which they reproduce! It was a fascinating discovery.

However, when I mentioned it to Echo...

"Master, the only reason why your creations are acting like this is that you haven't given them any orders, so they are just functioning based on instinct."

"Orders?" I asked, "And what do you mean acting like 'that'? Don't all animals have to eat and reproduce? Why do you think I decided on my first species to be animals? I need them to create the base of a food chain!"

It was then that I felt confusion in Echo.

"But Master..."

Oh no... I could sense that she was going to say something that might bring down my logic.

"Master, you didn't need to do that? Dungeon creations are perfectly capable of surviving on just the mana that exists in your dungeon."

I felt my heart break a little at those words. My carefully laid out plan...was it all for nothing then? Could I have chosen a much more powerful option, such as elemental spirits or constructs?

It was at that moment that my thoughts were interrupted by a window that popped into existence.

Congratulations! For creating a basic ecosystem where your creations fight for survival, you have met the special requirements for the secret title "Guide of the Bloody Evolution"! Title increases growth rate of living creations in your dungeon, allowing a faster natural evolution!

I cheered to myself and smugly showed Echo the notification windows that had appeared for me.

"See? It was not pointless." I am not sure if I was speaking to her or to myself when I said that, but it made me feel better, regardless, so who cares?

Anyway, I was pretty happy about the title. According to Echo, evolution is usually a lengthy process, since the creature must survive long enough to accumulate enough experience and power to evolve, let alone to evolve into a variant that requires special criteria to be met. Anything that speeds that up is very welcome indeed.

IT WAS another four days since I received the notification about my evolution title before I was confident enough to start creating kobolds. By this time, I had already experimented to my heart's content with the mice. I even managed to create a variant called "black dungeon mouse," which, as the name suggests, is a black mouse whose body is roughly 30 cm long, and the tail is another 30 cm long. It's not very threatening on its own, but it is quite a decent hunter if I do say so myself. A single black dungeon mouse is capable of beating back five full-grown brown mice on its own. I made this little guy able to prey on the smaller brown mice too, just to help keep their numbers down.

Anyway! Back to the important stuff, today I would be building my first kobolds! Hurrah!

Thanks to the mice being so cheap (only 15 MP per brown mouse), I had managed to save up quite a bit of MP. Additionally, every time someone or something died in my dungeon, I could absorb most of them back. I figured I was getting a good 99% of a creature's energy back into my system when I absorbed them. The remaining 1% of the energy went to whatever other creature killed it. Ergo, monsters could also act like mana batteries for me! While the rate at which I gained mana was fixed, the fact that I could "store" mana in a creature without letting it dissipate was great! Thanks to this, I had managed to save up about 1,100 MP, meaning that I had plenty of mana to start creating kobolds.

I mentally steadied myself, and prepared to create my first kobold. I stilled my mind and thought about all the information I had stored in my mind about kobolds. Short creatures, about 150 cm in height for females, 155 cm for males on average. Mostly reptilian in appearance, like a lizard that walks on its hind legs...

except that its legs are longer, and the arms more like those of a human, and they walk more hunched over, almost like an ape. They have scales that are slightly tougher than human skin, which offers them some basic protection. Their teeth are short but sharp, defining them as mainly carnivores.

I focused my mana and started crafting the first kobold. Carefully, gently, and slowly, I moved my mana in sync with my inherent skills, guiding it, slowing down the process enough so that I could manipulate the details of my creation. I imagined the scales, perfectly aligned, fitting next to each other flawlessly. The teeth pearly white and well aligned. The eyes would be the color of honey. The scales a deep forest green.

As I worked, I didn't notice that hours slipped by and I barely noticed that I added a bit of extra mana here and there, making sure that everything was working well. After what was probably three hours of non-stop concentration, I finally finished. The kobold was created.

The creature took a deep shuddering breath and looked around confused for a moment, before laying eyes on me. His eyes opened wide and he emitted a shuddering hiss before dropping to his knees before me, clearly submitting himself to my will. I looked at him and felt truly satisfied. For the standards of a lizard man, this specimen was beautiful. Scales perfectly wrapping around him, a strong and thick tail, not a single blemish on his forest green hide, no crooked teeth, no dull eyes... yes, I was pleased.

Checking my MP, I noticed I had used up exactly 110MP. It would appear kobolds are more expensive, even though I created him by hand. This was probably because I manipulated the details of creation, which increased the cost. Oh well, it was worth it!

I created three more kobolds, two female and one male. They were all gorgeous specimens of their race, and I felt quite proud of my creations, despite the fact that I spent about nine hours total creating all of them. Thankfully, the creation of the other three was far quicker, since I used my first kobold as a template for the rest of them.

<<<>>>
Congratulations! You have created enough creatures in your dungeon to complete the second step of your dungeon setup! Step 2 of 3 complete.
<<<>>>

Once again the mysterious window had appeared! It seemed that I was one step closer to completing this dungeon now. At least, now I wouldn't be completely defenseless.

<<<>>>
Congratulations! Due to your advanced self-awareness, you have now entered the final step. Please choose your name.
<<<>>>

For a second I was surprised by the request. I was about to reply with Mak'rit, before I thought better of it. Perhaps it was not such a good idea to name a dungeon heart with the name of the most famous blacksmith and craftsman in the last thousand years.

I thought about it for a moment, before I settled for an old nickname that felt appropriate.

"Smit. My name is Smit."

The window popped out of existence from my mind, but I felt a sudden happiness now, like a wave of warm water bathing my soul. A name. I had a name now.

<<<>>>
Acknowledged. Dungeon of Smit accepted. Welcome to the world as a fully fledged dungeon!
<<<>>>

Smirking to myself mentally, I looked around, and realized that all the creatures in the dungeon were looking at me, kneeling as if in reverence. I basked in my accomplishment for a minute, before coming back to the real world. I didn't have much time to relax after all. It was a small miracle that I hadn't had anything come into my dungeon yet. By now, someone or something must have detected the mana fluctuations that were coming from my dungeon.

I frowned at that thought. I should start stepping things up now that I had the basics covered. Looking around, I figured that this main room was fine enough for now. I would leave what used to be my forge room and my bedroom as they were, and turn them into my main chamber. But I couldn't create much more with just these few rooms and a long hallway. Any experienced adventurer would crush me if they decided to investigate this place seriously as it was right now.

With this in mind, I nodded to myself and set myself a list of things to do.

It was time to expand.

<<<>>>
Status

Species: True Dungeon
Rank: 0
Name: Smit
Age: 34 days
Mana: 760 MP
Anima: 12
Floors: 1
Inhabitants: 13 Species
Titles: Eager Creator; Guide of the Bloody Evolution; Legendary Craftsman; Reincarnated One
Abilities: Absorb matter; Alter environment; Break down

components; Craftsmanship; Creation; Digging; Destroy creation; Enhancement; Equivalent exchange; Ether manipulation; Evolution; Interdimensional storage; Life bestowal; Life-energy harnessing; Mana absorption; Masterful mana manipulation; Modification of creations; Monster link; Telepathy; Trap building; Transfer dungeon

Resistances: Magic (general); Mind control

CHAPTER FOUR

S mit wasted no time at all in getting to work with the dungeon itself. He let his creations have their fight for survival while he focused on expanding his domain. Naturally, the four kobolds quickly asserted themselves as the apex predators, hunting rats and eating them raw regularly. Smit wished that he had larger animals for them to hunt, and thus that way they could grow quicker, but that was not to be... not yet, at least. When he grew enough, he would unlock even more creatures, so he was confident that it wouldn't be long before he could do that.

Now that Smit had created a decent environment with "survival of the fittest" as the core value, he set about to work on the dungeon itself. He quickly discovered a few things between experimenting and talking with Echo. First, there was a theoretical limit to how extensive he could make each floor of his dungeon, and it depended on how much mana he produced. The more mana he produced, the more mana could permeate the stone that surrounded him, and the further he could expand his territory. One fun fact that he discovered as he let mana permeate the stone around him was that, once he created a room and let his mana permeate the stone, the stone became much harder than usual.

Secondly, he became aware that by deconstructing rock to create a room, he could analyze anything he deconstructed to produce more of it. Oddly enough, when he deconstructed the rock he could either store the stone he had removed in a sort of pocket dimension inside of him, or break it down into smaller components, and even use it to create mana. This was a fantastic surprise for him since it allowed him to store matter that he could use for the future instead of crafting everything out of raw mana. Interestingly enough, Echo had never had the ability to convert stone into mana, or store stone. Instead, she had been able to store specific items such as swords, but she could not revert the process of creation to degrade stone into mana.

The last discovery he had made was probably the most significant of them all, however. By expanding his dungeon and creating new rooms, he could increase the regeneration of his mana! That was a major discovery for him. Creating what he would call a "standard room unit," which was a cubic room in which each side was two meters long, he felt his regeneration rate for mana increase slightly. He was fairly certain that it was less than even one MP per hour, but that was fine. This discovery meant that as long as he increased the size of his dungeon, he could increase his natural production of mana, and therefore he could create more things!

Smit lost no time in expanding everything that his mana had permeated through. He began with a simple design. Since his first floor was currently a kilometer-long hallway and his core room, he decided to simply expand along that hallway. Had he not been in a rush he would have taken his time in creating a miniature maze right from the start, but given that he could have unexpected visitors at any moment, he didn't really have the luxury to be fancy. Safety first, appearances later.

He decided on creating three rooms first. One near the entrance, one in the middle of the hallway, and one near the core room. Each room was oval in shape, reaching seventeen meters in the long axis of the oval, and ten in the short axis. The ceiling was fairly low too, reaching a height of only three meters. He had a sudden inspiration, however, and he opted to make all the rooms look unrefined for the moment, leaving a few stalagmites protruding from the ground haphazardly and some stalactites hanging from the ceiling in such a way that anyone swinging a large weapon might find their attack interrupted by a stalactite if the person wasn't careful.

Admittedly, he did toy with his new rooms a little. As a craftsman, he couldn't help but to have some standards of appearances, even if he was going for the "natural cave" look.

He started off with the stalagmites and stalactites, adjusting them just a little so that they were a bit more smooth than normal, and giving them a bit of a pearly shine. Next, he spread moss in the rooms, using a thin layer to cover the sides of the room. This of course, gave the rooms a look of being ancient, which would play in well with the intimidating look of the stalagmites and stalactites.

And yet it was missing... something. He pondered this dilemma for a while, before he snapped his fingers with a grin. Water. It was missing water.

Stalagmites and stalactites could only be produced by water anyway, so he decided to add some dripping water to create puddles, and this should help create a better atmosphere in the dungeon. However, the problem lay in how to maintain a slow and constant water flow into his dungeon without making it excessive. He eventually concluded that he should just do it through the simplest method that would work underground, without the need to modify the entire mountain: water stones.

Water stones were a type of elemental magic stone that, as the name suggested, produced water in nature. As a craftsman, he knew that these stones were valuable, as once refined they were fantastic conductors for water-attribute spells. These stones were rarely found in large sizes, and thus expensive.

Nevertheless, Smit was a dungeon! He could create any kind of mineral as long as he had enough mana. He willed himself to create a small pebble about the size of a pea. It would be a deep blue color, no impurities of course, as he would rather a good conductor for the mana to produce adequate pure water. It took him a good hour to get it right, since he had to create the stone from scratch instead of using knowledge given to him through absorption. Thankfully, as he had worked with elemental stones extensively, he knew them down to their last detail. Had he not known them so extensively, reproducing one would have been nearly impossible.

Once he had produced one such stone, and tested that it worked properly, he produced several of them at the same time using his creation skill. Soon, one hundred and thirty-five stones were created, costing just over 250 mana. He then embedded those stones across the ceiling of the three rooms, making them appear as tiny glowing blue stars in the darkness of the cave. Of course, he made sure to wedge the water stones tightly in the ceiling, making it nearly impossible to pull one out.

With this, he modified the rate at which the stones produced water from the air that permeated the rooms, and he managed to bring to life the atmosphere he wanted, creating a few puddles in the process. With one last flare of creativity, he made a meter-wide puddle in the last of the three rooms, right against one of the walls. On the wall just above the puddle, he placed a small cluster of five water stones, creating a miniature spring that flowed down the side of the wall to refill the puddle whenever it was low on water. The puddle was only about ten centimeters deep, but it was a nice touch, and big enough for the kobolds to have a drink. He was sure they would appreciate pure water instead of only drinking the blood of their raw prey. At least he thought it would be a welcome change.

Satisfied for the moment with these adjustments, he barely noticed that two days had passed while he toyed with the details of his new rooms. Then again, the fact that he was a dungeon core meant he needed no sleep, so he could hardly be faulted for losing track of time.

There was one thing that surprised Smit, however, and that was the cost of the rooms. They had not been expensive at all, at least in comparison to what he expected them to be. Each room had cost about 237 MP, and each room was roughly four hundred and one cubic meters in volume. That was large enough to fit three peasant houses from a human village side by side, although it would have been a tight squeeze. Proportionally, creating a monster was actually vastly more expensive than creating a room. Even when he added in the cost of the stalagmites and stalactites, the cost of each room did not exceed 260 MP.

Apparently, creating life was a much more intricate process and thus required more energy. When he thought about it, it made sense though. Any living organism had to grow, adapt, develop, reproduce, survive, and well... live. You could not compare that to a simple rock.

As he contemplated this newfound knowledge, he was brought back to reality by a sudden tingling feeling in the back of his mind. Something had come into his dungeon.

I QUICKLY FOCUSED on the intruder, anxiety flaring for only a moment before relaxing. It was only a snake. It was probably a young one too, as it couldn't have been longer than seventy centimeters at most. Sighing with relief, I watched the creature cautiously slither into my dungeon. However, its presence made me... hungry, so to speak? I suppose that the feeling I got must be the work of my dungeon instincts.

I decided this would be a good time to test out the strength of my dungeon mouse. I chuckled at the thought of a snake getting destroyed by a mouse, but I was fairly confident that a small group of them could take out the snake. Sending out a kobold would be overkill after all.

With a mental command, three of my black dungeon mice converged near the snake, and marched towards it. They are simply animals, so they couldn't create any sort of formation on their own. I had to mentally guide each of them so that they surrounded the snake from a distance. The snake was clearly confused though, as it hesitated, trying to keep an eye on all three mice. I chuckled, and simply let the mice swarm the snake from three different sides.

The result? Easy victory. The snake seemed to have some sort of paralyzing poison, but could only attack one of the mice at a time. One of the mice died, but the other two managed to tear apart the snake's throat while it was distracted. I let the mice eat part of it, before I started to consume its body.

Congratulations! You have absorbed your first creature that is not from your dungeon. You have absorbed a [Green Sap Snake]. You now have broken down and analyzed the snake, allowing you to create more of them under your command.

I hummed curiously at this. Information certainly flowed into my mind regarding the snake. It was a common snake that has weak paralyzing poison. It can kill rodents, maybe even foxes if the snake reaches its adult stages... but I seriously doubted that it could kill anything larger than that. Perhaps I would be able to play around with the species and change it like I did with the mice, but that would come later.

Even though I increased my mana regeneration rate by 14 MP per hour, I still couldn't play with this as much as I wanted. A snake would cost about 23 MP, so I thought I would just create a few and let them wander around the dungeon. Hopefully they would grow stronger.

Speaking of stronger, the two mice that survived the encounter with the snake were clearly a bit larger now. They were two of my most vicious mice to begin with, having hunted on their brethren constantly, growing stronger by the day. But now I felt that they had gained a bit of strength. I hypothesized that if they can keep this up, I might be able to trigger an evolution in one of them soon.

GAT MOVED through the mountain quietly, tracking the game that he had been hunting for the last few hours. He was quite far from the village, already almost two days away. But that was unavoidable as he could not come back with a common rabbit or deer for the ascension ceremony, specially not when he was the youngest hunter in the village. In four days a new village chief would be selected, and a feast would be in place. He needed to bring something special.

Such was his luck that he finally stumbled upon the tracks of a deer hare. This was perfect. Deer hare are essentially very large hares with antlers that resemble those of a deer, and known for their magnificently tender meat. By the size of the tracks, this delicious animal must be at minimum as big as a medium sized dog, and probably even larger than that. It was perfect.

The only trouble lay in killing the sly creature before he was noticed. If the hare caught wind of Gat before he could take him out, he might never find the critter again in time, especially considering their notorious running speed. That was the thing about hunting; one could not underestimate their prey.

However, Gat became puzzled. The tracks led further and further up the mountain, which was rather unusual for this breed of hare. They much preferred the depths of the forest, where there were a lot more trees and roots to hide and the herbs they were known to prefer. After another hour tracking the hare, Gat saw him about two hundred meters away between some small trees, near the mouth of a cave.

Pausing to look around, Gat felt an odd sensation wash over him that he had not noticed before. It was almost like a gentle breeze that caused a slight tingle on his skin. Except that there was no wind blowing at the time. He looked around curiously, pushing his orange-red hair out of his eyes. He could see nothing that stood out. The trees were more scattered and a bit smaller than at the foot of the mountain, but that was normal when you are halfway up a large mountain like this one. The only things that looked out of place were that hare and the cave.

Frowning, he tried to shake the feeling off but it still remained at the back of his mind. He took a deep breath and focused. He couldn't let the hare escape him here. Kill it, take it, and get out. The rest could be sorted out later.

Carefully he started making his way towards the hare, minding his steps to make as little noise as possible. His thirteen years of accumulated experience hunting served him well, as he managed to halve the distance to the hare, which seemed to be feasting on something. He creeped closer still, but the hare's ears start to twitch, and it raised its head in alarm. Cursing mentally, Gat froze. Deer hares have great hearing.

Time slipped by slowly while he tried to still his beating heart. His hand instinctively reached towards the bow across his back. Every movement he made had to be done with utmost care in order to produce as little sound as possible.

First get the bow. Then grab the arrow. Gently lift the bow, and hold it with a firm grip. Ready the arrow, Gat, and pull the string. The lessons of his father from thirteen years ago resounded within his head as he focused to the limit. He had one shot. If he missed, the hare would run.

Just as he was about to release the arrow, the hare started to move slowly towards the cave. He gritted his teeth, slowed his breath, and timed the shot. Thankfully, there was no wind. A killshot would be difficult to make at about seventy meters distance, but he believed he could do it.

The arrow was released from his fingers, aimed just a little higher than where the top of the hare's head should be and...

Thwack!

Right through the head!

Gat let out a cheer of happiness and rushed towards the hare, which had fallen right before entering the cave. He moved quickly, and retrieved it, but he froze at the entrance of the cave. That feeling was back. The cave was clearly the source of this; he could feel it in his very bones. Looking up from his hare, he was greeted by the eyes of several small creatures staring at him from within. Mice and snakes just... staring at him unblinkingly. It was unnerving.

They slowly retreated back into the cave without uttering a sound, and Gat was left there stunned as his prey bled through the hole in its head. He grabbed the hare and ran away. That cave wasn't natural, and he could only think of one thing that would cause animals that would normally be enemies to act like that.

A dungeon.

IN THE DEPTHS of the dungeon, I grinned mentally at myself. Today had been quite the eventful day indeed. First I obtained a snake, and now I'd been discovered by a human. I was a little upset that I had lost the opportunity to obtain that hare, but at the same time... Now I could get some people coming in to see my dungeon. Adventurers soon would make their way here I bet.

Why was I so excited about that? Because of what that could do for me! I could syphon mana from creatures that visited me, and if I killed others, I could obtain mana and anima too. Anima apparently is what you would call raw life power. It's the basic component for any complex and sentient living organism, and it's the component that allowed me to place souls into my creations. I could generate a small amount of anima from ether as is, but at this rate it might be months or years before I could produce anything worthwhile.

Lastly, if I could devour more things, I would grow more, and create more. What kind of self-respecting dungeon does not want to grow? That said, I didn't intend to kill everything that came in my dungeon, but I definitely would not shy away from taking down some fools. Especially those that upset me. Thinking about it, I shouldn't kill everyone anyway; otherwise, people wouldn't visit my dungeon.

I suppose that the best setup would be one that gets progressively more challenging, which would weed out the weak and the foolish naturally. In addition to that, I should modify my dungeon so that I could move my creatures in secret between the rooms, which would allow me maneuverability if I decided to take down a particularly dangerous (or unsavory) group of intruders.

Hmm... this might be a good time to start crafting some Dungeon Laws, before I get visitors. I should probably sort out how to organize my defenses and I should add more rooms too. My crystalline body glowed eagerly while I grinned in my head.

Let the games begin!

Status

Species: True Dungeon
Rank: 0
Name: Smit
Age: 37 days
Mana: 1,600 MP
Anima: 42
Mana Reg.: 35 MP/h
Anima Reg.: 0.9 AP/day

Floors: 1

Inhabitants: 14 Species

Titles: Eager Creator; Guide of the Bloody Evolution; Legendary Craftsman; Reincarnated One

Abilities: Absorb matter; Alter environment; Break down components; Craftsmanship; Creation; Digging; Destroy creation; Enhancement; Equivalent exchange; Ether manipulation; Evolution; Interdimensional storage; Life bestowal; Life-energy harnessing; Mana absorption; Masterful mana manipulation; Modification of creations; Monster link; Telepathy; Trap building; Transfer dungeon

Resistances: Magic (general); Mind control

<<<>>>

CHAPTER FIVE

Since the day that the hunter found me, about two days had passed, and I was getting very frustrated at this point. Why? Because I found some limits to what I can do. It's easy enough to modify and adjust creatures within a certain range of what they already are. Spider for example, I could make more poisonous, grow twice as large, or make their spider silk more resistant. I couldn't, however, deviate too far from certain standards. For example, I couldn't make a normal spider I already created grow two heads. Or at least, I couldn't do it yet. From what I understood, doing a large change would require a large reconstruction of the creature. They would need to have gathered enough energy and experience to evolve. At that point, I could modify them more thoroughly.

There was one exception to this rule, however... if I could create a creature from the start with the modifications I wanted, then I wouldn't have to worry about deviating from the pre-set norm of the species. This was probably because in that case, I would be creating an entirely new species. That said, I tried experimenting a bit and the results were... grotesque.

My first experiment was a simple spider who I tried to give two heads. It was a spectacular failure. The result was simply foul, as the two heads were fused at the side of their face, causing their mandibles to tangle up and their eyes to become grossly glued together where their faces met. The poor creature died within minutes. I am assuming that even their brains got mixed up together and caused massive hemorrhaging in the brain.

The second and third experiments failed similarly. I eventually came to the conclusion that I could not just modify *one* part of the spider. I had to restructure it entirely for it to be able to survive. For the case of the two-headed spider, it took thirty-two different experiments to produce functional results. I had to restructure the entirety of the size of the spider. Then, the strength and length of the legs had to be altered to support it properly, the muscles had to be realigned, the hydraulic system that they used to move had to be adjusted, the exoskeleton had to be reshaped, and even its base instincts had to be changed so that the heads did not kill each other in their hunger for prey.

It took me an entire twenty-five hours of nonstop work to do this. Exactly one day.

All of that to get a slightly more lethal spider. It really gave me mixed feelings about the amount of effort it required. On one hand, this new creature was not much better at the moment. But if I could evolve it... it might become a deadly addition to my arsenal. For now, I would refrain from creating too many creatures from scratch. I didn't think I had enough time to create more than a handful of them anyway before someone came to explore my dungeon, and that was only if I ignored working on my pitifully small dungeon the entire time.

That would not do.

Looking over the expanse of my dungeon, it was not too bad in terms of overall surface area... but it was hardly what I would call deadly as of yet. Only one way to fix that quickly: Traps!

However, I couldn't simply start creating things willy-nilly. Though my overall regeneration rate of mana was quite high, it was still not large enough for me to frivolously spend my mana on creating all the traps I would like. As a matter of fact, it would be ideal to increase my MP regeneration rate right now, which would enable me to recover more quickly after I spend my mana.

If I recall correctly... the closest village is about two days from here. It shouldn't have an adventurers guild due to its small size though. From that village to the nearest guild it would easily be five days, even by horseback. Therefore, just to get a messenger to the guild would be seven days. I should have roughly fourteen days, give or take a couple of days depending on how rushed the adventurers moved and the speed of the messenger. I thought this over for a while, conscious of the fact that I had limited time to ready myself.

I checked my status... 1,700 MP...What an absurd amount of magic power. Even a lord magus would not be able to have this much magic power at one time. I calculated that with my current base regeneration rate of 35 MP each hour, it would take me roughly two and a half days to regenerate my MP back to my current position. However, assuming that the increase of my mana really did occur as a result of expanding the territory covered by my dungeon, I might be able to double my regeneration rate... which was very desirable.

"Hey Echo." I reached out to her mentally. I didn't know when I started calling Echo a "her" since I didn't think dungeons have a gender... at least not low ranked ones like her. But it seemed to suit her well.

"Yes Master?"

"If I expand my dungeon... how much will it expand the regeneration rate for my MP?"

Echo was silent for a moment, as if evaluating the progress I had made so far... in fact I was sure that's what she was doing. Echo seemed to have a very... mechanical mind. Similar to that of an advanced automata golem, it was capable of analyzing a number of factors in detail.

"Master," she finally replied, "the influence of your concentrated mana is large enough to reach a size of approximately 2.75 the size of your current dungeon. I believe that would be roughly the limit of what your dungeon would be allowed to grow."

This instantly piqued my attention, as I turned to focus on her entirely. "The limit? What do you mean by that?"

"There is a limit to which a dungeon core can grow their dungeon. Though the dungeon core can capture more ether by expanding the volume of their dungeon, the core still processes nearly all the ether. The dungeon itself can process some of the ether passively, but the core accounts for roughly 91% of the production of the mana in the dungeon. Despite Master's large core size, it will not be able to process much more ether before Master ranks up as a dungeon core."

I groaned mentally, not liking the sound of that at all. "Then what happens if I try to expand beyond that without ranking up?"

"Control over mana is weakened, causing severe inefficiency of its use when creating new objects or creatures. Mana also takes longer to permeate the environment, as the rate of production of mana is below optimal levels for the size of the dungeon. This is the reason why most dungeons develop slowly, as they often over-stretch their boundaries as they instinctively seek to conquer more of the space around them."

I growled at myself with distaste, considering the implication. This would mean that even if I made a second floor, I would have to limit the expanse of it as well. Forcefully expanding my area of control sounded like it would cost me in the future too, so it would be best to avoid it. Only one way out of this, then. "What do you mean rank up? How do I do it?"

"Ranking up is a method of growth. It allows your core to grow and develop, allowing for greater processing of ether, and learning of new skills and abilities. It occurs whenever the dungeon has obtained enough experience and energy to grow, as it requires the consolidation of mana in the core itself while internal energy expands through the core to allow an increase in size."

Mentally I stroked my imaginary beard, an old habit I had developed as my beard grew in length when I was a dwarf. *So... you need both an internal and an external energy source to converge in the dungeon core to expand it... And a dungeon core grows through the use of mana and qi?*

I contemplated that thought for a moment. If that was true, then it would explain a lot. No one really knows how dungeon cores develop. The most promising theory suggests that a dungeon core is a mana-stone that became infused with several elemental spirits, which would explain why a dungeon core is such a rare and powerful magic item. However, if a dungeon core has the ability to grow and develop through experiences, mana, and qi, it suggests that it's more than just a mana-stone infused with a multitude of simple elemental spirits. Especially since it can manipulate mana consciously, a feat impossible for a simple mana-stone, not to mention that elemental spirits cannot use qi.

If you consider that solidifying qi into a permanent structure would be impossible for even a master cultivator, then this must mean that a dungeon core has a strong spiritual connection that can control qi to an unbelievable extent. In fact, this points to dungeon cores being a very rare fusion between a mineral and a spiritual essence that can solidify mana and qi in itself. In other words, a dungeon core is a creature that can be considered a link between the spirit world and the physical world.

I contemplated this revelation for few more moments, and lost myself in the implications this would have for the utilities of dungeon core as a magic item. *What would a master wizard do if he knew this... what power could he obtain if he could utilize this knowledge?*

A link between the spirit realm and the physical realm... A source of unimaginable power, if my theory was correct. Necromancers and summoners in particular would certainly be willing to kill to gain access to a living dungeon core if I was right.

I let out a mental sigh and pushed those thoughts to the back of my mind. Perhaps this knowledge would have helped me in the past and my craft would have reached even greater heights... but that was beside the point now. I had to focus on the task at hand.

Three things required my attention immediately:

- Expand the dungeon
- Make traps
- Try to evolve my creatures

Ideally, I should create a system where my traps and monsters complement the structure of my dungeon. This way, I could optimize my chance of survival and reduce the amount of mana necessary to do so.

In this line of thought, I should consider the monsters I had available and then create a dungeon floor where their strengths could be used to the fullest. That said, I currently only had available to me one type of snake, two rodents, and about ten insects and bugs... plus my kobolds. I didn't have a particularly large selection to utilize, so I didn't really need to worry too much about creating an environment specific floor yet.

This was going to be tricky. I had no doubt that if I swarmed people with my dungeon mice, I could take down a modestly large group of poorly prepared visitors at first but that's about it. If there was a mage in that group of people, my rodents would suffer very large casualties and would likely be annihilated. I needed more species under my command.

I decided that my first floor should attract and capture more creatures into my dungeon. I would use the first room to host the majority of my bugs and some common mice. With any luck, their scent would passively attract any animal that was just outside my dungeon. Next I would just send a few creatures out to run around, get the attention of a few animals, and then lure them here.

I expanded my will, and reached out to a handful of common

mice around the first room. Instantly they stopped what they were doing and turned their focus towards my presence.

"Go out and lure some animals here. Try not to die," was my command.

They instantly rushed forth and tried to exit my dungeon. I kept my consciousness following them all the way to the entrance, and I found I could extend my senses to about a dozen meters past my entrance but that was the limit. However, that was enough, as I could watch how my monsters began to dissolve into particles of light the further they got from my dungeon.

"Wait! Return immediately!" I urged them, and they streaked back like furry bolts of lightning. Two of them didn't make it, their heads partially dissolved, and by the time they came back, they collapsed, their brains now exposed.

"What in Odar's great moustache was that!?" I asked out loud.

"The monster left your area of influence. Living creations may not exit the dungeon without a monster core; they will dissolve back into mana, otherwise," Echo explained.

"And *why* did you not mention this?" I asked icily.

"It's common sense. No dungeon would attempt otherwise." Echo replied simply, but... did I hear a hint of sheepishness in her voice? No... Likely not. Echo had next to no emotion.

I grunted at her response with exasperation. Great. I had to spend more mana now.

With resignation I turned my attention to the three remaining mice. A monster core huh? Another item that was a rare commodity, especially useful for alchemy, creating elemental golems, and even summoning. It could be used for forging of magical weapons, but often not practical due to the requirements of it.

I searched my knowledge and I found that I indeed knew how to create a monster core instinctively. My inquisitive mind disliked the fact that I knew things but I wasn't aware of this knowledge unless I actually *looked* for the information in my mind, but well... not much I could do about that.

Ironically, even though the cost for the core varied depending on the creature I was placing it in, for a mouse it was still more expensive than the mouse itself, as it cost twenty-two MP. I sighed and created one core for each of the three mice, and sent them out once again. Hopefully they wouldn't all die before bringing me some new critters.

Alright. That's one item crossed off the list, I thought tiredly. *God, I need a pint of ale... Ugh, no time for that. Now let's remodel this floor.*

This part should be fairly simple, now that I had an estimated limit of expansion thanks to Echo's analysis. Any dwarf that had waged a large underground battle knew the importance of choke points. Choke points were the difference between annihilation and survival when one was facing a large number of enemies. Thus I devised a simple but effective setup for the expansion of my dungeon.

I would add four rooms. Starting on the first room, I added two tunnels, one at each side of the main path towards the next room, and each tunnel veered away from the main path at a roughly forty-degree angle. Each of these tunnels would lead to a new room that was roughly the same size as the original three rooms. Then, I would create an additional tunnel that stretched from each of those rooms back towards what was the original second room. This resulted in a symmetrical rhomb-shaped pattern, which I copied by connecting the original second room to the original third room in the dungeon. The shape of my dungeon now reminded me a bit of the shape of the number 8, if more angular.

Of course, every room had been decorated with moss, small burrows and dens for the animals, and polished stalagmites and stalactites, as well as with water stones, which gave my dungeon a bit of an unreal look. It appeared... mystical and ancient due to the faint blue glow of the water stones, which was just enough to cast shadows over the rocky surfaces. It was eerie and gorgeous at the same time. However, just doing that had cost me a large sum of mana, even though I tried to do it by guiding the mana myself. Altogether, it had been a whopping 1,600 MP. It brutally decreased my MP to only a fraction of what I'd had, but in exchange, I had increased my mana regeneration rate to 89 MP/hour! Even though each room increased my MP recovery by roughly 4.5 MP/hour, I had made the hallways large enough to fit up to four people side by side comfortably, and that apparently had had a large effect on the sheer amount of mana I could gather.

This meant that the hallways themselves accounted for roughly 38 MP/hour of the total gains I had made. This was very odd to me, however, as the main hallway I had claimed produced nowhere near that amount of mana. Perhaps there was an optimal ratio I had to find to optimize the production of Mana? Hmm... food for thought.

Regardless, I spent all day working on that. Coupled with the day I'd spent messing about with critters, it meant I had only a dozen days left to work with.

I sighed at myself mentally, and decided to meditate. Perhaps I could use my cultivation techniques to gather qi inside this core of mine and start my trip towards this "ranking up" thing. Ranking up would certainly be desirable.

Letting go of that last thought, I turned my consciousness inwards, reaching towards serenity and enlightenment.

GAT ARRIVED at the village sweating and exhausted after a day-and-a-half of rushing through the vast green known as the forest of Nevermore. His quarry slung across his shoulder, looking a bit worse for wear than when he killed it, but otherwise it was still a fine looking piece of meat. He couldn't remember ever moving that quickly through the green, but then again, he had never been in such a rush before.

When he had arrived, he had been greeted with much fanfare once he revealed the wrapped up deer hare, but despite the celebratory mood, he had asked to meet with the village chief quickly. Curious at this request and the anxious face of the hunter, a number of people walked him to the village chief, who as usual was seated in a small room in his home.

"Chief!" Gat practically burst into the room, startling the sixty-year-old Gerald from the midst of his work, almost making him drop a vial of oily amber fluid.

"Gat!" he said as he turned around quickly, somehow managing to keep his grip on the vial. "How many times must I tell you to *not* startle me while I am working? Apothecary is a delicate art, and I don't have much to work with!"

Gat briefly nodded but quickly dismissed the annoyance of the chief. There was exciting news to be had... or terrifying news, depending on who you asked.

"I understand Chief, but this is urgent," Gat blurted out, barely registering the mass of people that had followed him and was listening in on the conversation. "There is a dungeon in the mountain!"

A collective gasp rose from the crowd behind him, and for once, the chief seemed to be stunned into silence.

"Impossible. We have explored most of this side of the mountain, and never have we seen anything like that. Where did you go?"

"Halfway up the mountain, about two days from here by foot, north from the village," he spoke quickly. "I know that there isn't *supposed* to be a dungeon, but I saw it myself."

"And how are you so sure that it was a dungeon?" the chief asked skeptically.

"Chief, the hare guided me to it. I found it right by the entrance of the dungeon, as if was attracted to it. When I shot the hare and went to retrieve it, I was greeted by the most peculiar sight... Snakes and large mice were waiting for me inside the dungeon. They stood side by side and stared at me. They are predator and prey and they stood there side by side! And then there was this... feeling. An eerie sense of power emanating from the cave that made my hair stand on end. It felt like a phantom wind that vibrated with an energy that is beyond my grasp."

There was a mutter from the crowd, and the village chief sank into thought for a moment.

"Are you sure Gat?" he asked, weighing the options in his mind.

"As sure as the sun rising every morning," Gat replied flatly. "There is something in that cave that can control creatures, and it's alive. I feel it in my bones."

Murmurs began to grow from the crowd, words of worry leaping from mouth to mouth. The uncertainty was palpable in the air. Gerald knew that this could easily turn into fear, and thus he spoke quickly but with conviction.

"I see. Then this must be a new dungeon, if it only has control over two types of animals. Well! I say that this calls for having professionals brought in. If there is a dungeon, then this is a chance to grow our hundred-person village. If it isn't, then at least we won't have to worry about it anymore."

There were murmurs of agreement in the crowd, and several nods of approval. That was a reasonable answer. Let the Adventurers Guild have a look at it. With any luck, it would be a harmless new dungeon and they would get some commerce out of it.

"Now Gat," Gerald continued, "I understand that there is some sort of reward for finding new dungeons, so you should be one of the people to go to the Guild. But first we have the ascension ceremony! We were going to do it two days from now, but in light of this, we shall move the date to tonight, when I will decide on my successor. This way you can be sent out tomorrow with a few men. Let's begin the preparations. We only have a few hours to prepare a proper feast! Let's go people!"

The village burst into activity, a sense of energy coursing

through everyone. They could worry about the dungeon later; tonight it was time to feast!

I SPENT a full day cycle in meditation. My dungeon core could gather both qi and mana much faster than my previous body, and thus the speed at which I gathered energy was... outstanding. If you combined that with the fact that I don't need sleep, well... the results were quite extraordinary. Of course, there was a problem in qi gathering, as some techniques for it (especially those requiring breathing) became obsolete for me. However, since the theory to gather qi still applied, I managed to cultivate my qi with my meditation technique. In the one single day that I meditated, I advanced more than a normal human or dwarf could in a month. I could already feel myself approaching the first breakthrough.

I felt quite satisfied by this progress, but I couldn't be sure how I measured up compared to other dungeons. Or I wouldn't have been able to, if I didn't have Echo to help me out here.

"Master, your progress is much faster than the average dungeon. The average dungeon requires either a year to rank up on its own without intruders, or several consecutive deaths of larger creatures in the dungeon over the span of several weeks to reach the level you have reached. How is this possible?"

If I had eyes, I would have blinked in confusion. How was it possible that dungeons, whose cores were so perfect for acquiring mana and qi, were slower at cultivating qi than average mortals? Thinking upon this, I asked Echo, explaining I had used a cultivation technique. Unsurprisingly, she told me that dungeons didn't use any type of technique to gather qi.

Well that explains everything... I thought to myself. It doesn't matter how talented you are at something, if you don't know how to properly exploit that talent it will be wasted. Still, the fact that a dungeon could gather qi and maintain it without doing *anything* was nothing short of amazing. A hundred-year-old dungeon that doesn't know how to cultivate could still rank up several times, while a human that doesn't cultivate will never reach the first breakthrough of cultivation even if he lives to be a hundred.

I pushed those thoughts to the side for now, and decided to check on my mana. I was pleasantly surprised to see that it was a massive 2,044 MP. This was a glorious amount of mana that I could work with.

Expansion of the dungeon? Check. Next order of business: protecting the shortest path towards my core.

The main path that led through the first three rooms directly to my core room was quite small and narrow compared to the new paths I had carved out, which was to be expected. After all, it was built to fit a single dwarf. However, it was too small to provide me with any reasonable amount of mana. The plan was to expand the hallway to a reasonable size, and then place several traps along that path. If I left the path as it was, no one would use it, and that would defeat the purpose of creating a "short" path towards me that would lure the dumber and more overconfident fellows to their doom.

I nodded my head mentally, and prepared to reach out to the walls of my dungeon with my will. Since I have been in this place for well over a month, my mana has seeped deep into the stone, allowing me to bend the stone to my will more easily.

First, I increased the height of the entire main hallway. The ceiling now varied in elevation, ranging between two and three meters above the ground. Like the rooms, it had a few short stalagmites and stalactites decorating its length. Next, I doubled the width of the tunnel, making it about 2.8 meters. It was a simple adjustment, but I felt an odd strain in my mana once I did that, losing 514 MP. That was definitely more than it should have been.

"Master, you have touched upon the limit of the current size of your dungeon. The limit was higher than calculated, but I advise against increasing the size of this dungeon floor any more than this," Echo's voice rang out.

"Hellfire and damnation, I forgot about the limit," I growled out at nobody in particular. On the plus side, my rate of regeneration of MP did increase to 93 MP/hour. I suppose I was correct about there being an ideal ratio for the increase of my mana regeneration. I would experiment with that later.

Still grumbling about the loss of my MP, I set myself to work on the traps. I focused on the knowledge I should have naturally about traps and...

"What in tarnation is this?" I asked myself with irritation.

"Master?" Echo asked with what I suspected was a hint of genuine curiosity.

"Is this a joke? Do dungeons really call these things traps?"

"Please elaborate Master, I am not sure about your inquiry."

"Open pits? Loose rocks? These are the starting traps of a dungeon?" I asked, feeling rather insulted. These barely qualified as traps!

"Yes Master? Later on you will be able to unlock larger mechanisms like tripwire traps, though those are more advanced."

I gaped at her mentally. "That's it? I have to *unlock* such simple mechanisms? For shame! This is an insult! I will craft better traps myself."

I harrumphed at the confused Echo and set to work. I would be damned if I was going to trust my protection to some simple *pit* in the ground. Any adventurer worth their salt would keep an eye out for random pits, even if they were concealed by poor lighting. This might be a beginner's level dungeon, and I might want to attract more prey, but I refused to have such poorly crafted monstrosities in my dungeon.

I took a moment to cool myself down, but the irritation in the back of my mind was still present. First, I would modify these monstrosities called "pit traps" and turn them into something that was at least partially disguised.

I started by making the pit in the hallway between the first room and the second room along the main path. It was a four-meter-deep and two-meter-wide hole that might not be lethal, but it would certainly deal injury. This was the so called "trap" that I was given. Next, it was time to modify it. First, I made the walls of the pit smooth like glass. That should make climbing the walls of the hole much harder. Additionally, I changed the ground within the hole to be very uneven and full of all sorts of rocks, from the size of pebbles to blunt stalagmites. Fall into this trap, and you are almost guaranteed to break some bones when you land, maybe die if you hit your head. And last, I made a thin layer of rock right over it to disguise it. Anything (or more likely, anyone) that was too heavy would cause that thin layer of rock to collapse, sending the person down into the pit.

I nodded, more satisfied by this. It was still a very basic trap, but it was definitely a step up from that simple hole in the ground. I wanted to make some pits with blades and trigger traps at the bottom of them, but I didn't wish to scare away potential prey. I knew enough about dungeons to know that they should become harder progressively, as to invite people that seek challenges deeper into itself.

Next I looked at the "trap" called loose rocks. It was worse than the pit really. It literally was a loose rock that would collapse upon contact with the enemy. It was a terrible excuse for a trap.

Unless you combined it with the pit.

I grinned at myself and created a few more of my modified basic pit traps, in the tunnels leading from the main path, and further modified the few that lay between the second room and my last room. First, I would create a small pit trap that was just as deep as the other pits, but only one-and-a-half meters wide. I left the top of the pit wide open, with jagged rocks at the edges of the top so that it looked as if it were another pit trap that had been previously collapsed. But here was the tricky part. The far wall of the pit was created using entirely a thin layer of "loose rock" trap, which concealed a second 2.2-meter-wide pit right behind it. Any person that tried to leap across the dud pit would land right on the loose rock trap, which would collapse, and reveal the *real* pit below. Of course, the person would tumble right down into it, with the added bonus of crashing down onto the jagged pieces of rock that fell with them as the fake wall collapsed.

I made only two of these dud pits, as I doubted any half-decent adventurers would fall for that more than twice in a row. Of course, I wasn't completely unreasonable. The pits were all pressed at either one side of the walls of the tunnel or the other, meaning that if the person could identify the trap, they could walk along that 60-cm ledge that was actually solid rock to avoid the trap... or just leap across it if they felt like it, though the low ceilings might make it hard for tall people.

I used up another 190 MP creating a total of four modified pits and two dud pits. They were surprisingly cheap to create, and it only took me about an hour to get it all set up the way I like it. The feature of being able to copy your creations and replicate them exactly is a very useful application of the creation skill. I quite like it when I am in a rush.

Then I simply created a couple of random modified pit traps in the second room along the main path, just for the hell of it, before judging that there were sufficient traps for now.

Traps set? Check, I thought to myself. *Next, check on—*

I was disturbed out of my thoughts as I sensed two of the three mice I'd sent out into the forest approach quickly towards my dungeon. I could feel their cores only a few dozen meters away, and judging from the feelings that I could detect from them, they were running for their lives.

Instantly I burst into action, ordering the kobolds to go into the second room and wait, along with nearly every other snake and dungeon mice I had. I also ordered the mice in the first room to congregate in the middle, and whatever snakes I had in that room would hide near them.

The plan was simple, but it was all I had ready. First, have the predators come towards the mice in the first room. When they got close, have the mice run to the second room along the main path. The snakes would try to bite at the predators as they passed the first room, and hopefully weaken them. In the second room, I would launch a full offensive battle against whatever was chasing the mice. It might be overkill, but I was not taking any chances.

No sooner than my creatures were in position in the first room, the mice being chased burst into it, followed by a pack of black wolves. How they had outrun a pack of predators like wolves was beyond me, but if I had to guess, my modifications were more successful than I expected... and the wolves probably had been nearby to my dungeon.

Instantly I ordered all the congregated mice to flee towards the second room, giving the pack of wolves a nice view of a lot more prey so close to their maws. They were so distracted by their hunting that they failed to notice the snakes. The snakes pounced on a few select wolves at the rear end of the pack, biting them again and again until they were paralyzed by the venom. Soon they would die from the overdose of poison that ran through their veins. That took care of three of them.

Two more wolves fell to the pits I had created recently, killing them as they landed on their heads against the jagged stones at the bottom of the pit, splattering their brains. Unfortunately, the rest of the wolves were more than capable enough to avoid the traps by leaping right over them.

Then a dozen wolves leaped right into the second room, and everything turned to chaos. Every single one of my creatures attacked. The dungeon mice leapt at them viciously, the snakes attacking at their ankles, and my kobolds leaped at them from behind. It was a massacre, with the greatest victory being the death of the Alpha wolf, which got killed single-handedly in the surprise attack carried out by my first kobold, which tore at the wolf's neck from the start.

A total of seventeen wolves were consumed that day, at the cost of one scout mouse that never made it back. Additional casualties came in the form of seven snakes and thirteen common mice that got trampled during the massacre. I will admit, I enjoyed watching my creatures emerge victorious against intruders such as wolves. It gave me a joyful feeling, and I suspect that is part of the dungeon instincts I had inherited.

Anyway. From the deaths of the wolves I obtained 1,088 MP total, and about 97 anima. Considering that some of the anima and mana is transferred to whoever killed the creature, I would say that it's fairly certain that my creatures gained a significant amount of mana and anima thanks to the wolves.

In fact, I could feel the energy inside some of my creatures had definitely increased. Specifically, two dungeon mice, three snakes, and my first kobold had dramatically increased their energy. The snakes and mice were nearly ready to evolve, while the kobold still needed a bit more.

Hmmm... I thought to myself. *If I could just rush their energy gain... maybe I could evolve my monsters?*

That seemed plausible. Now it was a matter of figuring out how to rush that energy gain. I inspected my status and looked through all of it. Maybe an idea would pop out at me.

And pop up it did.

I looked at my title "Guide of the Bloody Evolution" and it became clear what I had to do. Combined with my dungeon trait "Monster Loyalty," which essentially made my monsters flawlessly loyal towards me, I could command the start of a hunting frenzy. I could command them to hunt each other viciously, increasing the rate at which evolution occurs.

I would do that. But first...

I willed myself to bring up the image of the wolves, and recreated them without any modifications. I made eleven of them like that, and then I created what would be the Alpha. I chose as a model the male wolf that had been killed by my kobold, and made him bigger. I carefully crafted his snout and his canine teeth, making them harder, and reinforced the muscles of his jaw while trying to reduce the change in his appearance. The claws were hardened, and I made his hind legs and shoulders stronger too. But most importantly, I made his skull and brain larger. I wanted a true predator, a creature that was the king among its peers. And I succeeded. Standing at 1.2 meters tall to the shoulder, this wolf was 30% larger than the others, and much more deadly. The finishing touch was his eyes. I gave him gorgeous deep green eyes whose vibrancy seemed to contain a jade wildfire within them.

Satisfied, I divided the wolves into three small packs and dispersed them in the dungeon. Once everything was in place, I ran through my plan one last time in my mind.

Step one, every day create more creatures until you run out of mana. Step two, have them all fight until only a few of each species are alive... except for the kobolds, I needed at least three of them at all times. Step three, meditate all day until the next day. Rinse and repeat until you can actually evolve your creatures... Seems good to me.

The last thing I had to do before I began everything was use up my remaining mana. I created mostly bugs, snakes, and mice, littering them all over the dungeon. The only two creatures exempt from the slaughterhouse were my two scouting mice, which I sent out again in search of more prey for me. Hopefully they would return with something new.

"Alright boys!" I sent out a mental echo through the entire dungeon, grabbing the attention of every creature in there. "We are about to have a nice all-out war here. Good luck!"

The signal was given. The massacre started.

And I slipped back into meditation.

Status

Species: True Dungeon
Rank: 0
Name: Smit
Age: 42 days
Mana: 7 MP
Anima: 45
Mana Reg.: 93 MP/h
Anima Reg.: 0.9 AP/day
Floors: 1
Inhabitants: 16 Species
Titles: Eager Creator; Guide of the Bloody Evolution; Legendary Craftsman; Reincarnated One
Abilities: Absorb matter; Alter environment; Break down components; Craftsmanship; Creation; Digging; Destroy creation; Enhancement; Equivalent exchange; Ether manipulation; Evolution; Interdimensional storage; Life bestowal; Life-energy harnessing; Mana absorption; Masterful mana manipulation; Modification of creations; Monster link; Telepathy; Trap building; Transfer dungeon
Resistances: Magic (general); Mind control

<<<>>>

CHAPTER SIX

S mit had been meditating for seven days in a row, pausing exclusively to spawn more creatures every time the population became too low. Had it not been for the dungeon's passive ability to absorb everything after a certain amount of time, there would undoubtedly be a disturbing amount of animal corpses and gore all over the place. Every day he had to respawn his creatures at least once, sometimes even twice. On the flip side, the blood and sacrifice were paying off quite well. A handful of veterans from every species were ready for their evolution; however, he let them accumulate more energy and experience, in hopes that some special variant might arise from them.

Surprisingly, the wolves were not very effective in their hunting, probably because of the small hunting area they had and the small numbers. After all, wolves excelled in chasing their prey and taking it down with exceptional teamwork. The problem was obvious: The dungeon was too small and the prey was too small to provide proper use of their tactics and strengths. Still, all was not lost. They offered excellent training for the kobolds, and perhaps he would turn them into a sort of pet in the future.

But that was just a secondary matter. The most important

thing was Smit himself. Every time he slipped into meditation, he felt an odd sense of relief. Every hour that passed, his mind became clearer, as if a fog that he had not been aware of was slowly evaporating. At first, he didn't even see the change. But as the hours became days, he noticed. His mind became sharper, his thoughts became his own, his thought processes seemed to flow more freely. And above all, he felt as if he returned to his senses, as if he were waking from a long, drawn-out dream.

It wasn't until the midnight of the seventh day that he finally grasped the first stage of cultivation, triggering his rank up. In a bright light tinged with a jade color, everything began all at once.

<<<>>>
Congratulations! You have gathered the required energy for the first breakthrough. Rank up initiated.
<<<>>>

<<<>>>
Congratulations! By cultivating yourself, mind and spirit have been restored.
<<<>>>

<<<>>>
Warning! Anomaly in dungeon personality detected! Reverting to default dungeon personality.
<<<>>>

<<<>>>
Warning! Default dungeon personality annexed by integrated spiritual entity. Overriding default personality. Spiritual entity [Smit] empowered.
<<<>>>

Even while all these notifications blinked into existence in succession, Smit could feel his body expand, and his mind seemingly unbending from a warped state. It was a surreal feeling that almost overwhelmed him.

<<<>>>
Alert! Dominance established. [Smit] has undertaken permanent sovereignty. Original dungeon personality Overwritten. Original dungeon personality accepted as [Echo].
<<<>>>

<<<>>>
[Echo] has accepted full and total subservience to [Smit].
<<<>>>

<<<>>>
Due to prior interactions with the true dungeon core [Smit], entity [Echo] has spontaneously evolved to Origin Spirit. Origin entity may be placed into any body created by [Smit].
<<<>>>

<<<>>>
Congratulations! The rank up was successful, allowing for a significant increase to the size of the dungeon. Additional floors may be created now. Maximum floor size increased.
<<<>>>

<<<>>>
Congratulations! Due to the speed of your rank up, special conditions have been met. Due to your newfound spiritual stability, special conditions have been met. You may select two of the following options.
<<<>>>

<<<>>>

Contract Monster [limited]; Dungeon Abilities; Fame Increase;
Monster Traits; New Species [Monster]; New Species [Plant]

<<<>>>

Smit's mind, which had just become clear, instantly became flooded by even more information as a bunch of windows opened up in his mind, causing him to have a headache. Growling in annoyance, he mentally pushed them to the side, allowing his head to clear for a moment. Thanks to those damnable windows, he now felt like he was waking up from a hangover rather than awakening from a lucid dream.

Gods curse it all, he grumbled mentally. Why did the voice of the world always do that? It was like it freaked out when someone did something outside the norm. Even when he was a dwarf, it did the same damn thing when he crafted his first legendary weapon, earning him the title of "Legendary Blacksmith."

Once his head stopped ringing, he brought back the windows into focus, and started reading them one by one, with the patience that only an old dwarf could have. Sturdy, unyielding, and enduring. That was the essence of a dwarf, their very personality representing the stone of the mountains they dwelled in. Of course, one could add secretive, possessive, and hoarding a trove of treasures, but that thought did not pass through the mind of the old dwarf at the time.

He began to understand what had happened with more clarity. Even in his... impaired state of mind, he had deduced that he had fused with the dungeon core. However, it was not until now that he understood what had occurred.

The initial conflict between him and the original dungeon core, which was now Echo, had resulted in his soul battling with hers for dominance, a battle that he had clearly won. However, he had not escaped unscathed. His mind and soul had been exhausted and perhaps even damaged in the process, creating a disparity in his personality that was inflated by the elation of being alive again.

Add to this a confusing spiritual connection with another soul that used to own the body you now inhabit and voila: You get a fiasco of a confusing personality without any real sense of direction. Just a childish personality with the bare minimum of what actually constitutes a dwarven soul; an entity that tries everything at random with whatever happens to be interesting at the time.

What a bloody atrocious mess, Smit thought to himself with a grunt. Even his own voice in his head sounded closer to what it should. A deep, barreling voice that no one would mistake as childish.

He looked around briefly with a critical eye, examining what he had created during his state of immature mucking about. He had to confess that he was not impressed. Though all things considered, he was not entirely disappointed either.

The layout of the dungeon was fine enough for a general design, though it clearly lacked the beauty that he wanted in any dwelling of his. He would amend that later.

The problem that he found was the lack of preparation. Any dwarven craftsman worth his salt knew that preparation was the key to success. For example, if armor was to be effective, it had to be as perfectly crafted as possible, with as little excess material as possible, with as few weak spots as possible, and handled by someone that could clearly make the best use of it as possible. The current state of affairs was... mediocre. If his ancestors knew he had carved something as careless as this, they would surely mock him.

The one saving grace he had, however, was that all his crafted items were still intact. Every finely crafted item, all of them seemed to still be in place, hanging from the walls or stored away in his room. Though something worried him... Where was his spatial ring? Frantically he expanded his consciousness to search the room, until he sensed a weak magical signature right beneath him. His own mana seemed to have been interfering with the aura radiated by the small item.

Sighing with relief, he looked at what was now left of his body:

a pile of bones covered in dusty blankets. He absorbed the bones into himself, and tried to use mana to reach for the ring... except he couldn't actually interact with it properly. Frowning, he reached out, and found that though his mana could wrap and bind around the ring, he couldn't even lift it up, let alone actually activate it.

Growling at this, he felt like he wanted to bash his head against the wall. *Of course it won't work you blithering fool, you don't have a corporal body to use the ring!* As if anyone would make a spatial ring that could be manipulated by anyone with mana from the distance. If anyone found out, they could just empty the ring remotely!

Reluctantly, Smit called in a mouse and had him dig a shallow hole right under his levitating mana core, and bury his ring there. *That should be fine for now.*

He could figure out how to craft himself a body later to use that ring, but for now, he had bigger fish to fry. He had only a few days at best before he got visited by adventurers, and he was not going to be caught with his beard stuck in his belt. He had work to do.

First, things first though: he had to finish his rank up.

He observed the options for a moment, and put his whole thought into it, examining all the windows one by one. "Contract Monster" was interesting; however, it was a gamble. Essentially, it allowed you to contract a random monster or animal within a 10-km radius of your dungeon. The creature had to accept your contract, but there was no guarantee that whatever you contracted was useful. He skipped that without a second thought.

He also discarded "Fame Increase," as he didn't need to increase his fame at the moment. In fact, now that he had come to his senses he didn't even feel ready to be discovered yet, so why on earth would he want to attract more attention to himself at the moment?

"New Species [Plants]" seemed interesting at first, except that he had no use for the selections that were given to him. They were different types of moss, grass, and mushrooms, which he knew for a fact grew around the mountain anyway. He could get those himself later, if he needed them.

The decision came down to the last three options. Out of these, the decision was not difficult for him, as he chose "New Species [Monster]," which revealed the original monster list he had received when he became a dungeon, asking him to choose one additional species.

There was no need to think about it. "Constructs" was his choice. The childish planning of his previous self was overridden completely by his desire to work with stone and metal. It was the calling of his ancestors, and he would not deny it. Even if he had no arms and legs to forge constructs as it should be done, he would still craft them, one way or another. Of course, he would not mass-produce them as he would produce the mice or the insects, but he would take his time in crafting his constructs. After all, he would only be willing to create true works of art.

Satisfied with this decision, he went through the last two options. However, there was only one thing that really picked up his interest, right under the Dungeon Abilities.

The ability was called "Bestow Knowledge [rare]," and it allowed the dungeon to bestow some knowledge to one of his creations about something, provided that his creation had the capacity to process this knowledge.

In other words, he could teach them skills.

If the blacksmith had had a face, he would have been grinning from ear to ear. Imagine the possibilities. He could teach the kobolds how to smith for example! Or how to cultivate. He could teach them how to mine or any number of things.

Sure, creating things with just a thought was fun, but he suspected that there was a limit to the quality of what he could create through this method, as convenient as it was. And besides, how could he forgo the love of the hearth and the clanging of steel? The best weapons were those created in a dwarven forge after all.

And once he had a body, he would need assistants to speed the process.

He chuckled at his thoughts. He sounded like a youngling again, with dreams of grandeur. He had never taken on an apprentice before, mainly because he didn't trust anyone to stay as faithful to the art as he was, nor did he want to share his techniques with some stranger so easily. But now he could create the perfect apprentice to help him. That thought alone made him smile. The idea of relighting his forge and creating anew. That sounded like a pleasant dream.

OUT IN THE WILDERNESS, minutes away from Smit, a group of people approached the dungeon. They were dressed in patched over clothes, leathers, and furs, with knives strapped to their belts. Every single one of them looked ragged and dirty, and not one of them looked like the sort of man you would like to meet in a dark alley at night. Most of these strangers had used short swords or axes simply strapped to their belts. One even had a bow that seemed to have seen better days. These men were not adventurers, to be sure; they were bandits. Highwaymen of the truest sense.

"Oi, Buck," the largest of the men called out, "are you sure it was around here?"

"Yeas boss!" a stringy looking fellow with large ears piped up, his raspy voice dripping with enthusiasm. "It's definitely around here. I heard it all with me own ears. That half-wit hunter should have been smarter. Who goes talking about a new dungeon in a tavern before he even reaches the Adventurers Guild? But all is well. I heard it from the twit himself. Halfway up the mountain, directly north from Nam village. It shouldn't be too far now."

The leader, a burly man named Badack, grunted and stroked his dirty black beard in thought. "I didn't ask for the whole story, Buck," he grunted as he analyzed the situation as best as he could.

"But this be good!" he said energetically. "We must be a few days ahead of the adventurers. If the dungeon be new, then it must still be weak. One of them cores be worth a fortune boys!"

He heard a cheer from the men behind him, but still one of them nervously stuttered out: "B-but boss, that's still a dungeon. I heard 'orrible things abou' them. Just awful. Monsters everywhere, traps that'll poke out your guts, and slimes that eat you alive. Should we really go?"

"Shut up, Muck," the leader grunted without looking at him. "It's a new dungeon. It probably only has something as dangerous as squirrels protecting it. And what if it has a slime or two? If adventurers can handle them, then we can handle them too, eh lads?!"

Another cheer came from the bandits, shutting up the self-conscious Muck. He had a bad feeling about this. All of it. Ever since they had stepped on the mountain he had had a bad feeling about this adventure. And his gut had never led him astray. Last time he didn't listen to it he lost half of his left ear to a stray arrow. If he had left that trash woman to die from blood loss that wouldn't have happened, but noooo, he had to ignore the warning from his instinct.

"Eh! Look over 'ere!" One of the bandits shouted, pointing at a dark hole that was dug out of the mountain itself.

Muck shuddered at the sight of it. He had a bad feeling before, but now? Now he felt a foreboding that permeated his bones. Something was going to go wrong. He just knew it.

SMIT HAD JUST BARELY STARTED to play with his new species, the constructs, when he sensed a group of people approaching. He quickly moved his consciousness to the entrance of the dungeon, and found about fourteen men making their way towards him. They wore dirty clothing, devoid of armor other than a few scrapped, mismatched pieces that seemed to be stitched together by leather strings. Anyone with eyes could tell that they were most certainly *not* adventurers, and anyone with more than a handful of active brain cells could guess that they were bandits of some sort.

He felt anger flare up inside of him as he realized this. As a crafter, few things irked him more than thieves. They were a natural enemy of crafters, who were always a prime target for thieves. Not to mention that *these* thieves were filthy looking things whose presence would do nothing more than tarnish and damage the dungeon that he had built so far. Just looking at them repulsed him.

Still, even as his anger simmered in his mind, he saw an opportunity. He could use this filth as an experiment of sorts. While he was no scholar or military mastermind, as a dwarven craftsman of many years of age, he had a sharp mind. He had scant minutes before the enemy showed up, and hence he rushed to create some last-minute preparations.

He called in his kobolds, ordering them to meet him immediately. Like loyal dogs, the four kobolds assembled before him within a minute of receiving the message.

Good, he thought to himself. *Let us test this new skill.*

"[Bestow Knowledge]," Smit said, and focused on the kobolds.

Right away he understood that the extent of their capacity to understand was low, but it was sufficient for his needs. He passed onto them basic knowledge on how to handle spears.

As a craftsman, particularly one that specialized as a smith, Smit had trained himself on how to use every weapon he was capable of crafting to a degree. While a normal smith might forge a sword and hand it to a soldier, the soldier using it would be able to test it and see the strengths and flaws of a weapon better than the blacksmith himself. As a lone and reclusive craftsman, Smit had not always had someone to test his creations and therefore he had trained in weaponry enough to be able to discern any flaws in his own craftsmanship, which would then allow him to craft a better weapon in the future. In this way, he heightened his art beyond that of other blacksmiths once upon a time.

And now, he passed some of this basic knowledge to his kobolds.

The beauty of the spear is that it was a simple weapon to craft and easy to use, while offering great advantages. Even in the army, a peon armed with a spear with only a week of practice was more effective than a squire that had spent a month training with the sword. The reason for this was quite simple, as the spear offered three great advantages:

First of all, a spear had superior reach to that of a common sword or axe, allowing the spearman to stay out of the range of damage of the opponent. Secondly, the spear was easy to handle, as simple stabbing and slashing was all that was needed to keep an enemy at a bay, and the length the enemy had to cross to reach the spearman gave the spearman more time to react even if an attack got through. Last of all, spears could be thrown fairly accurately, even with little practice.

These advantages made spears one of the best weapons for true beginners that had never held a weapon before. Smit had kept all of this in mind as he passed the basic knowledge onto his kobolds. In all fairness, given that he was not a master spearman and the fact that kobolds were at the level of intelligence of cavemen, he only was able to pass onto them simple things like "hold the spear like this," "stab like this," "step back like this," and "don't stretch forwards too far like this."

Any normal person could have gotten that much knowledge from a month of practice, but for the kobolds, this was a treasure trove of information. The experience left them staring at Smit as if he was a sage of some sort.

The entire process of bestow knowledge only took about a minute, but that was precious time he was lacking now. The invaders would be here any minute.

"Here, grab these," Smit said quickly, willing four simple

spears made of iron and oak-wood to float down from one of the walls. These weapons were old, but well kept, and enchanted to fight off the rust. Though they had been crafted as a simple project a long time ago, the slightly rounded sides of the blade made these spears a bit different from the basic triangular tip. It allowed for a slight increase in the efficiency of a slicing attack, but other than that, the spears were not very remarkable from Smit's point of view.

With the seconds ticking down, he organized his dungeon, pulling back most of his dungeon mice and evolved snakes to the central second room, which he would use as a choke point to tear down the enemy.

Seconds after he had done this, the intruders stepped into his dungeon.

FOURTEEN BANDITS slowly crept into the dungeon, each of them shivering slightly as they felt an intangible breeze of power wash over them. As they looked around them, they saw the first room of the dungeon, giving way to three separate corridors. All around them, a few mice and insects scattered at their approach, hiding behind rocks or in the mossy outcrops that littered the room.

"This place gives me the chills," one of the bandits muttered. "It don't feel natural here."

A murmur of agreement went through the group, but it was quickly waved away by their gorilla-like leader. "Shut up you lot. Instead of making a big fuss over some small 'feeling' like a little girl that saw her shadow move, why don't you have a look at the damn room? It's as empty as that head of yours, Muck. The only things are insects and rodents around here. Now man up like the cutthroats you are supposed to be."

The words seemed to encourage some of the bandits, reassuring them, though a few of the more superstitious ones were still somewhat skittish. Naturally, the leader ignored them completely.

"Now, we got three hallways. I'm taking four of you boys with me through the middle. Buck, you take three more on the right, and Quag, you take the rest on the left. I don't want to waste time exploring this damnable thing so let's find that core and get the hell out before the Guild gets here."

With mutters of agreement, the assortment of bandits split up, unaware that Smit had been watching them the entire time. In the moments he had observed them, Smit had decided they were all going to die. Not only had they invaded him and disregarded his abilities, they had come with the full intent of capturing and killing him. He had no doubt that they would loot the entirety of his collection of weapons and armors in the process too.

Smit wouldn't even let them get close to him.

He focused on the first encounter the bandits would have. Their enemy would be the few snakes that had been left in the hallways, which had been tasked with hiding. They would be sacrificial lambs for the good of his dungeon, as he doubted those bandits had even bothered to prepare healing items or antidotes.

Smit waited patiently, observing the groups split up in his dungeon. Fear would have to be instilled in them, and they had just made his life a whole lot easier by splitting up. His patience was rewarded when a few minutes later the halls of his dungeon echoed with surprised shouting from all three groups of bandits. As expected, they had come within range of the snakes. These were just the common snakes in his dungeon, whose poison was not very powerful. But even if it wasn't strong, it would serve a purpose, reducing the balance of the bandits and their bodily control.

Several of the bandits got bit, some of them being on the receiving end of those snake bites multiple times, before the snakes were cut down, but that was fine. He could see the bandits were weary now, their heart rates increasing and moving the poison through their veins faster.

So far so good, Smit thought to himself with an invisible smile.

He would cut them down one at the time.

AN HOUR LATER, Badack was running with the remnants of his once glorious gang. They ran away as fast as they could, taking the middle path of the dungeon. They had been had by the dungeon. They had been completely outmatched.

The entrance had looked harmless enough, but that was only a front for the true horrors of the dungeon. First, snakes had attacked them, their poison shaving away at their reaction time and dexterity. Then they had encountered traps, pits with sharp rocks at the bottom, which had broken the legs or arms of several members and killed two. Even then they would have been fine, especially since the side rooms seemed to be devoid of life aside from insects and mice, just like the first room. They felt their hope increase as they delved deeper and deeper into the dungeon.

But then they entered the second room of the middle path, and they knew something was amiss. They had been ambushed. Snakes that had been coiled around the stalactites in the ceiling dropped down on them, wolves had pounced on them the minute they had been distracted, and even large, vicious mice latched on to them and began to tear at their legs and groins with their sharp teeth. To make matters worse, the stalactites had dropped so low that more than once they had interrupted an overhead attack from the bandits, causing them to lose their stance and become off balance.

It was a simple swarm attack by the dungeon, but the poisoned and injured bandits could offer little resistance. In the end, Badack sounded the retreat within minutes of the fight beginning, but by then it was too late. Many had been injured, and by sounding the retreat, he had effectively condemned them to expose their backs to the ravenous inhabitants of the dungeon.

Out of fourteen, only three remained. Three men running like demons being chased by a holy man. They didn't even turn to look back to see if anyone else had made it.

Bleeding and terrified, the three bandits were met with four short figures guarding the entrance they'd come through, with spears at the ready.

Desperate in their charge, the three bandits drew their weapons without slowing down, ready to cut down the short monsters in their way. But alas, that was not meant to be.

The kobolds stood in a line in front of the only entrance and exit to the dungeon, blocking it entirely as their spears faced their enemies. By virtue of the very nature of the charge by the bandits, the kobolds held the advantage as they lowered their spears. The spears thrust at their midsection violently, and one of the bandits was pierced through his gut, blood splattering out of the open wound as the kobold retracted its spear and thrust it into his eye.

The other two bandits, one of whom was Badack, fared better, only suffering shallow cuts to their ribs or arms before they jumped back. The kobolds, though unversed in the ways of war, were well versed in the art of hunting within the halls of the dungeon. Slowly they rounded up their two wounded enemies, pushing them back towards one of the walls. As per Smit's orders, the kobolds prioritized wounding to killing their enemy. Bit by bit the kobolds sliced and pierced their prey, bleeding them, letting them tire and weaken with every moment that slipped by.

The remaining thieves, now too weak to even parry properly, were left to despair. Not for the first time, Badack attempted to hack at the spears that pushed against him, only to be met with unexpected resistance from the wood. He had no idea how these creatures had gotten their hands on such finely worked weapons, but he was certain that even in the army of the kingdom, few below the rank of captain would even be found holding weapons such as these.

Just as he thought of this, a spear found its way to his neck and Badack was no more.

<<<>>>
Status

Species: True Dungeon
Rank: 1
Name: Smit
Age: 49 days
Mana: 1,870 MP
Anima: 286
Mana Reg.: 110 MP/h
Anima Reg.: 1.75 AP/day
Floors: 1
Inhabitants: 23 Species
Titles: Eager Creator; Guide of the Bloody Evolution; Legendary Craftsman; Reincarnated One
Abilities: Absorb matter; Alter environment; Bestow knowledge; Break down components; Craftsmanship; Creation; Digging; Destroy creation; Dungeon laws; Enhancement; Equivalent exchange; Ether manipulation; Evolution; Interdimensional storage; Life bestowal; Life-energy harnessing; Mana absorption; Masterful mana manipulation; Modification of creations; Monster link; Telepathy; Trap building; Transfer dungeon.
Resistances: Magic (general); Mind control

<<<>>>
Bonus info

Bestow knowledge: Allows you to pass on knowledge to a targeted creation or subordinate. Knowledge passed on dependent on your own understanding and the intellectual capacity of the targeted creature. Chance of failure if the knowledge is far too extensive or targeted creature is unable to process all the information.

<u>Dungeon laws</u>: Allows you to set rules or laws for your dungeon or for specific parts of your dungeon. Creates an automatic system in which certain actions will occur if the laws are followed or broken.

<u>Monster loyalty</u>: Animals, plants, monsters, and other creations are extremely loyal to the dungeon core. Intelligent creations are particularly entranced and dedicated to the dungeon core, protecting it more fiercely.

<u>Enhancement</u>: Allows dungeon core to modify, enhance, and manipulate creations (both living and nonliving) with much more precision than otherwise expected. This process is semi-passive, as more complicated enhancements must be carried out consciously by the dungeon. Previously done enhancements can be remembered and applied automatically.

CHAPTER SEVEN

In the village of Nam, a commotion was in progress. There was a certain static to the air, a curious jovial mood that seemed to be charged with excitement. Gat had finally returned to the village, looking a bit worse for wear with how tired he looked, and with him he had a full team of adventurers. A team of five, a reasonable, standard party set up of two front line members, with the rest acting as support from the backline. All the members were considered high C rank, which was to say they had considerable strength.

Add to that the fact that most villagers had never seen adventurers before, and one could understand why everyone was buzzing with excitement. To such common folk on the border of the kingdom, a high C rank individual was equal to a heroic figure head and shoulders above the common folk.

At the lead of the group, there was a red-haired lady with a rapier at her hip. The young woman was a bit on the short side, slim, with wiry muscles and a sharp face and green eyes that seemed to radiate a no-nonsense stare. Her armor was marginal. A chest plate that covered her upper torso, while the rest of her body was protected by what seemed to be thick leather armor. With her analytical gaze and aura of authority, she looked every bit the hero that every child had imagined an adventurer would be.

Before her stood a gentleman with a thick short beard, wearing modest clothes. His hair was taking on a silver color at the edges. Though the man must have been in his early forties, his eyes were already showing signs of more advanced age, looking even more wizened than a man his age would be expected to have. He bowed to the adventurer party with a small bend at his waist, his right hand curled into a fist that was pressed lightly against his chest. A common greeting of respect.

"Welcome, honored adventurers, to the village of Nam. We are grateful for your prompt arrival. I am the new village chief, Rowe Sheppard. I hope your journey here transpired without issues."

The party leader bent her head towards the elder in a small bow, acknowledging him. "I am Ella Graz, high C rank adventurer, leader of the Azure Arrow adventurer's party. I am here to lead my party in the investigation of the new dungeon. The journey here transpired without incident, thankfully."

Stroking his lush beard, Rowe nodded at her words with a small satisfied smile. "Good, good. It eases my heart to hear that. Come, let us talk about your stay with us in a more suitable location than the village square. I have to apologize for the crowd; it seems my people are quite intrigued by you and your comrades."

Ella nodded at the man simply, seemingly not even minding the stares of the local population. Her back was straight as a ruler, her eyes determined and focused. A consummate professional in her career in the eyes of the people. Strong, attractive, and determined. More than one of the village's men were intimidated and attracted to her at the same time.

The adventurers soon found themselves in the home of the village chief, seated at his dinner table with him while tea was prepared by his wife. The home was rustic, but charming, containing few luxuries, but cozy enough nonetheless.

"Right," Rowe said as he looked at the adventurers. "So, may I ask about your comrades, Ms. Ella?"

"Certainly," she replied, starting to wave her hand towards her team members, and began by introducing the biggest of them all, a large man that was easily 210 cm in height, dwarfing even the tallest man of the village by a fair bit. The man looked like he had been working out since the day he left his mother's womb. "The big guy is James, our defense specialist. He doesn't talk too much, but there are few people in our rank that can take him and his tower shield down."

Rowe had little doubt about that. He saw the man lift the 120 cm shield that was as wide as a man as if he were lifting a common stick. Add to that that the man was covered mostly in iron scaled armor, and he made an impressive figure.

"Then we have our ranger, Mei. She is a fantastic shot with her bow and arrow, and able to track almost any creature under the heavens. Together with Adder, our rogue who specializes in knives and trap detection, she keeps us safe from the back."

Rowe's eyes turned to see a female that was the counterpart to the large and burly James. She was small and lithe, but with sharp eyes and firm shoulders. Mix that with her pixie-cut hair and her bow and she had an interesting and alluring look. Beside her sat a roguish looking man with a well-kept moustache and several knives strapped across his belt. His tight leather armor clearly was designed to allow the best freedom of movement possible.

"And lastly, this is Ziggurd, our healer. He is well versed in healing magic."

That was when Rowe's eyes almost seemed to pop out of his skull. Healing magic was a difficult craft, and fairly rare even amongst magic users. Out here, in the edges of the kingdom of Mussol, a magic healer was rare beyond compare. Most people got their healing from a priest or apothecaries, or perhaps from some ranger that had some basic knowledge of how to tend to wounds.

This was the reason why Rowe looked at the stout mage with

curiosity. The man was a little plump around the middle, but his grey eyes and blonde beard gave him a bit of a jovial look. However, the staff he carried was gnarled and it radiated power. This man was clearly not someone to underestimate, despite his warm eyes and soft looking robe.

Rowe took a second to rearrange his thoughts before clearing his throat.

"I see. It seems your party is well balanced," he said carefully, a bit of awe slipping into his voice. These people were warriors to be true, seasoned veterans that hunted monsters for a living.

Ella seemed to perk up slightly at that, her lips twitching upwards into a small smile. "Yes, we have been quite successful with this setup. Now then, shall we get on to the preparations with regards to our stay here?"

"Certainly," Rowe assented with his head, his fingers intertwining before him as he looked at her with a serious face that was reserved for business only. "We are in your debt for your aid, and as such you are welcome to lodge at our local tavern free of charge. However, food would not be provided."

"We are agreeable to such terms," Ella nodded. "As you should know, should we determine there to be a dungeon, you should expect a guild hall of the Adventurers Guild to be built in the town. Depending on the level and development of the dungeon, the king may be informed and growth of the village should be expected in that event, unless the danger of the dungeon exceeds its use."

Rowe nodded with professional ease, before she continued. "Excellent. In addition to this, I require any and all information that you may have regarding the dungeon."

"We have limited information, as none of the villagers have dared to step close to the dungeon."

"All the same, I would like to hear everything you know," she insisted, keeping her face carefully neutral.

"Yes. Well to summarize, the dungeon is very near our village, but it takes about two days easy walk to reach the dungeon. Though the terrain varies somewhat in the trajectory of the journey, it is in general steep and cluttered with wildlife, which is why it takes time to get there. The dungeon seems to appear as a cave with a mouth that looks to have been carved out rather than naturally created. As Gat surely told you, we are under the impression that there are rodents and snakes in the dungeon, but we are unsure as to monsters or more creatures. However, we have lived in this area for generations and never come across it, so it must be young. That sums it up."

Ella sighed briefly. No idea of the traps, number of monsters, species, the number of floors, or number of rooms. The only thing that she could hope is that the dungeon was really that young and not anything to worry about, in which case, they could set up an outpost for the guild and expand it slowly as the dungeon grew. That would be ideal.

"If that's the case," Ella followed up, "then the exploration should be done quickly. We will rest here for the night and set out tomorrow for the dungeon. Is there any way to get to the dungeon faster than in two days?"

Rowe sat there and thought for a moment, considering things. "Not at the moment. If we built a road, it would be significantly faster, but as it is now, even horses won't do you much good in the forest. Although the dungeon is directly north of us, there are a number of obstacles in the way, such as rivers and cliffs, which require you to go around them."

Accepting this information, Ella thanked the chief for his help. She had much to think about as Gat led her and her team to the small tavern of the village, where they would be lodging for the night.

At least they would sleep in a proper bed for the night after such a long ride to this isolated place. And tomorrow, with the assistance of Gat, the adventurer team would head to the presumed location of the dungeon, and start their exploration.

Hopefully, there wouldn't be any surprises and everything would be smooth sailing.

"Master?" Echo's voice sounded in his head again. Ever since her evolution, she had started to act differently, showing more interest in her surroundings, herself, the creatures of the dungeon, and pretty much everything else. It was starting to get annoying for Smit. Couldn't she see he was a busy dwarf?

"What is it this time?" he grunted at her as he kept working, only idly listening to her while he guided his mana.

"What is the purpose of your work? The golems that Master is creating are clearly weak and of inferior quality. Why waste mana creating them?"

"Aesthetics, you fool," he grunted at her again. "I was a dwarf, and a craftsman at that. Every dwarf appreciates beauty, and I more so than others. I may be a dungeon core now, but I will not have anyone slander my dungeon and call it ugly. In fact, I will make it the most mesmerizing dungeon that anyone will lay their eyes on."

"But Master, this one is of the opinion that those golems are a waste of—"

"Yes, you've said that before, and I don't care," Smit replied bluntly. "Now hush up unless you have something else to talk about. I am busy."

Smit had worked and worked relentlessly since the defeat of the bandits to improve his dungeon, splitting his attention between evolving his creatures and fixing his dungeon. While the natural ambiance of the dungeon was nice, it was lacking in décor. He would be damned if his new home would be called mundane.

He started with his golem project to create statues. Unfortunately, the golems he could create were rather limited to whatever materials he had in the dungeon, namely dirt and claystone rock.

The MP cost for a stone golem was easily ten times that of one made of dirt, and the cost of the golem further increased by the size and complexity of the golem, not to mention that the specific rock type could influence the cost too.

For the purpose of decorating, he practiced his golem creation with hardened dirt golems, which would serve as statues to put on the walls of the dungeon. With the delicacy and accuracy that only a seasoned dwarven artisan could muster, Smit created replicas of the creatures found in his dungeon and placed them on the walls of his dungeon. Snakes, mice, wolves, insects, and kobolds were scattered around the dungeon, decorating the halls in a subtle matter, separated far enough apart as to not crowd the walls.

Ideally, once his guests stepped into his dungeon with a torch, the golems that doubled as statues would catch the light in such a way as to add a mystical aura to the place. It wasn't nearly as beautiful as he wanted it to be, but he resolved to make his second floor something far more suitable for his tastes. Let the first floor stay like this, a gateway to the rest of his dungeon.

As for his creatures, amongst the most notable evolutions were the dungeon mice, which evolved to dungeon rats, bigger than cats and with elongated claws that could slice through wood better than an axe. The second evolution that was worthy of note were the kobolds, which had achieved three evolutions, kobold chief, kobold warrior, and kobold shaman. The kobold warrior was about 10 cm taller than the original kobolds, but his mastery with weapons was higher, and his strength increased. The kobold shaman had acquired a bit of a blue tinge to her scales, her intelligence had increased, and she manipulated simple magic of water and earth, allowing her to heal and buff her allies with modest spells, in addition to allowing her to cast simple offensive spells.

Lastly, the kobold chief. He was by far the most impressive evolution. He had grown to an impressive 180 cm in height, dwarfing even the kobold warriors, managing to look far more ferocious. He seemed to have increased his strength and intelligence, demonstrating clear abilities to lead. Smit quite liked him, as he seemed to be a no-nonsense kobold, smacking the two kobold warriors if they started to argue. Much to Smit's delight, the kobold collectively gained the ability to communicate with speech.

The implications of their speech with regard to their intelligence were promising. Hopefully, soon they would be intelligent enough to start learning things in a more organized form. As it was, they could barely utter more than a handful of words, but that was commendable considering that they had been "born" recently.

Smit sighed quietly inwardly, considering the next steps he should take, when a voice intruded upon his mind.

"Master? This one has a request," Echo chimed in, her voice speaking hesitantly, but catching his attention quickly.

The sound of her voice irritated Smit briefly as she interrupted his thoughts, before her words truly registered in his mind. Echo had never requested anything. While he wasn't sure if this request was a good or bad sign, or perhaps neither, he was curious enough to hear her out. Ever since her evolution, she seemed more like an individual as opposed to a robotic entity, so perhaps this was just another manifestation of her individuality.

"What is it, Echo?"

"This one would like to request a body."

Smit frowned mentally at the idea. That was... an odd request. But one he could relate to. He also longed for a body, but he refused to take the form of anything that would not let him use his forge as he desired. A common kobold was far too weak, as were his current golems. As a matter of fact, a golem would be worse, as they normally had no sense of touch, which was detrimental for his work.

"I see..." Smit replied, mulling over the request. He didn't see any harm in this, but creating a body might prove difficult. "I could do that. Why do you want a body?"

"Master, this one wishes to be of use beyond the occasional

question. This one requests a body as an alternative to further aid Master in the future."

"I see. Well, you are my first creation, technically, so I suppose you do deserve a body of a sort. But what kind of body do you desire?"

Echo followed up flawlessly, almost as if she had rehearsed what to say beforehand. "This one requests a body with hands, preferably humanoid form. This one requests the body to be feminine."

Smit sat pensive for a moment, considering his options. Despite the drain on his MP to the numerous dirt golems, he still had a massive mana pool due to the bandits, and some leftover materials from when he had been a dwarf in his core room. He could certainly create a higher quality golem with that. However, using it now would postpone the second floor that he had been hoping to start on.

Bah, forget the second floor! Smit thought as excitement began to make his core shine. If he had a face, a large smirk would have been visible on his face. It had been far too long since this old dwarf had been able to craft a proper golem. Letting loose after all this time would be good.

"Alright. I shall accept your request."

He could feel Echo radiate a happy aura as she began to thank him earnestly. She quipped about her gratefulness and his great benevolence until he had to turn to her and fix her with a glare. Or that's what he would have done if he had eyes anyway. As it stood, he couldn't exactly do that, but he emanated a stern aura that demanded her attention, making her stop her words.

"Quiet. I need to focus for this."

He closed his mind to his surroundings, isolating himself until the feelings of being a dungeon ran in the back of his mind, freeing him to focus on the task at hand. First, he would envision Echo's form. As per her request, he would make a feminine form, but he needed to decide upon the shape, the materials, and the purpose of the new body for Echo.

Frowning, he contemplated the possibilities. Echo was relatively young, but her voice had shifted from emotionless and gender neutral to a younger and more high-pitched feminine voice. She clearly had some desires and thoughts, and had shown signs of self-awareness. What could that inspire him to create?

He settled for her voice. He would use her voice rather than her attitude to inspire her body. Young, crisp, but lacking the elating vigor of young children. Echo would not be aged or a child, but her voice did not inspire in him the body of a mother. Her voice... what could that voice inspire?

An idea came to him, and quickly, he reached for his power, drawing up on his mana. He would create her out of stone and metal, and will those to a masterpiece.

He summoned his last slab of labradorite, a blue rock that looked as if the sky and oceans themselves had frozen and solidified into stone. This stone was favored by diviners and healers, famed for its ability to give guidance when the right magic was applied to it. Best of all, it was as hard as granite, making it extremely durable.

Then he summoned the leftover iron and gold that his previous self had left behind, fusing the two metals at great cost of his mana, but worth it for the alloy that he needed. Guiding his mana to create a body from stone, his mana became depleted by the second. He made graceful and slender arms, toned legs that connected to attractive, yet not too prominent hips, which were attached to a toned belly. The shoulders were sensibly broad but delicate in appearance, breasts that seemed perky but not obscenely large, and a slender face without lips or eyes but with a cute sharp nose.

With the base completed, he set about the details. The eyes and lips were crafted out of his metal alloy, as were the nails on her hands and feet, and the braided hair that wove its way down to the spot just below her shoulder blades. Her neck, elbows, knees, and spine all sported the delicate cover of alloy that seemed to adorn the beautiful blue mannequin. This was the image he had selected for Echo. A girl, perhaps seventeen years of age, measuring roughly 157 cm, and human enough in appearance to fool anyone had it not been for the fact that she was made of stone and metal. A true masterpiece that any king would kill to have adorn his halls.

He wouldn't leave it at that though. Now she needed to be armed. He would not have this creation fighting nude. Fortunately, that was a more simple matter, as her body didn't truly need much protection considering the toughness of the material he had used. Thus, he simply willed the alloy of gold and iron to form into a metal crown for her head, gauntlets that covered her forearms and the backs of her hands, a skirt of chainmail, and a breastplate that left her midsection exposed. The finishing touch was a halberd that he plucked from his walls, an elegant weapon crafted of Damascus steel.

He looked over the body and smiled, satisfied with his stone Valkyrie. He didn't even mind that he had spent twenty hours working on it, or the fact that he had spent a grand total of 31,450 MP in her creation, draining nearly the entirety of his reserves, leaving him with a meagre 1,034 MP.

He smirked, pleased with his first masterpiece. Truly a vessel fit for his first creation.

"It is done," Smit said with satisfaction. He could almost feel the awe radiate from Echo. But before she had a chance to speak, he reached out and held her essence, and pushed it towards the golem on instinct.

Warning! You are about to bestow a body to [Echo]. Cost: 250 Anima. Are you sure you would like to proceed?

Smit briefly checked his reserves and smirked again. 286 Anima was at his disposal. Without any hesitation, he accepted the procedure.

And on that day, the stone Valkyrie was born.

Status

Species: True Dungeon
Rank: 1
Name: Smit
Age: 51 days
Mana: 1,030 MP
Anima: 39
Mana Reg.: 110 MP/h
Anima Reg.: 1.75 AP/day
Floors: 1
Inhabitants: 30 Species

Titles: Eager Creator; Guide of the Bloody Evolution; Legendary Craftsman; Reincarnated One

Abilities: Absorb matter; Alter environment; Bestow knowledge; Break down components; Craftsmanship; Creation; Digging; Destroy creation; Dungeon laws; Enhancement; Equivalent exchange; Ether manipulation; Evolution; Interdimensional storage; Life bestowal; Life-energy harnessing; Mana absorption; Masterful mana manipulation; Modification of creations; Monster link; Telepathy; Trap building; Transfer dungeon.

Resistances: Magic (general); Mind control

<<<>>>

CHAPTER EIGHT

Echo tested her body slowly, moving around the dungeon with cautious movements. Though she had received a body that was masterfully created with such detail that she even had an esophagus, the fact was that Echo had never had a mobile body before. Even if she was created to be a perfect replica of a human, crafted with loving detail, she was not sure how to make use of it.

Everything needed to be regulated consciously by Echo. From the movement of her toes to the angle of her hips as she walked, she had to manipulate every piece of her body to simply manage to take a step forward. This wouldn't usually be an issue for a regular golem, as they are more or less created with a predetermined amount of functions, but since Echo had taken over all aspects of the golem, this did not apply. The good news, however, was that her body had been created with excellent weight distribution in mind, in such a way that simulating the movements of a bipedal creature, such as a human, would not cause too many issues.

The bad news, however, was that since her body was crafted out of stone, it was stiffer than a body of flesh and bone. As a golem, the stone itself had far more flexibility than should be possible for a body of stone, but the fact remained that stone could not bend, twist, and stretch under normal circumstances. According to Smit, with enough practice it was possible that she could regulate certain properties of her body to an extent, allowing her to be more flexible and even replicate the feeling of having skin... in theory anyway. But that possibility was far, far into the future.

At any rate, in exchange for the lack of mobility, a golem was a very hardy existence, not needing food or air to survive, not to mention the fact that they did not become fatigued and that their natural defenses were not easily breached. Moreover, as long as golems did not run out of a power source (most commonly mana), then they could in theory function indefinitely, if their bodies permitted it.

Fortunately for Echo, as a former dungeon core she could channel more than sufficient mana from the dungeon she inhabited to power her new body. She hoped that eventually she could create a mana core in her body and store mana in it, but for the moment that was nothing more than a dream.

Just as she thought that, she stumbled to the floor due to an errant step on her part, her arms flailing as she tried to keep her balance in vain. She braced for impact as she felt the shock of her heavy body slamming onto the earthen floor, and felt a dull sensation that one might identify vaguely as pain. This was one of the mysteries of her new body.

Her body had a shallow perception of what constituted as touch. She could feel if she was grabbing something, but it was muted, as if the feeling itself was a distant thing. For all intents and purposes, a normal golem had no sense of touch, for they had no nervous system. However, Echo had some semblance of the sense of touch. Her only theory was that though her body was a magically crafted golem, by imbuing said body with a soul it had acquired special attributes. She couldn't explain how or why, but it was the only thing that made sense to her.

Pushing such thoughts aside, Echo mechanically pushed

herself up from the floor, dusting the beautiful armor that had been given to her. Smit had stated that he hadn't been satisfied by the armor he had crafted for her, and that he would upgrade it at some point, but he had not given her any idea as to what the upgrade would entail. Hopefully the creator could make enchanted armor that would enhance her sense of balance, or something along those lines, if that was even possible. She was getting tired of falling down.

As always, Smit was getting busy with work. Though his first floor was what he would consider as barely passable, he had decided to let it be, in favor of working on his second floor. Since his rank up, he had ignored the second floor as he tried to set up his defenses in the first floor, but now that his creatures had evolved, he was confident enough in his own safety to turn his attention away from them. He had charged the kobolds with train-ing, trying to get them used to their own bodies as soon as possi-ble, and he had Echo get to work too... though in a different manner.

He was disappointed at the fact that Echo could not use her body naturally from the start, but on hindsight it would have been very weird if she was able to. After all, she used to be a rock that had no limbs. With that in mind, the fact that she could walk at all, or swing a weapon was commendable. Still, he would probably keep her close to his core for now, making her a meat shield (or in this case, a stone shield) in case someone got too close to him. At this point, her lack of coordination made her more useful as a wrestler than as a warrior. If she could latch on to a person, and make them take the fight to the floor, then her superior weight and strength would give her the advantage. Otherwise, any experienced warrior with a decent weapon would simply dance around her with very few issues.

Now, if only she could get used to her body and learn to wield a weapon, then that would be fantastic...

Setting those thoughts aside, he focused on his current project. He had already transferred the entirety of his core room to the second floor, replacing the space it occupied in the first floor with a regular empty room. It would act as a faux core room for the time being, preventing his soon-to-arrive guests from exploring his unfinished work. He would have them wait until the second floor was done properly, and not a second before that.

His vision for the setup of the second floor was to create a sort of... reception hall. A very beautiful and dangerous reception hall.

At the moment, the second floor was little more than a long and broad hallway, about two hundred meters long in a straight line that connected to his core room at the end. The walls and the floor were polished evenly, using granite as the base material for them. The granite around this area of the mountain was rather nice, mostly a clean white color from quartz with a few pink and red tinges from the feldspar, and even a few dots of black biotite that decorated the surface. All in all, it was a beautiful setting.

Now if he could only get the ceiling to—

His thoughts were cut short at that moment, a prickling sensation in his mind alerting him that a group of intruders were entering the perimeter of his dungeon. He immediately abandoned the task at hand, and rushed his consciousness towards the entrance of his dungeon.

By the love of all metals, I need to fix this entrance too. I had forgotten it's literally just a hole right now, Smit grumbled in his mind, irritated by his oversight of such an important thing. The entrance to his dungeon would be the first thing people saw after all. Since adventurers were bound to come in anyway, he might as well try to make a good impression. Maybe something opulent and imperial would work. But that was a project for some other time, when he didn't have a five-person crew armed to their teeth marching towards him.

Heaving a mental sigh of exasperation, he focused on the adventurers before him. By the way that the redhead woman carried herself, she was likely the leader of the group. She was attractive enough to be called pretty, though not enough to be called a beauty in his mind. His senses stretched over her and her party like a blanket, allowing him to roughly analyze them, starting with Ella.

Short, by human standards. Leather armor, light tan color, seems to be worked decently, but with a particular stretchiness to it... Probably hind-bear leather then. Small short sword that appears to be made of common steel. The rapier looks to be of an alloy, given its slight green color, perhaps steel with some plant ingredient? Hmm... not your standard weapon set.

It took him only a minute to roughly analyze the properties of her armor and weapons. He acted similarly with the rest of the party as they stared into the entrance of his cave, talking amongst themselves. Based on what he saw, he assumed that they were at least a fairly experienced bunch.

Judging by their equipment, it was simple enough to guess their specializations, or at least make an approximation of them. The leader was clearly a damage dealer that specialized in piercing and slashing, armed with a rapier and short sword as her main weapons. The tall man was obviously a vanguard that was meant to primarily absorb damage and draw the attention of the enemy, while the other woman with pointy ears was probably a ranger or at least an archer of respectable ability, judging by the bow.

The last two members he was not entirely sure about. The one with knives could be a middle ground player, looking to cover the shortcomings of the others, considering the array of knives he held. Smit easily spotted different sets of knives, of which at least one set was specifically designed for throwing. The last member of the team looked to be a magic user of some sort, but he could not place his specialization. Most likely, he was a mage who specialized in the traditional style of casting, and therefore was not a shaman or summoner, given his lack of specialized tools and his rather standard looking staff. He was most likely specialized in something related to light or water magic, given the aura he radiated, but that was just a guess.

While he mulled over this, he caught snippets of a conversation between the adventurers, only listening to them partially.

"—odd isn't it? It seems just like a hole in the mountain," the big guy said carefully.

Smit snapped his attention towards the adventurers, a bit of anger starting to burn in him with indignation. What did these whelps know? The oldest was probably in his thirties at best! He would love to see them try to build their own dungeon if they were so great at it. He hadn't even been working for two months yet! What did they expect? A castle in the mountain?

"No, this is definitely a dungeon," the mage said with conviction. "I can feel the mana rolling out of this entrance in waves. It is hard to believe that this thing was just found. The mana seems to be of high purity for a brand new dungeon too. It's quite peculiar."

"Is that so? From the look of things I would've thought it was barely a couple of months old," the leader spoke up.

"That's why I say it's peculiar. Dungeons generally produce more mana as they grow in size, but the quality of the mana seems to improve exclusively as the dungeon evolves. For the mana to be like this... This might be a higher quality dungeon in the making."

Smit snorted at those words. Higher quality is it? By the time he was done with his dungeon, people would marvel at it. It wouldn't be just "higher quality," it would be the best of the best. Still, the mage seemed like he had a sharp enough mind. Smit decided he liked him the best out of the group. Hopefully he wouldn't die.

"Right," the leader announced. "Well, now that we have confirmed that this is a dungeon, let us begin the exploration. Adder, map our progress. The dungeon might be new, but if what

Zig says is true, then the dungeon might be more extensive than we expected. Everyone, standard formation. James, take the lead."

The group assembled quickly, creating an arrow-like shape in which the largest man was up at the front, followed by the redhead and the man called Adder, while the ranger and mage followed behind them closely. A moment later, the mage created a small orb of light that levitated right above the man named James, and the party began to move.

Come, my dear guests. Let me see how you deal with my dungeon. Smit needed to know how he stacked up. They might well be strong enough to clear his dungeon, but with any luck, they would not attempt anything... rash.

EVER SINCE I entered this dungeon things feel... odd. At times like this, the weight of my two swords at my hip is especially reassuring. True, we have only been exploring for perhaps a few hours, and due to the fact that we are trying to create a rough map of the area we are taking longer than usual, but even so, this feels more intricate than the first floor of any new dungeon has the right to be. Usually, the first floor of a dungeon contains only one main path that might curve a bit with a few rooms in the way and maybe a side room every so often. But not this one. This dungeon presents you with three pathways from the start, almost identical in shape and size at a glance.

There are glittering things that illuminate the dungeon dimly in the distance, the floor is uneven, the ceiling is rather low, and the moss creates an intricate tapestry with the polished protrusions of rock. That alone makes this dungeon odd in appearance, but the most unnerving part of this dungeon is the statues.

Hundreds of statues of dozens of animals are scattered around the walls, a few even carved out of the natural stalagmites and stalactites that dot the halls and rooms. It's rather unnerving the detail with which they were carved, and in dim light, one might confuse them for the real thing. James already smashed two of them with his hammer, confusing them for real snakes.

That's the other thing. So far, we have only encountered snakes and mice. Really big mice, but just mice nonetheless. Once or twice we have heard the growling of some sort of canine beast, but we haven't caught sight of even a tail. I am willing to bet that the dungeon has either foxes or wolves roaming around, but they seem to be smart. They are not attacking us as of yet. Maybe I am overthinking, but I can't help it. As team leader, worrying is part of my job.

"Can you not do something about mapping faster?" Ziggurd spoke up with a rather hushed voice. "We don't need a perfect layout yet Adder, just draw some rough hallways and let us get going. Something about this place is not normal. It's too beautiful and too... quiet."

"Quiet you, details are important," Adder hissed back at him, his charcoal pencil moving constantly on the page. "It is not like we have to hurry anyway. Do mice and snakes unman you so much, oh great sorcerer?"

"Listen here you!" Ziggurd hissed back. "You don't understand. I feel the mana here. There should be more than insects, mice, and snakes. There should be more... of everything with these sorts of mana levels. You may have found some pitfalls with your skills, but I wager that this dungeon has more in store than what we are seeing."

Adder snorted loudly, and turned to look at the mage with a grin. "I wager ten silver coins that the best this dungeon has are wolves, and you are just being an overly cautious pansy."

Ziggurd bristled up slightly, his eyes narrowing as he looked at Adder. "Fine. I bet ten silver that this dungeon has something more deadly than wolves."

I rolled my eyes, resisting the urge to smack them both. "Quiet both of you. We are here to do a job, not to bicker like old housewives. Now keep your wits about you. Last thing we need is someone falling into some obvious trap and breaking their neck. Adder, Ziggurd is right, less artistry, more efficiency. I want to be done before nightfall."

I sighed internally as Adder complained something about people not understanding art. The man was a bona fide expert on trap detection and mapping, but he had a bad habit of spending too much time on his sketches. Truly, these maps did not need to mark the location of every single statue, nor did they need to note the location of every large puddle they came across.

I allowed myself to leave that thought behind me, professionalism at the forefront of my mind now. The dungeon so far was not overly complex, but it certainly had more than enough locations to hide its creations. Lack of attention could earn me a snake bite that I would rather not have.

"Halt!" Mei hissed, her voice just loud enough for the rest of our group to hear, causing all of us to freeze up in mid stride. One of the main rules of our team: If the ranger calls for a halt, stop and listen to her. Usually there is a very good reason for it. This time it was no different.

I barely had time to turn to look at Mei inquisitively before she started explaining. "I hear movement behind us. It's faint, but there are multiple paws hitting the ground. They will be on us in a minute if they keep stalking us like that."

Superb hearing as always. Being half-elf had its perks, and excellent hearing was one of them.

Thinking quickly, I sorted through our options. We were in a corridor at the moment, just about to enter a large room. If we could enter the room and hold whatever creature it was in the corridor, we could cut them down efficiently. I barked out the order, and we started moving quickly towards the room. And as we neared it, a bloodcurdling howl rang out behind us, and the creatures abandoned all sense of stealth, rushing towards us instead.

Too slow! I grinned, and James and I turned around as we entered the large room. Between the two of us, we could cover roughly the entire entrance of the hallway. It is during times such as these that I am glad to have the big guy with us. James made for an imposing figure to the enemy, and a reliable partner. He also made for an impressive one-man blockade.

We stood facing about nine wolves, all of which looked rather hungry and pissed off. I glared into those yellow eyes that seemed to promise blood, trying my best to release all the bloodlust I could gather. Unfortunately, it seemed that I wasn't skilled enough to cower these creatures into retreat, though I gave them pause for a few seconds. Enough for our backline to get ready.

At an unknown signal the attack began, and we crashed against a wave of wolves. Highly unusual, as wolves would rather test things and slowly create an opening. But not these wolves. They rushed at us without regard, latching onto us as we cut them down. Had it been James and me fighting them on our own, we might have been in trouble, but we had our backline.

Steel sang as it pierced flesh, and arrows whistled in the wind along with knives. It was hardly a battle, though the aggressive wolves did manage to latch onto me and James more than once. Tenacious mutts.

"Argh!"

A shout from behind us made my attention snap back towards my other allies, only to see Adder hacking off the neck of a snake that had struck at his thigh. I cursed as I dispatched the last wolf and sped towards Adder, reaching him in two rushed steps.

"Zig, status?"

Ziggurd was already muttering a diagnosis spell, and within a handful of seconds he had an answer. "Hmm... some sort of paralysis poison. It is somewhat stronger than that of the previous snakes we encountered. Nothing too serious as long as we treat it quickly, but otherwise it seems it would take a day to break down on its own. The snake managed to pierce your thigh quite close to a vein. You are lucky the snake didn't sink its fangs directly into it."

"Yeah, yeah. *Real* lucky," Adder grumbled under his breath. "Fix me up... please."

"Of course," Ziggurd said with a sigh, casting a detoxification spell and mending his wounds. The entire thing took no more than a minute, chants and all.

"Have I ever told you how glad I am that you are a healer?" Adder mentioned as he stood up and shook his leg.

"Yes, but it is my job after all," Zig replied with a smirk. "Try to not get bitten too much."

"I hear yah," Adder grunted as he turned to face me. "Ready to go boss?"

I stared at Adder for a second. It's hard to believe that this man is also a high C rank adventurer sometimes. Moody, whiny, a cad in some aspects too... but I doubt anyone else amongst any of the C rank adventurers is more skilled at trap detection and knife throwing.

"Form up then." At my direction, we flowed into our standard formation again, and proceeded with caution. Seems like the dungeon creatures were a bit trickier than we had expected. If what Zig said was true, then that snake was a variant or a more deadly species of snake. Of course, this meant that the dungeon was either evolving faster than expected, or had specialized in some way with snakes. Or at least, those were the most desirable options. If a sorcerer was trying to manipulate the dungeon...

Well, that was only a very rare scenario. One that might involve a whole crusade against said dungeon and sorcerer.

However, there was no point worrying about that right now. "Ready? Advance."

SMIT KEPT an eye on the intruders, watching them progress inch by inch through his dungeon. Truth be told, they were taking quite a while, but that was just a sign of professionalism in his eyes. They did not rush in blindly, they took note of their surroundings, and they assessed their ability to flee. They were professionals to be sure.

However, he had mixed feelings about their treatment of his statues. On one hand, his statues had been realistic enough that the intruders had attacked a few before realizing they were statues and not the real thing. On the other hand, they had wrecked his statues.

I wonder if I can make things like those statues respawn on their own.

That would be a handy little trick.

In any case, he was pleased at his discoveries so far. By the looks of it, these adventurers were clearing his dungeon with a fair bit of ease; however, they were not unscathed. Several bites from his creatures had managed to reach them, though in all three occasions it had been the product of swarming them or ambushes. He was also pleased with his assessment of the sorcerer, as he turned out to be a healer that used mostly light element spells, and a few water element spells. He didn't have much in the way of offensive capabilities, but his buffs and healing skills were decent enough.

However, now that he had seen how useless pitfalls would be against moderately experienced adventurers, he was glad that he had taken pains to evolve his creatures. Had he just chosen to exclusively expand his dungeon, they would have passed through virtually unobstructed, as the man called Adder seemed to be able to guide them around any traps without much difficulty and none of his normal creatures would have caused them harm.

But now, the time to play had just about finished. They were approaching his last two rooms of the first floor, and he was not eager to let himself be found. Adventurers they may be, but they were still human, and humans could easily succumb to greed. They might let him be and return to their guild dutifully, or they might decide to fabricate a lie and kill him, stealing his core and selling it to the black market. One should never discount that dark possibility.

Thinking like this, he assembled his elites. The kobold chief and his entourage would be at the forefront, aided by the remaining three wolves that had not been cut down already. Unfortunately, he had sent the last of his evolved snakes to the hallway that the adventurers were using to buy some time. They were managing to hold out admirably, but even his greatest three-meter-long snake could do nothing against that hulking metal giant that they called James. The adventurers would dispatch them sooner rather than later at this rate.

"Right," Smit thought towards his creations, his voice gruff as it was carried into their minds. "We got powerful intruders coming straight towards me. You lot will work together to repel them, understood?"

"Yesss, Father," the chief kobold spoke, bending a knee towards the floating gem that was Smit. The rest of the creatures present bowed as well, showing him great respect.

Smit for his part simply stared at the kobold for a moment, at a loss of words. Father? That had not been a word he had expected the kobolds to learn, nor had he ever expected said word to be directed at him. However, this was not the time to contemplate the mysteries of where the kobolds were obtaining this knowledge, nor was it the time to sit around idly to try to sort out how he felt about being referred to as Father.

"Right. Good," he grunted, glossing over the entire father business. "Now go, assemble in the next room. Try to make sure they don't come in my core room, understood?"

"Yesss, Father," The kobold chief spoke again with that rough voice of his.

"Good. Get going then. We don't exactly have all day, move it!"

The group rose as one and dashed out of his room. He

couldn't decide if they were running like that out of eagerness to follow his instructions, or because perhaps they were eager for blood... maybe it was both.

"Master? No, Father?" A second voice called out to Smit, interrupting his thoughts.

"What is it Echo?"

"What about me? Shall I go with them and fight them as well?"

Though her voice was neutral, Smit, who had hundreds of years of experience with dealing with people, could sense a subdued eagerness in her voice. It was almost like a child that was too anxious to ask for something she really wanted, unsure of how to go about it.

"Hell no," Smit grunted at her, his words blunt as a hammer.

As he suspected, Echo's shoulders drooped down slightly. Smit suspected that if she could breathe, she might have sighed.

"You are my last line of defense, you fool. Why would I let you go fight with the rest?"

Her eyes seemed to focus on him, giving him a penetrating stare as if trying to unravel a deeper meaning to his words. Understanding her unspoken question, he sighed and began to explain.

"Look, my foolish Echo. As you are, your dexterity and balance are subpar at best, useless at worst. Thankfully, your body is sturdy enough to take quite the beating. From what I can see, their weapons will dull and crack long before they can destroy your body, unless they have some trump card that they have not played yet. Considering that they seem to be experienced, that is a possibility. Hopefully, if they do have a trump card, they will expend it during their fight with the kobolds, which will allow you to survive anything else they have planned. Get it now? You are my personal shield right now."

Her golden eyes went wide at the explanation, irises shining brightly upon carefully carved eyes that displayed their full radiance. Clearly she had not considered that as a possibility. Most likely, she had thought of maximizing their fighting potential to take down the intruders. That would be a good plan, *if* she knew how to control her body or fight in a team. As she was, she would most likely get in the way of the others. She was more intelligent than the rest of his creations, but she was hardly a tactician, it seemed.

"If you get it come over here. I am not sure how fragile my body is at the moment, so take care to hold it carefully."

Echo made her way closer and reached out to grab the core that levitated only a scant few centimeters from the ground, lifting it gently upon her open palms. His core, which was now larger than his fist when he was a dwarf, seemed to rest easily upon her open palms. She looked down at him with an odd expression, as if she was entranced, weary, and awed at the same time. It made him feel uncomfortable while he tried to focus on the fight that had just begun between the kobolds and the adventurers.

"Don't just stand there. Sit down. What if they knock you over and you fall on top of me? Also stop staring at me like I grew two heads and a beard out of my armpits. I am trying to focus."

"Yes... Father." Her voice was softer this time, more relaxed as she crossed her legs and sat down, cradling his core next to her chest.

"Good." Smit replied with a grunt, completely trying to ignore her now. He had to focus.

"This place is just full of surprises isn't it?" Adder said drily, his forehead shining as a film of sweat continued to grow slowly. While Ella and James took care of the getting up close and personal with three kobolds, Adder was doing his best to fend off three wolves that were constantly trying to sneak around them to target their backline, seeming particularly interested in Ziggurd. He was alone in this task, as Mei could not afford to let the kobold magic caster have too much time. She kept firing sniping shots that should have ended the fight quickly, had it not been for the fact that the kobold mage refused to stay in a clear line of sight, working to stay behind the chaos of the melee fighters.

A wolf let out a growl to his right, and Adder reflexively threw a knife before he could even see the creature, his actions rewarded with a gratifying yelp from the creature.

His eyes darted towards the enemy he had struck, briefly inspecting the damage. *Left flank. Right on the leg. He won't be moving as quickly now.*

No time for further thoughts was granted to him, as a second wolf made a lunge for his neck. Eyes going wide, Adder pulled a knife in time to slice into the beast, opening its throat with a swipe of the blade. Still, the dying wolf slammed into him, throwing him off balance. Two wolves pounced upon him, sensing the chance.

An arrow sprouted from the back of one of them, killing it instantly as the arrow pierced both the spine and the heart, though the other wolf managed to tear up the arm of the rogue pretty badly before Adder could end its life with a knife to the eye.

Gasping for breath, he swallowed his pain as he gave a wordless look of thanks to Mei, only to watch her get stumble to the ground as a water bullet smashed onto her left shoulder.

Nearby, James dealt with what could only be an abnormally large specimen of a kobold chief, while Ella fended off two warrior kobolds. How the kobolds had gotten their hands on such good quality spears was anyone's guess, but she could ill afford to think of such things. Despite the fact that these kobolds were only mediocre with their use of the spears, they held three advantages on her: weapon range, numbers, and strength. Though she was certain she could match the strength of either of her assailants individually, the fact that she had to use two weapons while they each used one meant that she effectively had to fend off a two-handed spear thrust with only one hand. As if that wasn't enough, both of her weapons were far shorter than the spears, which allowed the kobolds to keep her in check as long as they worked together. It was truly unlucky that she had to deal with them on her own.

James seemed to be faring better, dealing with the kobold chief on his own, but the creature was both more nimble and craftier than its brethren, making it hard for James to land a decisive blow. Every time the kobold chief launched an attack, it glanced off James' armor or the shield. Meanwhile, James continued to try to close in on him to land a strike with his hammer, only to strike empty air.

In other words, they were at a stalemate.

Minutes slipped by unnoticed as the combatants struggled for survival, steel against steel. Cuts accumulated and fatigue started to set in. Hours of exploration were taking their toll upon the adventurers as the fight stretched out, making their muscles burn with exertion. It was only through Ziggurd's efforts that none of them collapsed, as he kept trying to invigorate them with his magic, keeping them in the fight.

Salvation came to the adventurers in the form of a knife, imbedding itself in the shoulder of the kobold shaman and eliciting a shriek. It distracted the two kobold warriors for only a second. Plenty of time for Ella to slip past one of them and pierce its belly with her rapier, letting the blade penetrate clean through to the other side of the kobold.

It was at this point that the tables began to turn. Slowly, with the death of one of their comrades, the kobolds were pushed back as arrows rained upon them and a third combatant with a knife joined the front line. Restricted and outnumbered, the kobolds started to fall to the onslaught, despite the number of injuries they had managed to deal to their enemies.

"HEY, HEY, HEY," Smit muttered to himself as he watched as only the chief remained, scrambling all over the place as he did everything possible to dodge the incoming attacks, only able to make the smallest aggressive movements to nick his enemies with his spear. His allies all dead, he struggled to stay alive as he was riddled with arrows.

Smit had to admit he was impressed by his devotion and survival skills, managing to stay alive for even a few seconds against five opponents of that caliber was quite something for someone like the kobold chief, and yet the chief seemed to somehow survive as the seconds stretched out.

It would be a shame to lose him.

As if that thought had a will of its own, Smit felt his connection with the kobold strengthen, solidifying into something more tangible.

<<<>>>
Warning! Creating a direct link to the essence of [Kobold Chief].
Do you wish to upgrade [Kobold Chief] and grant it a proper soul? This will allow you to store the soul of the creature even after it dies, and recreate it later.
<<<>>>

Without any time to hesitate, Smit accepted. It truly would be a shame to lose this child.

<<<>>>
Warning! [Kobold Chief] is a semi-sentient being, and as such has developed naturally a pseudo-soul. Cost of soul granting drastically reduced. Anima available is inadequate, expending mana to gather required Anima. Using mana to supplement link to essence of [Kobold Chief].
<<<>>>

Wait what?
Before Smit had even the chance to process the information,

mana started draining out of him in waves, and he could feel his core starting to heat up several degrees as Anima was forcefully drawn out from the world and rushed into him. It felt as if he was sitting too close to a fire, and it was slowly starting to burn his flesh.

Hellfire and brimstone, that is not pleasant, Smit growled mentally, trying to suppress the pain through sheer willpower. Fortunately, the sensation was short-lived, only lasting a few seconds before it began to die down.

Focusing again on the fight, he managed to see the last few seconds of it, as the kobold chief threw his spear at James despite being off balance, a last attempt to take the armored giant down with him. The attack was moderately successful, knocking off James' helmet and slicing his eye. Unfortunately, inflicting that shallow wound cost the kobold chief dearly, earning him a rapier to the gut and a hammer to the face.

Congratulations! A true soul has been granted to [Kobold Chief]. You can store the souls of any creature that has a proper soul inside your body and revive them at a later time, keeping their memories intact up to the point of their death.

A moment later he felt a presence rushing towards him, only to be met with a small cloud of *something* that stopped before him. Of course, he could sense that it was the soul of the kobold chief. Satisfied, he drew him in, and stored him away for the moment.

Sigh. Well, they did a good enough job. I expected a defeat, but the fact that they couldn't even take one of them down is disappointing.

It was all up to Echo now.

GROANING, James kneeled down as he clutched at his eye. The beast had managed to wound him at the end. He was lucky, however. Had the angle been any better, or had the creature been in the proper position, the spear might not have just nicked his eye and knocked off his helmet. It might have pierced his eye and embedded itself in his brain. It would have been instant death.

"Zig? Can I get some help here?" James called out, his deep voice marked with tired tones as the adrenaline of the battle wore off. The lack of adrenaline caused his body to shudder briefly, as the realization of his narrow escape from death set in. He had been very lucky.

"I'm coming. I need a moment, please," Ziggurd replied as he hobbled over to James, using his staff as a walking stick to reach James. "That battle drained me far more than I expected. I don't have much left in me. Let me have a look at your eye."

James removed his hand from his face and looked at Ziggurd, who grimaced at the view.

"Ugh. Split eyeballs are always rather unnerving. Give me a second," Ziggurd began to mutter his spell, taking his time to word things properly. "—and by the grace of the moon and the power of the tides, [Mend Wounds]."

James felt energy start to flow towards his eye, causing it to feel hot and uncomfortable, painful even. But he didn't utter a single word as he held himself still, allowing Ziggurd to work his magic.

Barely half a minute had transpired before the healing was done. Ziggurd had turned pale by the end of it, seeming to falter for a moment, almost ready to faint.

"Don't push yourself, Zig," Ella ordered. "You were casting constant invigorating magic on multiple targets for a while, and you've healed Mei, Adder, and James with detoxifying magic. Not to mention you healed multiple minor wounds before that. It's a wonder you haven't fainted yet, even with your mana pool."

"Don't mind me," Ziggurd gasped out, letting himself plop down onto the floor, sitting down for a few seconds of rest. He should have brought some potions with him, but he had not foreseen this level of difficulty in a dungeon that had just spawned. He had never even heard of a dungeon this young that had this level of difficulty. "I can still walk if you give me a moment to catch my breath, but I won't be casting any more healing spells any time soon. Even in such a mana rich environment, it will take a while to recover from the mental fatigue and to recharge my mana."

"That looked a lot like a final stand to me," Mei spoke up. "I expect that fighting will likely be a non-issue, as it's likely that the next room shall be the last. The dungeon core will be there."

Her words rang true to her teammates, as that had been by far the most aggressive attack from the dungeon monsters. It was oddly coordinated too, making it almost seemed planned out. It was hard to believe that something similar to that would be waiting for them up ahead, considering the level of their previous fights.

"We better get a move on then, huh?" Ziggurd smiled weakly, standing up with the aid of his staff. "Let us get going and finish this."

Relaxing slightly after their last struggle, the team nonetheless got into formation once more as they stared at what they expected to be the final pathway. Together, they stepped into the short hallway to the last room. The hallway twisted and turned in an S-like shape, but it was hardly more than thirty meters in length, if that. However, when they stepped into the room, they held their breath as they were greeted by an unprecedented sight.

An empty room, at the center of which sat the most exquisite statue that anyone present had ever seen. The stone work was superb; the stone itself was of a color unmatched in beauty as light shined from the stone it held in its hands, reflecting the light of the statues surface as if it were the ocean made stone. Even the golden metal that created her hair, her eyes, and her lips seemed so real that one might wonder if those lips were as soft as those of a real woman.

It was as if the statue would come to life at any second, a goddess that gazed gently upon a large gem she held in her hands. They could only assume that the gem was the dungeon core.

They stared in silence for a moment, enchanted by the statue of the young goddess of battle before them. It even took Ella a few seconds to come to her senses enough to approach the statue. Carefully, almost fearfully, Ella inched towards the statue, followed by her party members who had begun to copy her.

A handful of minutes or only an instant, she couldn't really tell the length of time it took her to be within arm's reach of the statue of this beautiful battle goddess.

"Hey..." Behind her she heard Adder speaking in a hushed voice. It was almost unconceivable for that rogue to feel awe towards art, but she could hardly blame him on this occasion. "Who do you figure made this?"

"How would I know, fool?" she hissed back at him, her eyes never leaving the statue. She was not one for pretty paintings or fancy sculptures, but this? She could make an exception for something like this. How much would a nobleman be willing to pay for such an exquisite piece of work? Would they even be able to pay for it? Forget noblemen, she would wager that kings would probably bid for it against each other.

"It's beautiful..." James muttered somewhere behind her, shuffling closer to crouch down beside Ella. That was the understatement of a lifetime.

James slowly took off his metal glove, baring his hand as he slowly reached out towards the statue. "It looks so... *real*."

His hand was mere inches away from the face of the statue when it looked up, eliciting shrieks from everyone in the party as they bolted away from it, as if they had been electrocuted.

Gathering their weapons, they scrambled to huddle into a defensive formation in a matter of seconds, with James at the front protected by his tower shield. Two projectiles launched themselves at the creature that had induced panic into the adventurers, only for the knife and arrow to bounce off harmlessly from it.

The deadly projectiles clattered loudly onto the floor, and not a soul moved as the golem and the adventurers stared at each other for a few tense seconds. The piercing golden eyes seemed guarded, undecipherable, as if resisting the urge to do... something. Or perhaps the golem just did not know what to think of them. Either way, the adventurers were locked into a staring contest with the creature, and they were unsure if they should make a move.

Several seconds slipped by, and their hearts regained some semblance of calmness as they stopped beating like war drums, regaining a somewhat less aggressive rhythm. A couple of seconds more went by before the goddess carved out of stone looked slowly down at the dungeon core for a moment, before looking back up at them. Her eyes, though not made of flesh, seemed to convey a slight feeling of uncertainty as she unhurriedly raised one of the hands that cradled the core, shifting the core so that her other hand could support it fully.

The adventurers tensed up, wondering what would happen next, considering all sorts of possibilities before the statue simply... waved them off?

Wave them off she did. Slowly, the statue stretched her arm out towards the entrance they had come through, and made a hand gesture that was clearly meant to shoo them out. Confused by the gesture, the adventurers stood in place, shocked, while the statue looked back down at the gem in her hand, and then back up at them, repeating the gesture with her hand.

There was no mistaking it; she just wanted them to leave.

The first to react was Ziggurd, who started to chuckle softly, before bursting out laughing, laughing hard until tears started to well up in his eyes. He was tired but the unexpected turn of events was so out of the ordinary that he could not help but laugh.

"Ah for the love of...," Adder exclaimed as he collapsed onto the floor, sitting down as he threw his head back. "This is too much. I am done. Here, take your ten silvers too. You win."

Ziggurd grunted as Adder slapped a small pouch containing ten silver pieces against Ziggurd's chest, and started turning on his heel without another word. Ella for her part could feel a headache starting to form as she sighed in defeat. How would she even explain this to her superiors? "I am with you. This seems to be the last room anyway, and I am in no mood to fight something that deflected an arrow with her face. We are done here. Let's go."

They gathered themselves up and started to head out, though they always kept an eye on the beautiful construct that had moved their hearts with but a glance.

"Hey, you." Ella called back to the construct as they all started walking into the hall they had come through. "Not sure if you can understand me, but we will be back. Take care of that core."

Without another word, Azure Arrow began their walk back towards the exit, only stopping to pick up the three spears that the kobolds had left behind.

They had quite the story to tell now.

Status

Species: True Dungeon
Rank: 1
Name: Smit
Age: 53 days
Mana: 343 MP
Anima: 0
Mana Reg.: 119 MP/h
Anima Reg.: 2 AP/day
Floors: 2
Inhabitants: 30 Species

Titles: Eager Creator; Guide of the Bloody Evolution; Legendary Craftsman; Reincarnated One

Abilities: Absorb matter; Alter environment; Bestow knowledge; Break down components; Craftsmanship; Creation; Digging; Destroy creation; Dungeon laws; Enhancement; Equivalent exchange; Ether manipulation; Evolution; Interdimensional storage; Life bestowal; Life-energy harnessing; Mana absorption; Masterful mana manipulation; Modification of creations; Monster link; Telepathy; Trap building; Transfer dungeon.

Resistances: Magic (general); Mind control

CHAPTER NINE

S mit sighed in relief as he watched the invading adventurers take their leave, red-faced and tired, their armors scarred in many places by the trials that they were forced to face by Smit. Snakes, wolves, kobolds, rats, mice, and ambushes had left their mark on the adventurers. It would not be wrong to say that if the party had not had a healer several of them would have died. But then again, if they had not had a healer and pushed in so deeply with so little trouble, perhaps Smit would not have been forced to make a last stand with all his remaining kobolds and wolves.

Regardless, the dice had been cast and the outcome had been decided. Smit was safe. At least for now.

Smit had to admit, he was worried when the adventurers met Echo. Thankfully, Echo did not behave aggressively, which gave pause to the adventurers. Had she decided to react to the knife and arrow that were launched at her, things could have easily deteriorated into a fight.

As confident as he was in the toughness of her body, he was still very glad to avoid the fight, especially since her dexterity was not up to par. If a fight had broken out, there was a definite possibility that his dungeon core could have been knocked out of Echo's hands and been damaged or stolen.

However, thanks to her lack of reaction and their shock, Smit had time to intervene. Well, not that his intervention was anything spectacular. He had simply ordered Echo to wave them all away. Though he had gotten a confused reply from Echo at the time, she had carried out his order, albeit with a fair share of uncertainty in her initial movements. Thankfully, the adventurers had reacted well to this improvised method of communication. He was pretty sure that such a thing would not happen ninety-nine times out of a hundred.

He had been lucky, and he knew it.

And by god, did he ever hate relying on luck.

Well. I suppose I have my work cut out for me. These brats were not even B ranked yet and I got pushed to this extent. I need to get to work. He grunted to himself internally, clearly unhappy with the result, even though he had expected it. No one was more critical about his own work than himself.

He began to analyze the situation with a critical eye, while ordering the few creatures that had not been slaughtered by the adventurers to not attack the retreating invaders. Though he should regain the great majority of the mana expended on his creations when they die, he still did not wish to have to spend more time than necessary recreating every single thing that the adventurers had killed. By his tally, they had killed over a hundred and fifty creatures, which were more than four-fifths of his combat force.

"Mas—I mean, Father?" A feminine voice rang in his mind, pulling him back from his thoughts.

"What is it Echo?" he asked, giving her a piece of his attention.

"Why did the... invaders leave? They had the upper hand." There was clear confusion in her voice. As expected, someone that had knowledge but no experience would be confused. Intelligence without wisdom was a rather interesting thing to behold. "They could have very likely won the fight too."

"Simple," Smit grunted. "It wasn't worth it."

"It wasn't worth it?" Echo repeated, still clearly confused. "I was under the impression that Father's core was magnificent and very coveted."

"You are not wrong. But you need to consider their point of view beyond that."

"What could possibly be more important than your core, Father?"

The question itself made Smit stare at her, wondering if she was serious about her words. Unfortunately, it seemed she truly meant that. It was easy to forget that Echo was one of his creations, which meant that due to his *Monster Loyalty* trait, she instinctively held him in high regard. And in addition to this, he was fairly certain that without his core, the dungeon would just cease to be a dungeon, leaving behind a set of caverns underground. So of course, from her point of view his core was probably the most important thing that there could possibly be.

Sighing, Smit began his explanation. "Consider this: First, their healer was out of mana. This alone means two important things. One, they can't get healed in battle quickly. Even if they use something like a healing potion, the effect is not as instantaneous as magic. And two, it means that since the mage can't use magic, he can't even defend himself well, which means that he must be protected. This limits their actions as a team, unless they are willing to let him fend for himself, which would probably end with him dead. Do you understand? A magic user without magic is usually worse for a team than not having one, since they must protect them without anything to be gained from it.

"That's not all, however. Consider this too: You are an unknown creature that deflected an iron dagger and an arrow with just your skin without even blinking. They have no idea of the extent of your fighting abilities, or if there are any tricks associated with this room. For all they know you could be an immortal warrior that can cast fireballs with a flick of your wrist. Add to that the fact that they are exhausted mentally from long hours of exploration and fighting, and that their weapons and armors are not in optimal condition. Do you see now? Their confidence waned. They were completely unsure that they could get out of this alive. And lastly, their job was to identify the dungeon, not to take me away. From their point of view, their mission was accomplished the minute they laid eyes on me."

Echo tilted her head slightly, processing this new information with interest. He could almost hear the imaginary cogs in her brain turning, working over his words and absorbing them.

"I understand," Echo said after a while, nodding her head slowly. The movement made Smit chuckle lightly. Tilting her head, nodding... those were very... organic reactions. It was the sort of thing you would expect from a being of flesh and blood, not from a golem. But then again, Echo was beyond your average golem. After all, how many golems had an actual soul?

Speaking of souls... Smit hummed thoughtfully as he thought about his kobold chief, its soul standing in suspended animation within the unknown space that Smit held within his core. He could feel the soul of the kobold chief, ready to be called upon.

Thinking over it briefly, he decided that he should create a proper body for him as soon as possible. After all, the kobold chief was his greatest warrior to date. Having him around would grant him some peace of mind while he restored the rest of the dungeon.

He promptly began to gather his mana, remembering the kobold chief. Hmm... perhaps he should improve him too. *Maybe I should give him denser muscles, a stronger tail, harder bones...*

But just as he readied himself to activate his mana, he was greeted by an information box.

<<<>>>

Warning! Invaders are still present in your dungeon. Cost for creating new creatures tripled. Are you sure you would like to continue?

<<<>>>

Smit just stared at the text box for a moment before growling. These restrictions... who came up with these? Some annoying god probably. Maybe more than one had a hand in it. He hadn't had any trouble creating creatures when something like a snake came into his dungeon... so perhaps it was limited to things that could be seen as a threat then? Or was it limited to sentient creatures? If it was the later, he would bet the gods of each respective species had a hand in it. After all, which god would like to see their people at a disadvantage?

Grumbling at the unfairness of it all, he stayed his hand and waited until the adventurers shuffled their way out of his dungeon. Thankfully, he didn't need to wait too long. It barely took the adventurers two hours to walk out, following the path with the least number of traps. The second they stepped out of his dungeon's entrance, Smit noticed that the slain creatures were recycled entirely, their mana breaking down and partially refilling Smit's now diminished reserves. For a moment he wondered if there was also a reason for this, but pushed this thought out of his mind as he gathered his mana and the soul of the kobold chief.

He used the soul of the kobold chief as the centerpiece, wrapping it in mana and molding it into the proper shape. Bigger, better, faster, stronger... he wanted to create a more deadly kobold, but unfortunately there was a limit to his enhancements despite all his skills related to the matter. To begin with, he had already enhanced the kobolds when he created them, so the current enhancements were not as effective as he would have liked them to be, but it still worked to an extent.

Of course, Smit made his enhancements consciously, guiding his mana rather than letting it work on its own. It was the only way to decrease the mana expenditure when he created things, and right now, he really could not afford to waste a single iota of mana. Not when he was so defenseless.

Interestingly enough, it seemed like creating a body for him was faster this time around, and Smit suspected it was the presence of a soul that facilitated the process. Just over an hour after starting to create a new body, Smit had finished his task. Overall, he looked like the same kobold chief he was before, except he was... stronger to put it simply. More muscular without being bulky, standing a little taller than before at 185 cm in height. His scales seemed tougher, and he even managed to look more masculine at the same time. But perhaps Smit's favorite change was made to the eyes of his reborn kobold chief, which now seemed less... feral, holding a certain wisdom in them. He hadn't intentionally created that, though he assumed that it was due to the fact that the kobold chief had obtained a proper soul. After all, they do say that the eyes are the windows to the soul, do they not?

Whatever the reason, Smit was quite satisfied with his creation, even if it had cost him more than twice the amount of mana than for an average kobold, leaving him with a significant 6,988 MP. Between him and Echo, he could sit down to cultivate, gathering his mana at a much faster rate.

As he thought of this, the kobold chief opened his eyes again, and looked around him slowly, before gazing upon his own body. For a few seconds he marveled at his hands, his arms, legs, even going as far as to lift his tail and feel it with his hands. The kobold chief once more turned to his creator, and kowtowed towards him, letting his forehead touch the ground in reverence.

"Thank yousss, Father," the kobold chief muttered, just loud enough for Smit to hear. The words seemed heartfelt and shaky, almost as if the monstrous creature was choking back his tears. Or trying to, as his eyes watered up despite his efforts. Smit was fairly certain that if the kobold chief had a larger vocabulary, he would have said more.

"Raise your head," Smit ordered, looking upon the golden eyes of his creation, noticing the tears that streamed down his face. Who knew that kobolds could cry?

Pushing such thoughts aside, Smit felt the need to respond towards the feelings of his creation. Though he might have been a mindless monster before, the spark of wisdom and knowledge had risen within this creation, and it had even acquired a soul. This kobold had fought, bled, and died for him, while being fully conscious that the chances of survival were next to none. And it had done so, if only to protect him for a few seconds longer. Considering this, how could Smit not spare a few words for his beautiful creation?

Gathering his thoughts for a second, Smit spoke again. "You fought well. You made me proud, and so I decided to save you, and give you a soul. You are my greatest warrior, and I shall call you Pala, the kobold lord."

<<<>>>

Alert! You are about to bestow a name upon your created creature. This will render this creature a [Named Monster]. Would you like to proceed? Current limit of named monsters: 2

<<<>>>

Accepting the notification, Smit felt his magic leave him, pouring towards the kobold lord, wrapping him in tendrils of faintly visible white. It was as if vines made of clouds coiled around the kobold chief, seeping into his skin.

A moment passed, and the kobold chief closed his eyes, allowing the power granted by Smit to become his. Before Smit's eyes, the kobold changed. His forest green scales became marked with a hint of gold, his shoulders became broader, he seemed to stand up straighter, and his height rose another 5 centimeters. He had retained all the enhancements that Smit had crafted for him upon recreating him but he now looked more... elegant, for lack of a better word.

For the second time in a day, the kobold lord opened his eyes, and this time his eyes let the tears flow freely, basking upon the honor of obtaining his own name while silently worshiping the name of his creator as he remained kneeled. His heart beat loudly as these emotions washed through him, beholding his beloved creator, whom had deemed him worthy.

<<<>>>
Alert! Limit of named monsters reached. Limit will increase upon ranking up.
<<<>>>

Smit however, remained oblivious to the thoughts of Pala, simply dismissing the text window after having a quick glance over it.

"Now then," Smit said as he addressed both Pala and Echo. "I am going to have to sit down and meditate to gather mana quickly. Your job is to protect me until I wake up again. Understood?"

"By your will, Father," Echo spoke up as she cradled his core.

"By youuur will, Father," Pala repeated, jumping up to stand once more.

"Good. Echo. Carry me to the real core room. We have no time to waste. Pala, follow Echo and guard me."

Finished dealing out instructions, Smit wasted no time in slipping off to find his balance, meditating as he drew in the ether that surrounded him. He had things to do and things to create.

LOOKING DOWN AT MY SHIELD, I can't help but think that it has seen better days. Never in my life would I have expected a new dungeon to be capable of giving our party such a hard time. This dungeon is truly a mystery, and rather unnerving, truth be told. By all accounts, a group of high C rank adventurers should be far more than capable of clearing a brand-new dungeon on their own, on the first try. In fact, even a group of D rank adventurers should be able to do it on their first try, albeit with a lot more trouble and perhaps with a couple of missing limbs.

And yet here we are, coming out of this looking like we got worked over with sticks. My shield hasn't been this scratched and banged up in a long time, and everyone's armor will need some repairs. Ella in particular has several locations where the kobold warriors managed to slice up her hind-bear leathers. It wasn't as if they had gone into the dungeon willy-nilly either. They had properly spoken with the locals to gather what little information they could, assessed the situation, and prepared accordingly. The dungeon had simply been too far out of their expectations. Perhaps the most disturbing thing of the entire ordeal was the blue golem lady. By the gods, did she ever scare the living hell out of all of us.

The mystery of her creation was beyond me. Dungeons were rarely known for being able to create anything in fine detail that was not a monster, and even those that can make statues are a rare enough find. But that golem? It was a veritable goddess. The skill behind that workmanship must be unmatched under the heavens. I wouldn't be surprised if it was created by a god. But... why would a god create a statue like that? Why would a dungeon have it? Could it be that this dungeon has already been marked by a god? But if so, why would a god claim such a miniscule dungeon? Moreover, no god would mark a dungeon without leaving his name, or at least his mark, behind. Did this mean that the dungeon had truly created that magnificent golem?

"Focus, James," Ella barked at me, causing me to snap out of my internal monologue. "This dungeon is weird, and I don't trust it even if we were allowed to leave without a fight."

"She's right," Mei spoke up, her voice a bit unsteady as she looked around. "The creatures of the dungeon... they are all staring at us. None of them have made a move as far as I can tell, they are just... staring."

Those words sent a cold shiver down my spine as I tried to look around me without being too obvious. Indeed, in the darkness I could faintly make out the eyes of what might have been a large rat. It didn't move. It simply followed our progress with its eyes.

I guess this dungeon can be more disturbing than I thought.

Step by aching step we made our way out of the dungeon, and the closer we got to the entrance, the more creatures we began to make out. All of them were lower tier creatures, like mice, rats, or small snakes. But the fact that they would openly let us go was by far the most unnatural thing I'd seen in this dungeon, aside from that golem.

Under the scrutiny of all those critters we reached the exit, and I breathed in deeply the moment I stepped outside the dungeon. The sweet scent of fresh mountain air greeted my lungs and I felt alive once more.

"Right then," Ella said as she looked up to the sun, which was already getting low on the horizon. "This took a lot longer than we expected. Let us go down the mountain some ways and find a somewhat flatter spot to make our camp. We will set out in the morning and try to reach the village."

Getting a general consensus of agreement, we all began to move, ignoring the protests of our legs. Thankfully, walking to the village from the dungeon was faster than doing the opposite. There would be enough time to rest soon enough.

TIME SLIPPED OUT of Smit's mind as he focused on his progress, drinking in copious amounts of ether, feeling it enter his core and become mana. The process was much more effective when he meditated, more than doubling his already impressive mana regeneration. He spent 24 hours completely submerged in his meditative state before he finally stopped, opening his eyes to realize he had increased his mana pool by 7,512 MP. He had practically doubled the amount of mana available to him.

Upon awakening, he noticed Echo had not set him down on the ground as he had always been, but rather she had sat down cross legged again, holding him in the palm of her hands. Nearby, Pala stood guard, pacing the room silently, and his eyes constantly darted back towards the hallway that led to the core room.

The first order of business was to repopulate his dungeon, expending a grand total of 7,135 MP to recreate creatures, enhancing some of them in small ways in hopes of triggering an evolution at a later date. He additionally created his first dungeon law, [Respawn]. It was a simple thing really. Simply put, it would respawn creatures on a floor once the floor was free of invaders, saving Smit the trouble of having to respawn all the common creatures himself. Of course, the [Respawn] law only applied to common creations. Special entities such as Echo or Pala were not included.

<<<>>>

Warning! To use dungeon law, you must verbalize the law you wish to create. Various effects can be achieved through intonation and modulation of emotions and speech.

<<<>>>

Just as he tried to utilize his dungeon law ability, a window popped up again. The warning had some interesting implications, but for the sake of efficiency, he ignored it at the time. Or rather, it wasn't so much ignored as forcibly pushed aside and forgotten.

The second step for Smit was crafting the skeleton of his second floor. Currently it was little more than a long hallway with pretty walls. But he would fix that.

Grinning broadly to himself, Smit threw himself at his work determined to turn his second floor into the ideal floor he had imagined. First, he lengthened his hallway, making it an impressive 500 meters long, with high ceilings. He also increased the width of the hall, making it broad enough to allow ten people to walk side by side comfortably. He turned the ground into a polished tiled floor using basalt—black, heavy stone that would not be easily damaged. The contrast between the pearly walls of granite and the black floor created a stunning effect. Instantly he decided to make the ceiling of white granite too, to increase the contrast.

White on black. Simple, yet beautiful, resulting in a cultured and elegant look.

Then he began to add the fun part.

First, he created a few wide columns, scattering them over the length of the hallway. The columns were made of the same polished basalt as the tiles on the floor, adding a bit of a mysterious look to them. Each column had a little surprise associated with it. But of course, he would have to tinker with them. In essence, his plan for this hallway was simple: The tiles on the floor would contain triggers for the traps within the columns of stone. One tile would trigger arrows, another would cause a column to release a cloud of noxious gas, and yet another tile would cause a column to collapse onto the intruder.

He had five types of traps ready to set, and a few more that he was already considering to place, but he had yet to decide upon them. He would leave the trap making for later, however, as he had to continue creating the skeleton of his floor before he could work the details.

Leaving the columns of stone behind him, he began to work on the second part of the floor. The hallway would end at a doorway carved out of heavy wood, which would then lead to the main room of this floor. He would call this room the reception hall.

The reception hall would be one hundred meters wide by one hundred meters long. The ceiling would be high above the ground, rising a good six meters above the floor. The materials for the creation of the room were once again polished granite and basalt. But now, he would add beauty to this. First, he crafted spiraling columns that reached the ceiling at the four corners of the room. The columns were beautifully designed, carving leaves and vines along their lengths to decorate them.

Next he added a little detail. The walls themselves were carved to produce charming ledges that could be used as benches, creating a sort of polished indentation in the wall so that people could sit comfortably and rest. Above each bench, he added decorations. Lions, bears, eagles, and fish were carved beautifully, one specific carving per bench. He followed up by creating a small circular pond in the middle of the room, making it cover roughly two-thirds of the space of the room. The pond deepened gradually towards its center, reaching a depth of five meters at its deepest point. The ground would be basaltic for the pond, except for the deepest part, which would contain rocks and sand, ideal for housing fishes.

Lastly, on the far end of the room, he created a raised platform. The platform was not very high, only about 40 cm above the ground, but it was wide enough to host a small orchestra. Above the platform he created luminous crystals that lighted the stage sufficiently, making it stand out. It was from this stage that he would perhaps have a few creatures pepper the invaders with some kind of projectile... or perhaps he would use kobold mages. Either way, the stage was ideal for harassing the enemy as they tried to go around the pond.

The pond would contain a surprise, however. He planned to house there some kind of monster, be it kobolds or something else, which would be able to leap out and contain the invading forces. This room itself would be the centerpiece of this floor. Here, every adventurer would have to prove themselves to proceed any further. In fact, the entire floor was more of an obstacle course designed to deter weak adventurers from proceeding. However, those that could survive this room would be welcomed to sit upon the benches he created, and relax as they watched the fish dance in the pond.

He chuckled at the progress he was making, enjoying the idea of testing any invader that would be brave (or foolish) enough to step into his domain. The idea of watching them stare in awe at his creations, followed by a struggle to survive sounded like a fun plan indeed.

But before he could continue, he ran out of mana. The extent of detail he was using, and the materials involved, were draining his reserves of mana much faster than he expected, swallowing over 7,000 MP in the creation of a mere hallway and a room. Granted, his hallway and room would be enough to humble a noble once he was done, but it still annoyed him that he had run out of mana when he was in the full swing of things. It was like someone had snatched a cake away from his plate when he was only halfway done eating it.

Grumbling at his dilemma, he decided to spend this time resting, and thinking of his next move. To begin with, he needed an aquatic species to place in the pond. His rank up had unlocked a handful of species from his animal races, two of which were simple fishes.

Oddly enough, his rank up had not unlocked any new variations of golems or kobold. Perhaps it had something to do with the rarity rating of the species? He would make a note to ask Echo about that.

At any rate, one or two species of fish would not be enough. He needed some aquatic plants, and he also required some kind of more... fierce creature. Perhaps a giant carnivorous frog. Or a water snake. Hell, he would settle for a man-eating plant that lived in water. Kobolds would work as well, but he craved some variety. Plus, it was never a bad idea to have more species available to him. The worst-case scenario would be that he would not use them, and the best-case scenario would be that he would implement them, and then they would evolve into something even better.

Thinking upon it, he would not be able to send his dungeon mice to gather creatures like he had before in that case, for obvious reasons. He was going to have to send out kobolds to look for plants and fishes in the rivers of the mountain, and hope that they could find something useful.

The problem would lie in making sure that the fish survived long enough to die in Smit's dungeon. If they didn't make it here, then he would not automatically absorb the information of said creature.

Right... so first, create a handful of kobolds. Then create monster cores for them. Follow up by sending them out with tools to gather fish and plants that live in freshwater. Then have them return without killing the fish or plants.

Now that he thought about it... Did he have aquatic plants already? Also, plants don't necessarily die right away after being cut. Could they survive long enough to come to him after being cut?

Questions like these started popping up in his mind left, right, and center, distracting him for a moment. Soon enough he returned to the real world though and he pushed those thoughts aside as he settled down into meditation again.

Those thoughts can wait. First I must finish the setup. Then I can go about the details.

He couldn't help but to think of the surprise of the adventurers when they came back, diving deeper and realizing a whole new floor was waiting for them.

Thinking this, Smit chuckled before he let himself sing into his mind, reaching out towards balance and inner peace.

<<<>>>
Status

Species: True Dungeon
Rank: 1

Name: Smit
Age: 54 days
Mana: 343 MP
Anima: 2
Mana Reg.: 151 MP/h
Anima Reg.: 2.5 AP/day
Floors: 2
Inhabitants: 30 Species

Titles: Eager Creator; Guide of the Bloody Evolution; Legendary Craftsman; Reincarnated One

Abilities: Absorb matter; Alter environment; Bestow knowledge; Break down components; Craftsmanship; Creation; Digging; Destroy creation; Dungeon laws; Enhancement; Equivalent exchange; Ether manipulation; Evolution; Interdimensional storage; Life bestowal; Life-energy harnessing; Mana absorption; Masterful mana manipulation; Modification of creations; Monster link; Telepathy; Trap building; Transfer dungeon.

Resistances: Magic (general); Mind control

CHAPTER TEN

S mit hummed mentally as he worked, his mind sending a subconscious echo across the entirety of the dungeon. It was the deep reverberations of the voice of the earth itself as he worked, lulling the population of his dungeon into a gentle sway that spoke to them of home.

As he hummed his song, Smit carefully set up the mechanism for triggering the traps from the pillars of stone. The work was delicate and required time to set up, though in truth it did not require too much mana to set up. As a craftsman of considerable age, he had the skills needed to build the internal mechanism for these traps. It was a simple mechanism really. The floor was turned from solid stone into tiled stone. Some of the tiles were turned into trigger traps, which would activate whenever enough weight pressed on them. The weight would sink the tile, which would trigger an internal mechanism (some of which acted like switches; others contained levers or ropes). The internal mechanism would then induce mechanical motion that would activate the trap of the pillar.

Truth be told, the system was simple in majority. Most traps contained darts, arrows, or knives that would be thrown at the invaders from the pillars. A couple of the more nasty traps included being sprayed with needles coated with poison extracted from the insects grown in the dungeon, or the exploding pillar, which would detonate the entire pillar like a grenade. The exploding pillar was particularly vicious, as the sound alone could rupture eardrums, not to mention that the chunks of stone flew out fast enough to penetrate bronze armor with little trouble. It was probably the most deadly of all the pillar traps, which is why he had limited the number of exploding pillars to only a few.

Let there be the steel animal
Let the forge be the jungle it wants
Let the hammer forge the clavicle
The guard for the wielder's hands

Words consolidated into the minds of everyone in the dungeon as Smit lost himself in his work, singing an old song he had sung last long ago. The mana of the dungeon seemed to pulse at the rhythm of his song, the words causing the mana that permeated the air to thump slightly, like a drum in the distance.

The hammer of creation is swung
In hot flames, the metal obeyed
Metal meets metal, the sparks sprung
Unveiling the formation of the blade

Simple words painted a picture of his younger days, as the apprentice surpassed the master. Images of a short, bearded man flashed through the minds of the more intelligent species of the dungeon. Snippets of a memory more ancient than any of their young minds could dare to imagine. Arms as thick as logs, rippling with enough muscle to crush stone. Rugged hands that seemed powerful enough to bend steel. And a pair of deep green eyes that bore into his work with an intensity that dwelled in the realm of obsession.

They knew that this had once been their king, at a time before their personal god became what he was now.

Strike, strike, and strike again
Between the anvil and the hammer
The creation of steel and men
The naked blade of metallic glamour

An image took form in the minds of Smit's creations, becoming so vibrant that it seemed real. A hammer beat down on a blade that shined red and yellow, sparks flew as if he were smiting a star rather than a crafting a blade. Sweat trickled down his eyes, slowly steaming out of existence before the heat of the forge. Muscles bulged as they flexed and exploded into action with every swing of the hammer.

The blacksmith grinned as he lifted the sword from the anvil, and dunked it into chilled water, producing a cloud of steam. And just as fast as the image came to mind it vanished, leaving behind nothing but the memory of its passing.

Oblivious to all of this, Smit simply sighed contentedly as he finished the engineering for the last pillar, nodding with satisfaction at his work. It felt good to complete a job properly; a job well done brought its own rewards.

He had spent a grand total of ten days crafting his pillars lovingly, each mechanism tested time and time again at the sacrifice of several wolves. But eventually, the mechanisms were perfected, and the appearance of the pillars had been mostly retained as to not easily give away the type of trap to the enemy.

Leaving the pillars to stand on their own proudly, he gave them a once-over examination, carefully assessing how they looked. Aesthetics was paramount for his dungeon. He would not be living in anything but the best, and that was not negotiable. Whatever he crafted would be of high quality. Even a mere pillar had to be properly polished and refined.

Finding nothing to displease him, he deemed the situation to be satisfactory, and perhaps even a bit shocking to anyone unread in art. The pillars varied in diameter between the width of a man to twice that, scattered seemingly at random, but in an oddly pleasing fashion, giving the sense that there was a hidden pattern. The white walls only served to make the pillars stand out more, and acted like a canvas, while his pillars were the paint.

Now it was time for the finishing touch in this reception hall: the Dungeon Law.

He pulled at the mana in the environment, and infused it with his own mana. Willing the mana to swirl around the room, it gathered and it began to create a lining over the reception hall.

Warning! To use dungeon law, you must verbalize the law you wish to create. Various effects can be achieved through intonation and modulation of emotions and speech.

<<<>>>

Smit almost faltered as he received this information, but managed to keep hold of the mana as he digested this news. He recalled that this warning had appeared last time, but he had suppressed the notification and ignored the information. Now that he thought about it properly, the notification gave him pause. Saying what he wanted would be easy, but... from the sound of it, the same Dungeon Law could have a range of effectiveness, and even variations in power and other effects based on how one stated it.

If it talks about speech and emotions... Is that not just singing? Smit thought to himself, considering how obvious this seemed... but then again, how many dungeon cores knew how to sing? How many knew how to manifest their emotions? Perhaps it was obvious only to him, but other dungeons would have to figure it out the hard way.

Oh well... Not my problem. He chuckled at that thought, and proceeded to finish up gathering the mana necessary for the law, letting it coat the entire hallway and its pillars. He held the mana in place and began to mull over the wording he would use for this law. As it was only his second dungeon law, he should not make it too complicated. Probably it would be best if he could summarize it with a single thought.

And do I ever have the right word. Smit grinned internally as he solidified a single word into his mind.

Reset.

He wanted every single pillar, and every single trap to be reset soon after a group of adventurers made their way through. That would be ideal, as it would serve two purposes. First, it would be ready in case more adventurers came back to challenge his dungeon, as he had no doubt that more than one adventurer group would show up from time to time. Second, it would keep the room looking nice and tidy, which was of utmost importance.

Having decided on the proper focus of his Dungeon Law, Smit set himself to work. His deep voice started to hum out loud, emanating through the entire second floor. A deep hum seemed to hail from the very walls of the dungeon, making the entire floor vibrate with power as the mana that covered every surface stirred.

Traps of stone
Dead turned to bone
Consume the broken
The room is awoken
Reset the stone
Mend what's blown
Fixed the room
Absorb the fumes

DUNGEON LAW

In an instant, the entire room seemed to dim, as if the light from the new torches was absorbed by every surface for just a moment. The mana that permeated everything seemed to sink into every object in the room, as if it was water drunk by the sand of a desert. It all lasted only a brief moment, before the room settled back into its original appearance.

An eerie silence seemed to settle over the room for an instant, before Smit grinned. He could feel the power from every surface in this room. Every single pillar and wall was marked by the power of his skill. It was a costly experiment, but one that he would gladly do again for the future benefit he could reap from it.

Congratulations! New title earned: [Creator of Dungeon Laws].
Title has been awarded for successfully creating a fairly complex
Dungeon Law through advanced voice manipulation techniques.

<<<>>>

Blinking at his new title, Smit snorted in amusement, barely keeping himself from laughing out loud.

Advanced voice manipulation techniques my ass, he chuckled. *All I did was make up a little song. I suppose that my guess was right. Normally dungeons wouldn't ever think about singing.*

Satisfied with his experiment, he moved his consciousness away from the pillars and began to focus on the next order of business: the pond.

As a result of his desire to create a more realistic body of water, Smit had increased the kobold population of his dungeon to a grand total of seventeen, including Pala. He could feel them approaching the dungeon, coming to him with the latest fruits of their foraging and gathering.

Of the sixteen new kobolds, Smit had created four of them as warrior kobolds, four as mages, and eight regular kobolds. While it might have improved his war potential to have created more warriors or mages, Smit speculated that there were more evolutions to be obtained from a simple kobold other than the three initially discovered.

Most importantly, he hoped to trigger an evolution that would be related to a craftsman class or at least an evolution with enough intelligence and dexterity to start to learn some crafting skills. The dream of creating a perfect apprentice still swam in his mind, floating in the depths of his thoughts. The only problem was that he feared modifying the kobolds too much, thus wasting valuable time and mana to modify a kobold, only to discover that his creation was worthless.

As such, he had decided it would be best to take a slower but steadier approach. In his dungeon, he could trigger evolutions in his own creatures without having to completely redesign them himself. Though that was a significantly slower process, it could be sped up to an extent if he slowly modified his creations over time as they grew and gathered experience. Ideally, this would allow him to somewhat guide the path of evolution that a creature took rather than leave it up to chance, or whatever unknown rules of evolution monsters followed.

He had tried to explain this vein of thought to Echo, who had simply asked why he did not just create them as he wished, as he had done with her body. His reply, of course, had been blunt and short.

"I am a craftsman. I know blacksmithing, I know gadgets, and I know stone, wood, and clay. But I am not a physician. How would I know how to modify a living being?"

That was far outside the realm of his knowledge. He knew how to create golems and automata, but they were worlds apart from a true living thing. He would leave the extreme modifications on living beings alone for now. As it was, he killed dozens upon dozens of spiders to create a single functional two-headed spider that, aside from looking significantly scarier, was not particularly much more dangerous than its cousins who were the same size. All in all, his two-headed spider was not a failure but not a success either. It simply was a different species of spider that was marginally more dangerous than the others in his cave.

He couldn't imagine trying to manipulate kobolds to that extent, and especially not to produce something so detailed as a kobold that had high intelligence and high dexterity. Sure, he could do general changes. Stronger, faster, taller... those were general changes that he could manage, and even then, he had a limit. Perhaps he could even give them two tails with some experimentation, but that was the extent of his power right now. He could not even imagine how much reworking and experimenting he would need to manipulate something as delicate and elusive as natural dexterity, let alone mental abilities.

In the massive lifespan of his previous life, encompassing centuries of experience, he had never gone through the trouble of reading a single book of biology of any species. Hailed as a genius of the crafts, he had labored to memorize entire encyclopedias about construction, blacksmithing, engineering, and leatherworking. He had even studied blueprints for an untold number of gadgets, and trained in the fields of masonry, mining, blacksmithing, weapon development, and woodwork... but never had he ever thought about studying the art of medicine.

Enough of that, he grunted to himself mentally, focusing on the task at hand. *Let us see what the kobolds brought this time.*

He didn't need to wait long. The seventeen kobolds entered the dungeon, panting with exertion as they carried entire buckets filled with fish and plants. Smit grinned to himself as he watched the kobolds make their way into the first room of his dungeon, setting down those heavy buckets. In them he could see a variety of fish and plants, ranging from simple water grasses to algae for plants, and from little guppies to small salmon.

He wished that he could have given his kobolds better tools to carry more weight, but as it was, even a wheelbarrow would be ineffective with all the trees and rocks in the way. There were no roads to speak of this deep in the mountain, nor was there an easy path to his dungeon. Any transport that he could have provided was effectively rendered more of a pain than an actual useful tool, and hence Smit was forced to provide his troops with only buckets.

Still, all things considered, the kobolds had done a terrific job gathering this many samples without killing them. Sure, it had taken them a while to accomplish, but it was more than he had hoped they would achieve.

"Good job lads," Smit said jovially. "Now, go ahead and eat all the fish. Since they are here and alive, as long as they die in the dungeon I should be able to absorb the information on them. As for the plants, they are already dying. You can eat them or dump them on the floor. I have no use for them as they are now."

Following his instructions, seventeen kobolds proceeded to devour the fish they had carried, consuming them bones and all. Some of the algae were devoured too, though other species of plant were simply thrown out and stomped into a paste.

Soon, several windows of information appeared before Smit, flooding his field of view as a multitude of fish and plants came up in blue windows. As always, he obtained an automatic understanding of how to bring into being the creatures in question, understanding them but yet not comprehending the information. It was an odd sensation, similar to knowing how to breathe, but not understanding the process.

Pushing such thoughts out of mind, Smit gave his kobolds leave to rest and recover, allowing them to be free to hunt in the dungeon.

For now, he had nothing more for them to do, and he himself had plenty of work before him. His goal was to finish this second floor as quickly as possible, and begin working on the next project with haste. Though he had significantly increased the size of his dungeon since the adventurers showed up, he had no doubt that they would be back, with friends next time. Once the Adventurers Guild confirmed that a useful dungeon had appeared, there would be little doubt that a settlement would be built nearby, and an Adventurers Guild hall would be set up.

After that, as per the laws of the kingdom, the dungeon would often be exploited to train both adventurers and soldiers, and used to gather resources. Given that dungeons acted as giant mana producing pumps, a variety of alchemists and magic users would also flood to the settlement, increasing the number of people and possibly giving rise to a town that might grow into a city in the future.

In other words, it was only a matter of time until people began to flood his dungeon, and he had no doubt some of those people would be less than honest. As his popularity increased, so did the possibility of him being a target while he was weak. Hence, his best hope was to become strong while he still could, setting up as many defenses and protective layers between himself and any future enemy as possible.

Smit grinned at the challenge, reveling in it with as much intensity as he despised it. On one hand, he would have to deal with all sorts of unsavory characters in the future. But on the other hand, he would be able to put himself and his creations to the test.

And there were very few things that Smit preferred to a challenge.

Humming, he set himself to work again, ignoring kobolds who had hurried down the halls of his dungeon to hunt for food.

ECHO HAD SPENT her days training constantly, spending hours upon hours on a daily basis trying to master the control of her body. Her issue with simple balance had been resolved, as she could now walk and even jog without tripping easily. However, Smit had asserted that that could only be considered a standard level of balance at best. Most people without disabilities should be able to manage to do that much by the time they were children, and thus she still had a ways to go. With that in mind, her greatest challenge was improving her dexterity. This was particularly vexing for Echo, as it was much more difficult to do fine movements that required precision than large movements that one could do mindlessly.

Tasks such as writing, for instance, were arduous tasks that required rigorous concentration to get right for her. Of course, considering that most golems could barely do more than close and open their hands around a weapon, this signified that Echo was leagues ahead of them; she was still far behind a practiced human, not to mention a dwarf.

Today, she had been practicing her balance, going through a few of the simple motions she had seen the kobolds use to pierce with her halberd. Though her body sensed the weight of the weapon, she found it extremely difficult to control it even to the extent of a common kobold. Once again, Echo was awed at the amount of physical control that organic lifeforms had. In a simple forward thrust with her halberd, there were a number of things that were integrated into it. She was required to step forwards while rotating her torso, shift her weight, move her arms, strengthen her wrists, angle the strike, *and* she had to keep her balance on top of that.

Worse, she had to be able to do this in seconds to have a chance in a battle. She had to be able to deliver a killing blow faster than someone could finish saying "watch out!" to be effective.

As of yet she hadn't mastered the secrets of balance or dexterity, but she had managed to speed up the movement to only taking a few minutes per thrust. It was excruciatingly boring to watch her attempt to replicate a single movement for hours on end, but progress was starting to show in Echo. She walked straighter, more gracefully, her attacks were sharper, less weak, carrying some weight that seemed to have been absent in her early days of practice.

However, a noise entered her mind, and she faltered for a moment. It was a deep hum that originated from the dungeon itself. Looking back at the heart of her father, she could see it glow, pulsating gently to the sound of the humming.

Instinctively she knew what was going on. It was her father, the creator, who was causing this sound. It was his voice, the one who was altering the dungeon so, causing the very energy that permeated the entire dungeon to sway back and forth to the power of his voice. The sound was deep and invigorating, soothing but entrancing. She had heard insects chirp, wolves howl, and birds chirp, but this? This was different. It was the voice of an artist as he painted a whole new world.

Echo could not help but stop completely and just stand listening in awe. She was sure she was not alone in this. Any creature in the dungeon would likely stop and listen to the voice of the father.

Her body seemed to resonate with his voice, swaying to the musical tune. Slowly, gently, her body instinctively sought out the music, as if trying to do it justice with a visual representation of the emotions it stirred within her.

Step, step, turn, dip of the waist, rise, and retrace the steps.

Simple combinations of movements were created, and balance was reached between the forms. Each movement was rough, unpolished, but the movement was steady and unrushed. It felt natural and real. It made her feel... alive.

Echo's heart sang with joy as she thanked Smit in her heart for allowing her to discover this... dance. She moved, slowly but surely, allowing her body to take her through the motions without thought. It felt more liberating than anything she had ever experienced before. She had no need to worry and no reason to hesitate, not as long as the music guided her steps.

But then it all changed when humming turned to words.

Smit's verses reverberated through the minds over every being on the floor, and even her dance was forced to stop as the music took her breath away. She corrected her previous thoughts.

This wasn't the voice of a master artist.

This was the voice of a veritable god as he shared the joy of creating a whole new world.

Too soon the song ended, and Echo found herself wavering on the spot, struggling to stay upright as she was taken in by a wave of emotions. She, who was new to the whole idea of emotions and freedom of thought, found herself drowning in a sea of relief and happiness.

She turned towards the core of Smit, and got on her knees. She clasped her hands before her, and bowed her head.

And she prayed.

It was a simple prayer that consisted of two words: Thank you.

<<<>>>
Status

Species: True Dungeon
Rank: 1
Name: Smit
Age: 2 months
Mana: 26,743 MP
Anima: 20
Mana Reg.: 200 MP/h
Anima Reg.: 5 AP/day
Floors: 2
Inhabitants: 51 Species
Titles: Creator of Dungeon Laws; Creator; Guide of the Bloody Evolution; Legendary Craftsman; Reincarnated One.
Abilities: Absorb matter; Alter environment; Bestow knowledge; Break down components; Craftsmanship; Creation; Digging; Destroy creation; Dungeon laws; Enhancement; Equiva-

lent exchange; Ether manipulation; Evolution; Interdimensional Storage; Life bestowal; Life-energy harnessing; Mana absorption; Masterful mana manipulation; Modification of creations; Monster Link; Telepathy; Trap building; Transfer dungeon.

Resistances: Magic (general); Mind control

CHAPTER ELEVEN

S low breaths emit from my scaled nose as I regulate my breath, my.... instincts are guiding me in my hunt. The father has entrusted my clan with the search for new specimens as he continues to create our home, or as he calls it, the "Dungeon." After witnessing Father's work, I am in awe of his power. He can will the very earth to shift for him, he can carve items of untold beauty with his mind, he can bring to life the air with his voice, and he can will life into existence with a thought. He is as close as you could get to a god without being labeled as one in your species.

A rustle of leaves in a bush catches my attention from the other bank of the river. I can practically taste the tension build up inside my brethren as a large animal makes its way out of the leaves. The creature is large, maybe twice the height of Father's wolves, and by the looks of the creature, it was many times heavier too. This creature is one that we have not taken to Father yet, but it looks formidable. The animal is clearly powerful, judging by the way it carries itself. Father will be pleased.

I signal to my brothers and sisters with a hiss, and we all rise from the bushes as one. It has been many cycles of light since the enemy that slayed me left the dungeon, and I've spent every day hunting and training, refining myself with the spear that Father gave me. My brethren too have spent many cycles working to develop their skills, and today we see the fruits of our labor.

Seventeen spears soar through the air, arcing as they hit the lumbering creature on the other side of the river. Half of the spears miss completely, and of the other half, several hit the limbs of the beast. However, our control is lacking. Three hit the back of the beast, impaling themselves on the thick fur. My spear imbeds itself in the spine of the beast, close to the tail. It's a mighty fine throw if I do say so myself, but unfortunately, it seems to have been lacking.

The creature roars in frustration, and its deep howls of pain and anger alert us that the fight is not over. We approach the river and swim across the moving waters, eyes fixed on the creature as it bleeds, its legs too injured to flee properly.

It seems that the creature cannot move effectively, seeing as it merely watches us and trembles as we cautiously surround it. I start approaching it with measured steps, and it seems to turn towards me painfully slowly, its back legs quivering before they give out. I tilt my head as I watch it pant, curious at this. I approach a little more and the animal roars pitifully as it tries to take a swipe at my body, which I easily dodge. The creature, in its current state, is slow and weak. The time we spent crossing the river had taken a toll on the creature as it dealt with both pain and blood loss.

"We wait," I called out to my brethren. "Shamansss. Use water. Suffocate him."

It was a simple command but all I could manage to make them understand. They are learning the mysteries of speech still, as am I. Though I seem to have progressed more than they have. I understand more at least.

The command is effective, and the shamans labor to control a large ball of water, and ram it at the creature, holding the water on its head as it tries to shake it off for a minute. However, soon the animal stops moving and slowly collapses to the ground. The shamans sigh with relief, panting slightly. Holding a large ball of water in the air for any period of time is harder than just launching it, especially if they try to maintain it on something that resists like this animal.

We approach the animal and tie it up, leaving all the weapons that pierced its hide stuck upon the creature. Father had explained that removing a weapon from a body would create an open wound, which would cause the wound to bleed more than if you left the weapon stuck in the body.

Considering we had to travel all the way back to the dungeon without letting the animal die, we needed to refrain from letting it bleed too much. Otherwise we would have to find another animal like it and try again so it could die in Father's dungeon for him to comprehend the animal and recreate it. Thus, keeping the animal alive is an absolute necessity for our mission.

About half of my brethren are appointed to carry the hulking beast, dragging it on a sled made of wood and ropes, while the rest of them gather the weapons that did not strike the beast, and carry them. Three kobolds including myself are in charge of defending the rest of the group for now, and we take turns dragging the wounded animal to the dungeon. Thankfully, the creature was found uphill of the dungeon, so we are not forced to carry the creature uphill the entire journey.

Grunting can be heard as we drag our prize home, but there is not a word of complaint to be heard amongst the sounds of exertion. Rather, there is an excitement in the air. We are all eager to return home after our longest excursion yet, two full days out in the open, away from home. We are all eager to return to the father, and show him the fruits of our labor. Moreover, we are all curious what the father has created in our absence. Who knows what wonders he has crafted in this expanse of time?

Excitement wells up in me at the thought of this, and I begin to hum. I can't do it like Father can, not with the same depth, meaning, or power. But I suppose that is to be expected, as no one can be like Father. Father is in a league of his own after all.

I SHIFTED my weight to the side, causing the knives on my belt to rustle lightly. I sat with my team through another meeting with the guild master Ikfes, my mind wandering off somewhere into the distance as Ella and the rest of the people present focused on the conversation. It had been close to twenty days since we exited the unknown dungeon, and it had been close to a week and a half since we had gotten back to the city. Unfortunately, we have had several meetings due to the nature of the dungeon. This was the third meeting, something that was highly unusual.

"...you are saying that the dungeon has developed to this extent?" Ikfes asked, my mind barely registering the words that had left the mouth of the speaker and found their way to my ears. I was never one to enjoy meetings too much.

"Yes sir," Ella replied, watching the guild master and the advisors beside him. "The dungeon has expanded far beyond the scope of a recently born dungeon, completing an extensive first floor. By the looks of things, it should be ready to start creating a second floor. Usually, a newborn dungeon would require at least year to do this, and this one seems to be not yet even a third of that, as we mentioned in the report."

"This is quite the unexpected development," a man with a red goatee said, folding his arms behind his back. If memory served me right, this is Alester Griff, a representative for the king himself.

No shit, I retorted to him mentally. If he was shocked to simply *hear* of that issue, imagine how surprised we were when we had to go through this blind. We were a not a squad of greenhorns, the fact that a new dungeon gave us this much trouble is a testament to how powerful that dungeon could become.

"I concur," Ikfes nodded, humming in thought. "This could

be a Phantom or Heroic level dungeon in the making. This could be a great boon for our country."

It would be for any country really. Any dungeon of Phantom rank or higher was considered very valuable. Typically, dungeons of higher ranks have a number of benefits, turning it into a large exploitable resource that could provide a number of things, from raw materials to processed items. A higher rank not only meant a higher difficulty for the dungeon, it also meant higher rewards were awarded.

"As you all may know," Alester spoke up, "our country is on the small side of the scale compared to our neighbors, and it contains merely five dungeons in total, of which only one is Phantom level, and none that are above that level. If this dungeon has a chance at growing to be a Phantom level dungeon, then it is a resource that must be carefully monitored."

"Naturally," Ikfes replied, "a resource of this magnitude would surely be a boon to the kingdom. I assume that measures will be taken by the king to expand the village that already exists near the dungeon?"

"But of course," Alester replied, fixing up his collar before looking back at Ikfes. "The expenses of the initial exploration will also be covered by the crown as per usual, plus additional compensation for the mapping of the first floor and the discovery of a higher tier dungeon. The man who reported the dungeon will also be adequately compensated."

"Good, good," Ikfes said with a nod. "I request permission for the Adventurers Guild to construct a guild hall in the village by the dungeon. If this dungeon is going to elevate itself to Phantom status, I want to be ready."

"Request approved," Alester nodded. "I will ask that you refrain from sending anything beyond a B level team to oversee the situation. We do not need to stir up rumors or to attack the dungeon too earnestly at the moment, or else we might weaken it."

"Naturally," Ikfes acknowledged smoothly. "I will ready the

area, then. Tell his majesty that we will start gathering budding talents to send to this new dungeon."

"Understood."

The guild master and the representative shook hands, and exchanged a short goodbye, before the representative left. It was baffling. Usually any dealings with the crown had a shroud of politics that floated about, with subtle shifts in power. This, however, was not that in the slightest. It was quick, and spartanly short, as if the discussion had been hacked down to the bare minimum without being rude.

Most curious indeed.

Questioning back end politics would have to wait though, considering we all needed to rise from our seats out of respect to the king's representative. I hated all the manners and decorum that came with it when you are meeting someone of status, but it was a necessity. Especially when it came to royalty, they can be quite finicky about how they are treated. On that note, however, nothing was worse than noblemen when it comes to saving face and vengeance. Entire wars had been waged between nobles for simply being denied saving some face.

Worthless rats with wigs the lot of them.

"Adder," Ella's voice brings me back to earth from my own thoughts.

"Yes?" I reply nonchalantly, knowing that she knows that I was completely distracted. It's fine though: it wasn't like I was expected to say much through the entire conversation, but Ella could be quite stern about all of that meeting your superiors business.

Ella looked at me with a well-practiced disapproving stare.

"Focus. The guild master asked a question."

"Right. What was the question?"

Ella looked like she wanted to strangle me, and it almost made me smirk in amusement. Almost.

Ikfes chuckled at my response, stroking his short full beard. His amber eyes seemed to glint with amusement, but yet I felt as if they are staring through me. He gave me the chills sometimes. Those eyes of his seemed to stare through everything. Though that was to be expected; you didn't get to be an S rank adventurer without obtaining some sort of exceptional aura about you.

"I asked if you noticed anything about the dungeon other than what was written in the reports," Ikfes repeated. "More specifically, if there was anything that was unusually out of the ordinary. Dungeons can develop in mysterious ways, and the early stages of the dungeon can reveal a lot about their future. Any little oddity could prove significant."

"How would I know?" I asked dismissively. I really don't want to have an interrogation session right now. I wished that he would had just ask someone else.

"Adder." The tone of his voice went from mildly amused to deadly serious, and a cold chill ran up the length of my spine, zapping me into an alert state. By the looks of things, I was not the only one to feel this, because everyone in the room suddenly was sitting ramrod straight.

"Alright, alright, boss. Sorry about that," I chuckled nervously. The odd thing about Ikfes was that his face looked like he was in his late forties, but he stood at an impressive 181 cm in height and had a body like an experienced knight in his prime. It threw me off at first, coming off as almost comical, but when he put that sort of pressure on you, it was anything *but* comical. He looked downright scary in a nonthreatening way, if that is even possible.

I sighed internally. This sucked.

"Right. Weird, out of place, et cetera," I mumbled out as I start to think.

What would you have considered out of place in a dungeon like that? Half of it was out of place to begin with. Statues everywhere, traps inside traps, water stones, and let's not even talk about the golem. That was a thing of beauty.

"Well, there wasn't anything that was really *more* out of place than the quick growth of the dungeon or the statues all over the damn place, well except for the blue golem beauty."

"Blue?" Ikfes asked with confusion.

"Yeah, blue. It's made of some sort of blue stone. It was really hard, too. As I said, it deflected my knives without a single scratch."

"That is... outstanding," Ikfes said with mouth agape, staring directly at me.

"...What? How is that outstanding?" Was the old man finally going senile or what?

"You fool!" Ikfes roared as he threw his hands in the air, startling everyone in the room. "Do you not see? Quickly, tell me what you know about golems."

"Um..." I hesitated for a moment as I tried to figure what the old man is going on about. "Golems are constructs that function entirely based on the material they are made of and magic that they were created with."

"Yes, and...?" Ikfes urged me on.

"Um... unlike automata, which have mechanical parts to them and can carry out more complex movements, golems are usually more... simple?" I thought that's right. Golems normally were made of hardened clay or wood, or sometimes common stone, so they did not really have much in the way of joints or ligaments, which in turn means that they can't handle certain tasks, such as writing or fencing. They were more about raw power and endurance than about anything else. Automata, on the other hand, were more delicate due to the number of moving parts inside them, but this gives them outstanding dexterity and finesse.

"Yes and no," Ikfes said impatiently, waving his hand dismissively. "Both automata and golems are technologically fairly advanced, and capable of doing almost the exact same thing... in theory. Of course, due to the fact that golems are made without many moving parts, more often than not just a giant lump of material that moves by the power of magic, golems are usually what we would consider tanks, which soak up damage and can dispense high amounts of damage. Conversely, automata are typically able to be more graceful and dexterous. It is like comparing a tiger to an elephant in that sense."

The guild master paused for a second after confirming my knowledge, before resuming his explanation. "However, think boy, think. Golems are usually crude creations, made of whatever simple material is available. In the case of the golems in this dungeon, golems would most likely be made of clay, and at best whatever soft rock would be most readily available, as they are the easiest to shape and work with. So, tell me what does this tell you?"

I took time to think for a moment. And then it clicked.

"There isn't any hard blue rock around the mountain, or at least not that was easily accessible."

"Good! What else?" Ikfes encouraged me to say more.

"And the stone was really hard, but the movements of that golem were rather fluid."

"Excellent! What does that mean?"

"That the amount of work and skill needed to make a golem, not an automata, to act like that is very high, especially if the material is difficult to work with. That the golem is special. It is unique in all its aspects. It's a unique monster!"

"Bravo! Took you long enough," Ikfes said with satisfaction. "It is as you say, that creature is, in all likelihood, unique. This dungeon already has a unique monster while only having one floor and being less than a year in age! This is unheard of!"

Ikfes started to walk about the room, one hand clenched tight behind his back with a pensive look upon his face while he muttered something under his breath. I only managed to catch a couple of words when he came close enough, but the words "king" and "resources" seemed to stand out among them.

"Ladies and gentlemen!" Ikfes barked out as he suddenly stopped passing and turned to us with a serious expression, his hand flaring into the air dramatically and catching the attention of everyone. "I have a new mission for you. You will depart at once to the dungeon again. You will be there to observe the dungeon and note changes. You may explore it more deeply if you feel the need, but do not risk your lives foolishly until more adventurers arrive. Ask the receptionist for healing potions. This time, the potions will be on the house."

I gawked at the guild master, as healing potions were rather rare even for us C ranks. Hell, as C ranks we usually carry only one small healing potion each for emergencies, and even then, the quality of it is not that great. Healing potions were an expensive luxury.

"Dismissed." And with that, the guild master turned around and waved his hand, leaving us to see ourselves out.

SMIT HAD GONE through his fair share of work already, processing, altering, creating, and destroying. He worked tirelessly, finding new projects to expand upon while he tried to rank up again. The gap between his current rank and the next one was significantly larger than the gap of power needed for his first rank up. The process to rank up was slow for his tastes, but steady. It was like building a boat inside a bottle, piece by piece.

He was sure he could rank up before the month was out at this rate, considering the speed at which he progressed. He certainly could gather more qi and mana now that he had completed the expansion of his second floor, and thanks to his cultivation techniques, the progress was far more efficient than it should have been for a dungeon core. And for him, this was just fine. The faster he ranked up, the better things would be for him in the long run.

Currently, Smit focused upon the details of his dungeon, decorating it a bit more. Though his idea of "decorating"' was giving the entrance of the dungeon a full makeover.

Ever since Smit noticed how rustic and unrefined the entrance to his dungeon was, it had been weighing on his mind like an invisible elephant standing on his head. It irked him to no end that the first impression that people would have about his dungeon was that it was a simple hole in the mountain. It was an itch he just had to scratch.

This had given rise to the current situation, in which Smit was currently erecting the most detailed entrance possible. Smit had managed to create a porch of stone that rose two feet above the ground around it, crafted of green quartzite rock. The rock was beautifully laminated with different intonations of green, seeming like the greens of the forest had solidified into a solid stone. Moreover, Smit had taken his time to permeate the stone with his mana, filling it to the brim and hardening it to the limit of his abilities.

The porch had two columns that stretched upwards, bounding the edges of the entrance to the dungeon, and was capped off by a small roof that attached itself to the rocky wall of the mountain right above the entrance to the dungeon. Overall, the new porch had the look of an ancient, dignified temple. But that was not enough for Smit. The entrance, the hole itself, still needed to be fixed.

And this is where Smit decided to add some... flare to his work. The old hole was replaced by a proper doorway made of jet-black stone, and both sides were decorated by figures of carved weapons, like hammers, swords, and arrows. The weapons seemed to be held together by vines and waves, making the weapons seem to grow out of the nature itself. On the upper side of the doorway, he crafted a sign in the stone. It would be the name of his dungeon. He had kept it nice and simple, yet elegant. The name was derived from the very moment when he became a dungeon, "The Dungeon of Origins." It was perfect in his mind. This dungeon was his new beginning, the origin of his new life, the start of his new world, and the root of what gave birth to his creations. This dungeon was truly a dungeon of origins for him.

And then, Smit added the finishing touch. Above the sign for his dungeon, he carved a pair of old, sagely green eyes that looked down upon the place where the people entering the dungeon would pass through, as if judging their worth. He modeled the eyes after the ones that he had had when he had been a dwarf, making them as lifelike as possible.

He stepped back and looked upon his creation, and felt that it was appropriate. Moreover, he felt proud of his work, considering that it was barely within his range of influence, just skirting the boundary, and it had cost him much more mana than it should have due to this.

Yet, he could not be bothered to be upset by this expenditure of mana. He had satisfied his craving for his entrance, fixing it appropriately and making it far more resistant than it was originally. In all likelihood, any other dungeon would have outright rejected the idea of wasting so much mana on an entrance, but not Smit. Smit would create the most beautiful dungeon possible.

Humming to himself in satisfaction, he was about to retreat his consciousness into his dungeon again when he sensed the approach of his kobolds. Smirking, he decided to stick around until he saw their expressions.

This might be entertaining.

Status

Species: True Dungeon
Rank: 1
Name: Smit
Age: 2 months
Mana: 30,845 MP
Anima: 65
Mana Reg.: 210 MP/h
Anima Reg.: 5.1 AP/day
Floors: 2

Inhabitants: 51 Species

Titles: Creator of Dungeon Laws; Creator; Guide of the Bloody Evolution; Legendary Craftsman; Reincarnated One.

Abilities: Absorb matter; Alter environment; Bestow Knowledge; Break down components; Craftsmanship; Creation; Digging; Destroy creation; Dungeon laws; Enhancement; Equivalent exchange; Ether manipulation; Evolution; Interdimensional storage; Life bestowal; Life-energy harnessing; Mana absorption; Masterful mana manipulation; Modification of creations; Monster link; Telepathy; Trap building; Transfer dungeon.

Resistances: Magic (general); Mind control

CHAPTER TWELVE

S mit sat in meditation upon the hands of Echo, cultivating his
mana and qi. Echo had progressed admirably in the past
month since the creation of her body. However, there was more
work to be done. Though she had established a connection
between her mind and body, and she had mastered the art of
walking normally, any aggressive or vigorous movements were still
dangerously unbalanced. Hell, the grip of her hand was still so stiff
that Smit would not be surprised if she crushed a wine glass by just
trying to hold it.

Still, considering that a month ago she was essentially as
capable of walking as a human toddler, she had improved by leaps
and bounds. Now that she could jog at a moderate pace without
crashing into everything in sight, he was confident that she could
start to get a proper handle on her body if she learned more focus
and control. As such, he had decided to include meditation in her
training, forcing her to sit down with him and activate her mind in
order to focus on her body. In other words, he had her focus on
individual parts of her body one at the time, and allowed her to
slowly but surely understand how her body functioned.

The training had only been ongoing for roughly a week, but

there were results already showing. Her movements seemed to look smoother, and less jerky or mechanical. Moreover, his presence seemed to have a calming effect on her mind, which further enhanced the speed of her meditation. He suspected that his presence had nothing to do with the enhancement of her training *directly*. Instead, his presence likely soothed her, which allowed her to relax and focus better.

Whatever the real reason for her sped-up progress was, for who knew if her progress was even remotely related to him after all, he felt that there was no drawback to having her be nearby as he cultivated anyway. Besides, if she felt that his presence helped her, he would more than gladly stick around her to improve her growth. She had the potential to be his greatest defender at the moment, and he would take every advantage to improve upon her.

Hence, they both sat in silence, each focused upon their respective tasks. Echo worked on feeling her body mentally, focusing extensively upon her fingers, which gently cradled the heart of her father. Meanwhile Smit absorbed power, creating a miniature whirlpool of power around them as mana and anima were drawn to him.

Within Smit, the storm of powers intensified as anima broke down into qi and was absorbed into the core itself along with the mana that Smit absorbed. Slowly but surely Smit's core grew in Echo's hands, crystalizing the powers of the world and expanding as if it were alive. The progress was gruelingly slow, so much so that it was undiscernible to the untrained eye. However, if one could zoom down to microscopic level, one would be able to witness the miracle that should not occur naturally. Tiny crystals grew upon the seemingly flawless surface of Smit's core, like tiny, blocky needles that emerged without notice and were woven into an incredibly complex tapestry of solid crystal.

Layer after layer of crystal grew to surround the original surface of Smit's core in a breath-taking display that would be invisible to all but those with the sharpest eyesight and greatest patience.

Smit himself could feel his power growing bit by bit, a slow process whose speed matched the crystallization speed upon the surface of his core, but it made him feel greatly achieved. Once more he was pleasantly shocked at the incredible speed at which a core could cultivate. The fact that he could *feel* his power grow, however slowly, was just a statement to that prodigious cultivating ability that dungeon cores had. Even as a talented cultivator in his lifetime, cultivating was a painfully slow process, so much so that often weeks, if not months, were needed to note any progress at all.

Soon he would gather enough power within himself to reach his second breakthrough, and he would once more be able to expand his dungeon. According to Echo, the second breakthrough was different from the first. It sounded odd to him that the breakthrough would be significantly different, but he supposed that the first breakthrough acted as a "gateway" to his future evolutionary paths, while the later breakthroughs would help him evolve and define himself. Or at least that's what it sounded like.

According to Echo, the process of ranking up would take into account his achievements and his progress, which sounded a lot like what the voice of the world did when he ranked up as a dwarf. However, he was certain that the process would deviate, as his skills did not have any levels or proficiency scores, and he could not easily acquire new abilities like other humanoid creatures could. It would be interesting to see how the system would acknowledge his progress, and perhaps he would be able to work the system such that he could maximize the benefits of his rank ups in the future... but that was yet to be seen.

As of now Smit was fully devoted to his ranking up task, without a single worry in his mind. He had completed the second floor after all, setting it up with all sorts of new traps, while the large room with the pond had become the temporary home for his kobolds. Of course, once the special plant that had been recently planted at the bottom of the pond grew appropriately, the kobolds might have to be moved somewhere else, but for now, they served as an excellent protective barrier between himself and any would-be invaders that could attempt to harm him.

He chuckled briefly at the thought of anyone meeting his heavily modified plant once it was ready to go. It had taken a lot of work, and a lot of testing to get the plant to become what he wanted it to become, but eventually he had gotten it right. The only drawback was that due to his limited abilities, he had not been able to create a fully grown version of it. But that would be fine for now. After all, the plant only needed some time to grow.

Pushing these thoughts out of his mind, Smit got comfortable and started to cultivate to the best of his abilities once more, drawing in as much power as he could hold before directing it into his own self, permeating his very core with it until it crystallized and grew. The benefits of ranking up early would translate to a massive leg up later on, when he would inevitably meet stronger foes.

Time was of the essence.

ALESTER STRUTTED through the halls of the royal palace with confidence, his fine red cape flowing behind him as if alive, following him through the winding halls of stone. The palace was well decorated as always. Silken tapestries of various colors, many crafted with depictions of epic battles or mighty warriors, or grandiose views of mountains, were scattered across the walls, covering large portions of the halls. The ceiling itself was a work of art, carefully painted with depictions of animals, monsters, demons, and angels alike, creating images like the sequences of a dream. The ceiling was painted four hundred years ago by a group of dwarven master painters, and every seventy years it was repainted by another group of dwarven masters. The event itself was so rare that it would create a buzz around the palace when it occurred. The staff and the royal family would sneak peeks or openly stare at the dwarves while they worked, lying on their backs as they carefully restored the massive expanse of space that was the ceiling of the main hall in the palace.

Of course, the process required months of attention to detail, and it was expensive too, but the quality could not be denied. But then again, that was to be expected of dwarves. Their craftsmanship eclipsed that of any other race, even that of the elves. Few members of the human race could claim to be on par with a master craftsman of the dwarven race, and to be compared to a dwarven master was nothing short of an honor. It was the equivalent of a human mage being compared to an elf in terms of raw magical power, or to an ogre in terms of raw strength.

Alester sighed as he looked up at the ceiling and marveled at it briefly before he continued on his way to the audience chamber, where he would meet the king. A shame that it was so difficult to get a hold of a dwarven master. Despite being the best craftsmen, dwarves were generally notorious for being reclusive in nature, and this seemed to be especially true for craftsmen, who followed their passion with surprising stubbornness.

Furthermore, even if you managed to find a master dwarf, you would need to convince it to sell some of its crafts, which was an entirely separate challenge in itself. When a dwarven master crafts an item, they craft them with unbelievable care and detail, with the intent of making them last as long as the mountains themselves. Each item is an advancement of their craft, and it is created with a devotion that borders on the realm of the devoutly religious. Hence, you must earn their trust and their respect in order for them to even consider selling you a single piece of finely crafted armor, or a lovingly forged blade of blue steel.

Even then, the most that merchants can successfully obtain from dwarves are what they consider "failure" products. But although dwarven masters consider them to be failures, these items are still above the normal quality of masterwork armor from a human black-smith, and are sold for a considerable sum of money. Usually, the majority of the dwarven products one finds in the market are those produced by dwarf apprentices, or these so-called failure products.

Alester shook his head vigorously now, attempting to get rid of such thoughts. While he might be an avid fan of dwarven crafts-men, he had work to do right now. The king might consider him a close friend, but there was a clear division between business and leisurely time, and right now he had to deal with the former of the two.

He soon arrived at the large double doors of carved redwood, and stopped before them. He took a minute to adjust his cape and his jacket, before looking at one of the two guards by the door. "Ahem. Announce my presence to the court. King Vas is waiting for me."

The guard saluted, and turned on his heel as he pushed open one of the doors slowly, revealing the grand audience chamber. The place could easily hold three hundred people, and was deco-rated with magical chandeliers. Large windows allowed the light to flood in from the outside during the day, giving the appearance that the audience chamber was wider than it actually was.

Alester stepped right up to the foot of the raised platform that held the royal throne, where the king was seated, bounded at each side by an aide and a member of the royal guard. Lowering himself down on one knee, Alester bowed his head. "Your majesty."

"Alester, rise." Alester raised his head and stood up to face his king, a man whose dark red hair always reminded him of the untamed mane of a lion. As a matter of fact, the man's features were sharp but robust, as if an artist had taken the features of a lion and placed them upon the face of a human. This was largely the reason why the king was known as the "Red Lion" of duels. Not only was the man an accomplished duelist, with lightning quick attacks and fantastic reflexes, but he was also a capable ruler, able to run his country without giving in to the temptation of thinking himself superior to all of mankind.

If Alester had to describe his king, he would call him a bastion of hope. Everything about King Vas seemed to speak of a man with an unyielding sense of duty and strong character. Exactly as a leader should be.

"I read the report, Alester. Is this dungeon truly as amazing as you make it seem?"

"It is indeed, my liege," Alester confirmed with a short bow of his head. "It seems like the dungeon is progressing quite rapidly, possibly approaching the creation of the second floor. Allegedly, the dungeon has already created kobolds, animals, insects, and even a golem."

"A golem, you say?" King Vas sharpened his focus on Alester, his eyes searching him for answers. "Most unusual. That is also a very large selection of creatures for such a young dungeon. Are you certain that the adventurers did not miss the entrance to the second floor? Surely this cannot be correct..."

"No, my king. They were experienced C rank adventurers, not amateurs at all. In fact, they attest to having even seen the dungeon's heart itself on the first floor. I am sure you understand sire, but the dungeon heart is always on the last floor of any dungeon, thus it shouldn't be possible that the dungeon has more than one floor at the moment."

"How can we be sure that the adventurers really saw the dungeon heart, however?" King Vas inquired logically. "It could have easily been a dud or a trap."

"That is very unlikely, as the adventurers had a mage in the party. The mage swears that he felt mana emanating from the crystal in waves, which is a very good indication that this was the dungeon heart. Moreover, the rogue says he didn't spot any traps, and the ranger attests to the sturdiness of the golem that was protecting the crystal. For all intents and purposes, the Adventurers Guild is completely certain that the dungeon core really was found by the exploration team."

"I see. Well then, that is good. Considering how extensive the dungeon seemed to be in the report, I suppose it won't be long before it starts creating a second floor."

"I concur, your highness. The progress of the dungeon seems to indicate that it should occur soon."

"Hmm..." King Vas leaned back on his throne and closed his eyes, thinking about the situation calmly. The kingdom only had a handful of dungeons, each one of them an incredible resource of sorts. Even the weakest of them all was an excellent training ground for the country's militia and aspiring knights, teaching them more about survival and combat than could be explained in simple practices. This dungeon, however, seemed to have already reached a considerable amount of strength if it was this advanced in its progress.

"Good job getting the village expansion pre-work ready," King Vas said, as he opened his eyes. "Every dungeon is good for something, and this one might be a particularly useful one, especially if it gives items such as weapons. Strong opponents for my knights, and weapons to boot? Excellent. I want a report on the quality of those weapons that the adventurers picked up as quickly as possible. I need to know what we are working with here."

"Yes, my lord." Alester nodded, making a mental note of that.

"Now then..." King Vas said with a small smirk, his eye twinkling with a mischievous light. "Join me for a drink old friend! I believe we have much to talk about!"

Barking a laugh, Alester nodded graciously as the king walked down off his throne. He had missed the wonderful wine that the king always kept in store, along with the snacks that only the royal chef could prepare with the local fruits. The combination of those excellent tarts along with a perfectly aged wine was just heavenly.

It was good to be friends with a king.

<<<>>>

Status

Species: True Dungeon
Rank: 1
Name: Smit
Age: 2 months
Mana: 90,889 MP
Anima: 124
Mana Reg.: 210 MP/h
Anima Reg.: 5.1 AP/day
Floors: 2
Inhabitants: 55 Species

Titles: Creator of Dungeon Laws; Creator; Guide of the Bloody Evolution; Legendary Craftsman; Reincarnated One.

Abilities: Absorb matter; Alter environment; Bestow knowledge; Break down components; Craftsmanship; Creation; Digging; Destroy creation; Dungeon laws; Enhancement; Equivalent exchange; Ether manipulation; Evolution; Interdimensional storage; Life bestowal; Life-energy harnessing; Mana absorption; Masterful mana manipulation; Modification of creations; Monster link; Telepathy; Trap building; Transfer dungeon.

Resistances: Magic (general); Mind control

<<<>>>

CHAPTER THIRTEEN

P ala took a deep breath as he readied himself up again, taking a stance as he faced off against his formidable foe. Standing upon two thick hind legs, the fearsome creature he had hunted only days ago with his tribe, this so called "bear," roared out a challenge.

Pala would likely recall that day for the rest of his days. He and his tribe had returned exhausted, injured, and sore. They had been attacked by a number of creatures seeking to make short work of them, but somehow Pala and his tribe had persevered. However, what awaited them was not what they had expected at all once they arrived back at what should have been home.

Instead of finding a literal hole in the wall, they were greeted with an architectural masterpiece carved in many shades of green. If Pala had had any knowledge of what a temple should be, he would have immediately agreed that this was an entrance that would make even the mightiest temples feel inferior if one looked exclusively at the workmanship.

For Pala, who had never seen a temple or any buildings for that matter, this was nothing short of a wondrous view. How else could he describe the graceful curves or the detailed carvings? It was simply a feast for the eyes. It moved him, and it made him admire his father all the more. In Pala's mind, only the father was capable of imprinting such an emotion upon the soul of someone else with mere carved stone.

His thoughts were interrupted as the bear roared again, as if offended to be left waiting. He cursed himself silently, and turned to face the bear. "Sorry, brother. I am ready now."

Pala sharpened his mind and let his other thoughts fade into the background. He had been given a direct order from the father. Every creature in the dungeon was to be put in a fighting frenzy, in which the survivors would accumulate power and experience. Pala in particular was to train with the bear that the father created, and they would each attempt to kill each other without dying themselves. This was the Spartan training that he had received from the father, in order to increase both his strength and experience at the same time.

For his part, Pala had welcomed the order with open arms. After his defeat at the hands of the adventurers, he was made aware of his own weakness, and he was mortified by the thought that he would be too weak to protect his home, and most importantly, the father himself. Pala didn't fear his own death, for as long as the father lived, he could be revived. This meant he could throw himself at his newest brother and nemesis, the grizzly bear, and fight and die as often as he needed to, which in turn would allow him to gain experience.

Every day since his return from death, Pala had spent three hours sparring with the bear. He would sometimes die and be reborn through the will of the father, and then he would jump right back into the fray. Unfortunately, his ratio of wins versus losses was abysmal. Fourteen wins to eighty-three losses. And most of his wins occurred after he had exhausted the bear through previous encounters. But this time, Pala would make sure it would be different.

The bear snorted, looked at Pala dead on, and issued one last roar before it dropped to all fours, and started to circle Pala, weary of the spear held by the kobold.

Both predators circled each other slowly, inching closer to one another as they looked for the perfect opportunity to strike. At an unseen signal, they both rushed in, and the clash began in earnest.

Though Pala had a good advantage with the range of his weapon, it did little to stop a bear that was not afraid to get cut. The bear was weary enough to avoid being struck in his head, but he clearly did not mind a few cuts and slices. This, coupled with the fact that the bear could bat away Pala's spear too, meant that the kobold had a hard fight ahead of him.

Hence, Pala had decided on the following strategy: bleed the beast first, and then hack at it until it died.

It was a simple and rudimentary strategy, but it was a logical strategy as well. With the range provided by his spear, he could cut and wound the beast, frustrate him, and maybe even bleed him enough that he could not react properly. The more wounds the better, as it would give Pala more opportunities to kill the beast. The only problem was that he also needed to stay alive through the entire process.

The clash continued to expand from seconds into minutes. Long, excruciatingly tense minutes in which both creatures bloodied one another, tooth and claw versus steel. As the battle drew to a close, Pala threw his weapon at the beast, intending to end it once and for all. His aim was true, but the bear lifted his arms to protect his face, and had his arm skewered, the blade only nicking the side of his neck as the forearm deflected the blow partially.

But he was not dead.

Roaring with defiance, the bear tried to approach the kobold, rising on two legs as he showed his full height... only to collapse awkwardly onto the ground. Breathing heavily, Pala observed the scene before him numbly, watching the blood ooze from a hundred cuts he had inflicted upon the bear. The final straw had been his last blow. His spear had nicked a major artery in the bear's neck and he was finally dying of blood loss. Pala struggled to his feet, wounded and bruised. Some of his scales had been ripped clean off as he had been thrown about the room. But through all his pain, Pala managed to approach the bear and kneel beside him.

"Thank you, brother," Pala said, conveying a deep sense of appreciation. "Thanks to you, I have finally gotten my first real success against your kind. May you find comfort in knowing your sacrifice has protected the father."

Pala saw the bear close his eyes in satisfaction. This was for the father, for their home, and for their way of life. The bear knew his fate would be to die, and he had welcomed it readily. Everything was for the sake of the father. It did not matter that the bear was not sentient enough to understand Pala. All that mattered was that the bear was satisfied with his end. He instinctively knew that this was necessary.

Smiling, Pala stroked the head of the bear one last time, before bending over and biting into the beast's neck with his sharp teeth, ending the life of the bear in seconds. He chewed and swallowed a few mouthfuls of bear meat, before the bear started to dissolve into particles of light as the dungeon reclaimed his body. But just like every time Pala had had a victory within the dungeon, a tiny portion of the light came to him. He basked in the invigorating feeling of the light as new power entered his body. It was not a dramatic increase in power, but he could feel his strength had taken a step forward. He could fight a little harder, for a little longer now. And that was good. Bit by bit Pala would claw his way to the summit, and claim the right to stand beside the father as his protector.

That was his only wish.

My sharp ears picked up the sounds that resounded through the village of Nam easily as I strolled down the streets, the lively sound of people milling about as I inspected the area at a leisurely pace. This place was good, imbedded deep within nature, and with abundant mana, thanks to the nearby dungeon. As far as magical races such as elves would be concerned, this place would be a fantastic location for a town... if you ignored the noisy humans or the fact that the location fell within a human kingdom.

I was followed by a small group of people that are in charge of planning the expansion of the town. Apparently, I'd been given the "honor" of helping pick out the best location for the future Adventurers Guild hall. I couldn't see what difference it made where we put the guild right now, considering that there were barely over a hundred people in this village. By the time that the expansion was done, the guild would not be that distant from the center of the village anyway. The guild could literally pick any empty plot of land around here and that would be good enough in my mind.

But of course, I couldn't say that. I had been chosen to pick the most "accessible location for civilians, while remaining strategically located in case of a major threat"—which, in other words, meant "Pick a place that everyone can find easily but if we get attacked by monsters we can defend it or run away easily like beaten dogs."

It was a sensible train of thought, save that this place was little more than a large clearing at the foot of the mountains. There was really no place that you could say was more strategically feasible than the other at this point in time. Personally, I thought that if a wave of monsters decided to surge out of the forest all at once, this village would be razed to the ground within the hour.

Well, a job is a job, so I had to do it, no two ways around it. I sighed and put my mind to it as I wandered around the small village. Ideally, I would find a place that was wide enough to create fortifications and a training ground. Of course, it should not be too close to any houses or the forest in case of a fire, and I should look into having it made on as even ground as possible. That's about all I had to worry about, considering that the village is miniscule and offered little protection or strategical advantages.

Speaking of protection, how had these people survived so far? I got that the village was barely four decades old, but they didn't have any walls around the village perimeter, and they barely had patrols. The most that some of these people had were flimsy wooden fences around their cattle. Granted, it had been enough to keep the local wolves from having a feast, but if they ever encountered a real threat, they would be turned into food in the blink of an eye.

Grimacing at the lack of fortifications that were placed around the village, I finally decided on a location. It wasn't ideal, but it seemed to be the most promising spot at the north end of the village. It was a bit separated from the other residential buildings, but it had fairly flat ground and a lot of space to work with. It would need a bit of work, but it could be made to work. There was plenty of stone and lumber around this part of the mountain too, which meant that they would have plenty of available resources to reinforce and expand both the village and the Adventurers Guild if needed.

"Alright, this place looks good," I nodded with satisfaction, pointing at the floor with a wide smile. "Right here."

There was a collective murmur of agreement, and the squad of people I was guiding set about to work, pulling out tools of all kinds to take measurements, test the ground consistency, and to do calculations. It was almost impressive seeing them utilize their tools so nimbly despite how complicated those things looked. But then again, with practice comes perfection. All these men working on the guild were easily in their forties, and they had plenty of experience with their craft.

Satisfied that I had completed my task, I turned on my heel and I was about to march away confidently when a nearly imperceptible sound suddenly caught my attention. It started as softly as if it was a breeze of cool air, but with a hint of... something that made my brain do a double take. The sound that I could barely hear even with my enhanced hearing at first seemed to be laced with some other power I could not identify.

I held my breath as my skin started to perceive this sensation as well. Within seconds, I noticed that the volume of the whispered noise was increasing ever so slightly, but enough that I could start to distinguish a tone to the sound. I could not quite understand it, nor could I tell if there were words, but there was definitely a rhythm to this sound. This melody began to change as time wore on. Slowly, gently, and delicately, the sound began to take a shape, as if molded by invisible hands.

"Lady Me-"

"Shh!" I spun around to quiet down the man that had tried to interrupt my focus, a finger pressed to my lips as I glared at him. "Do. Not. Move."

I didn't even wait to hear his reply. I simply closed my eyes and tried to hear that whispered melody that was carried by that unusual wind. My ears picked it up again in a matter of seconds, but the tone had changed just a bit again. It was not quite so gentle or mellow. Rather, the sound was more firm, as if the gods of the wind had decided to give shape to a single thought within the tone of the wind. I swayed slightly in place as the rhythm moved around me, inviting me to a slow waltz of unknown emotions.

And then it ended.

The mysterious sound that moved my heart just... ceased to be. I strained my ears and swung my head around, trying to catch another second of that whispered melody, but it was all for naught. The music had stopped.

"Rats!"

I opened my eyes with disappointment, and puffed my cheeks in frustration. What was that anyway? Where did it come from?

"Lady...Mei?" the same man from earlier asked in confusion,

one foot suspended in the air as he quivered, trying to keep his balance.

"What is it?" I asked, sullen that I missed out on the musical tune that had ridden the wind to reach me.

"Can I move now?" he asked, and I realized that the man had no clue what was going on. He had just stopped because he thought there was something seriously wrong. I suppose anyone would, if an adventurer just turned around and told them to shut up and stop moving with a very serious voice.

"Yes, yes, you can move," I grumbled, watching as the man sighed in relief, and placed his foot down on the floor comfortably.

"Lady Mei, may I ask why I had to... freeze?"

I sighed in frustration and rubbed my temple with one hand. He probably didn't hear it at all. It's only due to my superior hearing that I even caught wind of it.

"There was a... noise. A very strange and melodic noise. I have never heard anything like it in all my life."

The man's eyes widened, but before he had a chance to make any odd assumptions, I interjected, stopping his train of thought. It would not do to have this man start imagining all sorts of wild things and alarming everyone else around the camp.

"Just to be clear, it did not sound malevolent or dangerous. Rather... it sounded soothing and beautiful. It could be a good omen of some sort, or it could be that we are near a colony of wind fairies. I have heard that they are excellent musicians," though I doubt that it is either of those things. I would have sensed something more with the fairies, and they are usually more playful too. "I just asked you to freeze so I could try to identify the sound and its source."

The man visibly calmed down, sighing in relief as he smiled at me again. "Well that's good... It's always a welcomed thing if we can have a good omen at the beginning of a project like this. Perhaps one of the gods smiles upon us."

I nodded at his optimism, but merely nodded my head at this. Perhaps he was right after all.

Still, it wouldn't hurt to go have a look, right?

I excused myself, and ran back to find Ella and the rest of my party. The sound seemed to be coming from uphill. Perhaps the dungeon was to blame, and it would do us no harm to check it out. We had to go back in there soon anyway—might as well investigate a bit while we were at it.

If Smit could sweat, he would be soaked right now. His constant cultivating with such absurd speed, in addition to constantly trying to heal creatures, was taking its toll on him. Smit was gambling here. Though he had placed the dungeon law [Respawn] to refill his dungeon when it got dangerously low on creatures to defend him, he had realized that there was something to be said for keeping some of his defenders alive out of their sheer potential. Hence, he had created his third law amidst his cultivation.

Dungeon law [Scoreboard]. Put simply, it was a law that acted as a pseudo skill for Smit. It kept track of who were his best fighters, and if they seemed to be in critical danger during the fighting frenzy, he would aid them by funneling mana to their bodies, which would boost their abilities momentarily, in addition to helping treat their wounds to some extent. Basically, this was a safety net for Smit.

In frenzies, there were no rules. It was kill or be killed, and it allowed his creatures to improve quickly... if they survived. But because of the lack of rules, he had noticed that several weaker members would sometimes stumble upon a stronger, injured foe, and they would attack it as a group. Of course, this meant that now the strength gained by defeating that one injured creature would be divided into the weaker creatures. In other words, there was a dissipation of power, which he wanted to avoid.

The whole point of the frenzy was to do only two things: to speed up evolutionary progress (which required large accumulations of power in a member of a species), and to create experienced fighters that could help him defend his dungeon. If his best fighters died a useless death like that, it would make achieving those two goals much harder.

Thus, by adding [Scoreboard], he could give his most promising troops a chance to survive and keep progressing. It eliminated some of the "luck" aspect of his original method. Of course, because he was only funneling mana to them to momentarily boost their abilities, and to just do some patchwork first aid on them, the creatures could still die, but it gave them a fighting chance.

However, there was one drawback to this.

It required intense amounts of focus to heal multiple creatures at once and to cultivate simultaneously. The mental strain was something he had not expected, but his pride and his sense of urgency would not let him stop his cultivation for much more than a few minutes per day. His scouting dungeon mice had already detected movement in recent days at the village of Nam, and he knew that he had only a limited amount of time before more men arrived again at his doorstep.

But this time, things would be different. He would dazzle them in ways they had never expected, and he would force his trials upon them. The victors would be rewarded, and the losers would be punished. Such was the way of his dungeon.

CHAPTER FOURTEEN

G at strode through his little village, staring at the sudden change that was going on throughout it. It was odd to see so many people that he didn't know in his village. The village, though it had been founded less than a century ago, did not have much traffic from foreign entities. Even merchants were a rarity that only visited the town a handful of times a year, and even then only a few would come at the time.

Today, the population of the village had grown over the course of a few days by an additional sixty people, increasing it by fifty percent. For a village as small as Nam, an influx of sixty people was a staggering increase in population density. By order of the king, the village of Nam was to be expanded into a more fitting settlement, given its proximity to the dungeon. The village itself would get more than just a basic expansion of living quarters. Several facilities would be opened, including an inn and tavern, an Adventurers Guild hall, a barracks, supply stores, and even an apothecary with medical facilities.

The plan seemed quite grand for the villagers, especially since the expansion was going to be a large boon for them, as the demand for their crops and cattle had suddenly increased, raising the amount of profit they could gather. Moreover, the crown was sponsoring their expansion to a certain degree, which meant that they would be compensated for facilitating the growth of their town. In fact, the crown had even granted the villagers more territory for farming, encouraging them to prepare for the future growth of their village.

The only real downside for the original inhabitants of Nam village was that they were going to get a lot of visitors really quickly, and they didn't have much of a say as to who would come. However, the benefits of expanding their village would prove to be astronomical in comparison to what they currently had. More people meant more money, which meant a more prosperous settlement in the long run, if it was managed appropriately of course.

The deal had been too sweet to pass up, and the entire village had thrown their support behind the expansion, working overtime to increase their farmland, craft shop stands, or to house the new arrivals.

Though the new arrivals consisted mostly of carpenters, architects, and generally any laborers that were tasked with readying the basic facilities that were promised the town (most notably the Adventurers Guild and the barracks), the true stars of the show had been the Azure Arrow team, who had returned from the dungeon looking rather worn out on the first time that anyone had approached the dungeon.

Interestingly enough, Azure Arrow had been quite tight lipped about the first dungeon dive, only citing that it was lurking with all manner of creatures, but that they were unable to say more than that until they had discussed it with their superiors at the time. But now? Now they freely talked about it to anyone that would ask.

Gat could not help but daydream about the adventure every time he heard about it from the adventurers. Snakes that hid in the shadows, rats the size of cats that pounced at your face, pitfalls that could cripple you, and kobolds that swung spears at your heart. All of it placed neatly in a realm of fairy tales, where the beauty could fool you into a false sense of security.

He had heard the story of how the members of Azure Arrow dove into the dungeon at least half a dozen times over the last week, and still he could not get tired of it. His favorite part was the final battle with the kobolds. The kobolds had been adversaries so fearsome that they had manage to wound the members of Azure Arrow multiple times, going as far as pushing them back, if only for a moment.

At first, Gat had found the story rather... lacking. In his mind, it was natural that a monster had been able to push back a human, even if they were adventurers. Adventurers were still human after all, only that they were a bit stronger and wiser than the average human when it came to fighting monsters.

Or that's what he had thought anyway.

The day after Azure Arrow returned, he had awoken to the sound of wood clashing against wood, in a series of thumping sounds. Tired but curious, Gat got himself dressed and went to check on the disturbance, only to be baffled at his findings. Before him, two members of Azure Arrow sparred with wooden weapons. A roguish man with wooden knives and the redheaded leader with her wooden sword dashed around the clearing at quick speeds, engaging and disengaging in a flurry of blows that lasted only moments at a time. Each movement was precise and determined, and seemed aimed at injuring the opponent, if not disabling them.

The rogue was clearly the more slippery of the two of them, dodging as many blows as he could rather than taking the attacks head on. He reminded Gat of a snake that coiled up to attack, retreating quickly when its offensive was blocked or diverted. On the other hand, the redhead was more like a wolf, carefully circling her prey, diverting the blow of the attacks or blocking them entirely, only to retaliate with powerful hits that pushed the rogue back every time they connected.

One opponent was slippery and vicious, the other was steady

and tenacious. The two were evenly matched in a dance of adrenaline and sweat, until their partner, the large man called James, stepped in to stop them.

The sight of the two warriors facing off had changed Gat's perspective of them completely, and it had caused him to realize how dangerous those kobolds truly were. It didn't matter if the kobolds had had aid from wolves in that last stand. Considering the speed and strength of Azure Arrow, he was surprised that the kobolds had managed to even slow down these adventurers, much less injure them or push them back, however fleeting that moment had been.

He shuddered to think what would have happened if he had entered that dungeon on his own the day he discovered it. He had no doubt in his mind that he would have ended up as a corpse before he had even been halfway through the first floor. It was a terrifying thought.

However, at the same time, the idea of challenging the dungeon excited him greatly. Just imagining the adrenaline, the challenge, the pure excitement of diving into the unknown stimulated something deep inside of him. It was a feeling that sang to blood, and pulled at something deep in his heart.

...Perhaps it was time for a career change after all.

I HELD my staff in my hand loosely as I looked around. It was interesting to see how the little village I'd come to know recently had begun to change. Within one week, the Adventurers Guild's main building was already half completed, though the training grounds were mostly just fenced off and used to spar at the moment. The training grounds would require little time to be completed, however, as they would mostly consist of stationary targets to train against and wide open spaces for group drills to be carried out.

On that note, I suppose I shouldn't be surprised, but the inn with the tavern was well on its way to being completed too. In fact, the tavern area of the inn was nearly done, and it would be open for business soon. This was even more impressive considering that the tavern and inn only started to be constructed three days after the Adventurers Guild, and it was being built by a relatively small group of people.

Then again, perhaps it would be weird if the inn wasn't one of the first things to open up. Adventurers are largely known for their need to drink and party after a long day of adventuring, after all. As an adventurer myself though, I could certainly understand why that was the case. Sometimes you were risking your life for days out in the bush, hunting down dangerous monsters or stopping criminal groups for a good sum of money. In those occasions where you could die at any moment, where a single missed blow could end your life, or a wrong sound could reveal your location to a wandering beast... Who wouldn't accumulate stress?

Mental stress was one of the eternal enemies of adventurers. There was a need to relieve stress regularly, and few outlets were more available to people than good company and good drink. As a matter of fact, the guild encouraged us to go and relax at the tavern, as it relieves mental stress. And everyone knows that living in constant high alert and high stress is detrimental for a person over the long term.

I chuckled at myself at the sudden turn of my thoughts. My mind went from marveling at the speed at which the town was changing... to death. Funny how that happens sometimes.

I let my morbid thoughts slide out of my mind without resistance, and returned to walking towards my destination whilst inspecting the progress occurring throughout the village. Soon I approached a tent that had been pitched amongst the construction zones for various residences, and I heard the familiar voices of my teammates.

"About time you got here Ziggy," Adder blurted out, grinning with that odd, tilted, mocking smile of his. "What happened? Got lost on your way to the washroom?"

"Just admiring the progress around here. These guys are working quickly," I replied as I stepped into the ten-man tent. It wasn't very big, but it was enough for the five of us plus the table that held a map of the village and the dungeon. Adder must have drawn it. He didn't have many talents other than fighting with his knives and drawing... unless you counted his ability to make people want to strangle him as a talent.

"Of course they are being quick," Ella chimed in. "A total of fifty carpenters and laborers. That is plenty to build a basic structure in a few days. Besides, there are a few master crafters sent by the king himself. They should drastically increase the rate at which the entire thing progresses."

"Hmm... how much do you figure that those two master craftsmen cost?" James asked, sounding mildly curious. "I would love to have something designed by them."

Snorting loudly, Adder was the one to reply to James, clearly amused. "Boy, James, buddy, friend. Master craftsmen charge in gold pieces. Often upwards of double digits. Does that answer your question?"

"Ugh... They get paid better than we do," James grumbled with a dissatisfied scowl.

"There is a reason why they are called master craftsmen, James," I added. "There is only a handful in the entire kingdom. The whole continent has about a hundred... maybe two hundred, at best. The fact that we could get two master carpenters all the way out here is already an achievement in itself. The king must have had a hand in acquiring them directly."

"The king really wants this place to be up and running quickly huh?" Mei spoke up offhandedly, her eyes looking down at the map of the area around the village.

"Well, sure he does," Ella replied with a matter-of-fact tone. "There are very few dungeons in the kingdom. Every dungeon is a useful resource for training people and for gathering materials. It wouldn't be an exaggeration to say that dungeons are directly tied to the economic growth of a nation. A single dungeon can provide a vast amount of resources over the years. Of course, this largely depends on the size and quality of the dungeon. A large dungeon that provides high quality materials will obviously have a higher impact on the economy than a small dungeon that provides lower quality materials. Moreover, you need to consider that every dungeon can provide a kingdom with live training for adventurers and the military. Experience fighting living things is very valuable, even though it doesn't have a price tag attached to it."

"I suppose you are right," Mei sighed as she looked up. "The quicker we can get this place up and running, the better it will be for the kingdom as a whole. I am curious to see if this dungeon will have a specialty though."

"A specialty?" I asked, confused for a second, before it clicked in what she meant. "Oh, you mean a special product or resource it specializes in producing. Isn't that quite rare though? Most dungeons are only good for gaining fighting experience and perhaps gathering some common monster parts."

Mei looked up at me with those lovely grey-blue eyes. "That might be true. But aren't you forgetting something?"

"Hmm..." I murmured, stroking my short beard as I thought about it for a moment. "Ah, you mean the spears?"

"Correct," Mei nodded sharply.

"Didn't we just take that from the kobolds though?" I asked with a bit of confusion. "They should be just common spears."

James snorted at that, and turned to look at me dead on. "Trust me, they are not. Perhaps you didn't notice because you weren't fighting them upfront, but those were magnificently crafted weapons despite their simplicity. I tried one out before handing them over to the guild to get them identified. They were perfectly balanced, sharpened enough to retain an edge but not enough to make them brittle, and the tips were made with unique care. The spears were sturdy enough to withstand a blow from my hammer without breaking too."

I stood there, quiet for a moment as I digested this information. James was amongst us the strongest one physically. I have seen him use his hammer to crush the head of a wild boar as easily as if it were a melon, and yet the spears had somehow managed to withstand those blows. Say what you want about deflecting the blows or blocking them only partially. The fact that they could survive *a* blow from that steel hammer at all was a testament to their durability.

"I see... Now I am curious too," I hummed out, smiling at the news.

"Save that curiosity for later. The hawk is here," Ella interrupted as a hawk flew into the tent a second later, landing neatly on Ella's outstretched gloved hand. She quickly pulled on a little metal tube that the hawk had on its leg, and extracted a small roll of parchment from it. She cleared her throat and began to read it out.

"Members of Azure Arrow, you are hereby authorized to do a routine inspection on the recently confirmed dungeon that lies north of the village of Nam. You are to conduct a check dive, in order to determine the state of the dungeon, as it is possible it has begun to create a second floor now. Send a report once your check is done.

"Additionally, the examination of the spears you have handed in for inspection has been completed. The analysis concludes that the spears are masterwork level, in terms of quality. The tips are crafted with Damascus steel, with a technique that is unknown. The handles are also made of good quality wood that has some give to it, which helps absorb impacts to an extent. The price for each spear is quoted at around three and a half gold pieces..."

Ella stopped talking as she gaped at the sum of money, stopping to read it again. "Three and a half gold pieces... Lord, that's two gold pieces and ten silver for each of us!"

"That's more than some of the quests we take sometimes!" Adder said excitedly, "In one day we managed to get the same pay as a one-week-long mission! I love this dungeon already."

I whistled at the sum of money, stroking my beard again. "Two gold pieces is enough to make sure a commoner can eat well for a half a year easily. That's quite a sum to gather in a day."

"I hope that this is the specialty of the dungeon," Adder added in excitedly. "Just imagine, if we can get this much on just the first floor, once it develops more floors it will be a literal goldmine!"

"Don't get too excited yet," Ella interrupted. "These could have been a fluke. Or it could also be that the dungeon only produces a fixed amount of high quality items in a given amount of time."

"Shhhh.... Don't ruin the moment for me yet," Adder said happily, clearly disregarding her sensible words.

"Anyway," Ella said, as she ignored Adder as he went off into his own happy world, "let me just finish the letter. Let's see... It simply asks if we would wish to sell the spears to the Adventurers Guild or if we wish to retain them."

We all looked at each other for a moment, before we simply came to the agreement that we would just have them sold. None of us was a spear user anyway, so for us the money would be more beneficial. Though if it had been a staff for mages, and of the same quality as those spears, I would have immediately claimed one for myself. As much as I love my staff, it is just a tool, and if I can get myself a tool that is more likely to keep me alive, I will gladly take it.

"Right, we got our orders, people," Ella said with a nod. "Tomorrow we depart for the dungeon. Pack your things and have a good night's rest. The hike is rather long as we all know."

"We should really look into having a path cleared to the dungeon," James pitched in. "Two days to get to the dungeon is too long for the actual distance from here to there. If it weren't for all the winding paths we must follow and all the obstacles we have to avoid, I bet it would take us less than half of the time to reach it."

"That will have to wait, James," Ella said with a sigh. "Though I agree with your opinion, the expansion of the village comes first."

"I know," James said with a nod as he stood up and rolled his neck slowly. "I just wish there was some way to get there quicker. It's not pleasant to hike up that mountain for two days in full gear."

"Oh, hush up you big ox," I chuckled at him. "If there is anyone here that can carry a metric ton of weight for two days straight in our group, it's you. You will be fine."

"Easy for you to say, Zig. You carry a robe and a stick for weapons and armor, in addition to whatever food and water you need. You don't carry full plate armor," James grumbled like a child, making it all the more funny to me.

"I am sure you can manage. We've been through worse before. Remember the time we had to catch the cursed fire goat on that ridge? An entire week of hiking and you were fully armored. If you could do that, you can do this."

"Just because I *can* do it, it doesn't mean I like doing it," James replied. "A human can go for a number of weeks without food and live, but that doesn't mean anyone would enjoy doing it, you know?"

"Okay, point taken," I chuckled at this point, knowing fully well that what he said was true.

"So, we will meet here at the same time as always?" Mei interrupted, clearly eager to get out of this little meeting. Not that I could blame her. She'd been distracted ever since she heard a certain "ethereal tune in the wind," whatever that means. Whatever this tune was, it had her quite enchanted, and she'd been spending her days scouting the area around the village, searching for the source of it without any luck yet.

I have no doubt that the minute this meeting is over, she is going right back out there to those woods, and get down to business, searching once more. She can be adorable when she obsesses over little things like that... at least until she decides that whatever caused it is dangerous. Then she starts using her arrows, and I would hate to get in her way when that happens.

Ella smiled and nodded at Mei's question. "See you all at sunrise."

Chuckling, I departed from the tent and began to walk back to my tent, when I heard a little squeak as I set my foot down. Following the sound, I noticed a little mouse dart past me, running off into the bushes like a devil chased by a holy man. Poor thing, it's probably dying of anxiety due to all the activity around here.

CHAPTER FIFTEEN

Smit's core had grown significantly in the last couple of days, increasing his size by a good thirty percent. He could feel himself approach the second breakthrough. It was close enough that he could taste it, figuratively speaking. Soon he would cross over the threshold, and then he would be able to grow his dungeon. Perhaps more importantly, he would be able to increase his abilities.

However, now he had other things to contend with too. According to his scouting mice, the adventurers had come back to the village and they had brought company. A small vanguard of carpenters had accompanied them. Apparently, they were all getting to work right away. Led by two master level carpenters, the group had recruited several able-bodied men from the village to gather lumber, and had proceeded to create a frenzy of activity. Within a week, the groundwork for the Adventurers Guild and the entirety of the inn had been completed. They had even begun to flesh it out.

Smit was now racing the clock, as he knew that once the adventurers truly began to explore his dungeon, the amount of time he would have for cultivating would decrease significantly. More likely than not, he would have to start relying on his abilities to syphon energy and mana from his "guests" passively in order to gather the necessary resources to cultivate. However, as cultivation required one to gather and concentrate energy and then appropriate that energy as part of oneself, he suspected that relying completely on that system would cause his growth rate to drop substantially.

Just as he thought of this, he sensed a presence rush towards his dungeon, moving as fast as its tiny legs would allow. Naturally, this was one of his dungeon mice. Unfortunately, he did not have the ability to see through the eyes of his dungeon mice from a distance. However, he could feel their general location, and the accuracy of his ability to locate them increased the closer they got to his dungeon.

He paid no mind to the little thing though, opting to let the mouse race towards his dungeon core on its own as he continued to work on his cultivation. Thanks to the alterations that Smit had managed to give his mice, the little thing was significantly faster than a normal mouse, and it only took it about twenty to thirty minutes to reach his core.

As his creation raced into the room and came to an abrupt stop before him, Smit turned his attention to the small rodent. He reached out with his mind and made a link between his own mind and the mouse's, tapping into its memories.

The thing with dungeon mice, despite the fact that he had improved them, was that they had a limited memory span. Sure, given time they would be able to learn certain simple things, but to be able to recall more than a day's worth of stuff after only seeing it once was virtually impossible for their tiny brains. Perhaps the information was there, but Smit would have had to spend a long time rooting through their minds, trying to piece it all together. Hence, Smit had the mice report to him frequently.

As soon as the mind link with the mouse had been established, Smit began to sort through its memories lazily, still focusing upon gathering the energies necessary for cultivation. That came to an end abruptly, however, as Smit stumbled upon a particular memory from his little spy.

"Damnation," Smit huffed as his concentration got broken. He quickly calculated the speed at which the adventurers should be moving, reaching a rough estimate. "Pala, Echo, to me! I need to discuss something with you."

He didn't even need to wait for a response; he could feel his creations rush towards him, the seriousness in his voice demanding their urgency to meet him. Within minutes they reached him, the first to arrive being Pala, despite the distance he had to cover being greater than that of Echo. It was to be expected, however, considering Echo still was not on par with organic beings when it came to movement, although she was making large strides towards that goal. At this point, Smit was confident enough to say that Echo could probably eat with utensils if she had any need to eat, but it would not look refined by any stretch of the imagination.

"Father!" Pala spoke out loudly as he skidded to a stop, his clawed feet finding purchase upon the rocky ground. "I heard your call, Father, I came as quick as I could."

"I as well, Father!" Echo called out from behind as she entered the room, trying to stop her forward momentum as she headed straight for Pala. She stumbled a bit in the process, but deadened most of her momentum before Pala reached out to help her stop.

"Oof!" Pala grunted, stopping the moving Echo. "I forget sometimes that your body is entirely made of dense stone. You are heavier than you look."

Echo huffed at the comment, but thanked him for his assistance.

"Right," Smit said, ignoring the brief exchange just now, bulldozing ahead. "I have news. Urgent news," Smit said sternly as he began to talk to his captive audience. "The adventurers are back, as you both know, and they have started to expand the settlement that is closest to us. That in itself is fine, but the problem lies in the readiness factor. While we have improved compared to when we experienced our first dungeon dive, we are still far from safe. Don't forget, last time most creatures got annihilated despite all our efforts and strategy. Even Pala and his comrades died back then. Therefore, we can't let down our guard."

He paused to gather his thoughts, letting his mind organize the information he wanted to relate to them properly before opening his mouth again. "As you can imagine, the completion of the second floor is a huge asset for us, but the new species at the pond hasn't matured enough. As a result, I would like to ensure it isn't destroyed yet. We retrieved a young specimen, and I cannot recreate it as a full-grown adult if it dies. I would have to start from scratch, again from a young thing since it's simply so... different. Unique even. I need that pond room well protected. Pala, it will be your job to secure that room. You and your fighters may train, but stay in fighting condition."

If Smit had a beard, he would be stroking it right now as he contemplated his next course of action. "Echo, I need you on protective duty as well. If needed, you will act as my mouthpiece to the adventurers. I would rather avoid that if possible, as it would cause complications, but it is an option we have to consider. We have perhaps a day and a half to prepare for their arrival. I want everything ready by then."

"By your will, Father!" Pala is the first to respond, sensing that Smit's speech has come to an end. Like an arrow shot from a bow, Pala dashed out of the room, speeding towards his brethren in a rush to follow through with his new orders.

"Echo, I will need you to do some basic practice with your halberd. You are not at a level where you can fight with it, but if you can manage to carry it around at least naturally, it will do for a good show of intimidation."

"As you order, Father," Echo replied, nodding her head as she moved to retrieve her weapon. Smit, for his part, had a look around his room. The entire room was covered with all sorts of armor, weapons, and artifacts he had crafted. Of course, his most valuable stuff was stored in his dimensional ring, but that was beside the point. The fact that anyone would be able to try to take any of his creations without even earning them was rather insulting. A finely crafted sword wouldn't display its true capabilities in the hands of an amateur.

Smit could not stand his creations going to people that were not worthy of them. The last adventurers were decently capable, and had taken three of his spears, which, to be fair, they had earned by combat. Still, the trial felt a little too... simple for his taste.

Well, at least with two floors I can start setting up a more proper trial now, he thought to himself. After all, he had to provide some sort of reward to divert people from aiming at his core. If the people saw him as a resource that was more useful alive than dead, the risk towards his own well-being would be reduced.

That said, the spears that the kobolds held would have to do as reward if they got to the second-floor room, for now.

Pushing these thoughts away from his mind for the moment, Smit focused on a more pressing matter: The fighting frenzy in the dungeon was still ongoing. A quick scan through his floors revealed that a handful of creatures had transcended into a previously discovered evolution, while a few more were ready to be evolved by his hand. He would have to look into evolving those few that would be able to take it a step higher.

From the first tier evolved species, some of the insects, snakes, and dungeon rats had gathered enough energy to evolve. The wolves were getting close, but they were not there yet. The bears were even further behind.

Interestingly enough, some of his plants were ready to evolve too.

He looked at the first patch of moss he had set up at the

entrance and he discovered that it had gathered significant amounts of energy, probably since every dying animal brought by the kobold was killed there so that Smit could absorb them. However, in the time frame that it had taken Smit to absorb the creatures, blood had been spilled constantly upon that moss. Apparently, it had unlocked certain secret conditions for it, as it now gave Smit the option to evolve this moss into "Blood Moss."

<<<>>>

Evolution Available: Blood Moss. Blood Moss is a rare ingredient that can help replenish blood when drunk as a tea, or help stop blood loss when turned into a paste with other ingredients.

<<<>>>

It sounded like a fairly valuable thing to have around, so Smit immediately evolved his little patch of moss into blood moss, and absorbed the knowledge of how to create it greedily.

He left the patch of blood moss at the entrance as a little gift for the first adventurers to come in, and proceeded to place a few more patches of blood moss deeper in the dungeon, to act as an incentive for adventurers. With any luck, this small reward would encourage quests for the collection of blood moss, which would in turn increase the value of the dungeon in the eyes of the public. Of course, this meant more adventurers visiting him, but it also meant he could test the mettle of more people.

He had to make sure that blood moss wasn't too abundant in his dungeon, or not yet, at least. If he created too much of one valuable resource, there wouldn't be any doubt that he would have hordes of people trying to acquire it. In his current state, though his dungeon was quite advanced for its age, he was aware that it would not be able to survive large, consecutive assaults from adventurers. He simply wouldn't have the resources to constantly create enough creatures to keep up with a large number of adventurers and constant attacks. That would change in time, but for now, he had to play it safe.

Keeping that in mind, his fastest method of strengthening himself and fortifying his dungeon was evolving his creatures. While a larger dungeon brought him more maneuverability and resources, it was ultimately his traps and creatures that had to stop intruders from waltzing through his dungeon.

Thus he began to examine his creations. Currently he had "original" species, such as mice, simple snakes, and wolves. Some of those had already undergone their first evolution, resulting in creatures such as dungeon rats and green snakes. First tier evolutions were a significant step up from their previous forms, but hardly a dramatic improvement. In terms of strength, it would be like comparing an eight-year-old child to the same child when he was eleven years old. It was considerable growth, but not overly impressive.

Smit hoped that these next evolutions would prove at least as useful as the last, and, ideally, even more so.

Smit began with his smallest creatures. The spiders, which had evolved mild hallucinogenic properties, had improved significantly, their power overflowing past what was required for a normal evolution. As such, Smit had a little extra to play around and enhance them with. To begin, he made their main body the size of a human male's fist. Rather a large body that was made easily twice as large again by the long legs that carried it. It was a large enough spider to induce fear, but not large enough to be easily cut down. Most of his focus went to their poison. Rather than making their poison more lethal, he redirected the evolution to make it so that the illusions created by the bite of the spider were more intense. Anyone with a weak constitution would start to feel the room waver and sway, and perhaps see things that were not truly there.

It was not a very lethal poison on its own, but the fact that one bite could affect your perception of space and reality for any extended period of time would be a serious boon for him. It could easily tip the balance in his favor in the long run, especially if he was facing a large armed force. A couple of confused and scared enemies amongst the ranks of the enemy could cause chaos in an organized formation.

He named these spiders Mirage Spiders.

Then he moved on to his two headed spider. The poor thing finally had gathered enough strength to evolve. It had taken quite some time, as she, for some reason, required almost twice as much energy as the original spiders. He looked at the spider carefully, noting that she had several scars along her chitin body. By the looks of things, the spider had had a hard time surviving but she had managed to progress along well. She was one of his earliest creations, and also one of his earliest experiments.

He looked at her closely for a moment, examining her before accepting the evolution. As his spider's poison was weak, he decided to focus instead on making her suited for close combat. He looked over his creature and increased her size dramatically, making her the size of a large domesticated cat. Her armor was tougher now too, thicker, able to resist more intense attacks, and the mandibles on both heads were made significantly stronger and larger. Lastly, he made sure that her joints were a little more flexible, making her movements stealthier. He hoped to make this spider a good assassin in the future.

He placed his two-headed spider on the second floor, amongst the pillars where she could hide with her black armor and perhaps pick off the remnants of some inexperienced adventurer group. With any luck, it would help his spider get some experience. He would be curious to see how effective his two-headed minion would become.

He placed his spider carefully, instructing her to use the dark pillars to her advantage, and then he moved on to the next creature in line to obtain an evolution: his snakes. In particular, the green snakes had improved enough to obtain an interesting evolution.

The most advanced of his green snakes managed to evolve into a green viper.

Green vipers were well known for their poison, which was capable of paralyzing a grown man. The cost for that evolution was surprisingly high, which made Smit wonder just how many creatures his green snake had consumed to gather that amount... Regardless, it was a significantly better evolution than the standard evolution option "sly green snake," which, in all honesty, seemed like a normal green snake that was simply better at being sneaky and hiding.

He looked over the wolves, the bears, and a handful of other creatures he had acquired, but those had yet to reach a high enough concentration of energies to evolve. Still, they were making good progress. He made a mental note to give the best of those specimens a little boost of energy, hopefully allowing them to escape if necessary in the future. He needed them alive if they were to evolve into the best possible versions of themselves.

Humming to himself, Smit observed his current new evolutions, and set them in place. Everything had to be perfect so that he could get more time to advance. He only had a bit further to go for his breakthrough and he would be damned if he would be interrupted before he could see it through.

With that final thought, Smit retracted his consciousness to his core, and threw himself into cultivating with renewed vigor. He had opted to leave his safety, and the security of the dungeon, in the hands of his creations. Of course, he would still have some faint awareness of his surroundings, but it was the first time he was placing this much faith in the hands of another being.

Then again, if he was going to leave his dungeon and his life in the hands of someone else, he could do a lot worse than leaving them in the hands of his own devout children.

THIS WAS IT. This was the moment he had been working towards.

Since he had been created, Pala had done as the creator, the father, had instructed. He had been witness to his miracles, and the wealth of knowledge. Pala had listened, learned, and he had trained and hunted under his instruction. Carefully groomed by Smit in a brutal yet oddly controlled form, Pala had catapulted himself forwards in terms of progress. He was far ahead of the rest of his brethren both physically and mentally, ensuring his position as the right hand of the father.

And yet, Pala had never received this level of *trust* before.

Sure, he had been given assignments in the past. He had been given hunts of several variations, foraging missions, and even defensive missions. But he never had had this level of free rein over such an important task. Yes, Father might have set up a few things, and evolved a few creatures here and there, but ultimately, the final offensive rested squarely upon his shoulders.

In Pala's mind, he had been given a precious gift. The trust bestowed upon him by the father was something that he had earned through his accomplishments, something that he had had to work himself to the bone to acquire. It was a symbol of the bond he shared with the father.

And that was precisely the reason for Pala's wide grin as he gathered his brothers and sisters, his sharp teeth in full display as he organized them in rows.

"Brothers! Sisters!" His voice boomed out, his tail twitching and jerking excitedly as he talked, easily catching the attention of his audience. "The father has given us a great honor!"

A mutter ran through his brethren, whispers of curiosity ensuing amongst the small crowd, but soon they were silenced as Pala spoke again.

"The father has given us the honor of being his personal guard for the next invasion!"

An excited chatter broke out from the kobolds, tails thrashing and twitching with excitement at the news. This was a position that had never been bestowed on anyone in the dungeon! It was quite obvious that the prospect of serving the creator directly tugged at the heartstrings of the devout kobolds.

"Father saysss that the invasion will occur in fewer than two days!" Pala continued, barely paying heed to the excitement in the crowd. "We are to guard the pond room, as it is the last room before his own. Prepare yourselves! We must let no one intrude upon the sanctum of the father."

A deafening cheer rose from the small crowd of kobolds, and they broke into a frenzy of motion as they ran to get their weapons.

They would fight for the father to the last man standing, and woe to the foes that stood before them.

<<<>>>
Status

Species: True Dungeon
Rank: 1
Name: Smit
Age: 2 months
Mana: 97,879 MP
Anima: 163
Mana Reg.: 215 MP/h
Anima Reg.: 5.12 AP/day
Floors: 2
Inhabitants: 63 Species
Titles: Creator of Dungeon Laws; Creator; Guide of the Bloody Evolution; Legendary Craftsman; Reincarnated One.
Abilities: Absorb matter; Alter environment; Bestow knowledge; Break down components; Craftsmanship; Creation; Digging; Destroy creation; Dungeon laws; Enhancement; Equivalent exchange; Ether manipulation; Evolution; Interdimensional

storage; Life bestowal; Life-energy harnessing; Mana absorption; Masterful mana manipulation; Modification of creations; Monster link; Telepathy; Trap building; Transfer dungeon.

Resistances: Magic (general); Mind control

CHAPTER SIXTEEN

I adjusted my bag over my shoulder while I trudged uphill, trusting Mei to lead us up the mountain. Despite coming here once before, I hated to admit it, but I was certain I would have gotten lost within the first hour of hiking. How did Mei even know which way was the right way? There were trees everywhere and the only real sense of direction we could get is that we were going in a generally upwards direction towards the top of the mountain. I could not even tell if the village of Nam was east or west down this hill.

I was half convinced that this "tracking" thing that rangers and hunters did was really just a different type of magic. I could not understand how they orient themselves in the wild with so few clues and tools. It was slightly maddening that I couldn't figure out the trick to it myself, but then again, that's the entire reason for having a team. It was just about impossible for a single person to be able to do everything. A team was supposed to be composed of people that cover each other's weaknesses, creating a group that would be able to surpass obstacles that an individual cannot.

"I swear this trip feels longer than last time," Adder grumbled aloud, making it no secret that he disliked carrying things. Even if they were his own things. Things he might have needed to survive.

"That's because it is," Mei replied simply.

"Why would you even do that?!" Adder replied indignantly, the rogue puffing up slightly as if he had been personally insulted.

"Because there are bear tracks on the original road," she said, her tone clearly signifying that she was not willing to elaborate.

"Good answer," Adder finally said after a long pause, seemingly calmer now that he had an explanation.

"We shouldn't be too far off," I said finally, looking up at the sky. We had been moving through the wilderness for the better part of the day, and we were just passing the point of noon. Considering the speed at which we were going, it was safe to say that we should have been arriving in less than an hour.

"She is right," Mei chipped in, turning to gaze at me with those intense grey-blue eyes. I swear, she had the prettiest eyes I had ever seen in my life. They are piercing and soft at the same time. How is that even possible?

Mei looked away after a moment, letting her eyes linger in the forest, scanning it slowly. "We should be there within the hour. I recommend stopping to eat now while we can. I haven't seen any signs of predators for a while, and we have a relatively clear view in this area. It would be best to eat here, before entering an animal and monster infested dungeon."

Considering that we had been hiking since the sun rose, I agreed with her suggestion and gave the order to rest and eat. If we had a moment to spare, it was better to use it to regain as much energy as possible. That dungeon was surprisingly energy consuming as far as new dungeons go. Going in at anything less than our best would just be asking for trouble.

Lunch was uneventful, save for this Grey Jay bird, the so called "Camp Robber" bird that tried to have a go at stealing a piece of my bread. Not that it was very successful in its attempt, of course.

No one took my food.

Other than that, we packed up our bags and set back out to find ourselves that odd dungeon. Never in my life had I seen kobolds that were just so... tenacious. Maybe that might be because I had never entered a dungeon that had kobolds, but I have met kobolds before. My team had been part of several extermination missions and a few of them dealt with aggressive kobold tribes.

However, those kobolds were more disorganized, more vicious, wilder, less... determined, I suppose? I am not even sure if it is possible for a kobold to be consciously determined to do more than just hunt for food or protect its young. Yet, these kobolds *felt* different. And they looked different! Even their teeth seemed to fit better and be less crooked, the scales more uniform, and their eyes seemed to hold a different type of determination that I just could not place.

To be honest, it was a bit unsettling and yet exciting.

To be fair, everything about that dungeon was weird. How did it grow so quickly in such a short time? Normally that would not be possible. And another thing worthy of note was that the level of the creatures was surprisingly high. The difficulty of clearing the first floor was higher than it should have been for a dungeon that young. Also, the statues... all the little statues that we found around the first level had a superb level of craftsmanship. How did the dungeon, which was a sort of monster-like creature, create so many of those little statues so quickly, with *that* level of detail?

I guess that would be a mystery for the ages, wouldn't it? Perhaps with time, and enough studying, we would discover the reason for these oddities. But for now, we had to focus on our task and gather information from the dungeon. The worst thing that could happen would be that our people went into this dungeon unprepared. Every single bit of information they could get was a higher chance for us, the adventurers, to return alive, which of course was a very desirable outcome. Nothing worse than losing a large number of adventurers to the same silly mistake.

A feminine gasp up ahead broke me out of my thoughts, and my instincts right away brought me into a cautious stance, my senses going up in high alert.

Mei was not one to be startled or surprised easily, especially not in the wilderness, the place where she was the most at home.

I moved towards her as quickly as I could, while keeping as quiet as possible, fully aware of the gentle rustling of leaves and the sound of small sticks breaking that reminded me that the rest of my team was right behind me.

I followed her gaze slowly, unsure if I wanted to know what sort of thing could have possibly made her stop. I didn't have much time to wonder, however, as my eyes quickly fell on a wondrously crafted structure.

I didn't know what it was made from, other than it seemed to be a type of stone. Never in my life had I seen rock of such beautiful green. It was as if the forests and the oceans themselves had blended into a solid structure crafted by the gods. Bewildered, I turned towards my team, whipping my head around so quickly that I heard my neck make a small popping sound.

They all looked just as shocked and speechless as I was.

Where could this structure have come from? Who created this in such a short time? Was it the dungeon itself? Or perhaps some devout villager? No that didn't sound right... no villager would spend this much time and effort on creating an entrance for a dungeon, much less with such detailed craftsmanship in such a short amount of time. Not even a master craftsman would have been able to pull this off so quickly. Even with all the skills and knowledge required to just *reach* this level of perfection, the time needed for a single person to create it should have been months at best.

Slowly, my team and I approached this pavilion of wonder. Wary for any sort of tricks or malicious intent, we kept an ear and an eye out for anything else that might seem off. But try as we might, the only thing that seemed off about the entire picture was the structure made of this weird green stone; everything else was exactly as we left it before. Talk about ominous.

The closer we got to the structure, the more we realized how amazing it was. Sure, from the distance it looked well crafted, sturdy, and fancy, but up close it was a whole different level of brilliant. The rock itself lent the structure amazing complexity, drawing your eyes in waves upon layered waves of green that twisted and flowed gently across the entire surface. But the second you were up close, you noticed that carved from those waves were figures. Weapons and vines of many kinds could be seen lovingly sculpted on the stone, and each figure demanded its own moment of attention.

It is amazing how well organized the entire piece was. This entrance was the single greatest piece of art I had ever seen in my life, and I come from a house that is considered lower nobility. Never had I witnessed such a well portrayed sculpture. Though every sculpted creature demanded to be noticed, none of the pieces fought with each other for attention when viewing the entire entrance as a whole. Rather, they acted in harmony to draw the eye towards the doorway and the large pair of ancient eyes that overlooked any who would stand before the entrance of the dungeon. It was as if a god were personally appraising us, judging us before we even set a foot into its domain.

"Well... Damn." Surprisingly, Ziggurd was the first to speak, whistling as he finished his sentence.

"No kidding," I agreed.

"Who do you think made that?" Adder asked, for once too stunned to add sarcasm or distaste to his tone of voice.

"Lightning strike me if I know," I replied.

"None of the villagers could have done this," Mei said, "and virtually no one knows about the dungeon yet," she added, shutting down any hope for an external force having anything to do with this.

"So that means..." Adder tried to say, but I could almost feel his mouth starting to go dry. It was easy to tell, because my own mouth was doing the exact same damn thing.

"...That the dungeon created this itself," James spoke up, finishing Adder's sentence for him.

For some reason, when James said something with that heavy, solemn voice, it really seemed to drive it home for me. I took a deep breath and accepted the fact that this dungeon was far beyond anything that I expected it to be. That was fine. Breathe in, breathe out... again... again... and again.

"So... Anyone have any clue what this could possibly mean?" I ventured, hoping someone had theories, ideas, guesses... anything really. Anything would help. I just needed to attribute this massive change to something. It would make it easier to swallow.

"Nope."

"Nuh-uh."

"Nada."

"None."

"Great," I groaned out, as four voices replied to my inquiry with a negative. Rubbing my head with my hands, I sighed and looked up at those deep green eyes that had been sculpted at the top of a sign.

I blinked for a second and realized I had been so caught up with the entire craftsmanship that I had completely ignored the sign below it.

"Well damn," I grumbled as I did a double take. "The dungeon is named, too."

For three full heartbeats, nobody said a thing. Everyone had their eyes fixed on the sign below those hauntingly beautiful green eyes.

The Dungeon of Origins

"The hell does that mean?" Adder blurted out, staring at the only part of the entire structure that was made of black stone.

"It means that either a god has named this dungeon or..." Ziggurd ventured slowly, hesitation in his voice. I could practically see the gears of his brain turning and working overtime to process all the information. It seemed that he had reached the same conclusion as I had.

"Or it means that this is an entirely new type of dungeon that no one has ever seen before," I finished for him with a frustrated sigh. I didn't know which was worse. Abnormalities such as these could be really good... or really, really bad.

"Great," Adder grunted, sighing loudly as he scratched his head in frustration. It seemed that he shared my concerns. "Why did we agree to this again? We should have just taken a vacation and enjoyed the money from our last dive."

"Indeed," James agreed, hefting his hammer over his shoulder. His eyebrows frowned in frustration. "Well. I say let us stop idling about. The night won't wait for us, so we best get going."

"Agreed," I replied, and shook off all the questions for a moment to organize my thoughts. "Everybody, standard formation. At the very least, I think it's safe to say that this dungeon has now started to create its second floor. Our objective is to just do a checkup on the dungeon, not to conquer it. Let's get it done without dying, people."

The speech concluded, I turned to face the empty doorway, and walked in, following James.

But despite all my determination, I couldn't help but feel a little apprehensive. I could already tell that this wouldn't be like the last time I was here. It would be something... more.

TIME SLIPPED through Smit's mind like sand slips through the fingers of an open hand. Time lost meaning as he focused exclusively on his cultivation. Absorbing qi and mana, owning it, solidifying it, conquering it... it all required so much attention and skill that he could barely afford to be vaguely aware of his surroundings, especially given the intensity with which he was focusing.

However, with such intense focus came certain benefits—namely, a significant boost to his cultivation speed. Of course, the speed at which he was forcing himself to cultivate was far beyond what most people would have ever been able to endure mentally, but thanks to his constitution as a dungeon core and his mental fortitude as a stubborn old dwarf that had passed the seven-hundred-year mark, he was more than capable of pushing himself past the boundaries of regular mortal men.

With this excessive cultivation speed, it was only a matter of time before he made his second breakthrough. And achieve a breakthrough he did.

Congratulations! You have gathered the required energy to rank up. Rank up initiated.
<<<>>>

Congratulations! By cultivating yourself with superhuman determination and willpower, your mind and spirit have been strengthened. Hidden conditions met, bonuses will be applied.
New title gained [Master of Concentration].
<<<>>>

<<<>>>
Second breakthrough accepted. New species have become available for creation. General improvements for all abilities and skills have taken place.

<<<>>>
Alert! Due to vastly increasing your repertoire of creatures available to you for creation through brutally evolving your

creatures, you have met hidden requirements. Bonuses to evolution and species manipulation have been applied.

Due to successfully advancing to the next dungeon rank in a record span of time while maintaining balance within the dungeon ecosystem, an award has been unlocked. Rare species [Elemental Spirits] has been awarded.

<<<>>>

Smit grinned as he opened his eyes, and felt power and knowledge flow into him. Before he could even utter a word, he turned his focus to look into his dungeon, and felt those five familiar foreign presences scurry through it. Smiling, he set himself to watch.

For now he would enjoy the show in silence, observing how his creations would act without him.

And later, he would celebrate.

<<<>>>
Status

Species: True Dungeon
Rank: 2
Name: Smit
Age: 2 months
Mana: 97,885 MP
Anima: 163
Mana Reg.: 215 MP/h
Anima Reg.: 5.12 AP/day
Floors: 2
Inhabitants: 63 Species
Titles: Creator of Dungeon Laws; Creator; Guide of the

Bloody Evolution; Legendary Craftsman; Master of Concentration; Reincarnated One.

Abilities: Absorb matter; Alter environment; Bestow knowledge; Break down components; Craftsmanship; Creation; Digging; Destroy creation; Dungeon laws; Enhancement; Equivalent exchange; Ether manipulation; Evolution; Interdimensional storage; Life bestowal; Life-energy harnessing; Mana absorption; Masterful mana manipulation; Modification of creations; Monster link; Telepathy; Trap building; Transfer dungeon.

Resistances: Magic (general); Mind control

CHAPTER SEVENTEEN

From the beginning, everything felt strange once again, just as it did the first time James had visited the dungeon. However, it was obvious to James that something had changed beyond obtaining a fancy new entrance. His instincts told him so. It was as if a mischievous ghost was breathing its chilly breath on the back of his neck.

As if to prove his thoughts correct, Mei let out a yelp of surprise, and streaked past the armored giant of a man, stopping only an arm's length away from him. Her hand was outstretched towards James, and her cheeks puffed slightly as she glared at him adorably.

"Stop!" she barked, though instead of sounding aggressive it sounded more like she was worried. James froze midstep, fearing that a trap might be ready to be triggered the moment he made a wrong move. She stared him down for a moment, only to turn away from him quickly and kneel down.

"Is it... a trap?" James asked carefully, trying to look over her shoulder as her hands pulled out a knife and she knelt down to scrape something off the ground.

"No!" she replied excitedly. "You almost stepped in blood moss! Do you have any idea of how valuable this is?"

"Um... no?" he replied uncertainly. To him it just looked like some odd colored red moss.

She threw her hands up in the air as if to say that only a fool wouldn't know what it was, but she continued to explain the details to him anyway.

"Blood moss has good healing properties. It has a strong vermillion color and a slightly sweet but citric smell. It is used in many healing potions and salves to replenish blood, clean infections, detoxify blood, and help stop bleeding, depending on how you prepare it. It is a valuable ingredient, you know?! Especially for us. Even eating it raw will help replenish and cleanse your blood in a pinch, though that's less effective than a well-prepared potion."

"Then... why did you stop me like that?" James asked confused. "It's not like I would have ground my feet and killed all the moss."

Sighing, she rolled her eyes at his words. "Blood moss is pretty sensitive, you know? If you, with your huge body and weight, had stepped on it, the moss would have definitely been crushed and torn. Sure, it might still work, but the quality and effectiveness would have dropped without a doubt."

"How valuable are we talking about here?" Adder interjected. As always, he was interested in the profit. It wasn't a bad attitude, but James couldn't help but think that it made him come across poorly. Adder did not even realize that he came across that way.

Relieved that they were not walking into a life-threatening trap, the rest of Azure Arrow was happy to wait for Mei to finish her harvesting. She was quite handy with her foraging skills, gathering the majority of the crimson moss into a leather pouch and tucking it away safely in her satchel.

"Next time," Ella said, her tone a bit irate by the delay, "do not scare us like that Mei. We are in a dungeon, and screams like that gets us all on edge."

"But the blood mo—"

"There are better ways of doing things," Ella said with a frosty tone, punctuating each word purposefully, causing Mei to slam her mouth shut, and nod slightly.

"Good. Let's go. We have a dungeon to explore," Ella said sharply. It was rare to see Mei speechless. She was usually very stoic, but on occasion she became childish when it came to certain rare plants or animals.

As per usual, Mei pouted after being scolded. She was an interesting woman, sometimes switching from mature to childish in the blink of an eye. It was a unique personality that made her stand out amongst her comrades. Chuckling, James consoled her by patting her shoulder and nodding his head towards the depths of the dungeon. "C'mon, we have a job to do."

As the team moved along the dungeon, James couldn't help but notice once more the statues that were scattered over the first floor. It was a touch unnerving and quite distracting. If it weren't for the bright light that Ziggurd provided for the team, distinguishing between the real dungeon critters and the statues would have been a challenge. James thought that amateur adventurers would have certainly wasted some of their energy smashing the statues by accident.

A hiss interrupted his thoughts, and the giant of a man swung his hammer instinctively to his left, in a perfectly horizontal motion that was followed by a crunching noise. His eyes followed his movements a fraction of a second later, only to see a common snake had its head crushed between the hammer and a stalagmite.

"Good reflexes," Ella said approvingly. "Let's keep going."

As the team progressed, things were moving along more smoothly than the last time they ventured in. Step over a trap, kill an enemy here and there, etc. And yet, they still had an uneasy feeling that whispered to them that something was different.

"Something is not right," Mei said after a while, echoing the thoughts of the rest of the group, "This seems a bit different from last time. I can't explain it but the creatures seem to be attacking differently."

"You think so?" Ziggurd asked, his eyes still scanning the area around him warily.

"I wouldn't have said anything if I didn't think so," Mei replied drily. "Last time they threw themselves at us as if trying to slow us down, remember? This time, we haven't come across any big groups like that. Mostly we have just encountered individual monsters, or monsters attacking in pairs. Don't you find that odd?"

"Hmm... you are right," Ella responded, a small frown appearing on her face as she processed the information. "Something has certainly changed in the dungeon. I can't quite place my finger on it."

"What gave it away? You know, besides the huge renovation effort of the entrance?" Adder added sarcastically. There was a hint of nervousness in his voice.

Rolling her eyes at him, Ella ignored his comment and paused to think for a few seconds. "We keep going as is. There is no point in trying to change our formation right now. We will adjust as needed. Let us proceed."

There was no murmur of agreement or grumbles of discontent. The rest of the team simply continued as instructed, making their way through the dungeon. Twice they encountered a nest of snakes and had to fight them down, acquiring only some scratches and minor injuries for their troubles, which Ziggurd deftly healed without a second thought. Mei took the time to skin a couple of the larger snakes, making sure to roll up the bright green skins into neat little bundles. They would surely sell well at the guild headquarters.

Deeper into the dungeon they ventured, and the further they progressed, the more creatures they encountered. Slowly but surely, the frequency of the attacks increased, along with the number of attackers. Soon they found themselves facing up to five snakes and four dungeon mice at once. They were pitifully weak compared to the veteran adventurers, but they still managed to scratch and bite them several times at the expense of their lives. It was as if they were determined to leave their mark on the adventurers before passing on into the void.

Once more they were reminded of how odd the dungeon was, as most animals wouldn't behave like this without a very good reason, such as protecting their young. It got to the point that James started to question his own logic, wondering if he was imagining things. But to him, it almost seemed like the creatures of this dungeon are a little bit insane... or perhaps they had a different mentality altogether, if that were even possible. Who has ever heard of a rat willing to die in order to give a man a mere bite after all? And yet... that was exactly what it felt like.

"The next room should be the one that had the kobolds last time," Adder said after they finished dispatching a particularly nasty group of dungeon rats, which had hidden in the shadows so well that they had managed to catch them by surprise. Thankfully, the worst injury that was suffered was to Ziggurd, when a rat bit deeply into the fleshy back of his lower leg, right above his Achilles tendon. Nothing that a little magic couldn't fix.

"It should be just down that tunnel and we should be there," Adder concluded, and the rest of the team moved at his direction.

Their steps resonated in the dungeon with every step they took, creating a dry echo that resounded softly around them. No one spoke, allowing the echoes of their steps to be the only sound that reached their ears. They were approaching the room in which they'd been taken by surprise by the kobolds and the wolves. This time, Azure Arrow would not give them the chance to entertain them for as long as last time.

Rule number one of being a true adventurer: Learn from your past mistakes.

Ella stepped in front of James and held up a hand, signaling for a stop just before they entered the large room. She took a moment to make a few hand signs to communicate to her team a brief message: "V formation. Slow advance. Pick them off one at a time."

James nodded to himself as he acknowledged her plan. He would step in and bait them into targeting him, while Adder and Ella picked them off when they attempted to flank him. Mei would take care of hitting them from the backline, and Ziggurd would play the role of crowd control and healing. It would be a quick and dirty tactic that had saved them several times in places that contained fairly narrow spaces, since it made use of James's large body and strong armor to block any frontal attacks, and the sides are easily protected by just two people in a confined space like the hallway they found themselves in.

James inched his way forwards now, falling into position. He held his tower shield in front of him like an iron wall, while he kept his war hammer at the ready in his other hand, poised above his head and ready to strike at any creature foolish enough to come straight at him on its own. He truly hoped that something would rush at him thoughtlessly. Inside a dungeon, James much preferred a quick and simple kill to struggling for a victory. Brushes with death might be exciting, but more often than not, he found that they were not conducive to the betterment of one's health.

Each step he took gave rise to the sound of metal rubbing against metal, and the crunching sound of iron boots grinding dirt and pebbles against the hard stone floor. He didn't even try to be stealthy, since his job was to get their attention after all, to make them grow bold and attack him. James was quite comfortable with this role. In his mind, the best way to act in this situation was to be loud enough to be heard, slow enough to seem weary, but not aggressive enough to make them grow cautious around him. Beasts were receptive to body language after all.

James had scarcely taken a couple of steps into the room before he was greeted by a series of growls. Around him, thirteen wolves had gathered in the room, scattered in different directions, all of their golden eyes fixated upon his figure. Despite the danger of the situation, he could not help but notice that their fur coats were a beautiful shade of grey, which made their eyes stand out like jewels crafted by an artisan.

For a brief moment, neither the wolves nor James moved. Only a single thought floated into his mind as he kept an eye on them. *Why does everything in this dungeon look so... pretty?*

Pushing aside the useless thought, he took a couple more steps forward, giving Adder and Ella enough room to step out of the hallway themselves, but only just barely. With this, the three of them were blocking the hallway, making sure none of the wolves could easily flank them and attack Mei or Ziggurd.

As the wolves started to pace around the room, their eyes were fixed upon the three people before them. They were clearly looking for a way to flank the adventurers, but that was nigh impossible with their current formation. Seconds slipped by and the wolves kept their slow pacing, clearly in no rush to attack in a blind blitz of hunger, much to James' disappointment. While thirteen wolves was hardly an army, a pack of that size was still fairly dangerous if you were unprepared. However, to a prepared team such as Azure Arrow, they were more of a nuisance than an actual threat, considering the circumstances. Their fangs would not be able to penetrate James' iron armor, nor would they be able to easily overpower him as long as his teammates could keep the wolves that tried to flank in check.

Considering their lack of aggression from the wolves, Ella gave Mei and Ziggurd the signal to attack. Because they were all well prepared, the attack only took a few seconds altogether. As one, they released their projectiles, a knife and an arrow embedding themselves in the skulls of two separate targets, dropping them instantly to the ground.

The sudden death of their comrades caused the wolves to panic briefly, and their eyes to deviate from the adventurers for a moment. Taking advantage of that, Mei drew another arrow and aimed it at the nearest wolf. Surprisingly, the wolf scrambled to the side, tripping over its own limbs like a panicked lamb, avoiding certain death only to receive a knife to the eye from Adder.

Adder and Mei seemed to have an uncanny sense for teamwork in situations like these. Mei had often told the others that it's just instinctive, that taking down the weakest link first is how any hunter would prefer to hunt after all. James, however thought that there was more to it than that. He couldn't explain how, but he thought that at some level, Adder and Mei shared some sort of rivalry that made them more attuned to each other. They would never admit it out loud, but it wouldn't be the first time that a rivalry unified people instead of dividing them.

The confused panic quickly turned into heated anger, and the wolves rushed at them as one. Ten canine beasts with sharp fangs and claws charged Azure Arrow, fully intent on rending them into strips of meat. Normally, a pack of wolves bearing down would be quite intimidating, but considering their experience and strategy, the adventurers were more tense than worried.

The distance between the two groups disappeared in the blink of an eye. A wolf pounced towards James, who swung his hammer down towards it. The creature's head was crushed like a melon, brains splattering out of its fractured skull in a gory mess. Beside him, Ella utilized her rapier to puncture a hole straight into the throat of a wolf trying to flank her, the end of her blade piercing through the spinal cord and exiting out the other end of the neck. With a flick of her wrist and a fluid motion she retracted her blade, and the battle continued. On the left, Adder kept the wolves at a bay with his knives, until Ziggurd utilized a simple magic that shone a bright light into the eyes of the wolves for a moment. It was just enough to surprise them, and the team gained the advantage. In that moment of confusion, Adder stepped forward and ended the lives of his two assailants, before retreating back to his original defensive position.

A single arrow flew just over Adder's head, and imbedded itself on an approaching wolf just beyond the reach of his knives. In a matter of seconds, half of the wolves were dead or dying. Within a minute, the adventurers cleaned up the rest of the pack. Best of all, most of the pelts seemed undamaged, so they could stand to gain a fair bit from skinning the wolves and gathering their pelts.

With the wolves taken care of, Mei and Adder pounced on their carcasses, eyes glinting. Ella sighed and rubbed her eyebrows with her thumb and index finger. "Just... get the least damaged ones. We are not here to gather resources right now."

Adder opened his mouth to argue, but was quickly shut down by a glare from the fiery leader of the group before he even made a sound. Looking away sadly from the most damaged wolves, he reached for one of the least damaged wolves and started to skin it as efficiently as possible. Between Adder and Mei, the two of them skinned three of the wolves. It was rough work, but with their practiced hands, they managed to speed through the process in under an hour.

"Alright, back into standard formation," Ella barked, gathering the attention of her comrades, and they responded by arranging themselves in a line, ready to continue. "That should be the last room of the first floor, where we met that weird blue golem. Ready up in case it is still there."

Steeling themselves for another weird encounter, they forged their way forward. They crossed the short hallway with determined steps, and soon come face to face with their next challengers: five kobolds, five wolves, and a handful of rather large snakes. But what caught their attention was a large archway that seemed to lead to what appeared to be a decorated vertical tunnel.

"Guess that the dungeon has a second floor now," Adder said, verbalizing the thoughts of the others.

"Well boys," Ella said with a bit of glee, "let us get on with it."

Seconds later, the sounds of battle rang through the last room of the first floor of the dungeon.

ADDER WAS QUITE disappointed that he had to leave the pelts of such beautiful wolves behind, but what else was he to do? He had known from the start, since before he even asked Ella, that it would have been a bad idea to skin them all before they continued, but a part of him could not help being a little heartbroken at the idea of leaving those precious pelts behind. A well skinned wolf pelt could be worth a silver coin, and depending on the size and quality of the fur, it could even be more than that. Considering all the factors, Adder calculated that they could have gotten somewhere around sixteen or seventeen silver coins for those pelts. Even though they were not that much larger than normal, the fur's color was a glossy and uniform grey, and it had a certain bounce to it that made it feel even better than it looked. It was certainly a higher quality item, and some people would have been willing to pay a higher price for them.

Unfortunately, Ella was correct. To skin those wolves would have taken a while, even if they were to just do a quick and dirty job with all five of the members of Azure Arrow. Moreover, the increased burden of carrying thirteen pelts would slow them down, and fatigue them faster, a deadly combination when they were not sure what they might find deeper in the dungeon. A good adventurer should always be ready to run if the need arises—that belief was firmly ingrained in Adder.

Not that he would ever admit it to anyone, of course.

Thus, he begrudgingly left his source of income behind him, taking his place in the simple, linear formation, smack in the center of the group. This was his favorite formation. It was, in his opinion, the least dangerous position of the group. He was protected in the front by James and Ella, and if someone sneaked from behind and was stealthy enough to fool Mei's hearing, he wouldn't be the first to die either. Quite convenient for him. Of course, his position meant that he would be expected to run and aid his teammates in case they encountered a heavy frontal assault or were ambushed from behind, but that was a small price to pay for not being first in the death toll.

This held especially true when entering unknown situations, such as when they were descending the spiral staircase to the second floor of the "Dungeon of Origins," as the dungeon had so chosen to call itself. Perhaps it had been named by a god of some sort... though that seemed highly unlikely to him. What god would look upon a new dungeon and try to take it under its wing right away? No matter how unusual the dungeon, no god or devil would try to claim a fledgling dungeon that had not even turned half a year old.

However, Adder couldn't help feeling that this dungeon was more than *just* unusual. Even as they climbed the finely carved spiral staircase, which had no railing, he kept his hand pressed lightly against the wall to which the spiral staircase was attached. His fingers brushed over the intricately carved surface, which depicted long shoots of vines crawling over the wall as if they were real. He could literally trace a single vine down the length of the stairs; following it down the base with just his fingers. Even the stone itself was colored a soft greyish-green, making it almost seem like they were real vines that had been petrified in time.

To top off the effect, the opposite wall to the stairs depicted a sweeping design of rolling waves, which spiraled along with the stairs. But the interesting thing with that was that the stone itself was not colored; it was just simple, polished grey stone. However, that stone had contained thousands of shiny blue stones of varying tones embedded in it. It held a certain resemblance to the night sky on a cloudless night... if the stars were arranged in the pattern of rolling waves, at least. How could something this gorgeous be created by a simple dungeon?

Adder was not the only one that was taken aback by the simple, but elegant design of the stairs that led straight down to the following floor. The entirety of the team was so busy absorbing the sight that they were subconsciously slowing down, walking gently as to not disrupt the peace of the environment. It was as if they had stepped into a gallery of some sort, a room designed in its entirety by an artist of incredible skill.

Before he noticed it, Adder had already reached the ground of the second level of the dungeon, and practically bumped into Ella before he realized where he was standing.

Before him, a wide archway bounded by two statues of wolves acted as the entrance to a new room. The room itself was... breathtaking to say the least. White on black, the entire room relied on this contrast of colors. Pillars of black stone created patterns with their own shadows upon a checkered floor, which sparkled in the light provided by Ziggurd.

"What in the world...?" Adder heard Ella ask to no one, her voice escaping her lips before even she had realized it.

"I know we have said this before but..." Adder chimed in, "this is *definitely* not a normal dungeon."

"No kidding..." Mei agreed, her own eyes glued onto the spectacle before her.

"Are we sure this is a dungeon and not the art gallery of a king?" James commented, looking at the room with honest curiosity.

There was no reply from Ziggurd for a moment, and Adder could have sworn that the magic caster was wondering the same thing James had said. Not that it surprised him; Adder was starting to think that the big guy might have had a point there.

"Well... It would be nice if it was, but it isn't," Ziggurd replied with a chuckle. "It's kind of depressing to think that a dungeon can outdo you completely when it comes to art, though. I can't even draw a tree without getting upset over how crooked the branches look."

That comment drew a snigger from Ella, a chuckle from James and Mei, and a full-blown guffaw from Adder, who snorted loudly in the process.

"Don't laugh too hard," Ziggurd said with a smirk. "The dungeon could probably outdo your drawing skills too, Adder."

That stopped Adder's laughter quickly. He felt somewhat indignant at the thought, but he knew that he couldn't deny it. From what he had seen so far, only a master level artist stood a chance at competing with the dungeon if it could paint as well as it could sculpt and design. Even then, Adder would bet on the dungeon winning ... assuming that a dungeon could consciously draw something, of course.

After taking their time contemplating how the hell all this art was popping up in the dungeon as if it had been purposefully planned, they regained their bearings and decided to make their way forwards once more. However, the dungeon had one more surprise in store for them.

The moment that they stepped into the room, its ceiling lit up as if it contained a million stars within it, giving the entire room good lighting. Interestingly enough, the shadows of the pillars still were split into two directions due to the lighting, causing the pattern of black and white to change into a more complex work of art.

"...Damn," Adder exclaimed, unable to verbalize his thoughts beyond that.

"Agreed," Ziggurd's voice rang behind him. Nothing else was said for a moment, probably because everyone had the exact same feeling.

"At some point we are going to have to stop being surprised by all the beauty," James breathed out with a sigh. "I am not even sure my brain can keep being in a constant state of admiration. This is a first for me."

"A first for everyone," Ella added. "I haven't been so awed since... actually I don't think I ever have been in awe of something for so long."

"Enough gawking," Mei interrupted, tearing us away from our

mellow musings. "We have to get moving or we are going to starve to death just staring at this room."

"Everyone, avoid touching the pillars," she ordered. "This is most likely a room full of traps, and I would wager my left hand that those pillars are not just decorations. They probably have something to do with the traps."

Following her direction, the adventurers began to make their way across the hall with cautious steps, wary of the polished black pillars. However, it wasn't more than a minute before the first trap was triggered.

Out of nowhere, a cone of fire burst from one of the pillars, and Mei let out a shout of surprise as she threw herself to the floor barely in time to avoid the raging fires that consumed the place where her head had been a mere second ago. The flames receded in a few moments, but the hearts of everyone present kept beating like drums well past that.

"What did you do?" Ella asked quickly, not daring to move herself until she knew what was going on.

"I... have no clue. I didn't touch the pillar at all. I think it might have been the floor, however. I think I felt my foot slide before the fire trap activated."

Cursing under his breath, Adder looked around at the floor. The tiled floor was polished perfectly evenly, with no obvious signs of which tile would trigger a trap. He would probably have to advance while testing the tiles... or risk trying to outrun whatever trap there was.

"Right," Ella said with a grunt. "Everyone, mind your steps. This place is definitely not friendly. Let's make sure it doesn't end up being the last place we see."

PALA SAT, waiting patiently in the pond room, and meditated as the father had taught him and Echo to do. It felt unnatural to him at first, but he was learning to appreciate the experience. Even though he lacked practice, he had begun to discover that it granted him a certain calmness that he was beginning to grow fond of. Moreover, it gave him a way to practice his exercises mentally, which meant he would be conserving energy for the upcoming fight.

But today, he was meditating for a different reason. He was not training in his mind, but instead he was focusing on the world around him. Even now he could hear the sounds of explosions and yelps of surprise and concern from the room that his creator had dubbed the reception hall and Pala was attempting to track their progress.

"Watch out!" A loud banging noise rang in the distance, as if something heavy had collapsed.

"Argh!" A second shout was heard, male by the sound of it, followed by a small thumping sound.

"Adder is down! Careful, I saw that trap launch some sort of darts!" a strong female voice joined the chorus, barking orders without hesitation. A leader perhaps.

"I am okay! Just... Ugh... Give me a minute. I am going to take some of that potion."

Kra-Boom!

Something exploded, and a chorus of metallic strikes could be heard shortly after. "Careful! Some of the pillars explode!" a deep male voice spoke up. "We shouldn't split up too much, just follow me! As long as I can absorb most of the damage, I doubt that the traps will hurt us."

Pala nodded to himself as he heard them progress, grinning slightly as he heard curses fly from their lips from time to time. Of course, he frowned more than once when they cursed the dungeon that the father had created, but he took some joy in hearing them struggle. After all, the father himself had created the dungeon to be a challenge, not to be a relaxing stroll. Pala made a mental note to let him know of the success of his reception hall, as he was sure that Smit would be more than happy to hear that.

Still, although the reception hall was only a few hundred meters in length, it did a terrific job at slowing the adventurers down. A distance that could have been covered in a fraction of the time, if there were to be no obstacles, was instead turned into an ordeal that lasted close to two-thirds of an hour. Clearly, the adventurers were taking their time after triggering the first few traps, slowly edging forward as they did their best to avoid any traps they could, and weather the rest of them.

More than once, Pala heard the sound of stone striking metal or the pained grunt of a man as he struggled to absorb the impact of something. It wasn't until he heard them approach the end of the reception hall that Pala opened his eyes and jumped to his feet. He looked around briefly and observed his troops with a quick glance. Fifteen kobolds, out of which four were warriors, five shamans, and the remaining six just regular kobolds. Every warrior had a spear in their hands crafted of wood and polished stone, while Pala himself carried a spear of redwood and Damascus steel.

Pala grinned at this, looking at his entourage with pride. Last time he had lost to the intruders, but this time it would be different. This time his forces were more numerous, and they had had time to train under the order of the father himself. Moreover, he himself had already danced with the enemy once and Pala had improved by leaps and bounds since their last encounter. No longer was he the naïve kobold chief that had thought himself at the apex of the world. Now he was Pala, kobold lord, who had been tempered in training and had even walked beyond the scope of the dungeon itself. There was a world of difference between his previous self, who barely could avoid being crushed by the massive hammer of the giant human, and the kobold that he was now.

And today he was looking for redemption.

"Brotherss! Sisterss! To arms!" Pala barked out, his eyes already shining with anticipation. It would be a glorious day for the kobolds; they would hold the line for the father and nothing would stand before them and their sacred duty.

The kobolds jumped to their feet, holding on to their weapons. Shamans with their wooden staves, everyone else with spears. As one, they faced the simple wooden door that led to the reception hall, staring at it silently. They all felt in their blood the need to defend this spot, for it was an honor given to them by the father himself.

Seconds ticked by, slipping into an infinitely long moment that lasted but an instant before the large wooden door started to swing inwards. With the door opened, the kobolds were able to clearly see the enemy before them. Five humans of different statures stepped into the room cautiously, eyeing them back.

"Well... I guess this is the welcoming committee," the thinner man with knives said drily, plucking two of them from a harness, palming one in each hand.

"We got no choice now," the metal-cased giant said. Pala's eyes had been glued on him from the moment he stepped into the room. That one was his target.

"James is right," the redhead spoke up. "If we try to run, we will probably die from the traps, or we will be skewered from behind by those spears."

"Only way out is through, huh?" The short girl with long ears said, hefting a long piece of wood from her shoulder. It wasn't lost on him that she was positioning herself behind everyone else, standing on a jutting rock to gain a better vantage point. He would let his shamans take care of her.

"Either that or at least tire them out enough that they won't be able to follow our retreat," the man with a staff said as he stroked his beard. "Either way, it looks like it's going to be tough."

"Well boys, let us get to it then," the redhead said with a large grin, and Pala matched that grin with his own.

"RAAAH!" Pala roared out, and all hell broke loose as he commanded his troops to charge.

Pala instantly threw himself to the side as something brushed past his cheek, plunging in the pond behind him as he rolled on the floor and bounced back to his feet.

"Tch," Mei clicked her tongue as she missed the shot by a fraction of a second. How the creature had avoided it she was not sure. However, she was not given a chance to wonder about it, as a tidal wave of kobolds rushed her and her teammates.

Spells flew from the shamans at the back, and she knew those would be priority targets. A duel between the kobold shamans and herself, with the aid of Ziggurd, had begun.

Meantime, the blood sang in Pala's veins as he bounded towards the iron giant, taking large strides to reach the man who held the massive iron hammer like a toy. Unfortunately, he was not the first to reach him. One of his common kobold brethren jumped at the giant first, and was swatted aside like a fly, spewing blood from his mouth as his ribs were crushed. Unfazed at the death of his brother, Pala leaped over his body, thrusting his spear towards James' face without mercy.

He would thank his brother for his sacrifice later; right now he had a duty to uphold.

"What—!" James exclaimed as he jerked his head to the side, narrowly missing a spear to the eye. However, Pala was not done yet. Taking advantage of his superior speed, the minute that his attack failed he pulled back his spear in mid-air, and readied himself to attack once more as he landed in front of James. Bringing his body low to the ground, Pala used his momentum to thrust the spear in an upward direction as his body moved forward, resulting in a powerful strike that caused James to stumble back in a panic in order to avoid a spear to the underside of his jaw. James dropped his shield in that movement, choosing to let go of the hefty shield in favor of surviving a killing blow.

Wise move, Pala observed briefly, before jumping back into the swing of things.

Without his shield, James met Pala in open combat, a battle

between the giants of both sides of the conflict. They danced a deadly dance of steel and iron, the two of them relying on two very different principles. James depended entirely on his power and the defense that his armor provided, while Pala leaned heavily on his speed and the reach of his spear. The two were at a stalemate, neither able to land a crippling blow on the other. They lost themselves in their deadly battle as if in a trance while chaos unfolded around them.

Meanwhile, Ella engaged herself in a dual fight once more with two warrior kobolds, swinging her rapier and short sword like a red cyclone, striking with precision but unable to land a killing blow on them. Occasionally she would disengage for a moment to strike at a common kobold that tried to join the fight, only to drive it back with an injury across its scaly hide for its intrusion.

Adder, Mei, and Ziggurd were all locked in their own personal battles too. Ziggurd countered enemy spells with his own, while Mei did her best to strike down the shamans. She had successfully taken down two of them, but the remaining three were proving a challenge, as they kept trying to pull up defenses created from water. Adder was not faring much better, playing the role of the main defense to Mei and Ziggurd, he was constantly throwing knives or engaging and disengaging kobolds. He had managed to surprise one warrior kobold with a knife to the eye, killing him instantly, but the other kobold was warier, pacing around him slowly as others distracted him.

The warrior kobold had struck at him twice already, and managed to injure Adder in the second strike. He was certain that this warrior kobold was bright, acting just like a wolf, waiting to strike its prey.

Minutes went by and the fight started to grind to a halt. More than half of the kobolds lay dead or dying, but Azure Arrow was not completely unharmed. Adder had lost his helmet somewhere along the fight, and the spear had found the gaps between the plates of his iron armor more than once, biting into his flesh. Ella had defeated her two warrior kobolds, but at the expense of a spear to her ribs. She was currently being healed by Ziggurd while Mei engaged herself in a battle of projectiles with the last kobold mage, finding herself low on arrows while Adder defended the three of them from the last kobold warrior and a couple of regular kobolds.

The fight was turning into a battle of attrition, and from the look of things, Azure Arrow was standing to lose the round.

"It should do for now," Ziggurd sighed as he wiped his brow clean from the blood that ran down an open wound on his forehead, putting away the empty flask of the potion he had used to help Ella recover faster. "Let us retreat. Most of them are dead, all of them are exhausted and so are we. We must retreat now, while we still can!"

Ella nodded weakly as she started to stand, wincing as she stood. "Retreat! Let us retreat! Mei, how many arrows do you have?"

"Only three," she replied tiredly, as she let go of an arrow, which struck the shoulder of the final kobold shaman, making the creature yelp and collapse. "Make that two."

"Ziggurd, how much mana do you have?" Ella asked wearily, flicking her eyes towards him.

"Enough for a big flash," he replied. "But after that, I am done. I already exhausted my mana potion to keep up with all the buffs and defenses I had to put up."

"Good enough," Ella replied. "Start chanting."

Following her instructions dutifully, Ziggurd began his chant, concentrating on articulating his words properly, and funneling the last of his power to the spell.

"Adder! James!" she called out loudly. "Close your eyes now!"

At that moment, James and Adder closed their eyes after parrying blows from their enemies. An instant later a flash of blinding light exploded across the room, blinding every kobold for a few seconds. By the time they opened their eyes, the adventurers were gone.

Looking around, Pala blinked with teary eyes as the pain of the flash faded away. It took him a second to understand, but when it finally clicked, he smiled. He stabbed his spear on the floor, and roared to the heavens.

They had won.

<<<>>>
Status

Species: True Dungeon
Rank: 2
Name: Smit
Age: 2 months
Mana: 98,392 MP
Anima: 165
Mana Reg.: 235 MP/h
Anima Reg.: 5.25 AP/day
Floors: 2
Inhabitants: 63 Species

Titles: Creator of Dungeon Laws; Creator; Guide of the Bloody Evolution; Legendary Craftsman; Master of Concentration; Reincarnated One.

Abilities: Absorb matter; Alter environment; Bestow knowledge; Break down components; Craftsmanship; Creation; Digging; Destroy creation; Dungeon laws; Enhancement; Equivalent exchange; Ether manipulation; Evolution; Interdimensional storage; Life bestowal; Life-energy harnessing; Mana absorption; Masterful mana manipulation; Modification of creations; Monster link; Telepathy; Trap building; Transfer dungeon.

Resistances: Magic (general); Mind control

<<<>>>

CHAPTER EIGHTEEN

I sat upon the ground with my legs crossed, meditating with my halberd across my lap. My hands held the true body of the father, which cycled the power of the world in a slow but unstoppable tide like the currents of a whirlpool. There was something comforting about being washed by the powers of the world. Mana and Anima, the two driving forces that allowed Father to grow and us to grow with him.

Perhaps it's because I myself used to be a dungeon core, but I can feel the powers of the world more clearly than anyone else in the dungeon, aside from Father himself. It's quite mesmerizing to see Father work these powers, like when he created my body. To this day this body he created for me still baffles me. The durability and strength of this body is definitely an advantage I should exploit, for the sake of the father and the dungeon. Ideally, I should be able to fight with my weapon up close and be able to mimic the abilities of magic users in some way.

I pushed these thoughts out of my mind after a moment, letting them slip out of my stream of consciousness as I refocus into my task of meditating. The training had been effective, increasing my proficiency at controlling my body appropriately, making my movements smoother and less... spasmodic. Thus, my mind settled into place, and I began my self-awareness practice. I focused on what the abdominal area of an organic body should be able to do. The tension, the flexibility, strength, and fluidity, everything I had noticed that organic creatures could do with a strong core. The abdomen was a nucleus of strength that gave any warrior the ability to perform certain moves with far more efficiency. It was the connector that allowed people to guide the strength of their legs to their upper body.

My meditation stretched from minutes into hours, a constant stream of wordless thought. Gradually, I felt myself reaching a new understanding of my own body, rehearsing the movements that I should be able to recreate in a battle.

In an instant, my training was disrupted by a resounding roar from the next room over, heralding the start of the real battle. As Father had predicted, the adventurers had succeeded in getting through the reception hall, and now they would face off with Pala and his people.

I listened intently as chaos ensued. I could hear all sorts of sounds, from metal on stone to that of bones breaking under pressure. Every sound indicated a different event that marked the battle that was just beyond my reach. How I yearned to prove my worth just as Pala and his brethren did... But my duty, should worst come to pass, would be the most crucial one of them all. At the moment I was the last line of defense. The final shield that can protect Father.

Time seemed to blur as the sounds of battle held me in a trance-like state. My mind was too busy trying to reconstruct the battle to be able to focus on my exercises properly. Though this showdown between Pala and the adventurers was to his honor, I couldn't help but desire a similar challenge to prove myself. How wonderful would it be to present the fruits of my labor to the father?

The orchestra of battle started to wind down after a while; an atmosphere of exhaustion seemed to permeate the air. It was as time itself were stretching out the fight, desiring to see a clear victor.

By this point, the noise had been reduced to a handful of sounds, with one continuous small duet of sounds that danced amongst the cacophony of the battlefield. It stood out just enough to grab the attention of a listener, but not enough to overshadow the ambiance that was created by the exhaustion of battle.

I heard a shout, a female voice, and then... nothing. For several seconds, silence reigned and my hearing would not pick up any sound that betrayed either winner or loser. If I had physical heart, it would have beaten like a drum as the suspense built up for those short seconds.

Rooaaar!

Pala's victorious howl resounded across the dungeon, and I let out a sigh of relief. Even though I don't need air to survive, I find the action of sighing to be reflexive in this situation. It was also oddly satisfying to me.

I let myself relax slowly now. My body had become taut without me realizing it. Closing my eyes, I let my mind sort through the entire series of events for a few moments.

Eventually, my turn to prove myself would come. I must be ready for that.

I will be ready.

SMIT OBSERVED the adventurers from the moment they set foot into the dungeon, tracking their movements with curiosity. It was rather satisfying to see their reactions to his improved dungeon. The looks on their faces when they had seen his new entrance had been particularly enjoyable. The spiral staircase he had designed had also evoked doe-eyes and dropping jaws, which was always a good sign as well.

However, though their reactions to his works of art were good, he was more interested in how they would fare against his new challenges. The idea was, after all, that all the creatures and obstacles he created would help keep him safe. Thus, Smit remained silent as he observed the adventurers with scientific interest, watching them work around his machinations, watching them as they overcame his obstacles and defeated his animals.

His excitement grew when the adventurers reached the reception hall, watching them stop entirely for a moment as they analyzed the situation, as they should have. Diving into the reception hall head-first would have been borderline suicidal for the adventurers, in his opinion. He had to approve of their quick thinking, and the accuracy of their analysis. However, he chuckled internally as they spread out to try to find a safe passage.

Though in theory it would be good to spread out in hopes of finding a passage that was not dangerous, the fact was that any intruder would encounter at least one trap in any route they chose to cross his hall, hence making the idea of spreading out useless. Rather, it would be more dangerous for them if they got significantly separated, as they would not be close enough to aid each other immediately. Worse, to reach the injured person, the closest team member would have to make their way to them blindly, and potentially activating more traps. Of course, if the would-be rescuer triggered more traps and got caught in them, the situation would only worsen for the invaders, as they would now be faced with two team members down instead of just one.

In other words, this reception hall was designed to slow and injure large groups of people. Should a flood of invaders try to force their way into the dungeon, this room on its own was guaranteed to deal large amounts of damage to the invading force. As a matter of fact, a small, organized group of people would be better suited to cross through the veritable minefield that was the reception hall. By making someone take the lead and absorb most of the damage, the rest of the party would be able to follow behind the person tanking the damage. Of course, he had set some delayed activation traps to hit the people that would be behind the tanker, but these traps were but a minority in the room.

Fortunately for the members of Azure Arrow, they realized that the best strategy was to have James tank and absorb the damage, though by that time, they had already consumed two health potions to avoid serious injuries that could have turned life threatening, costing the adventurers dearly for their mistakes.

It was oddly satisfying watching the adventurers struggle through his obstacles, almost like a game of sorts. Could they make it? Could they use their skills to survive his test? Or would they simply roll over and die? It was exciting in its own right. This feeling was amplified when he saw the adventurers approach his creations, his children. Now the real challenge began, and he mercilessly squashed down those emotions that were welling up within him as he focused in earnest. Right now, Pala and his brethren would test their mettle against the adventurers that dove into his dungeon.

As the clash began, he seared into his memory the actions and movements of both sides, observing every move and word that was utilized during the fight with surgical precision. This feat was only possible due to his ability as a dungeon core to be aware of anything occurring in his dungeon at any time. Any martial artist or warrior would have killed for the ability to analyze movements so exquisitely, even if just for a day.

With unshakeable focus, Smit absorbed everything he saw, making a mental note to break down the entire sequence of events in his mind later. To understand anything, it was important to deconstruct it first, break it into tiny little pieces, and then carefully reassemble it, piece by piece.

This is what Smit plotted to do with the movements he was witnessing. He would take it all in, memorize it, and then bit by bit he would break down all the movements to better comprehend the structure, the pattern, the flow of all the movements he witnessed today.

Then he would pass that on to his creations.

He would build a force to be reckoned with, and his enemy was going to help him do that.

As the fight reached the apex, Smit watched intently as Pala faced off with James, taking in the sight carefully. Both sides were exhausted, but the adventurers were running low on mana and ammunition, meaning that James, Ella, and Adder would have to fight the kobolds while protecting Mei and Ziggurd. Definitely not an advantageous position when they did not know how much more of the dungeon was left to explore. He could practically taste the victory coming his way. Regardless of if they stayed or ran, they would have to pull something out of their hat really soon if they wanted to survive.

True to his prediction, his thoughts were interrupted by the bright flash of light that stunned his kobolds and gave the adventurers time to turn and run. Naturally, the light did not affect him too much, as he was perfectly aware of their location and movements by virtue of the fact that the entire dungeon was an extension of him, allowing him to sense them in detail beyond the mere visual means.

Satisfaction spread across his soul as if he had drunk a tankard of hearty good ale. There was something extremely gratifying about successfully executing a plan. Be it a simple project, a competition, or a strategy to defeat adventurers, success had a sweet aftertaste.

He followed the adventurers in silence as they made their way out of the dungeon, instructing his remaining creatures to let them out without any fuss. He needed them to spread the news, after all... and perhaps he had grown a little attached to them. They *were* his first real visitors, and from their interactions, he could respect the professionalism that they shared when it really mattered.

A lesser group of adventurers would have hardly been able to face off against his squad of kobolds with such determination and unity. In all likelihood, a lesser squad would have panicked at the unprecedented unity and organization of well over a dozen kobolds rushing at them with sharp spears while said kobolds were being given fire support from kobold shamans.

Pushing that thought aside, Smit watched the adventurers finally leave his dungeon. He gave them an invisible nod, as if to acknowledge their ordeal, before deciding that it was time to talk with his children.

They had done a good job. It was only proper to praise them... but not too much; it wouldn't be good for them to get big heads about a single victory.

Focusing upon his children, he found Pala splayed on his back like a starfish, breathing heavily, but grinning from ear to ear, a toothy smile fixed on his face.

Chuckling, Smit's consciousness focused on Pala as he contacted him through the mental link that they shared.

"You seem satisfied," Smit said with a carefully crafted neutral tone.

"Father!" Pala yelped with surprise, as he attempted to stand, scrambling to his feet in a mess of limbs.

"Settle down, there is no need for that," Smit said soothingly in Pala's mind. In response, the kobold collapsed onto his rump, sitting on the hard ground with a slightly uncomfortable expression as he accidentally hit a sharp rock with his tail.

"Yes Father," he replied as he started to take deeper breaths.

"Let me have a look at you," Smit said as Pala began to relax.

A quick examination found several injuries of varying degrees of severity in Pala, bruised flesh and cracked bones being the majority of the damages. His hands seemed to be numbed and had a large number of minute fractures, probably from blocking and redirecting that giant hammer with his spear repeatedly.

"Father, did you manage it? Did you break through to the second stage?"

Smit snorted at the question, almost as if it were a joke.

"Of course I did it boy, who do you take me for?"

The response elicited a soft chuckle from Pala, who shook his head in amazement. He had heard from Echo herself that breaking through to another level was a difficult and time-consuming process that could take years to complete. And yet, in less than a couple of months, Smit had completed two breakthroughs. That was nothing short of a miracle in Pala's eyes.

On that note, Pala was convinced that Smit was a special existence even amongst others of his kind. Everything that he had seen his father do only served to reinforce that belief. He was a being that was the closest to a so-called "god" in Pala's eyes.

"Seems like you had an intense fight, didn't you?" Smit hummed at Pala, bringing the kobold back from his distracted thoughts. Smit, however, barely paid any mind to the distraction of the bipedal monstrous lizard before him as he started to direct the flow of mana into Pala, healing him at a steady pace.

"Yes," Pala mumbled as he closed his eyes, letting himself drift upon the feeling of mana circulation through his body. It was a very different feeling. The mana that circulated through his intact body was almost cool, relaxing, and soothing. But wherever the mana touched his injuries, the sensation switched from cool to warm, as if sunlight were concentrated upon a single spot in his body.

"I see. How did you find your opponent?"

"He was strong, Father. His blows were reserved as he did not want to be too separated from his clan, but even then, I could not use that to my advantage, nor could I strike a devastating blow in return. If he hadn't been restricted by his clan, I might have... lost."

Smit was silent for a moment, observing Pala as he healed him. The kobold lord before him seemed... ashamed. He studied Pala for a second, considering his words before he proceeded.

"I saw," Smit stated simply. Two words that caused Pala to snap his eyes upwards, to where he could sense vaguely the presence of Smit to be stronger. However, before Pala could respond, Smit continue to talk.

"It was a good fight, Pala. You have improved." He allowed his words to contain some pride and warmth. Pala was his child, and it warmed his heart to know that Pala had improved. One could say that Smit had begun to develop fatherly instincts towards a few of his creatures. "You could stand toe to toe this time, instead of bouncing and dodging around the entire room like a circus monkey."

The childish grin from earlier returned to Pala's face in full at Smit's words, causing the dungeon core to chuckle at his son. He allowed the moment to stretch out for a few seconds, giving Pala the acknowledgement that he so craved. However, that had to come to an end.

"However," Smit continued, "you must improve further. This time he could not move as he pleased, which evened the odds between you and him. Next time you might not be so lucky. You must improve, son! Your opponent this time was bigger and stronger than you were, with a defense that made using your spear efficiently far more challenging. You must learn to overcome these challenges. Become stronger; prove yourself even more, my son. Given time, I have faith that you can become a paragon of strength for my dungeon."

Pala looked straight up, and his eyes closed for a moment as he smiled broadly. His eyes, however, had changed a little from before. The innocent, childlike happiness seemed to have mixed with a certain flame of desire, like amber burned behind his golden eyes.

"Yes, Father!" The reply was filled with determination. They were the words of a warrior and son that wished to protect his father. "Give me time, and I will reach the apex of your dungeon, Father. This I swear!"

Smit chuckled at Pala's reply, and said no more as he continued to heal Pala. There was nothing more to be said.

For now.

Status

Species: True Dungeon
Rank: 2
Name: Smit
Age: 2 months
Mana: 98,892 MP
Anima: 171
Mana Reg.: 235 MP/h
Anima Reg.: 5.25 AP/day
Floors: 2
Inhabitants: 63 Species

Titles: Creator of Dungeon Laws; Creator; Guide of the Bloody Evolution; Legendary Craftsman; Master of Concentration; Reincarnated One.

Abilities: Absorb matter; Alter environment; Bestow Knowledge; Break down components; Craftsmanship; Creation; Digging; Destroy creation; Dungeon Laws; Enhancement; Equivalent exchange; Ether manipulation; Evolution; Interdimensional Storage; Life bestowal; Life-energy harnessing; Mana absorption; Masterful mana manipulation; Modification of creations; Monster Link; Telepathy; Trap building; Transfer dungeon.

Resistances: Magic (general); Mind control

<<<>>>

CHAPTER NINETEEN

E lla woke up groggy, squinting as the sunlight managed to find its way through the wooden blinds that covered the simple window of her tent. Staring blankly at it, she groaned as she tried to roll over in her bed, only to let out a hiss as a sharp pang of pain shot through her ribs.

As if struck by lightning, Ella recalled the last battle of her last dungeon dive. She lay in her bed reliving it piece by piece, moment by moment. It had been one of the most intense experiences of her adventuring life. Had it not been for the fact that Zig had been quick to heal her on three separate occasions, she was unsure of the extent of the damage she would have suffered. It was entirely possible that she would have been crippled, or worse. She was certain that of those three injuries, two might have caused her death during the battle if they had not been attended to quickly. It was moments like those that she wondered how other adventurer parties managed without a proper healer. Perhaps the reason why the great majority of high-level parties have at least one person that can act as healer is that those who don't simply... die.

Chuckling darkly at her morbid thoughts, she pushed them out of her mind. There were things to be done today, and morbid thoughts did not rank among the priorities. Instead, she hauled herself out of bed with a groan, and set herself to do her morning routine. She carried out her stretching exercises more slowly and carefully than normal. She longed for a hot bath, but time would not allow for such frivolous desires at the moment. She settled for washing her face with a bucket of fresh water, and then using a wet towel to wipe herself down too. She had to be mindful of her sore injuries, particularly the tender area in her gut, under her ribs. That last strike she had endured had been particularly nasty.

Still, a single thought had floated in her mind since their adventure and it buzzed around like an annoying fly that refused to be ignored... How had the dungeon changed so much in so little time? The time frame between the first dungeon dive and the second had been about a month. In one month, an entire new floor had been created, decorated, settled, and populated as if it had been there since the very beginning. How was that possible?

To begin with, dungeons rarely were so quick to expand at such a young age. A new dungeon could spend months creating a new floor, and they were particularly vulnerable as they did so, considering that the second floor was usually sparsely populated and rarely contained more than your usual pit traps. It was quickly becoming apparent that this... Dungeon of Origins did not play by the same rules as other dungeons did. Even if you ignored the fancy decoration and the intricate artwork that seemed to infuse the dungeon's very design, the way it developed was far too different from that of any other dungeon.

Moreover, she was certain that the kobold chief had been the same one that James had faced in the first dungeon dive, but his strength was in a different league altogether this time around. She would have described him as slippery and evasive last time, acting more like a cornered animal trying to survive. After seeing him in action again, however, she could not say the same thing. Though she had been preoccupied by her own enemies, from what she managed to observe of him, he was now much more agile and dexterous. The kobold clearly had a better idea of how to use his spear, which was demonstrated by how he managed to block and deflect the heavy war hammer that James utilized.

That kobold was not a slippery cornered animal anymore. He had changed from a cornered rat to a prowling wolf that was not afraid to bare its fangs at any intruder that would dare trespass into his territory.

A pang of jealousy surged through her for a moment. How unfair it was, to have a creature such as a common kobold chief advance so quickly in the martial path without any guidance while she, a lady raised from a young age to wield the sword, had been forced to struggle for years to reach her current level. Ten years of striving to build up her skills to her current level, ten years of blood, sweat, and tears. A decade of her life dedicated to the path of the sword.

In ten years she had advanced quickly, reaching a level of mastery of the sword that would allow her to stand toe to toe with even a consummate knight from the kingdom's army. She had been heralded as a talented youth with a bright future, one of the few who could one day be called an expert in the art of the sword.

And a common kobold chief had advanced more in a month than she had advanced in her past two years of hard work. How unfair.

She clicked her tongue and shook off those negative thoughts, chiding herself for being jealous of a monster that could barely be said to have a community with members of its own species. The dungeon itself was an oddity; it shouldn't be a surprise that its inhabitants fell outside the norm. Rather, it should be expected that the creatures from this dungeon were different from those of a common dungeon.

Putting such thoughts aside for the moment, she finished cleaning herself, and proceeded to get dressed. Her attire today was more casual, consisting of common trousers and a light blue shirt, which was then covered with a leather vest. She strapped her sword to a belt around her waist and put on her shoes. As for her hair, she decided that it would be too much trouble to properly comb that unwieldy mane of hair she had. Eventually she settled for fixing it up in a ponytail and ran a brush through it a few times to make herself presentable.

Satisfied with the results, she smiled and set off to check on her companions. Standing straight, showing no weakness, Ella walked out of her room and proceeded to gather her teammates, receiving answers from every member except James, who lay sprawled upon his bed, shirtless and dead to the world as he dreamed on.

Ella sighed and looked at the giant man with an amused half smirk. Not only was he as strong as a bear, he slept like a hibernating one, too.

"James? James," she called out to him as she shook his shoulder, merely managing to make the man roll over to the other side of the bed. Unwilling to waste any more time, or to be ignored, Ella drew back her hand and brought it down on his exposed back with a loud slapping noise. "James!"

With a yelp of surprise, James finally opened his eyes and turned around to look at Ella with a confused expression before he managed to process the cause of his wakefulness.

"Morning boss."

With a sigh, Ella pursed her lips and looked down at the man. "Get up James. We have a report to make. I expect everyone to be ready for the crystal call in an hour. We must be presentable."

"Aye, I hear and obey," James said with a yawn that made her want to give him a smack to the back of his head. However, she resisted the impulse as she knew that he meant no insult; it simply took him a bit more time to wake up than she liked. That and the fact that his thick skull might bruise her hand if she smacked it too hard.

"Go down to the tavern and eat as soon as you are able. We will do the crystal call after we've all had our breakfast."

Hearing him mumble his agreement on the matter, she turned

on her heel and left the room, her thoughts taking flight in another direction as she proceeded to the tavern for some much-needed breakfast. One of the less appreciated benefits of adventuring was the fact that, despite consuming more food than the average person, there were very few overweight adventurers. The very nature of the job was physically taxing, burning through more energy than the common man. Hence, it allowed her to indulge herself and more. For someone that enjoyed the pleasure of dining and drinking, this was a clear benefit.

Hopefully today the menu included something with a substantial bit of protein. While a well-prepared bowl of gruel was welcome, bread with some protein was a luxury that she was always happy to indulge in. Eggs, sausage, honey bread, and fresh goat milk were favorites of hers, but that might be asking too much for a small village in the middle of nowhere.

Still, a girl could dream...

WITH BREAKFAST TAKEN CARE OF, the team met in Ella's room, standing before a carefully placed fist-sized yellow crystal, which stood upon a small silver stand. The stand was decorated with a few runes, giving it a mysterious and unique aura. This little crystal was what was known as a communication crystal. A communication crystal was a very expensive magic tool that allowed for communication at long distance with those in possession of another magic crystal. Usually, a large magic crystal would be split in half after being treated through alchemical processes. Each half was placed on a metal stand that had been enchanted with rune magic that allowed for a visual projection of whatever stood a short distance away from the crystal, creating a hologram. Normally, Azure Arrow would not have such an important (and expensive) item with them; however, the guild master had loaned it to them for the purposes of the mission.

Ziggurd reached out to the crystal and ran his finger with utmost caution along a runic inscription on the metal stand, voicing the "Connect" command to the artifact. A humming noise originated from the crystal, and the crystal itself began to light up with little constellations of stars. A moment later, the crystal projected several thin beams of light, creating the three-dimensional appearance of the upper body of a person. This person was none other than their guild master, Ikfes Massan, former S ranked adventurer and leader of the adventurer guilds across the kingdom. The man was a legend that had completed many quests considered suicidal in nature, such as the legendary undertaking of the red basilisk.

"Ah, Azure Arrow!" Ikfes said with a smile, his soft amber eyes managing to retain that strange quality that seemed to see through everything, despite it being only a magically created hologram. "Right on time, as usual. So, tell me, how did your last dungeon dive go? That should have been... two days ago, yes?"

"Correct," Ella replied with a nod, her hands crossed behind her back, looking like the poster child of discipline. "We entered the dungeon two days ago, and found it significantly changed."

Ikfes' eyebrow arched upwards, his eyes glinting a little due to some sort of light source outside the scope of the crystal. Nevertheless, his expression was the very depiction of contained curiosity. "Oh? Do tell."

None of the members of Azure Arrow missed the fact that his last statement was not a request, but an order. Even if he had not ordered it, all of them would have been more than happy to talk about the dungeon, as it was far too great an oddity not to do so.

"Sir!" Ella replied with a nod, looking Ikfes in the eye as she began to report. "We entered the dungeon two days ago, with orders to check for any changes. However, we did not even have to enter the dungeon to notice that it had changed."

"Oh-ho?" Ikfes exclaimed as he leaned forwards slightly, listening intently to the report.

"Yes sir. The entrance to the dungeon has completely changed from the original hole-in-the-wall look it had. Rather than looking like the entrance to a cave, it now resembles what I could only describe as the ornate entrance to the tomb of some king. It's as if the dungeon itself erected a pavilion of green stone. I have never seen a more intricate design adorn the entrance of a dungeon. The dungeon also seems to have a name now."

Ikfes eyes seemed to widen slightly, becoming sharp at the same time. The intensity of his gaze seemed to cut into them like a knife. "A name you say? Has this dungeon been claimed by a god or demon?"

"I do not know, sir," Ella replied while shaking her head. "However, the name is the Dungeon of Origins."

"Origins, huh..."

Silence stretched between Ikfes and Azure Arrow as the guild master seemed to consider what he'd heard. You could almost hear the cogs in his mind spin as he sorted through a hundred possibilities and discarded them almost as quickly.

"We will set that aside for now," Ikfes said after a minute of silence. "I have a few ideas as to what that could be, but they are all inconclusive. I have trouble believing that a god or devil already claimed such a young dungeon. However, the possibility of someone powerful enough naming a dungeon that has just been discovered... Moving on. Continue your report."

Without missing a beat, Ella resumed her story, relating the little changes they noticed about the first floor, before getting on to the important stuff.

"Other than that," she stated, "the first floor is more or less the same as last time. However, we have confirmed that a second floor has already been created."

"Hmm..." Ikfes replied thoughtfully. "What is the level of completion for the second floor? It wasn't there last time, was it?"

"It seems to be fully developed."

A pause stretched between Ikfes and Ella, his eyes boring into her without a word. Soon enough, he broke the silence. "Fascinating. Tell me more about the second floor. In all my years, I have never heard of an entirely new second floor being developed in a month."

"Of course. At the final room of the first floor, there is an opening that leads to spiraling staircases down to the second floor. The stairs have no railing, and are connected to the walls of the vertical tunnel. There are some impressive decorations on the stairs, seemingly crafted with loving detail. At the bottom of the stairs, there is an entrance that leads to a long and wide corridor. I estimate the corridor to be over three hundred meters in length and easily thirty in width, but I am not certain of the exact dimensions.

"The hallway contains large stone pillars of varying widths and a black and white checkered floor. It seems that the pillars themselves contain traps that are triggered as you move through the hallway. We suspect that the tiles are the key triggers for the traps, but we did not have the chance to test the entire room. We experienced at least a dozen different traps within the hallway, and I believe that there are more that we simply did not trigger. The traps ranged from common darts, to gouts of fire that spew from the pillars and even detonating pillars that pepper you with shrapnel."

"That's quite a serious floor then," Ikfes hummed thoughtfully. "Do make sure to give me all the traps you can recall in writing. I want a written copy of all of this as soon as possible, with a map for the second floor."

"Yes sir. We also consumed two potions getting through the hallway, and had it not been for James taking the lead to tank most of the damage, we might have had to use more."

"Oh-ho! Quite serious indeed then," he said as he stroked his beard. That floor was certainly something to make note of. C+ adventurers were not exactly pushovers. For them to have trouble with one trapped floor despite having James to help them through it... he would have to put a warning about that floor for lower level adventurers.

"Yes. We managed to get through it, of course," Ella continued. "However, the next room is just as dangerous. The second room of the floor is large enough to contain a large pond in the middle. The room was infested with kobolds. We encountered fifteen kobolds and a kobold lord. The kobolds came in four varieties: common kobolds, kobold shamans, kobold warriors, and a kobold chief."

"I see. The dungeon is truly evolving beyond what we had expected. To be able to create those creatures already... Given the amount of time it has had, the kobolds shouldn't have been able to evolve on their own. The dungeon must be able to create them from scratch now."

"It's as you say, sir," Ella nodded.

"Good to know. Now then, what happened next?"

"We fought... and had to retreat."

"...Pardon me?" Ikfes looked at Ella like she had grown a second head. Not that she could blame him. A group of C+ ranked adventurers should be more than capable of taking down a band of kobolds three times their number, even with a kobold chief leading them.

"We... had to retreat. There were four warriors and five shamans, in addition to the six regular kobolds. We had our hands full, but the worst of the lot was the kobold chief. He is clearly superior to the average kobold chief, as he was able to duel James through the entirety of the ordeal. I've never seen a kobold chief that capable with a spear. He was able to parry and block James' hammer several times, and even managed to injure him. With our main tank partially blocking the entrance to the room, it limited our ability to use ranged attacks, which forced Adder and myself into close quarter combat with kobold warriors and common kobolds while we were peppered with magic from the enemy. The organization behind the entire thing was frankly astonishing, even considering the kobold chief leading the pack."

"I see..." Ikfes said with a pensive tone, his mind hard at work once again.

"I would like to propose that this kobold chief is the same one we defeated last time, sir," Ella ventured, making Ikfes look up at her sharply.

"So, you are saying that this kobold chief is a boss monster, huh."

"Potentially," Ella ventured. "He singled out James from the group, and proceeded to duel him without paying attention to his surroundings. Moreover, I find it hard to believe that even a dungeon as odd as this one would be able to create a second kobold chief within a month, especially one strong enough to survive a duel with James... unless it was a boss monster."

"So, you are saying that the kobold chief remembered James and singled him out for a rematch, is that it?"

"Yes sir."

"Hmm... It isn't unheard of, you know? There have been cases where dungeon bosses seem to retain memory of previous adventurer parties and reacted differently to them. It is quite possible that this is the case here. However..."

"However...?" Ella echoed after a few seconds of silence, hoping to encourage the guild master to continue his thought.

"However, that means that this dungeon is far more advanced than we had thought. Dungeon bosses should theoretically appear every ten floors. For this dungeon to be able to create one so early..." Ikfes paused as he considered things for a moment, "This must be more than even a Phantom dungeon. This dungeon has the potential of at the very least being ranked as Heroic!"

A collective gasp shot through the room. Heroic rank dungeons were almost unheard of. In the entire continent, Heroic dungeons only numbered a few dozen. Any dungeon considered to be "Heroic" was a potential treasure trove. Unlike the lower rank dungeons, which provided exclusively basic raw materials and combat experience, Heroic dungeons were an entirely different level. Once they developed past a certain point, they could directly improve the strength of a person, allowing someone to physically transcend the boundaries of a human.

Ikfes was proof of this. It was said that Ikfes and his party had managed to conquer a Heroic dungeon and, despite losing most of the party in the process, the three survivors had exited the dungeon with power that was incomparable to that of their previous selves, earning Ikfes the S rank in the Adventurers Guild. Ikfes had been catapulted from a formidable adventurer to the strongest man in the kingdom of Mussol as a result of his sudden increase in power after conquering that Heroic dungeon.

"I am sure you all know what this means," Ikfes said. The entire group nodded silently, understanding the impact of the news. "In the entire continent, there are only twenty-seven Heroic dungeons, and four Legendary dungeons. If this dungeon has the capacity to reach the heights of even a Heroic dungeon, this is a huge boon for our country. If even a fraction of our adventurers and knights can get their strength boosted by the dungeon, even by only ten percent, then our nation would become a force to be reckoned with. That's without mentioning the treasures that we have yet to find within this dungeon as it grows."

Ikfes looked at each individual member of Azure Arrow, who now stood ramrod straight, almost frozen on the spot. Had it not been for the subtle movements of their chests as they breathed, Ikfes might have been concerned that they had been hit by a petrification spell in secret.

"As of now," he continued, "I am placing a silence order on you all with regard to the official ranking of the dungeon. The dungeon is still too young to ascertain its true ranking, but the minute that it's ready, we will have it ranked. I'll also be sending my assistant to oversee this new hall of the Adventurers Guild. If this dungeon is truly as special as I think it is, it must be protected at all costs. Furthermore w—"

Whatever Ikfes was going to say next was suddenly cut short as he paused without a reason. His eyes shifted to focus on the side of the room as if staring at nothing.

"Sir?" Ella asked with confusion.

"Shush!" he hissed. "Silence child. Do you not hear it?"

"What do you—?"

"I hear it too," Mei replied, turning to look in the same direction where Ikfes was looking.

Everyone stood stock still, barely daring to breathe as the seconds melted away. Second after painful second, Ella, Adder, and James just stared in confusion at the spot where Ikfes and Mei were looking.

And then came a sound.

Distant at first, it grew into a soft melody that seeped into the bones of everyone present. The mountain where the dungeon resided seemed to resonate with the sound, as if the wind and the earth themselves wanted to carry the tune.

"What in the world...?" James whispered quietly, holding his breath as the deep tone of the melody permeated the entire village. It was unmistakably the voice of some living being, but it was also a voice that was clearly not human. It was too powerful. Too old. Too clear and mysterious.

"...The dungeon... it's alive..." Ikfes whispered, his voice full of awe.

No one doubted his words at the time. They instinctively accepted them as true.

The dungeon was conscious. Alive.

And it knew of them.

<<<>>>
Status

Species: True Dungeon
Rank: 2
Name: Smit

Age: 2 months
Mana: 98,892 MP
Anima: 171
Mana Reg.: 235 MP/h
Anima Reg.: 5.25 AP/day
Floors: 2
Inhabitants: 63 Species

Titles: Creator of Dungeon Laws; Creator; Guide of the Bloody Evolution; Legendary Craftsman; Master of Concentration; Reincarnated One.

Abilities: Absorb matter; Alter environment; Bestow knowledge; Break down components; Craftsmanship; Creation; Digging; Destroy creation; Dungeon laws; Enhancement; Equivalent exchange; Ether manipulation; Evolution; Interdimensional storage; Life bestowal; Life-energy harnessing; Mana absorption; Masterful mana manipulation; Modification of creations; Monster link; Telepathy; Trap building; Transfer dungeon.

Resistances: Magic (general); Mind control

CHAPTER TWENTY

K ing Vas sat at the dining table in his palace. The meal was all expertly prepared, with several dishes served for the king and his family, though there was not enough food on the table to label the moment as "excessive" by any means. Dinner was the king's favorite time of the day, simply because he could spend time with his beloved wife, Shana, and his two daughters, Emma and Dianna.

Because of his busy life ruling the kingdom, the king had less time than he would like with his family. However, the one moment that was guaranteed to have available to spend time with his family was at dinner. His entire family would gather and talk about their day while they enjoyed the delicacies of the royal kitchen. His wife was a fantastic scholar and enchanter, spending her time immersed in books and experiments between caring for their daughters, and she was always happy to talk about whatever book she had read or any experiment she had carried out with the help of the royal enchanters.

Their daughters, on the other hand, were mischievous little brats that he loved with all his heart. Though cheerful and adorable, they were a handful. Dianna was the oldest, who dreamed of adventuring and glory in duels. Talented with the sword, she spent her days training and honing her blade between her other duties. At the ripe age of eighteen, she had yet to accept a marriage proposal, much to the king's anxiousness. Usually, royalty would marry by seventeen, but his daughter was stubborn on this matter, refusing to marry a showy weakling that only cared about status or wealth. He had to admit, he was secretly proud of her standards, even if he could not voice that out loud.

His second daughter, however, a youngling of sixteen years, soon to be seventeen, had taken after her mother. Emma was a talented sorceress in training, capable of calling earth and fire to do her bidding. Born with dual affinities for both magics, she was a rarity that excelled in both defense and offense. When paired with her sister, the two of them were nearly unstoppable, each covering for the weakness of the other.

The king was mighty proud of his two adorable girls, and he had every reason to be. He had no doubt that within the decade, they would be more than a match for him in duels. Not a small feat, considering his strength was easily equal to an A ranked adventurer, if not an A+ rank. It gave him peace of mind knowing that his children would be strong and independent, able to handle whatever the world threw at them.

However, today this joyful moment was interrupted when the doors to his dining room were slammed opened roughly.

"Who dares!?" the king roared as he jumped up to his feet, his eyes looking furious as his mane swirled about his face. He looked at the source of the commotion, only to find Ikfes making his way towards him with long, hurried strides, being followed closely by Alester.

"Your majesty!" Ikfes said hurriedly, "I must speak with you."

"Ikfes! Old friend, what are you doing here now?" the king replied with shock, calming down at the sight of his old teammate.

"Your majesty, it's urgent news!" Alester said hurriedly, "It could mean a world of difference if—"

"Vas, that dungeon... It's alive!" Ikfes interjected, dropping a proverbial bomb on the heads of everyone present.

"Ikfes, slow down," Vas said slowly, taking a deep breath to calm himself in the process. "What do you mean? Which dungeon? Both of you, sit down and explain everything to me, carefully. Servants, you're dismissed. All of you. This is a private matter. You are all forbidden to speak of this to anyone."

Taking a deep breath Ikfes nodded and took a seat at the table, and Alester mimicked this. The servants who had been playing music or pouring wine for the king, nodded obediently and walked out of the room respectfully, closing the wall behind them.

Once the king was sure that they were out, he turned to gaze upon his guests. "Now, explain."

Nodding, Ikfes straightened up on his seat, and leaned forward. Everyone could tell that he was wound up, quivering almost. Whatever he had uncovered clearly had been important or exciting beyond measure... perhaps both.

"Forgiveness, my king, I know you hate being interrupted during your dinner time," Ikfes began, regaining some of his composure. "But I have urgent news. The new dungeon seems to be far more than we had ever expected. This dungeon probably has the potential to be a Heroic dungeon or higher. I can't know exactly the level as it has not matured enough to be tested yet, but all the signs point towards it being a powerful dungeon in the making."

The news left the entire room shocked, but Ikfes did not stop there. He powered through, not giving anyone even a moment to ask questions.

"Moreover, the dungeon *sings*. It changes and evolves at an unheard of rate, maximizing limited resources in a way I have never heard of. Your majesty, the dungeon is alive, I am sure of it."

Seconds of silence slipped by while the people present absorbed the information that had just been thrust into their faces.

"Ikfes," King Vas said slowly, "all dungeons are alive. We know this. They produce monsters and traps. What makes this one so different? So what if a room or two of the dungeon have weird noises? It could be a type of monster that we just have not met before."

Ikfes shook his head vigorously, denying that suggestion instantly.

"No, no, no. That's not what I mean at all. It wasn't a single room, or even a couple. The *entire mountain* resonated with the sound Vas! *ALL* the mountain! Do you understand? No monster could cause such a thing, not if it's confined within a dungeon. The sound was created by the dungeon itself. More importantly, even though all dungeons are alive, I mean to say that this one isn't *just* alive. It is aware. It is conscious! It is capable of thought. Do you see what I mean? A normal dungeon will expand and develop in a way that is static but logical. It's a simple design of tunnels and rooms that are protected by monsters and a few traps. Rarely is there a design that is created exclusively to mess with people, unless the dungeon was manipulated by a god or devil."

"This dungeon is different, though. It hasn't been claimed by anyone or anything, yet it is evolving and changing in such a way that it would leave several claimed dungeons to shame. Everything is calculated and developed in a specific way, and the sheer level of ingenuity that goes into creating what this dungeon has already done in two mere levels... It is conscious, Vas, conscious! To what extent it can think, I do not know, but I am willing to wager my title as guild master that it is sentient to some extent."

"Those are some serious claims, Ikfes," Vas finally said as he sat down, leaning back into his chair. He stroked his red beard, thinking about the situation. To begin with, Ikfes was never one to make wild claims without some evidence. If he was correct about this, it was going to open a whole lot of problems, and a host of opportunities. If it was handled correctly, this could be a great benefit to the entire country.

"The problem is," Alester interjected, with a serious voice, "that there could be a host of troubles stemming from this."

The king grunted in agreement, his mind running through a number of possibilities as quickly as it could. "You are right. A dungeon of this degree might be enough to spark a war if we do not handle it carefully. We are not on good terms with the kingdom of Illeb, nor the kingdom of Amiz, and they would be very interested in a dungeon that can potentially turn a normal soldier into a monstrous enemy, not to mention the physical rewards that they could reap over time."

"Indeed, it is as your majesty says," Alester nodded. "However, beyond that, other countries are not our only trouble. If the nobles were to hear about this, the internal struggle to possess the dungeon would wreak havoc amongst the noble families. It is practically guaranteed that this dungeon will create a prosperous city around it, and whoever rules over that land will gain power and profits that would dwarf that of most cities in the continent, let alone in the country. I would wager that it might even spark a war between the noble families behind the scenes, as I wouldn't put it past some of the nobles to attempt assassinations for such a price."

"You are right once more," the king conceded, knowing that what his advisor said was nothing but the truth. Though nobles seldom engaged in brutish acts of violence directly, they hid behind a carefully constructed game of words, sharpening their claws and striking when it was the most convenient for their schemes. "That does complicate matters significantly. I can think of a handful of people that would be also be dangerous to have in such an important position."

"You speak of Lord Ravoul?" Alester questioned, his tone dark at the mention of that man.

"He is certainly one of them," King Vas said with a grunt. "It is no secret that he is very interested in monetary gains, and he is not on great terms with the royal family. The rumors around that man are nothing if not ominous and unsavory. But besides him, I am also concerned about Count Lerron. The man is a master manipulator, exclusively interested in expanding his influence across the kingdom. If he were to gain control of a dungeon city, I shudder to think at how he would upset the balance of power in the kingdom."

"Dear," the queen interjected, "if that's the case, you should not forget about Lord Estaban. Though he is neutral, as a magus he would be a good candidate to place at the helm of a dungeon city. As a high magus, he is more than capable of guiding the city down a more beneficial path. With him at the head, he would lead the city to be a center of magical research!"

"My dear, that is an excellent suggestion," Vas said, "But if we were to simply hand it over to him, that man would undoubtedly focus on his research to the point of ignoring his duties. He is a brilliant man, but he is famous for becoming fixated upon his research."

"This is true, my dear," the queen agreed. "But that is exactly why he should be at the helm of this. None of the nobles would have to worry about him expanding his sphere of power, or abusing his position, as those things hold little meaning to him when compared to his research."

"Hmm..." Vas thought about this for a moment, stroking his red beard. "He is certainly a possibility."

"If that's the case," Ikfes jumped in, "what about the Duchess Bik'aard? She is a clever woman that has good ties with both the Adventurers Guild and the royal family. She should be able to make good use of the resources gained from the dungeon. Moreover, her command over the battlefield is well known, so she would be able to defend the city should the situation call for it."

"This is true, Ikfes" the king said, pausing for a moment before replying. "However, it is well known that she is a good friend of the royal family. Simply giving her the rights to a dungeon city would stir up a buzz in the noble families, not to mention that others will feel wronged as they have equal or greater qualifications as leaders in the battlefield."

Ideas were traded like this back and forth between the four adults while Emma and Dianna watched the proceedings like it was an intense sport, trying to understand all the implications and strategies that were being proposed. Although they were educated in the ways of dealing with nobility, the discussion that was occurring before them was on a whole different level. It required broad knowledge of the individual characters that could play a role in the situation, in addition to being able to foresee several difficulties that could arise from each decision. This is what it meant to be a ruler, the responsibility to guide your people down a better path.

"Perhaps we are going about this all wrong," the king suggested after a while. "Placing someone at the helm of this entire thing by force might produce more harm than good, wouldn't you say? Almost no one is aware of the dungeon, so there is no need to rush this decision. Perhaps we could even make it a contest of sorts."

"Your majesty? I am not sure I follow..." Alester said uncertainly, hoping that his king was not truly suggesting making a game out of such a precious resource.

"Alester, consider this," the king said as he opened up his palm as if weighing an invisible object. "On the one hand, we could place someone on the proverbial throne and thrust upon them the responsibility of creating a suitable dungeon city. The drawback to this would be that many families are likely to take offense, potentially resulting in a number of internal struggles."

Everyone nodded at this. Assassination was likely to occur if someone felt wronged or overlooked. Even if they were lucky and assassination did not occur, those families could stunt the growth of the dungeon city in numerous ways out of spite. Worse, it would make many nobles less willing to cooperate with the crown, which would cause numerous headaches for months.

"And on the other hand..." the king said as he stretched out his opposing hand, with the same gesture he had just used. "We could create an event to find an appropriate leader for the dungeon city. If we can make it seem like the town is nearly unprofitable to most, the majority of the high-ranking nobles will ignore it, while lower-ranking nobles that have less of a stake in politics might be attracted. If we can do such a thing, we might be able to attract people with a different set of skills, and groom them appropriately to take hold of their post in the most beneficial way possible. This might help us find some hidden jewels amongst our own people that we have overlooked. Though it's riskier for us, it avoids suspicion, and it would allow us to have a better control over who presides over the area. Though the risks are great, the benefits could be greater."

The room went silent for a moment while everyone weighed the options in their mind. The new suggestion presented to them was risky, to say the least. Just like there was a chance to find a hidden jewel, there was a chance for that jewel to be snatched up by another high-ranked noble if they were not careful about this. Worse, the rise of a prosperous dungeon city might upset the power balance in the region, leading to certain hostilities... but conversely, if the new ruler allied themselves with the crown, and was able to properly manage and defend the would-be dungeon city, then the entire kingdom could reap the benefits of this treasure trove. Better yet, the number of people that would feel cheated or overlooked would diminish greatly, reducing the number of hostilities in the future.

This was a gamble indeed. One that would have profound consequences on the kingdom if it were to fail. Yet, the benefits were certainly there. It was not always that one could create a chance for a new economic power to rise within the kingdom, and it was even less common to be able to choose who would rise. Even as a king, Vas could not foresee and manipulate every aspect of the kingdom.

"Are you certain, your majesty?" Alester asked tentatively, his words coming out cautiously, as if he doubted every step. "Though the plan has great potential, the shortcomings would be disastrous in a worst-case scenario."

"You're not wrong," Vas conceded, before grinning at his advisor. "However, it would be a simple matter to set up the event to be more suited to our needs. First, we will have spies find the connections between most lower nobles and see who has connections with the upper echelons of nobility. This will help us make informed decisions in the future. Second, we have to make the event skill based, eliminating the chance of outside help. Just this alone will help make our little contest much more difficult to influence."

"Not a bad plan," Ikfes said thoughtfully. "However, I must ask: What will be the basis of this... event of yours?"

The king leaned back in his chair once more, and pondered that thought for a moment before replying. "This dungeon will become the treasure of our country. It could easily spark conflicts with our neighboring nations. I say that whoever rules over the city must be capable of defending it, thus military prowess is a must. Moreover, whoever manages the city must be well versed in economics, as this dungeon will become a hub of trade."

"Dear," the queen added, "don't forget foresight. Whoever rules the city must have the ability to foresee potential issues that might arise in the future, not just the issues that they are facing at the moment."

"Absolutely correct, my love," the king nodded seriously, adding that to his mental checklist. "And above all, whoever rules the dungeon city must be resolute and loyal to the kingdom."

"That sounds reasonable," the queen nodded, accepting the criterion. "However, dear, how will we set up an event... no, a test for people to do this?"

"Well, dearest," Vas said with a grin, "with a few challenges, of course!"

Everyone raised their eyebrows at the king, wondering what

sort of challenges he would lay out. "I think that economic ability would be the least problematic, as nobles are normally taught the workings of economy. However, military prowess and foresight is a whole separate matter. I say that we set up a sort of war game to test this."

"A war game, you say?" Ikfes said with eyes shining brightly, clearly hooked on the idea.

"Well, not a war game as you think it, dear old friend," Vas said with a chuckle. "But the idea is simple. The noble must select from an assortment of adventurer groups, and must go with them to try to conquer the dungeon. Whoever can lead their team the deepest in the dungeon will win."

"Oh-ho," Alester said with a nod, seeing where this was going. "By handing them a unit that they are unfamiliar with, you want to see how adaptable they are to new and dangerous situations, is that it?"

"Precisely," the king said with satisfaction.

He gave a hearty laugh at this and smirks spread across the lips of his three conversation partners, while the princesses looked slightly confused, still trying to process all the information.

Meanwhile, they were unaware of a servant with his ear pressed to the locked door, trying his damn hardest to hear everything they said. Unfortunately, he had only caught snippets of the conversation. Still, though he had missed the importance of the dungeon city, he had gathered there would be a tournament of some sort to grant a territory to a noble. That itself could be worth a lot to the right person.

Smiling, the servant silently stood up and walked away, his eyes pausing over the fresh corpses of the two royal guards. He fixed his collar, and licked his lips, quietly humming to himself a simple, happy tune.

He could practically smell the money coming his way.

BACK IN THE DUNGEON, the atmosphere was tranquil. However, just a day ago, the atmosphere had been merry. The second floor had been a success, the intruders had been repelled, the lake had been protected, and Smit had ranked up. As a result, Smit had called a feast to take place, ordering Pala and the remaining kobolds to hunt for some prey in the forest surrounding the dungeon. Pala had brought back a couple of deer, which he and his brethren, along with what remained of the wolves and snakes, consumed with gusto.

Smit had sung a merry tune as everyone enjoyed themselves, eating and laughing as they enjoyed the atmosphere. Smit's only regrets were that there was no alcohol to be offered, and he had no physical body to enjoy food or alcohol.

However, now that the party was over, Smit was full of eagerness to continue his expansion. He was ready to create the third floor of his dungeon, and this one he would make a different sort of challenge.

He focused his powers on the wall behind him, and began to create a tunnel spiraled downwards without any steps. Instead, it was smooth, almost like a slide or a ramp. However, just as he began to work on his would-be next floor, an announcement rang out.

Congratulations! You have begun your next floor expansion after your second breakthrough. You are now able to create three more floors. Maximum floors possible to have at the moment: 5

Smit paused for a second taking in the information. He could have a maximum of five floors now.

It seems like once I reach a certain rank as a dungeon, more floors become available. It doesn't necessarily mean that I can build only one floor per rank up, but rather, each rank up will unlock a certain number of floors available to be created. Smit speculated on the reason for the sudden jump in the number of floors he could make.

Still... three more floors were available to him, which changed things significantly. He could create a theme for a set of floors if that were the case, which gave him more room to experiment with his own ideas. Considering this, he decided to change his previous idea for a third floor.

If this is how things are going to be... Smit thought again, and an idea popped into his mind. If Smit had had a physical face, it would have been grinning wickedly, its eyes alive with mischief.

His dungeon had been fairly straightforward so far, so perhaps it was time to challenge his guests with a bit of a childish game now. Humming to himself, Smit set to work, starting his expansion on the third floor properly. He could hardly wait to see the adventurers' faces once they reached this new level, only to find out that it was nothing like the previous two. Perhaps it would give him some enjoyment as well. There were bound to be a few adventurers that would get lost in this place once he was done with it, especially if he was creating three levels of it.

He chuckled at that thought, and lost himself in his own work, his mind set upon the task with unshakeable focus.

Status

Species: True Dungeon
Rank: 2
Name: Smit
Age: 2 months
Mana: 109,232
Anima: 402
Mana Reg.: 235 MP/h
Anima Reg.: 5.25 AP/day

Floors: 2 (Max Floors available: 5)

Inhabitants: 63 Species

Titles: Creator of Dungeon Laws; Creator; Guide of the Bloody Evolution; Legendary Craftsman; Master of Concentration; Reincarnated One.

Abilities: Absorb matter; Alter environment; Bestow knowledge; Break down components; Craftsmanship; Creation; Digging; Destroy creation; Dungeon laws; Enhancement; Equivalent exchange; Ether manipulation; Evolution; Interdimensional storage; Life bestowal; Life-energy harnessing; Mana absorption; Masterful mana manipulation; Modification of creations; Monster link; Telepathy; Trap building; Transfer dungeon.

Resistances: Magic (general); Mind control

CHAPTER TWENTY-ONE

S mit argued with himself as to how to carry out his plan. His choices were simple: He wished to create either a maze or a labyrinth. Although the terms were commonly used interchangeably, there were marked differences between the two of them. The main differences are rather basic. A labyrinth consists of only a single, long, and convoluted path that does not require much thought. A maze, on the other hand, has a multitude of branching hallways and paths that can be taken, resulting in a structure that is far more convoluted and complicated. Essentially, while it is possible to get lost in a labyrinth, it would only happen to the most directionally challenged. Whereas in a maze, it is almost certain that you would need to use your brain to get out of it.

For Smit, it would have been okay to use either idea; the only thing that would change would be his approach to dealing with invaders. If he created a labyrinth, he would just fill it with all sorts of traps, creating what was in essence an extremely long obstacle course. But if he created a maze, he could challenge his invaders mentally, forcing them to use their wits and instincts. This became the true deciding factor for Smit. He did not wish to have simple brutes force their way into his dungeon, or at the very least, he did not wish to make it easy on muscle-heads to travel through his dungeon unhindered. Thus, he decided to implement the maze, instead of the labyrinth.

Smit meticulously worked his way into the stone once he had chosen his desired plan, carving out vast swaths of stone faster than any mole could hope to burrow. Of course, he was determined to create a masterpiece of a maze, putting his would-be intruders to the test intellectually. Despite the inherent difficulty and challenge of the task at hand, and perhaps even because of it, Smit was highly motivated. He was quite excited, because it was the first time he had three new floors available to him at once. This was a unique opportunity for him.

Naturally, Smit would never settle for a common maze. He had his sights set on something much more ambitious than that: An extensive, multilayered, and trapped maze was his goal. He had no wish to make a shifting maze, where the walls moved around constantly, at least for the moment, but he wanted to test the patience and wit of his future guests. Hence, he settled on a type of maze that would be challenging, despite having some weaknesses.

To begin with, each floor would be quite large. He fully expected the first floor of the maze to have a surface area of nearly two square kilometers, while the second floor would double that at four square kilometers, and the third one would triple its predecessor at twelve square kilometers. The floors were aligned such that they were placed one on top of the other in a way that it resembled a pyramid, with each new floor being larger than the last, reaching deeper into the ground. The size alone would have warranted several hours of travel time if someone were to walk the shortest path from the beginning to the end of his maze. But considering the number of twists and turns, one could easily spend days in the maze if they were to get lost.

The reason for this absurdly long travel time for such a short area was primarily the clever design of the maze. The halls were barely wide enough for two men to walk side by side comfortably, though in certain areas the width of the corridors expanded by another meter or two. There were a number of triple or quadruple junctions, corridors that led in circles, winding halls that simply sent you back or made you fold upon your old path, or dud paths that led to empty rooms.

However, that was to be expected of a common maze. What made this maze stand out was the fact that there were several stairs that led up or down the maze's floors to reach the end of the maze. From the start, the invaders would have to move through the floors, sometimes doubling back to past floors, to reach the final boss battle. But that was not all. Throughout the maze there were a number of traps that were meant to either deter invaders from continuing or to disorient them. Even simple things like hidden pit traps that led down to a random section of the lower level could throw an entire party of adventurers into disarray, making them lose their way. To add to the difficulty, to be able to proceed through some of the stairwells, simple puzzles had to be solved. Failure to solve them would trigger traps or the release of monsters or animals into the room where the intruders were located.

In addition to this, though there were no traps designed to kill anyone, there was a definite possibility of injury or even death in the maze. A simple modified pit trap that dropped someone to the floor below was enough to break bones if the person was unprepared or weak. And a common trip wire was enough to make someone stumble on the floor and hit their head, not to mention the effect of hallucinogenic darts.

As a matter of fact, though hallucinogenic darts were non-lethal on their own, they could be counted as one of the most dangerous traps in the maze. As the name suggested, the darts were coated with a weak poison that induced hallucinations for roughly half an hour, causing the afflicted target to become confused. Depending on the nature of the person, the effects varied from causing them to wander aimlessly and take the wrong paths to causing them to attack their own party. In other words, a simple dart could create sufficient discord in a group to lead them completely astray from their goal. In a place like the maze, the hallucinogenic darts that confused the mind were truly a nightmare to deal with.

It would not be hard to imagine that the troubles that any adventurer group would have to go through were nothing short of trying, and perhaps even despairingly difficult, if the group's teamwork and overall skill were not up to par. One misplaced dart could ruin hours of tracing their steps in the maze. A single pit trap could render a heavy infantry unit to break its leg and become immobile. A failed puzzle could cause an unassuming party to fall prey to a common pack of wolves. This last one was particularly likely, as the puzzles were simple only by Smit's standards. Ordinary people would likely struggle greatly to solve the puzzles.

And of course, the most subtle, yet equally dangerous hazards were very simple ones: starvation and dehydration. If the intruders were to repeatedly fall for traps and were unprepared, it was entirely possible that they would start to starve or become dehydrated, which would slowly sap their strength, making every challenge that much more difficult. Of course, even without the other factors of the maze, becoming malnourished or dehydrated could lead to death.

All in all, it was a rather challenging maze that would certainly cause a number of headaches for the people that dared enter it.

But of course, Smit was not completely heartless. He had begun to enjoy the appearance of the Azure Arrow crew. They always provided him some sort of entertainment and they served to test his inventions nicely. In his mind, it would be a shame to kill them without a reason, particularly the magic user, who seemed to have a more appreciative perspective than the rest of his team. With this in mind, Smit had decided that his stance on the matter of adventurers would be neutral. He would certainly do his best to defend himself against invaders that would try to take his treasures, especially those who were greedily attempting to take what he had created for a meager profit. But as the adventurers were a source of entertainment, he would not go out of his way to destroy them. Or at least, he would not do so without a reason.

However, that was not to say that he would not react differently to certain people. He had no qualms about picking favorites or singling out bad apples. If someone dared to, for example, start smashing his decorations maliciously, they would certainly be met with retribution. But as no one had tried to do such a thing to date, Smit had no reason to create an impossible maze or a truly lethal floor for his dungeon. If one was prepared, careful, and skilled enough, the maze should not be of any real danger to them in Smit's opinion.

Still, Smit invested heavily in the number of halls that were present in his maze, making them wind, twist, and branch off exquisitely. Due to the fact that the majority of the maze consisted exclusively of hallways, the length of the maze was far greater than the mere surface area suggested. In fact, if one were to add the length of all paths in the maze together, the total length would be well over one hundred kilometers. When combined with all the traps and challenges, he estimated that the average adventurer would take about three days to make their way across the entirety of his dungeon if they decided to go for the old trick of placing a hand on a wall and following it all the way to the exit of the maze.

Though that old trick certainly would work, the party risked spending several days in his dungeon at walking speed, and they would undoubtedly be met with more hazards as they proceeded, as a longer route would naturally mean there were more traps and monsters to be encountered.

Overall, this little setup was rather hard to overcome with brute strength, unless the person was willing to put up with the numerous obstacles and hazards that Smit had designed to disorient people and obstruct their progress. However, since there were certain skills out there that would allow people to make their way through his maze with much more ease, Smit did not feel that his expectations were too unreasonable. What self-respecting adventurer could not deal with a simple maze anyway?

Following such lines of thought, Smit began working on the walls of his maze, taking care to make the surface smoother before he began modifying the bare bones that formed the skeleton of the maze. Though the halls and rooms were created along with the stairs, there was still much work to be done.

First, Smit created a few secret passages outside the regular network available to trespassers or adventurers. He had thought about creating such passages before, but only now that the dungeon had grown to this extent did these secret tunnels become a true necessity. The passages were connected to all five floors of the dungeon, and were rather small, barely able to fit a grown man inside them. However, these passages offered a shortcut for his creatures to move through his dungeon, just in case he ever needed them in a rush. These hidden emergency halls would also be connected to a few isolated rooms where certain creatures could rest if needed.

He hid these few emergency hallways with his stunning workmanship, making their location nearly impossible to find unless you knew they were there. Moreover, he even created a dungeon law that only allowed entry to these emergency halls to his creatures. Should anyone succeed in forcing their way into those tunnels (despite the very low odds of that happening), the emergency hall would collapse upon them, crushing them mercilessly under the weight of the stones. Of course, Smit could override the dungeon law, should he wish to let this person escape for whatever reason.

Next, it was time for Smit to focus on the decorations. Ironically, decorating the maze turned out to be the tricky bit.

Usually, decorations would have been unique, or leading up to a specific piece of art that would be the center of attention, thus enhancing the centerpiece of the hall. However, that could not be done in this case, as having a single, unique masterpiece would create a sort of landmark that could be used to navigate the maze.

Smit wished to avoid that possibility as much as possible, and thus came up with a countermeasure. Instead of making a center-piece, he would create designs that would form patterns— self-repeating patterns that were elegant, yet attractive to the eye. This would weave an aura of refined tranquility that would certainly relax anyone that stepped into his maze... or at least, it would help relax them when they weren't in an immediate threat of death.

This feature, of course, was also part of the danger of the dungeon. Something beautiful and elegant could make you drop your guard at the wrong moment, only to discover that it would be the last mistake you would ever make.

Smit chuckled lightly at that dramatic thought and let it fade away, regardless of the truth in it. He started to carve patterns of vines, branches, and leaves on the walls. Within the leaves and branches, he carved the figures of several small furry creatures and birds making their nests. He paid careful attention to the eyes of the creatures, sculpting them so they were as lifelike as possible, almost as if he were breathing life into those eyes.

Some of the creatures were actually golems created of packed dirt, which he embedded in the wall itself. The miniature golems would be useless in combat, but his reason for creating them was simple: He would have them stare at the adventurers that made their way down these halls. This would mess with the heads of the adventurers, making them believe that they were crazy for believing that small, cute carvings were following them with their eyes. However, as time went by and the feeling of being observed accu-mulated, those with weaker mental fortitude would start feeling nervous and eventually become mentally fatigued.

In other words, Smit was just creating an atmosphere that could disturb adventurers' minds at a deeper level, by using simple tactics.

As he progressed with crafting his maze, he looked up to the ceiling, and frowned at the dullness of it all. A simply polished ceiling without much to stare at would not be interesting. Therefore, he decided to change it up.

The ceiling was no longer made out of simple stone, but instead it displayed a pattern of narrow stripes of deep blues and greens, alternating as they twisted around each other like snakes. To accentuate this, he gave the borders of the ceiling a narrow, yet simple pattern that had a tribal feel to it, bounding the dance of dark greens and blues that dominated the majority of the ceiling. However, even with this, Smit felt that something was... missing.

Troubled by this lack of *something*, Smit carefully began inspecting his work on the third floor of his dungeon. Everything was beautiful, but finally it dawned on him: It was the darkness.

When the adventurers came down to his maze, there would only be darkness, making it nigh impossible to witness his works of art. Furthermore, if they brought a torch, and he had no doubt some of them would forget to bring one, the effect of his art would be greatly reduced, as only a small section of it would be visible at a time.

This made Smit deeply unsatisfied, causing him to click his tongue in his mind. While he wanted his maze to remain beautiful and mysterious, the idea of it looking gloomy under the dim, yellow-orange light of a torch distressed him. Worse, the clash of the orange flame against the deep greens and dark blues would disrupt the delicate balance of color that he had set up, and that was certainly not acceptable.

He meditated upon this for a while, pondering several possibilities until he reached a conclusion an hour later. The solution came to him in the form of the newest species available to him: elemental spirits.

Though elemental spirits, along with constructs, were a rare species, they were extremely hard to evolve. Elemental spirits had a vast range of possibilities, but they could hardly be called powerful in the beginning, as they were not even considered sentient at the most basic levels. In fact, they could even be compared to insects of the spirit world: small, weak, unintelligent, but hardworking.

However, Smit had found a use for them now.

Grinning internally, Smit allowed himself to use up a tiny fraction of his mana to call forth a fire spirit. Fire spirits were tiny and weak, not even the size of flies. This little spirit seemed to be a grain of sand that floated around slowly and aimlessly, glowing softly in the air. It shone with a small, pale yellow light that was pleasing to the eye.

Good, Smit thought as he observed the little fire spirit. Mentally, Smit guided the little spirit to the ceiling of the maze, before letting it rest there. The little spirit was perfectly content to stay there, basking in the vast amounts of mana that flowed through the halls of the dungeon.

Smit considered things for a moment, before he nodded to himself and summoned thousands of tiny fire spirits. Like little stars, he guided them to adorn the ceiling of his maze, letting them produce a dim glow that gave the halls just enough light to guide your way through them, and still make out the shapes of the decorations on the walls. It was as if the maze were in perpetual early twilight, in that splendid moment when the first few rays of sun touched the night sky and all its stars. However, the true beauty of it resonated deep within the blues and greens of the ceiling, which reminded Smit of the night sky of the north.

It was a truly lovely scene that gave Smit a deep sense of satisfaction. This was exactly what he wanted. He had managed to create a soothing, elegant, and mysterious atmosphere that could evoke both pleasing dreams and the worst of nightmares. There were enough shadows to mess with a person's head, making them believe that there could be danger at any corner, but enough beauty to enchant even the royal family. It was perfect.

Smit had spent nearly fifty thousand mana on the fire spirits needed to light up the first of his three new floors, giving it the look he needed. Then he spent another five thousand mana to bring forth earth spirits to imbue the eyes of the small golems hidden in the halls with a little bit of extra life, and, finally, another ten thousand mana to create small wind spirits that would provide fresh air for the maze, lest it became stagnant and it began to smell badly.

The thought of bad smells made Smit realize something that interrupted his preparations. If he expected people to spend over a day in this maze of his... would they not need to use a washroom to relieve themselves?

The idea made Smit pause his activities and sigh to himself. Yes, the adventurers surely would need an area where they could do their necessities, or his precious maze would end up being contaminated. Cringing at the thought of having feces litter his beautiful halls, Smit went out of his way to create a few small rooms in a few key locations in his maze. These rooms were only two- or three-square meters wide, but they were sufficient. In them, he created small pits in the floor, over which chairs with a large hole in the center could be used. In other words, he created primitive toilets.

He made sure to have a small beetle nest in each of the small rooms to help recycle the feces that would inevitably fall in the small pit. He also gave these washrooms a bed of soft moss on the floor, and even created a few plants on the edges of the room to ensure a better atmosphere. He created a few water spirits to water the plants periodically, away from the eyes of adventurers, to keep the plants looking fresh and healthy. Smit even went as far as having wind spirits ventilate the area, and brought in a small cluster of fire spirits so that the washrooms had a little more light than the rest of the maze.

All of this was done so that his maze would not suffer the shame of having someone relieve themselves in the middle of the hall. He would be damned if he was going to have excrement litter the beautiful halls of his maze.

Smit added a final touch to the dungeon when he created a few lightning spirits to spark randomly around the edges of the ceiling, where the pattern that bordered the blue and green was found. Small sparks of light could be seen occasionally running across the patterns, almost as if small shooting stars were streaking across the night sky.

Smit looked at this and smiled. This was good.

Smit looked at the first floor and nodded with satisfaction. The first floor of the maze was complete. Now it was time to repeat this process with the second and third floors of his maze.

BACK IN THE ROYAL PALACE, chaos reigned as a full-blown investigation was being launched into two murdered royal guards, who had their throats slit from behind without anyone noticing. The perpetrator was bold enough to even leave the corpses in full view, not even bothering to hide them in any way. During the search for the criminal, a royal servant's corpse was found in the sewers. The most disturbing part of it all was that his face seemed to have been cut off with surgical precision.

"Who could have done such a thing?" King Vas growled, pacing back and forth across his room without rest. "Who would even dare?!"

"Your majesty, please..." Ikfes said carefully, trying to placate the raging king with his words. "Though it is true that this is a grave matter, I doubt that they are after your life, or that of your family's."

The king looked sharply at Ikfes, demanding for his reasoning wordlessly. The words of the guild master had hit the nail on the head. For the king, his immediate concern was the safety of his family. How could he not be enraged when there could be a killer within his very castle? Should this mysterious assassin dare touch his family, he would move heaven and earth to find and destroy them and their employer. But the possibility of someone hurting his family still troubled his heart greatly.

"If they were targeting your highness or the royal family," Ikfes continued, "why would they leave the corpses like that? It's practically advertising the presence of a danger to your majesty. It would have been far more efficient to have the assassin stay hidden until the right moment was found."

"Ikfes is right, your majesty," Alester said with a nod. "There are few people that could hope to assassinate a member of the royal family anyway, considering the amount of protection provided within the castle walls. Rather than an attempt of an assassination, it seems far more likely that the goal of this unknown assailant was to disrupt your highness and the affairs of the royal palace. I am willing to wager this is a plot from some enemy kingdom to occupy your mind elsewhere, instead of focusing on international affairs."

"What makes you say that?" The king whirled around to face Alester, looking him dead in the eyes.

"It makes sense, your majesty. Our two largest neighbors are on good terms with us. How convenient would it be for them to destabilize the kingdom? Imagine the rumors, if it became known across the continent that someone assassinated royal guards right outside the doors of the royal dining area? There could be repercussions in ways we could not predict."

"I am not sure about that," Ikfes butted in. "This to me seems more like the work of someone that just wanted to create a distraction. I am more concerned about the fact that someone might have overheard our conversation about the dungeon."

"Impossible!" Alester retorted. "There were only a handful of people that were aware of the dungeon. All of them are trusted people! How could anyone have found out?!"

"Anything is possible, Alester," Ikfes pointed out. "There could have been numerous ways to find out, especially if magic is involved."

"Enough!" the king roared, clearly displeased. "Both of you have valid points. Let us deal with the most urgent matters first.

Ikfes! I expect you to go personally to the dungeon and oversee it. I want you to protect the dungeon until further notice. Regardless of whether it is our lovely neighbors or our own nobles, I do not want a single soul taking over that dungeon until further notice. You and your adventurers are free to use it as training grounds. This is effective immediately."

"By your will, your Highness," Ikfes said with a respectful bow.

"Alester!" The king called out to him roughly. "I want you to monitor the actions of the other countries. I want reports on their current states of affairs. Have a report ready for me as soon as possible."

"By your will, your highness," Alester said with an elegant bow.

"Good. You two, dismissed," The king said as he turned on his heel and gazed out a window looking out onto the royal city. He continued to gaze out the window in a pensive mood, brooding even as his two friends left the room, closing the doors behind them.

As the king stared out into the city, he couldn't help but feel as if a cloud was looming over him. He could not shake the feeling that something was coming his way, something big. It felt... ominous.

He was certain that whatever it was, it could only be trouble. Enough trouble to make his hands itch and long for the weight of his sword once more. However, he resisted the temptation, clenching his fists behind his back.

Grabbing his sword would only grant him momentary solace and, if his hunch was right, there was no time for idling around. He needed to make preparations. As to what kind of preparations, he was not sure yet, but at the very least he would inform his family to sharpen their skills and keep their eyes open. It was a prudent course of action, even if only due to the possibility of a murderer roaming the halls of his castle. He would also talk with his generals, and have them run more drills with the knights, under the pretext of noticing the knights having gotten lazy. That should be a good start for now.

"What tribulations will come my way?" the king murmured to himself, staring at his city as dusk approached, bathing everything in orange light.

IN A DARK LIT ROOM, an old man hummed out a slow, but happy tune. The sound of his voice resonated lightly against the damp walls of stone, creating an odd atmosphere in the old, dusty room. Yet, the man did not seem bothered at all by either the dampness or the darkness of the room, perfectly content to sit in his old wooden chair.

Resting upon a table of questionable integrity, a communication crystal with a sickly shade of purple stood upon a silver stand, right beside a lonesome candle.

Time ticked slowly by and the man continued his slow tune for minutes on end, seemingly unbothered by the slow passage of time. However, eventually a small humming sound could be heard coming from the crystal as it started to light up, generating a pale purple glow that created the holographic image of a thin older gentleman. The gentleman wore a hood, but underneath it, gold chains could be seen, along with embroidered clothes that seemed to be of high quality.

"Ah! My lord," the humming man said with a smile as he stood up and bowed to the figure. "Pleasure to see you once more."

"Hasef. Good to see you," the other man responded, nodding towards the humming man lightly. "I hear you have good news for me."

"Good news indeed!" Hasef said with a chuckle, rubbing his hands in an excited way. "I am sure this will certainly be worth your time."

"Get on with it, Hasef," the man replied sharply. "I did hire you at a steep price, under the condition that you could gather some useful information. Considering the mess you made in the royal palace, this better be worth blowing your cover. You might be an outstanding spy, but if I become compromised as a result of your actions, I swear to you that I will make sure you regret it for the rest of your life."

"Of course! Of course, my lord," Hasef said with a smile. His face gave the appearance of a pale, unhealthy man in his late fifties, but the features weren't quite right. Somehow the features seemed to be offset just a little. "I promise to make it worth your time... and your coin."

The hooded man grunted, and eyed Hasef suspiciously. "Fine. Out with it."

"You see, my lord, I overheard the king and his trusted fellows talk about a brand-new dungeon being discovered in the north."

The hooded man looked sharply at Hasef, so much so that he could almost feel the intensity of the hooded man's glare increase. Smiling, Hasef continued.

"More importantly, it seems that the dungeon is quite rare. I did not get the full details, but it seems that the dungeon is predicted to be quite a resource in the future and they are even considering creating a city around it. More shockingly, it seems that the region where it is currently located does not have a ruler yet. Hence, the king is going to create some sort of event to decide who will rule over the dungeon city in the future."

"Are you sure about this?" the hooded man asked sharply, his stare practically boring holes through Hasef, searching for any sign of deceit.

"But of course, my lord!" Hasef said with a grin. "With my ability, [Ears of the Bat], even magical barriers cannot fully block my hearing. Despite the strong wards of the dining room, I was able to make out the gist of the conversation. I assure you, my lord, they likely never suspected they could be overheard."

The hooded man slowly nodded and a twisted grin started to spread across his face.

"Good... Good!" The hooded man laughed, and slapped his knee happily. "Excellent news, Hasef. You will be handsomely compensated for this. I will make sure of it. Expect your reward at the usual place, under the bridge."

"I humbly accept your generosity to this humble servant, Lord Lerron," Hasef said with a deep bow, grinning widely. He knew very well of Lord Lerron's deep pockets and was already quite excited about the potential reward.

"Of course," Lerron said with a smile. "Loyal servants will be rewarded. One more thing, however."

"Yes, my lord?"

"Get rid of that disgusting face you have on. It seems it's starting to peel at the edges. It's rather unsightly."

"Ah! As you wish. It's a shame though, I just got it yesterday."

Lord Lerron grunted with distaste. "I will never understand your attachment to the faces you obtain. Wearing the flesh of a dead man is rather sickening to me."

"I understand, my lord. However, I beg that you indulge this servant a little bit. It is one of my few hobbies."

Sighing, Lord Lerron shook his head and sniffed.

"Do as you wish. Just get rid of the face before someone recognizes it."

"As you wish, my lord."

"Good. That is all for today."

And just like that, the conversation ended.

Status

Species: True Dungeon
Rank: 2
Name: Smit

Age: 2 months
Mana: 80,232
Anima: 452
Mana Reg.: 341 MP/h
Anima Reg.: 7.27 AP/day
Floors: 3 (Max Floors available: 5)
Inhabitants: 68 Species

Titles: Creator of Dungeon Laws; Creator; Guide of the Bloody Evolution; Legendary Craftsman; Master of Concentration; Reincarnated One.

Abilities: Absorb matter; Alter environment; Bestow knowledge; Break down components; Craftsmanship; Creation; Digging; Destroy creation; Dungeon laws; Enhancement; Equivalent exchange; Ether manipulation; Evolution; Interdimensional storage; Life bestowal; Life-energy harnessing; Mana absorption; Masterful mana manipulation; Modification of creations; Monster link; Telepathy; Trap building; Transfer dungeon.

Resistances: Magic (general); Mind control

CHAPTER TWENTY-TWO

After a full ten days of careful planning and intense work, Smit was just about to complete his maze. It was a massive network that spanned well over a thousand kilometers in length, if one was to measure the entire length of all the pathways and halls. It was truly a massive structure, which, if a normal person was to attempt to map it in its entirety, would require the better part of a year, by Smit's estimate.

This, of course, gave Smit a thorough sense of accomplishment. In his opinion, the traps were placed rather haphazardly, as if a giant had thrown the traps at random. Some halls had only one trap for several hundred meters, where others had numerous traps almost right next to each other, creating a truly painful experience for anyone unlucky enough to trigger them. The combination of pit traps with hallucinogenic darts was particularly terrifying, as it could create a situation where the victim would become disoriented and subsequently fall to an unknown level, increasing the risk of injury and becoming lost.

Additional traps, with effects such as inducing temporary paralysis or creating disturbing sounds, were also incorporated for the purpose of intimidation and demoralization. The fear of being paralyzed in a hostile environment whilst unsure what sort of creature will crawl up to you in the darkness is not to be underestimated. Even the slow scraping sound of stone grinding against stone, or a quick shuffling noise behind you is enough to make your hairs stand on end, as they force your imagination to go into overdrive, conjuring all sorts of horrors lurking in the dark.

These "harmless" traps were enough to render most people paranoid. The strain could cause them to make many mistakes that would otherwise easily have been avoided. Of course, this environment was the sort of place where one simple mistake could result in death.

Naturally, Smit was quite satisfied at the thought of the future mental strain these traps would cause.

However, he was not heartless. His dungeon was barely five floors, after all! It would not be fair to destroy all hope for the adventurers that dreamed of conquering his halls. Or rather, he didn't see the need to do so quite yet. Smit had no desire to mindlessly kill anyone that stuck their heads into his halls. Though he could benefit from taking the lives of his enemies, there would be no one to entertain him nor would anyone come to admire his creations, were he to gain a reputation for being nothing but a deathtrap.

In other words, the benefits of being a bit lenient towards adventurers far outweighed the drawbacks.

That being said, he was at a loss on how to add appropriate benefits to the adventurers for venturing into his maze. He had managed to add a few positive features, such as creating beneficial pitfalls that would let you skip an entire day's worth of walking if you managed to fall into them, as they would drop you on the correct pathway on the floor below. The catch to these "lucky" pitfalls would activate randomly if you stepped on them. As such, when maps would be produced, not every group of adventurers would be able to make use of these traps as shortcuts.

He had also made several safe zones. These were areas where

monsters and other dangerous animals would avoid wandering into and, of course, there were no traps there, making them ideal places to camp for a night. He had even added a few patches of blood moss in these rooms as a small boon for adventurers, allowing them a chance to treat their wounds.

However, despite these few mercies, Smit felt that something was... lacking.

He gazed upon his maze with a thoughtful stare and looked it over. There were countless creatures and traps in the halls of his dungeon, hundreds of walls and rooms, a multitude of dirt golems, hundreds of thousands of elemental spirits, dozens of bathrooms.... for the most part, one would not consider the maze to be extremely dangerous. One might even call it considerate. Even so, its sheer size was a weapon in and of itself, as it raised the level of difficulty many times over.

Smit was certain that once the adventurers came to realize the real danger of the maze that their interest in progressing would drop sharply. Who would willingly put themselves in such an unfavorable position for nothing in return?

He played with several ideas, such as leaving treasures for the adventurers to find, or creating rooms full of valuable plants, or even creating minable veins of ore along the walls of his maze. However, the idea of creating every weapon and armor individually and having to decide how to place it and who should get what... sounded thoroughly annoying and exhausting. Even for someone like Smit, who had the power to create almost anything that he could imagine by manipulating mana and the elements around him, it would be a very time-consuming process. He had no doubt that it would also be irritating to distribute all these treasures individually.

Smit had better things to do with his time than to craft hundreds of items for any common Joe that entered his dungeon. He wasn't some sort of mindless construct.

Thinking this, he decided to put the idea aside for now, as he focused back on the last detail of his fifth floor, the last floor of his maze: the boss room.

This time, the boss room was the location of his dungeon heart, as well. Therefore, he put a little more thought into it. He crafted a large room. The room was circular and dome shaped, about one hundred meters across. There were no pillars to support the weight of the stone above the dome, as there was no need for them. The magically infused stone of the dungeon walls, along with the masterful architecture crafted by Smit was more than sufficient to create a stable room like this.

Satisfied, Smit smiled as he finished carving the room.

Congratulations! You have completed the 5th floor of your dungeon. Abilities have been released.

Ability [Loot Craft] has been released. Native inhabitants of the dungeon (monster, animals, or constructs) will now drop loot after a fixed amount of time has passed after the death of the creature. The loot will be based on the type of creature that has been slain. As a superior species of dungeon core, you may also create customized loot.

Ability [Treasure Management] has been released. As a reward for completing five (5) floors in your dungeon, the ability to create treasure and loot, and the ability to manipulate the laws that revolve around both treasure and loot, have been granted.

Ability [Luck of the Draw] has been released. As a reward for completing five (5) floors in your dungeon, the ability to place fixed drop rates for items from your deceased creations is available. This ability may also be applied to treasure stashes or treasure chests.

<<<>>>

Blinking at the announcements, Smit hummed thoughtfully and looked over the abilities, examining them carefully. The abilities seemed to be awfully convenient to him, given that the troubles that had been plaguing his thoughts not but a few minutes ago had been solved with these abilities. However, perhaps these abilities were set to be released after a dungeon matures to a certain extent. If dungeons had the ability from the get-go, it wasn't hard to imagine a situation in which a young dungeon with only one floor would swiftly be plundered by small-time thieves, hindering its growth. Or perhaps the dungeon would be wholly ignored by the world, as the rewards would be too pitiful to be worth even traveling to, and after a while it would be forgotten in its entirety. After all, a dungeon with only one floor would only have what you could consider trash items or pocket change.

Either way, it was fortunate for him that these abilities came to him now when he felt they were truly needed. All three abilities sounded quite useful, and he particularly wished to try out [Loot Craft], considering that it might give him a new and enjoyable hobby. He would have to make time to experiment with his new abilities once he had finished decorating and adjusting the rest of the third floor of the maze. While he had the skeleton of his maze completed, the walls and rooms were not fully decorated yet, which would be amended by his hand in moments.

Satisfied with his new abilities for the moment, Smit set himself to finish all the details of his dungeon. He added the intricate designs that he had utilized for the previous two floors of the maze, carving the stone into intricate shapes that seemed impossibly lifelike.

The decoration process took a total of two more days for the third floor, and he finalized it by creating a cluster of fire spirits that lit up the boss room spectacularly, making it look as if it was bathed in a silvery-yellow light, as if the moon itself had blessed this spot in his dungeon. As a final touch, he added a simple set of bird golems that he located at the top of the dome. The four owls were placed right into the ceiling, making them seem as if they were stuck in the night sky. Their eyes were so lifelike that any normal person would have thought that they were truly real owls.

Congratulations! After creating a vast number of intricate dirt golems of many shapes and sizes, you have advanced your experience with constructs far beyond your level. As a reward, you are able to craft fully functional golems out of the following material: Wood.

<<<>>>

The announcement came as a surprise to Smit, who, in truth, had forgotten completely about the fact that he could create golems for battle. In reality, given that dirt golems were weak enough to be taken out by normal people, it made much more sense for him to use his animals or kobolds to fight invaders. Additionally, because his dirt golems had no real instincts of self-preservation or teamwork, not one of his dirt golems had survived long enough to evolve during the battle frenzies in his dungeon. In fact, most of them had not even survived an hour before being destroyed.

In reality, the only "golem" in the dungeon that had any significant fighting capabilities at all was Echo, but she was a clear exception to the rest. This was simply because she had not been created as a golem, but rather, she had been two separate and exceptional entities: a strong statue made of stone and a soul entity. Since the statue had later been infused with a soul, Echo could have been considered a type of possessed statue at the beginning, rather than a traditional golem. One could even say that Smit had cheated his way into creating a powerful golem far beyond his normal capabilities when he created the current Echo.

However, it seemed that creating an obscene number of golems of a variety of shapes and sizes had somehow unlocked some hidden requirements, which allowed him to advance his race of constructs, at least with regards to his golems. It didn't take a genius to realize that the step up from dirt to wood was huge in almost every aspect. To begin with, the durability of packed dirt was infinitesimal when compared to that of wood. Though wood would certainly prove vulnerable to fire attacks and the like, the basic abilities of a golem made of wood would skyrocket when compared to those of a golem of packed dirt.

In other words, his golems would finally be useful!

Excitement ran through Smit as a whole new set of possibilities suddenly opened up to him. Wood golems could be camouflaged in settings with lots of plants, particularly if there were trees there, making them excellent for surprise attacks. They could team up with other creatures as well, acting as shields that drew the enemy's fire, leaving other creatures free to terrorize the invaders with abandon. The only true weaknesses of the wooden golems would be their elemental vulnerability to fire, and, if the enemy was skilled enough, slashing attacks. On the flip side, the wood golems would be resistant to lightning and water-based attacks, and even normal penetrating attacks such as knives or arrows would simply get stuck without piercing too deeply.

Without hesitation, Smit decided to try out his new ability.

To begin with, he wanted his first golem to be the raw embodiment of the element of wood: slow, durable, and strong. He created a tall humanoid figure out of redwood, and he gave it a smooth, rounded head with no mouth or nose. The neck of this golem was short, but thick, leading into broad shoulders reminiscent of those of a boar or a bull. Dark tree bark covered it in armor, protecting its broad upper chest, forearms, and shins. Its arms were as thick as a man's thigh, making its upper body heavy and strong. Smit didn't add joints, however, letting the wood bend via magical forces beyond what the rigidity of the wood should have allowed.

In addition to this, he carved blank eyes into the golem, giving it an eerie look that made it hard to discern where the golem was looking. The weight of its upper body created an imbalance, but that was planned for. Smit made the arms quite long, allowing the golem to hunch over and rest thick fists on the ground. This golem would be able to walk similar to how a gorilla could, albeit without the same speed or flexibility.

Satisfied, Smit looked at his golem only to realize that it would not move. And then he added the final touch: a magic core, placed right where a real gorilla's heart would be.

Traditionally, magical golems all required a magic core to power them, otherwise known as the "heart," which was the center of their system. Even his dirt golems contained a miniscule magic core that allowed them to move. Of course, this magic core was also a weak point. Should it be destroyed, the golem would be destroyed as well. Thus, the challenge for the enemy was to find the magic core and destroy it. More often than not, however, the enemy simply would bombard a golem with enough strength to destroy the majority of the golem to compromise its structural integrity. If a golem was damaged sufficiently, it would simply cease to function.

Once the magic core was introduced into Smit's wood golem, its lifeless eyes changed. They glowed a bright green, showing that the golem had finally awoken like some ancient construct. In addition to this, its posture seemed to gain some vigor, making it stand a bit taller. Smit looked over the golem and nodded to himself. This creature would certainly be slow, but its power would be nothing to scoff at. He estimated that, in terms of sheer physical strength, the golem would be almost on par with the average black bears of the mountain. However, its durability far outstripped that of a common bear. In terms of raw strength, the only two creatures in his dungeon that had a half decent chance at beating this wooden golem in a one-on-one fight were Echo and Pala. Perhaps one of his grizzly bears could have pulled it off too, but those odds were slim.

He called this design "brute golem," because they were built for close combat and using their fists in a crude fashion, swinging them down onto their enemies like hammers, while they absorbed large amounts of damage.

Next, Smit proceeded to create a second type of golem, basing this one on a specific type of tree: the weeping willow.

This design was far different from the last. The golem was relatively tall for human standards, but rather thin. Standing at a hundred and eighty centimeters in height, the willow golem still stood a good thirty centimeters shorter than the brute golem. It also had only about half of its width. The willow golem's head was more elongated than the perfectly round head of the brute golem, and Smit even decorated it with long, flexible branches whose leaves extended down to the waist of the golem, like a mane of hair. Smit made the limbs of this willow golem long, and two long and flexible whip-like branches extended from each of its wrists so far down that they dragged on the floor. Since the willow golem could control these long appendages at will, they were meant to incapacitate or distract adventurers.

Furthermore, to increase the flexibility of the golem, Smit made sure to give the golem appropriate joints, allowing its range and flexibility to come much closer to that of a creature of flesh and blood, thereby improving its handling of its whip-like branches tremendously. Of course, these joints would also be weak spots, but it was a fair price to pay in exchange for the significant increase in its functionality.

He added the finishing touches by giving this golem two eyes, much like the previous golem, but this time he carved the outline of a nose upon its face, making it appear significantly more ghostly and gaunt in the dark twilight of the maze. Lastly, he placed the heart of his golem in the center of its head, where the brain of most organic creatures should have been.

The willow golem powered up, and a green shine came into its eyes. Smit decided to call this golem type a "whip golem" for obvious reasons. This golem was designed for mid-range support during combat and incapacitating enemies via immobilization or distraction. While its attacks where not very deadly on their own, the pain from a whipping from it certainly would be a good distraction.

Together, he suspected that these two golems could be rather effective, especially when supported by other creatures or traps, but the fact that they lacked the ability to function at a sentient level was quite the drawback. Still, they could carry out simple orders such as "defend this area" or "stay hidden until an enemy walks past you and then attack." However, anything more compli-cated than that would be nigh impossible for them to comprehend.

Still, this was good enough for now.

Grinning to himself, Smit decided that the fifth floor of his dungeon would see wooden golems. They would be a new hidden enemy that would appear occasionally, while Pala himself, along with some of his troops, would be the boss monsters for the fifth floor.

He would also be certain to make Pala and Echo practice their fighting skills with these new golems of his. Surely they would prove useful sparring partners that would help his two precious children increase their abilities.

With such thoughts, Smit smiled to himself as he turned back to work. He had lots of golems to create and new powers to play with.

IKFES HAD LEFT the capital days ago, under the order of the king. He had taken a number of adventurers with him and was already well on his way. Meanwhile, the search for the murderer of two royal guards was still in full swing.

One could describe the entire debacle as chaotic. However, this was not something that concerned Hasef. No, he was more than happy to let it all play out. Soon he would have his reward, and he would be well away from the royal city of Naref. Perhaps he would simply relocate to another nearby city, or he could leave the kingdom of Mussol entirely and seek his fortune elsewhere.

Both options had their up- and downsides, but he minded neither option. He had done his bit and in doing so earned enough gold to live comfortably for the rest of his life... or lavishly for a decade. He chuckled at that thought. Perhaps he would even get himself an elven slave and a mansion in the countryside. Elves were a beautiful race. If he could get his hands on one of those beauties he would make sure to thoroughly take advantage of the options his would-be slave opened up. Perhaps he could even get himself an illegitimate child or two to sell. Half breeds could still go for quite a good price, after all.

Grinning at these thoughts, Hasef slipped through the shadows in the dead of the night, approaching the place where he would be getting his reward. It had been painful being patient enough to get such a large sum of money, but payday was here at last, and he was going to collect.

The location was the same as always, under a rundown old bridge at the outskirts of the city, where the sewers of the capital ran off into a small river that carried the waste far away to irrigate some farms in the south. The moon cast shadows all over the area, giving the impression that anything could be hidden amongst the shadows, but Hasef paid it no mind. Who would even come this far from the city at this time, other than him, that is? Even if he encountered someone, he was quite confident that he would be more than capable of dealing with them. He was the man that had taken the lives of two armed guards in the middle of the royal palace, after all. Who could possibly beat him in a game of shadows? He was sure that he was the best in the city. He would bet his left arm that he was even amongst the best in the entire country, for that matter.

Thus, with a confident strut, Hasef walked into the sewer tunnel that was under the bridge. A few minutes of walking saw him to the designated location, marked by a pile of broken barrels and scraps of trash. It was the perfect place to hide such a payment.

Humming to himself, Hasef started pulling things aside, tossing them ever more roughly into the sewer, as his anticipation increased. His heart hammered with excitement as he imagined a treasure chest of coins, a bag full of bars of gold, an ingot of orichalcum, a magic item that could be sold for thousands of gold coins! Anything like that would have made all his troubles worth it and more. Thus he didn't leave a single scrap of trash left unchecked, no rag left unturned until he found it. There sat, below everything, a modestly decorated wooden chest the size of a cat. Grinning like a kid presented with cake, he hefted up the treasure chest and was pleased by the weight of it. Clearly it had been filled with something worthwhile, as it was heavy. Perhaps he would be lucky and he would actually get an orichalcum ingot!

Filled with excitement, Hasef hurriedly opened the treasure chest.

BOOM!

An explosion rocked the sewers violently, gouts of flame spreading down the halls of stone as the fire consumed everything in its path.

<<<>>>
Status

Species: True Dungeon
Rank: 2
Name: Smit
Age: 2 months
Mana: 11,233
Anima: 472
Mana Reg.: 861 MP/h
Anima Reg.: 19.27 AP/day
Floors: 5
Inhabitants: 70 Species

Titles: Creator of Dungeon Laws; Creator; Guide of the Bloody Evolution; Legendary Craftsman; Master of Concentration; Reincarnated One.

Abilities: Absorb matter; Alter environment; Bestow Knowledge; Break down components; Craftsmanship; Creation; Digging; Destroy creation; Dungeon Laws; Enhancement; Equivalent exchange; Ether manipulation; Evolution; Interdimensional Storage; Life bestowal; Life-energy harnessing; Mana absorption; Masterful mana manipulation; Modification of creations; Monster Link; Telepathy; Trap building; Transfer dungeon.

Resistances: Magic (general); Mind control

CHAPTER TWENTY-THREE

Smit clicked his tongue mentally as he observed the dungeon he had created so far. A grand total of five floors, which had a combined distance of well over a thousand kilometers to be traveled. Certainly, that sounded quite good to most people; it was a substantial achievement for a dungeon that had not even existed for half a year. Hell, Smit had heard of dungeons that were half a century old with only five floors!

However, despite the fact that he was quite advanced for a dungeon his age, he was not satisfied with his current dungeon, or to be more specific, he was dissatisfied with the inhabitants of his dungeon. Even though he had a significant variety of species already living in his dungeon, he had more in store due to his recent rank up. It seemed that dungeons received general improvements to their abilities through ranking up, which he found useful but less than ideal, as it meant that he did not get to select what he could specialize in at will.

This was a serious problem in Smit's opinion, as it meant that he was not in full control of his development, and therefore he could not improve as he desired. Unlike a human or dwarf or elf, he could not choose to work on a set of skills and raise their proficiency consistently as a result of his own effort. His rank up gave him fixed increases in his abilities, thus locking him in a format that would restrict his ability to grow quickly in any given direction he would have otherwise chosen.

This, of course, was the source of Smit's worries at the moment. While he would have preferred to work his way to specialize his dungeon and its creatures to grow in a specific direction, he found that he could not force the matter past a certain point. In other words, despite his rank up, he was limited in modifying and roughly guiding the evolution of his creatures. Moreover, he could not select what animals and plants became unlocked to him after his rank up. The knowledge simply came to him as if some unknown god decided to implant the blueprints into his mind on a whim.

What was he supposed to do with the knowledge of how to create a gopher? Or the power to bring pigeons into existence? Neither creature excelled at defense or offense and as such, barring an invasion of enhanced earthworms capable of digging their way through the mana-hardened stone of his dungeon, they were essentially useless for Smit.

The realization that he had so little control over what his rank up entailed and how it was managed was stressful to him, to say the least. He, who had lived for over seven centuries in his past life, spending untold decades to master each of his crafts so carefully by planning his future and overlapping knowledge, had now minimal control over his own development. It was madness!

The best he could currently do was modify creatures thanks to his abilities [Enhancement] and [Modification of Creations], both of which stemmed from his dungeon trait [Enhanced Monster Alterations].

He shuddered to think how much more difficult it would have been to manage everything if he had not chosen that trait when he came into being. Then he might have experienced true despair. At the very least, he might not have been able to create the current versions of Pala and Echo, which were heavily modified and enhanced. Pala in particular had been enhanced twice, and Smit had to push himself to the limit to make the modifications work. The only creature that had been more modified than Pala was his two-headed spider, and that had required many failed experiments to even achieve.

With his modifications, Smit could make his creations more dangerous, and he could certainly make them more viable to use. Pala himself was a testament to this, as without the enhancements, Smit doubted he would have been able to keep up with that giant adventurer last time. That alone made his selection of the dungeon trait [Enhanced Monster Alterations] well worth it.

That thought made Smit smile to himself, even if only a little. Perhaps there could be a way to make things work. There was always a way to make things work. Even if the materials were not ideal, a good blacksmith could still craft a brilliant axe if he used the right technique and the right tools.

Sinking deep into thought, Smit contemplated his options.

Option one was the most simple: rank up as fast as possible and gather as many new species as possible randomly. Eventually, he would get something good out of it. The downside of this was that he had no idea how many rank ups that would take, and that each rank up would take longer to reach.

Option two was instigating fighting frenzies. He could force his creatures to continuously develop through the bloody evolution method. This was guaranteed to be a more certain solution than option one, but the downside was that if anyone entered his dungeon during a fight, his forces would be weaker due to the very nature of the frenzy.

Option three was that he could send out Pala and his kobolds to hunt more creatures outside the dungeon, which would certainly benefit him by getting him new species faster than the rank up and the frenzy. However, he would also be sending out one of his most powerful forces into the wild. With so many adventurers starting to gather, they might simply hunt down Pala and his brethren, or worse, associate Pala with the dungeon and come in force to investigate the situation.

Smit sighed as he thought of this. None of the options was what he would call ideal, or even satisfactory, especially when he knew that the village down the mountain was starting expansion plans, further reminding him about his time constraint. He wouldn't be surprised if the village doubled its original size within a month at the rate that it was expanding. Smit had to praise the master craftsmen leading the workforce of the village, as they were truly guiding the other craftsmen skillfully, if the images by the scouting mice were anything to go by.

Suddenly, as if a switch had been flipped in Smit's head, an idea surged from within the recesses of his mind. Perhaps he could guide his creations? Perhaps he could at least partially guide his creations down a broad path that he wanted them to take. It should be doable, and it would increase the efficiency of his fighting frenzies too.

Smit speculated that his modifications could give a certain edge to his creations and his creations would, in turn, utilize his modifications to their advantage. By constantly utilizing these modifications and growing used to fighting with them, his creatures would be more likely to evolve into something that used those modifications as a strength. In theory, this should make his creatures more likely to evolve into other creatures more in line with what he desired them to be. With a bit of luck, he could potentially enhance the chances of creating a variant or a rare subspecies.

The idea sounded a little farfetched at first, but the more he thought about it, the more plausible it seemed. It made sense to him that, if a creature relied heavily on defense, its evolution would also rely on defense, whereas if another creature relied on the use of poison, its evolution would be more poisonous. In a way, his snakes and mice had already proven this. Smit had enhanced the constricting snakes previously and the evolutions of those snakes turned them into larger snakes with more powerful muscles. The same could be said for his mice evolving into dungeon rats, a more aggressive and powerful form created for the purpose of fighting.

As he considered this, he hoped his hypothesis would be correct. If it was, then it would allow him to enhance his current strength significantly. Even if he risked the fighting frenzy, he was confident that his maze would slow down his enemies enough for him to recuperate some of his troops, despite the fact that the cost of creating them was enhanced for the duration of the ordeal. After all, if the enemy spent upwards of a month in his dungeon at this point, even if the cost of recreating creatures in the dungeon increased, he would have plenty of time to regenerate his mana.

With this in mind, Smit swiftly took action. He was acutely aware that time was not on his side, and another group of adventurers could dive into his dungeon at any moment. He looked over the entire selection of creatures available to him. In total, he could create just over a hundred and ten different species of monsters and animals and fifty-two different types of plants. However, that included a large variety of creatures and plants he had not even attempted to create, such as pigeons, gophers, and cockroaches.

Frowning at his list, he looked over the new additions to his creations. He just recently had gotten the ability to create an additional twenty creatures, amongst which the only useful ones seemed to be dingoes, bobcats, iguanas, and an odd type of fish called "betta," which, despite being rather small, ranging between five and thirteen centimeters in length, seemed to be hardy fish that could ingest a large variety of things. Though not the strongest fish by any means, Smit approved of the hardiness of the species and hoped to make something useful out of them.

Other than that, the rest of the creatures seemed to be rather... underwhelming. Pigeons were hardly what he would consider a threatening creature, unless his invaders were deathly afraid of projectile bird poop landing on their gear. However, Smit might be able to find some use even for pigeons, but goldfish? Ladybugs? Dwarf rabbits? What was he supposed to do with those?

Particularly the goldfish got on Smit's nerves. Few things were less threatening than a goldfish. The little critters were not even that great, with stupid looking eyes and droopy lips. The only thing they had going for them was the color of their fish scales. He was willing to bet his beard that they probably didn't even taste good, either.

Sighing internally, Smit reminded himself that he didn't have a beard at the moment, as he was currently a stationary crystal that resided in the last room of his dungeon. Grunting to himself as he pushed that thought away, Smit calmed down and considered his possibilities.

He took a moment to settle himself, stilling his mind as he tried to attain perfect clarity of thought. As much as he hated to admit it, he had to consider every single possible creature at his disposal for evolution, even those dumb floating sacks of fool's gold. He had to remember that even his little harmless mice had managed to evolve into a pseudo monster called dungeon rats. Even if the dungeon rats were far from being the most powerful creature he could create, they were still capable of hunting snakes in packs, and with enough of them, even normal adventurers would face danger if they weren't prepared.

From cute little mice to predatory tiny killing machines, his dungeon rats were proof that even the weakest creatures could grow to be fearsome monsters, if they had enough time. Who knows, maybe in the future he would have a giant goldfish that could shoot magic lasers of fire from its eyes as a dungeon boss.

Smit chuckled and let the thought fade away as he returned his mind to the matter at hand. No matter how hard he thought about it, he did not have a foolproof way of determining how any of his creatures would evolve, even if his theory was correct. And even if his theory was correct, he could not be a hundred percent certain that a specific result would be reached. Even if he gave a snake horns, it didn't mean that it would turn into a horned-lightning snake down the line. It might evolve to use the horn as a drill to burrow underground for all he knew.

Ergo, now he had to decide how to enhance his creatures so that they might evolve down a more useful path to him. He suspected that if he were to be too outlandish, the animals might not realize how to use the enhancements to their full advantage, or use them erroneously, leading to deviations from the path he wanted them to take.

Based on this, perhaps the simplest enhancements would be the most effective. An increase in size, or hardness of their hide, or their speed might be the most basic enhancements that a creature could get, and that might be all it would take to get them to evolve in a certain way.

"Well," Smit said out loud, "no use in just guessing these things right now. It's all theoretical anyway. The fastest thing would be to experiment."

"Father?" Echo called out to him, pausing her exercises as she turned to look at the shining green gem that was Smit.

"Don't worry about it," Smit grunted. "I am going to be doing some experimentation, see if I can accelerate the growth of some of the inhabitants of the dungeon. Get back to training."

"Yes!" Echo said enthusiastically, throwing herself at her training once more, her halberd swinging through the air with energy.

Throwing Echo a glance, Smit nodded in her direction, before creating a common dungeon rat before him. The creature was a large, dark-furred rat, the size of a house cat, much like any other dungeon rat. Looking at the rat for a moment, Smit considered his options. If he was going to enhance a rat, he might as well enhance it in a way that would give it a serious advantage over its peers. However, what were rats good at? They were slippery creatures, nimble and adaptable. His dungeon rats were particularly hardy due to their already large size.

After considering the issue for a while, Smit set himself to work by increasing the size of the hind legs of his rat, making the muscles brim with power, hoping to increase its speed and agility. Additionally, he pushed his modification powers even further by giving the rat a short horn, no more than two or three centimeters in length.

It was hard work to rearrange the bone structure of the rat to the extent of giving it an actual horn, but he was hoping that the little thing learned to use its horn defensively. Even if it didn't though, the rat would certainly look more threatening if it had a horn, so there was no real downside to having the rat keep it.

Once he had finished creating the rat, Smit ordered it to go up to the first floor, where it could get ready for the next fighting frenzy.

"That's one upgrade," Smit grunted. "Let's get another nine, at least. I need more test subjects."

SMIT SPENT the following six hours simply enhancing creatures. He created ten separate species, from his repertoire of species, half of which already were in his dungeon, and from each species he created three members that he later enhanced. In short, he created a total of thirty different creatures, each enhanced to make them stronger in one way or another. His personal favorite was the grizzly bear that he had enhanced so that it had a thicker hide and longer arms. It had been difficult to rearrange the bone structure of the bear so that the shoulders were placed a bit more to the sides of his body, thus giving the bear a wider range of movement for his arms, costing Smit the same amount of mana to create that small change as it had cost him to create the entire bear, but he was confident that, if anything, this would give that bear a higher chance to become a hind bear... Probably.

Now that would be a fine addition to his repertoire.

Smit smirked to himself at the thought of some cocky adventurer trying to assault his dungeon on his lonesome, only to be met with the fury of a hind bear. The bear would, of course, tower over the adventurer, and show him that this dungeon was not a game for the amusement of pompous fools.

But alas, that was only a distant possibility at the moment. Not a single adventurer had ventured into his halls since the retreat of Azure Arrow. He was thankful for that, as it had granted him time to build one hell of a maze. He was rather proud of his work, as it resembled walking through a living museum in his opinion. Every detail of the halls was crafted to resemble the image of a forest. Leaves, vines, branches, and tiny creatures hiding amongst those gave the impression of an incredibly dense forest being trapped in the walls of the maze.

One could even call his maze a single, massive work of art, a unique gallery that displayed only one sculpture the admirers could walk through to observe. Well, or at least that's what they would be free to think when they weren't trying to find their way through it all, avoid traps, and all that.

The only thing that was left for him to do before the adventurers came into his dungeon was adjust the settings for the drop rates of his creatures.

He opened a blue window in his mind by willing it to appear and reviewed the details of his dropped items. Thankfully, the window could organize the information in multiple ways, the default of which was organizing the list by creature. By simply selecting a creature, Smit was able to see what the drops would be for that creature and the rate at which they dropped.

For instance, if Smit selected the dungeon rat, he could see that there was a sixty-five percent chance that the rat would not drop anything at all. Of the thirty-five percent chance that the rat did drop something, the rat had equal chances of dropping a dungeon rat tail, a tooth, or a leather pelt of random quality. There was also a small chance of earning a single copper coin from it.

Smit hummed as he looked over this, and spent a while looking through all the drops of his creatures. He noted that in general, the weaker the creature, the lower the chance that they dropped anything. A grizzly bear had a seventy percent chance of dropping something, which was vastly superior to the meager thirty-five percent offered by a dungeon rat. Moreover, better items became available with higher difficulty creatures. A grizzly bear could even drop nonorganic items such as silver coins or fur boots, though that seemed to be a rarity with a chance of occurrence of about one percent.

Smit felt mighty confused as he read some of the items that his creatures supposedly could drop, but there was little he could do about it other than adjusting some of the rates for his creatures to some extent. In the end, he didn't know enough about the rarity of certain items to change their rates too drastically, so he left the drop rates mostly untouched for the moment.

Instead, he decided to focus on his other skills, namely the ones related to actual loot and treasure chests.

To his disappointment the loot was... rather mediocre. Copper coins, rusted knives, brass bracelets... total junk for the first three floors, in his opinion. One would have to open about ten chests to make it worth anything more than pocket change. Calling this "treasure" mediocre almost seemed like a compliment to him. He could not care less if other dungeons with the same number of floors actually used this "treasure" in their dungeons; he found it simply unacceptable.

Shaking his head with disgust, Smit resolved to fix this immediately.

First, he erased any trace of treasure chests on the first floor of his dungeon. In his opinion, the first floor was little more than an introduction to the real dungeon and as such, he didn't feel that there should be any sort of distracting little chest for getting through that particular area, especially when it wasn't even all that dangerous.

Looking at his second floor, he felt it would be almost cruel to set a treasure chest in his reception hall. More likely than not, few people would even notice it, and those who did would probably get a nasty surprise from his traps for being distracted. However, he did put a sizeable treasure in the pond room. He dropped the treasure chest *in* the pond, beside his growing little surprise.

He paused and considered that his second floor would most likely be the first real challenge for most adventurer groups and decided to give them a little something for their troubles. He was aware that his dungeon did not have many treasure chests, so in exchange, he resolved to make the few that he did provide contain better loot instead. Opening up the option window in his mind that regulated the treasure chest loot, he made sure that the treasure had at least a half decent piece of equipment in it. He invested some time to create a set of leather armor out of the hide of his wolves.

Despite his best intentions, he had to spend quite a bit of time to create the armor and even then it wasn't up to his standards of what he would even consider a half-decent leather armor. At best, he would label it as mediocre in terms of its actual utility and effect. None of the five pieces of the armor had any enchantments to speak of, nor were they made of particularly expensive or durable materials. They were merely modified versions of the loot proposed by his new skill. Yet, he had endeavored to at least make his creations not just functional, but also quite effective, considering the materials.

The armor had been tanned excellently, with polished buckles made of brass holding the straps in place. The design was neither flattering, nor crude, but instead it gave the impression that it was made to be used on a regular basis by a respectable person. Smit even went out of his way to thicken the leather around the chest area, ensuring that the lungs and heart would be a bit more protected than the rest of the body. It was an armor that, while superior to most armors worn by rookie rangers or adventurers, was still not comparable to a high-end armor. However, Smit deemed it sufficient.

The treasure chest would contain at least one of the five pieces of armor at random, custom made for the person who managed to open the chest. Then the chest would disintegrate into nothing, only to respawn again in a few hours. He judged that this would be sufficient reward, especially for a lower leveled adventurer.

Satisfied with this, he moved on to his maze. He placed three treasure chests on the first floor of the maze, five in the second, and nine in the last. The treasures ranged from good quality iron ingots to a few silver coins, to even finely crafted steel knives. The knives in particular were designed to be thrown, a little inspiration he had taken from that mildly annoying fellow from Azure Arrow. He noted that his knives, while well-balanced, were much more limited in supply than his arrows. Hence, he decided to provide some small measure of support. At the very least, his knives could be used in an emergency if someone lost their main weapon, or it broke.

Smit almost patted himself on the back for helping out adventurers, even if it was only slightly. Though part of his decision was definitely the fact that he wanted people to see his creations. As much as he wished to remain safe, a part of him wanted his creations to be seen. It was a similar feeling to an artist who wished to have his pieces admired at a gallery, for the public to behold. More than that, he wanted people to not just witness his creations but to experience them in all their glory.

What use was a sword that would never be used to slice? Or a wand that would never cast a spell? What would the purpose be of an armor that would never be used? It would go from being a useful tool to a mere eccentric decoration.

Smit, as a true craftsman, did not wish for that. No self-respecting blacksmith would be satisfied by creating decorations.

Just the thought of someone utilizing the equipment that he created to its full potential brought a smile to Smit's lips.

He was about to start fussing over the details of his treasure chests when he recalled what he needed to do.

"Oh, that's right," he mumbled to himself. He had gotten so lost in his work that he had forgotten entirely the purpose of enhancing his creatures in the first place. "Enhancing them is not enough. They must evolve."

Resolving himself to set things in motion, he sent a pulse through his dungeon, fueling his creatures with energy. An instant later, he willed everything in his dungeon to fight. To fight and survive so that they could grow stronger as a whole. The response was almost instantaneous.

The entire dungeon exploded with activity; rats, mice, snakes, bears, wolves, kobolds, spiders, and a whole host of other creatures leapt into action, instantly seeking to devour one another. The only restrictions he placed on the frenzy were Echo and Pala fighting each other. He couldn't see that ending well for anyone. Instead, he ordered them to hunt within the dungeon the strongest creatures possible. Golems, bears, wolves needed to hunt as much as they could and increase their strength.

Of course, his two children agreed eagerly, rushing into the dungeon's halls to find their quarry. And as pandemonium erupted, Smit began to hum an energetic tune to himself as he continued to fine tune the details of his dungeon, adjusting, switching, and fussing over every detail.

Status

Species: True Dungeon
Rank: 2
Name: Smit
Age: 2 months
Mana: 17,036
Anima: 529

Mana Reg.: 861 MP/h

Anima Reg.: 19.27 AP/day

Floors: 5

Inhabitants: 75 Species

Titles: Creator of Dungeon Laws; Creator; Guide of the Bloody Evolution; Legendary Craftsman; Master of Concentration; Reincarnated One.

Abilities: Absorb matter; Alter environment; Bestow knowledge; Break down components; Craftsmanship; Creation; Digging; Destroy creation; Dungeon laws; Enhancement; Equivalent exchange; Ether manipulation; Evolution; Interdimensional storage; Life bestowal; Life-energy harnessing; Mana absorption; Masterful mana manipulation; Modification of creations; Monster link; Telepathy; Trap building; Transfer dungeon.

Resistances: Magic (general); Mind control

CHAPTER TWENTY-FOUR

The light of the sun shone down on the growing village of Nam at the bottom of the mountain, illuminating the crowd of men milling about. The crew of craftsmen had been working tirelessly to expand the village, as per the crown's orders. The inn and the guild had already been completed in record time under the supervision of the two master craftsmen. The guild and the inn both were very prominent structures for a village; even at a modest two stories in height they were giants amongst the single-floored original residences of the village.

The two buildings were even furnished with wooden cabinets, chairs, and tables, allowing each of them to comfortably host several dozen people at a time. Ikfes mourned the fact there were no cushions or proper mattresses yet available in either building, but that was not something that could be helped. The first order of business had been to start the development as quickly as possible. As such, the crown had opted to gather just the tools and the personnel required to start the project, leaving behind luxuries like feathered pillows or bulky mattresses to lighten the load on the horses that had brought the craftsmen. Though Ikfes knew that this was the most efficient way of going about things, he could not help but miss the comfort of a properly stuffed mattress and the soft feeling of a pillow stuffed with misty ivory swan feathers. He consoled himself with the thought that the next caravan of people to come to the Nam village would include merchants with some of the much needed mattresses and pillows; he only had to wait for them to arrive.

By the time the merchants got there, Ikfes hoped that the small army of craftsmen would have completed some of the buildings that were requested by the crown. If all went according to plan, there would be residences ready for some of the immigrants that were expected to come to the village, some of whom would undoubtedly be merchants and entrepreneurs seeking to live in the growing village.

Of course, this was all part of the plan that the king and queen had devised together. Ikfes had to admit that he was not as well versed in economics as either of them, and as such he still marveled at the simplicity of the plan that was expected to pay off in time.

The plan was to stimulate the market of the village by creating houses. The crown would pay the carpenters and the locals to create housing, thereby increasing the income of the small village significantly. By the time the merchants and entrepreneurs arrived, housing would be readily available for them to purchase at a rather cheap price. Seeing the opportunity to establish their base at a growing dungeon town, these people would purchase the housing, and set up shop in the village much faster. Then, since the villagers would have more money to spend thanks to crafting homes, they would be able to spend more money, which would encourage the merchants to restock their wares, thereby attracting more trade to the village.

Between the increased trade and the allure of the dungeon to adventurers and the military, one could expect a large influx in immigration, which then meant more tax money for the crown. In short, this plan aimed to jump-start the miniscule economy of the village into a significant economic engine for the kingdom.

Of course, this plan was only possible due to the fact that the dungeon was projected to be a great natural resource for the kingdom, and thanks to the fact that the village had a very small economy. It was far simpler to boost the economy of a small village such as Nam, as opposed to a large city such as the royal capital.

Knock knock.

The sound of a fist politely knocking on the wooden door of his office brought him back to reality swiftly. "Come in."

The door swung open, revealing the five members of Azure Arrow, who filed into the room neatly.

"Ah, welcome," Ikfes said with a smile, his eyes sparkling as he looked over his adventurer team. "How goes the task?"

"All goes well," Ella replied, bowing her head slightly in respect. "The new adventurers that arrived yesterday seem to have had no problems with the briefing that we provided them."

"Excellent. There are only four teams, but I expect a good showing from them," Ikfes replied. "They might be your juniors, but they are promising E and D ranks. Do be sure to look after them for now, but do not pamper them."

"Understood," Ella replied firmly.

"Good. Now, onto the next topic," Ikfes said with a smile. "I believe that it is time to go for a third dungeon dive, do you not agree?"

"Sir?" Ella replied curiously, looking at the guild master with a scrutinizing gaze as she tried to read his intentions. "Would that be wise? We have not determined how to best approach this sentient dungeon."

"That is true," Ikfes conceded with a nod. "However, it doesn't seem like the dungeon is particularly hostile, does it? As a matter of fact, it seems to be busy expanding itself rather than aiming for your deaths, if you consider that its monsters didn't try to jump on you on either occasion when you left the dungeon, isn't that right?"

"That is true..." Mei replied. "We didn't eliminate every creature on either occasion. I could feel the creatures staring at us as we left. It felt like... we were let go."

"Precisely," Ikfes nodded seriously. "If the dungeon is not particularly hostile, we should take advantage of the situation and gather information while we can, not to mention that it will help keep your skills sharp."

"And what should we do if the dungeon tries to... make contact with us?" James spoke up, voicing his thoughts with an unsure tone. He proceeded to hurriedly add, "I mean... *if* it does. If it really is sentient, maybe it would try to?"

"Be polite, of course," Ikfes replied without hesitation. "Though I very much doubt that the dungeon will bother talking to you unless it has to. Besides, even if it wanted to communicate, there is no guarantee that it could enter a dialog with you. Who knows if it can even speak anyway? As of now, the best policy is to proceed with caution. If the dungeon tries to make contact with you, then handle the matter carefully. That's about as much as I can suggest right now. Even I haven't ever tried to speak with a dungeon, so I do not know what to expect either."

"That makes sense," Adder said with a shrug. "It's a dungeon. Who knows how it thinks or how it acts. Does it have a sense of honor? Is it emotional? Does it behave in a cold and calculated form? Does it even care if we are dead or alive? For all we know it views us as no different than we view pigeons, just pesky creatures that flutter in and out of its domain... Or perhaps we are food?"

"Don't say that Adder," James retorted. "I dare say that if we were simply food, we wouldn't have gotten away last time so easily. Zig and Ella were particularly vulnerable at the end of it all, if you recall."

Adder replied with a grunt at that, but kept his mouth shut. Everyone was aware that they had been dancing with death in their last dungeon dive. Sure, they might have been able to push deeper into the dungeon and perhaps go to the last room once more, but the chances of everyone surviving were slim. If they had tried to continue, chances were that Ella and Ziggurd would have both died.

"Regardless of how the dungeon behaves or acts," Ikfes interrupted, "the most important thing right now is to gather the most information possible. I cannot stress that enough. There won't be any drawbacks to gathering information. In fact, there will only be benefits. If the dungeon turns hostile, then the information will help us exploit the resources it offers in the future. If the dungeon remains neutral, or becomes friendly, it is always good to be aware of the capabilities of a potential ally."

There was a general murmur of agreement from Azure Arrow and Ikfes smiled at them widely. "Excellent. I am glad to see you all understand. Now, in addition to all this, I am sure you know that the dungeon will be officially opened to the public today. As always, I expect some curious villagers to enter the dungeon, despite the warnings. Since the population of the village is in the low hundreds at the moment, I would like to avoid senseless deaths. Every able-bodied person is an asset right now. Therefore, if you happen to encounter any villagers that are in danger in the dungeon, I expect you to use your better judgment and help them if you are able to. Of course, your own safety is to be placed above theirs. Azure Arrow is currently the most invaluable team of adventurers in the entire village. Should anything happen, your strength may be needed."

"Guild master?" Ella asked, clearly picking up a hint he was dropping. "Are we expecting any situations?"

Ikfes paused for a moment and looked at Ella with a piercing stare, the soft and playful gaze replaced by the eyes of a warrior. The change lasted only a second, before those sharp eyes changed back into the very image of playfulness. The change was so sudden Ella felt a chill crawl up her spine.

"Not immediately," Ikfes replied with a gentle smile. "But we are in the wilderness and the magic from the dungeon might attract all sorts of beasts. It never hurts to be prepared, does it?"

"You are undoubtedly correct, guild master," Ella said with a small bow, her mind churning as she tried to decipher the meaning of Ikfes' words.

"Then it's settled!" Ikfes said with a youthful smile. "It's time for you to get going."

"Then, we will excuse ourselves, guild master," Ella said politely, before leading her team out.

A GIANT PAIR of wooden fists smashed down on the floor where Pala had been just seconds ago, making the ground shake slightly from the heavy impact. Stepping to the side with his powerful reptilian legs, Pala rotated quickly to change his momentum, his tail swinging around with the speed of a whip to slap against the bottom of the wooden brute's leg. The attack shattered the bark armor that surrounded the lower part of the leg. However, it was not enough to trip the golem. Leaping back, Pala adjusted his position and slashed with his spear, cutting into the wood of the golem shallowly, baiting the golem into attacking him again.

A few dozen meters further down the hall, Echo was fighting a wooden whip golem. Unlike Pala, who boasted the highest mobility in the dungeon, Echo relied on her weight and defense, resisting the onslaught of fast strikes from the enemy golem as she struggled to land a blow. Her halberd in hand, she had managed to use its axe blade of her halberd to slice partly into the whips a few times, but the movement of the enemy was clearly superior to her own. Her current strategy consisted in slowly pushing back her enemy until she could corner it and deliver a powerful blow. It was a difficult task considering that the whips tangled her up and inhibited her movement, but as she took no damage from them due to her high defense, she was inching her way to victory.

Slowly but surely, Pala and Echo chipped away at their enemies, crawling their way to victory. Smit had selected their adversaries as a way to train them against creatures that they could not achieve an immediate victory over, enemies who would force Pala and Echo to learn to fight differently.

The two fights lasted a while, well over fifteen minutes, but the result was satisfactory. Both Pala and Echo conquered their opponents and absorbed a portion of their energy into their bodies. Sighing with relief, Pala sat down on the floor of the dungeon as he munched on the core of the golem as if it was a candy. Being organic, he felt fatigue, even after his evolution.

"Hey, Echo," Pala called out.

"Yes?" Echo replied as she extracted the magic core of her fallen enemy.

"You used to be a dungeon too once, didn't you?"

"Yes. However, Father has taken that role now. He is far more suitable," she replied simply as she put the core in her mouth and began to slowly chew it.

"I don't doubt that," Pala replied as he leaned back against one of the walls of the dungeon, staring at the beautiful ceiling of the maze. "But I can't help but think that Father is too amazing. I am not even three months old yet, and I have grown so much. It is all thanks to him."

"That's true," Echo said as she took a seat beside Pala. "Father is indeed extraordinary. When I was a dungeon, I was considered a dungeon with respectable difficulty and growth speed. However, even at my prime, mine would pale in comparison to the speed of Father's growth and his ability."

A pause stretched between Pala and Echo as they both chewed on their prize, each lost in their own thoughts for a moment.

"Why do you say that?" Pala asked.

"Well," Echo started, "it took me a year to complete the first floor of my dungeon, even though it was a little smaller than Father's first floor. The speed at which I developed the first floor was fast enough that I was even granted a random species of lower-class monster. However, Father's speed outstripped my own by such a large margin that the voice of the world gave him unbelievable options. I did not see some of those options until my third breakthrough."

"Amazing..." Pala said as he continued to stare at the floating fire spirits, admiring the soft light that they radiated.

"Yes. Father is unbelievable."

"We must get stronger. Otherwise, we won't be able to stand beside Father, or bring glory to his name."

Echo turned her head to look at Pala, noting the resolute tone in his voice. Though she was still learning about emotions and reactions, she could tell that this desire burned brightly inside Pala. He wished nothing more but to stand beside the Father and be of use to him. Echo couldn't help but approve of this as a warm feeling spread across her heart. She herself felt the exact same way as Pala did.

"Hey, you are smiling," Pala exclaimed, looking at her with interest.

Blinking with surprise, Echo reached up to her face and lightly touched her lips, tracing them with her fingers. She indeed was smiling.

"I don't think I have ever seen you do that before," Pala commented.

"I don't think I have either," Echo replied, slightly confused.

"We should tell Father. I am sure he would be pleased," Pala said happily as he stood up, dusting his legs and the simple bear loincloth he wore.

"What is your basis for believing this?" Echo asked. She saw no reason why a smile would warrant the attention of the father.

"Isn't it obvious? Father may be constantly working, but he

still cares for us. I am sure he would be happy to know you've grown internally."

Echo tilted her head in confusion. Surely a smile wasn't much to get worked up about... but if the father was pleased, she would be very satisfied.

SMIT BUSIED HIMSELF WITH CULTIVATING, only periodically pausing to check on the state of his dungeon. He expected a third dungeon dive soon, as he had gotten reports from his spying mice that a group of armed people had arrived at the village. Now that his existence had been known to the kingdom for a while, he expected that these were more adventurers.

He was racing against time to try to complete his experiments with his blood frenzy, healing those creatures that he deemed as the most likely to survive and evolve in a useful way. Of course, he didn't overdo it with the healing. At most, he would give the creatures an infusion of mana and generally help mend their wounds to a limited extent, but should they be overwhelmed, Smit had no qualms about letting them be devoured by other creatures in his dungeon. Survival of the fittest would see to it that the best would move forward in their evolution.

Smit had gone as far as to create at least a handful of every creature available to him, even the useless looking ones like the goldfish and pigeons. As expected, the pigeons were promptly devoured. Though they were birds and very capable of flying, the small spaces in the dungeon ensured that they could not escape from their predators.

Still, other creatures were showing promise. The modified alpha wolf was showing signs of improved organization and leadership with his subordinates, and the modified grizzly bears were certainly learning to utilize their new bodies quicker than he anticipated. Even the iguanas were proving to be rather efficient hunters, though they did tend to cluster in areas where the fire spirits provided more light.

However, he was the most pleased with Pala and Echo.

Pala was steadily accumulating experience and energy, and his reflexes were extraordinary for someone who had been alive for such a short amount of time. The one thing that caught his attention, however, was that the amount of energy that Pala needed to consume to reach his next evolution was massive when compared to the amount he needed for his prior evolution. Perhaps it was the modifications, or perhaps it was simply his evolutionary pathway, but whatever the reason, it seemed doubtful that he would reach the required threshold soon, despite the frenzy. Still, Smit expected great things from his kobold lord.

Echo, on the other hand, had improved immensely, now attaining control over her body that was at the level of a normal human. Her agility and dexterity were still poor when compared to Pala's but she had improved sufficiently that Smit was confident that she could give even the average C rank adventurer a run for their money, thanks to her incredibly high defensive abilities. Moreover, her spiritual and mental capabilities had improved greatly. She had even managed a natural, genuine smile! He was very pleased with the news and had thoroughly congratulated her on her breakthrough.

Despite all this good news, he could not allow himself to relax. The adventurers had taken off from the village yesterday and he was expecting them to arrive at his doorstep in less than a day.

According to the intel he had managed to obtain from his mice, the group was significantly larger this time. If you included the five adventurers that he already had encountered twice, the total size of this expedition seemed to be twenty-two people. As he had no reference point to their level of skills, Smit had no direct way of knowing what level the adventurers were. However, he did notice that the seventeen new adventurers seemed to treat the members of Azure Arrow with respect, from which he deduced that the seventeen members were at least one rank below Azure Arrow.

If he used Azure Arrow as a point of reference, then the first floor would likely be conquered easily with the sheer number of people that were coming through this time.

He grimly considered the possibility that the adventurers had been requested to act as a subjugation force to destroy him and his creations. The chances of that were very slim, less than one percent if he had to guess. Most likely, Azure Arrow would educate the other adventurers on the basics of his dungeon. However, even with his furry little spies Smit had been unable to gather sufficient intelligence with regards to their motives. His spying mice simply had not been able to pick up any intelligence regarding the adventurers, as there had been minimal conversation between the new adventurers and anyone in the village. As a result of this lack of knowledge, Smit was preparing for the worst.

He was nowhere close to achieving his third breakthrough. However, he had decided to make the most of the remaining time he had before the adventurers arrived. He was very sure that from here on out, he would only see more and more adventurers diving into his dungeon, demanding his attention and interrupting his cultivation of energies.

A cold aura interrupted his worries without warning, causing Smit to shift his focus immediately. Extending his senses, he pushed his consciousness to the gates of his dungeon, peering into the open world as if he stood out in the open in the flesh. The sensation grew stronger as he watched, and soon he sensed the ground quake gently around him. Trees seemed to groan as something large or powerful, or perhaps both, forced its way through the forest.

Smit scowled as he narrowed down the possible creatures that could do this in this mountainous terrain and he did not like any of the results that his brain presented to him. At best, it would be some sort of wild beast like a dire boar, but at worst... he left that thought behind as he rushed to prepare.

Cursing internally, he growled at the awful timing of the creature. He had not stopped the blood frenzy in his dungeon. With his forces depleted and injured, and with the adventurers approaching by the minute, he was not in an enviable position by any means. Despite this, Smit was no stranger to working under pressure. Instantly he began to prepare for the assault of whatever creature was coming his way, starting by immediately cancelling the blood frenzy.

"Beware!" Smit's voice boomed across the minds of every creature in the dungeon, demanding their attention immediately. "A new foe is coming our way. Defend yourselves! Defend the dungeon!"

The words themselves were lost in most of the lesser creatures who could not understand what they meant; however, the intention behind the words was clearly transmitted to every single creature in the dungeon. Anyone who was inside the dungeon at the moment would have been startled by the sudden switch in the atmosphere. The creatures who all seemed to be hell-bent on devouring each other ceased their battles to the death and, in a matter of seconds, were rushing to different positions, accompanying each other as if they were brothers in arms.

Not one to idle, Smit let loose a massive surge of mana through his dungeon that targeted every one of his creatures in an attempt to mend injuries as quickly as possible. Under other situations, he might have done this in a more elegant and systematic form, healing his creatures in order of priority, but unfortunately, he had no time for that.

In addition to this, he attempted to recreate his fallen creatures, starting with the larger ones. Bears, golems, wolves, kobolds, and snakes were at the top of the list. It irritated him to waste mana by creating them automatically like this when he could reduce their cost by crafting them "by hand" as he liked to think of it, but he had little choice at this point. He didn't even have time to move his creatures across the large expanse of the dungeon, which forced him to fortify specific locations, where he believed he would have a greater chance of victory.

In a matter of seconds, most creatures had seen visible improvements in their physical condition thanks to his healing and, in minutes, multiple larger creations had already been formed at several locations across his dungeon. However, for all his speed and power, Smit still had his limits.

Exhaustion started to crawl into him, like a grub trying to eat away at his strength. Despite this, Smit ignored the fatigue entirely, his mental fortitude allowing him to shrug it off for the moment as easily as breathing.

And then his time ran out.

Smit focused on the entrance to his dungeon, and saw a grotesque looking head sticking its way inside. The creature was three meters tall and green, its eyes yellow and slit horizontally like those of a frog. Tusk-like fangs extended from its square jaw upwards, giving its bald head a brutish look. Thick fingers grasped a crude wooden club, and a disgustingly dirty loincloth was the only thing that gave the creature any semblance of modesty.

"Ogres," Smit hissed, a hint of rage expressing itself through his voice. "Father?" Pala exclaimed as he rushed into the core room, standing beside the dungeon heart that hosted Smit's soul. "What is it? What's wrong?"

"We have some vile visitors," Smit grunted with obvious distaste as he kept observing the gate. "Ogres, a lesser type of giant. We have three of these brutes and some of their henchmen goblins by the looks of it."

"Father, I heard your warning," Echo interrupted as she rushed into the room. "What is happening?"

"We have three ogres and about four dozen goblins running around the dungeon's first floor," Smit growled.

"What is wrong with ogres and goblins?" Echo asked curiously, clearly not seeing them as anything other than common monsters.

"The problem," Smit hissed, "is that those forsaken creatures are nothing more than crude, mindless, arrogant, vile, and disgusting monsters who live to pillage, rape, and consume other creatures. There are variants that are the exception to this, but these fellows are nothing more than common wild ogres and goblins. I detest their kind, and these brutes are sure to taint my dungeon with their foul presence!"

Hearing those words, the expressions of Pala and Echo switched from curiosity to surprise, and then to anger. They did not feel rage due to the loathsome acts that these creatures had committed, nor did they feel rage at the fact that they were known for being filthy and vile. Instead, the two of them were enraged that these creatures dared to set foot in the home of the father. They felt rage at the very thought of them tainting their home, and most importantly, they raged because the father himself had been angered.

"Leave it to us Father!" Pala exclaimed. "We will eradicate them from existence."

"Yes Father," Echo nodded eagerly. "Let us face them at once."

"Fools!" Smit replied bluntly. "Do not underestimate them. Though the goblins are little more than a nuisance, the ogres are lesser giants. Their strength is still a force to be respected. If you fought them one on one, your odds of beating them are perhaps sitting at around fifty percent. If you are lucky."

Pala growled in the back of his throat, frustrated at this newfound knowledge. Even after all this training, he was little more than a common small fry, it would seem.

"However, do not worry," Smit continued. "We will be rid of them before night falls."

Pala felt a chill go down his spine as Smit uttered those words. Never in his life had he seen Father this upset or bloodthirsty. It was a very different demeanor from his usual gruff, stoic, and hardworking attitude. This change in his attitude was nothing short of surprising for Pala, yet it was also fulfilling. He was certain that the only beings to have ever seen the father this upset were just he and Echo. It filled him with a sense of pride to know a different side of the father, something that the great majority of the other creatures were not able to witness.

"Now, my children..." Smit growled gently. "Let us hunt."

LUMBERING THROUGH THE MAZE, the three ogres noisily laughed and smashed into anything that looked remotely alive, spitting and belching as they snatched little morsels of food such as rats and snakes. The creatures were nothing short of filthy, and not very intelligent, considering that they called out to each other with such finesse that made pigs look like well-educated folk.

"Grunk!" One of them roared. "Share snake! Give!"

"No!" The uglier of the brutes roared back. "Ograk ate many rat! Snake belong to Grunk!"

"Grunk stupid! Ograk stupid! More food there!" The fattest of the three screamed at them as he rushed forward with large strides, swinging his club wildly, smashing through a goblin as he tried to strike at a wolf that swiftly leapt out of the way.

"Goblin stupid!" he growled as he picked up the remains of the goblin, taking a bite out of it. "Got in Krigis' way. Stupid!"

"Go go! Food there!" Ograk roared, and the entire horde of goblins and ogres ran right down the hall of the dungeon, chasing the wolf as they impotently tried to hit it by throwing rocks. They never noticed the fact that there were no creatures visible in any of the halls they passed, nor did they notice that a handful snakes and rats crawled out of their hiding spots to follow them.

Instead, the horde chased the wolf blindly into a large room, only to be met with several bears, wolves, and a handful of kobolds, along with Pala and Echo. A total of twenty-three against the goblin army and the ogres.

Stupefied by the sudden turn of events, the horde stopped and stared for a second, before the ogres grinned widely. "Food! Lots of food!"

"For the Father!" Pala roared, and his fellow creations roared in unison, only to be met with an opposing roar from the ogres.

The fight quickly began in earnest, both sides throwing themselves at the other in a savage, close combat brawl. Roars erupted as the enemy was assaulted from behind by poisonous snakes and aggressive horned dungeon rats. Most of the rats and snakes quickly became trampled under the heels of the enemy, but their job to poison and induce confusion was accomplished.

"Smash heads!" Grunk roared at the goblins. "Like this!"

The ogre geared back his hands over his head as he readied to land a devastating blow on the enemy, smashing the skull of a bear with the deadly blow. The ogre stretched his arms once more to repeat the feat, only to be met with a spear to the shoulder. His blow was thrown off balance, and the ogre ended up smashing into two kobold warriors, and Krigis, killing the kobolds and breaking Krigis' knee.

"Argh!" Krigis bellowed in pain, dropping on his other knee as he began to curse. "Stupid! Stupid Stupid Stupid Grunk! Krigis will—"

His voice was cut short as a spear pierced into his ear, sinking itself well into the brain of the ogre, killing it instantly. "Begone!" Pala howled as he withdrew his spear, turning to face Grunk.

Echo fought beside him, challenging the remaining ogre, whose name was apparently Ograk, to a contest of strength as they traded straightforward blows. Around them, the bears, wolves, and kobolds faced off with goblins of many castes. Goblin warriors and mages contended fiercely with their opponents, savagely throwing themselves into battle as they tried to take advantage of the chaos that had been created by the ogres.

Yet, despite all their savagery and outnumbering their enemies, the horde was cut down one monster at a time, repaying them for every injury they inflicted tenfold. Both sides took heavy losses, but after just an hour, only one side stood victorious.

Echo's victory over her ogre opponent had sealed the enemies' fate. Once she had taken down the monster, she moved to support Pala, who was fending off three goblins and the ogre named Grunk. Within minutes, the ogre fell, and all that was left to do was deal with the remaining goblins who attempted to flee. They were cut down like weeds, hunted by the wolves and skewered by the kobolds' spears.

The battle was hard fought and most of the troops had fallen to the enemy. Out of the original twenty-three, only seven remained.

"Well done," Smit's voice echoed in the minds of the survivors. "I had not expected them to be stopped on the first floor, even with this strategy. Congratulations, you all far exceeded my expectations."

Panting, but grinning from ear to ear, the seven survivors staggered down to the floor and collapsed.

Status

Species: True Dungeon
Rank: 2
Name: Smit
Age: 3 months
Mana: 13,036
Anima: 549
Mana Reg.: 861 MP/h
Anima Reg.: 19.27 AP/day
Floors: 5
Inhabitants: 79 Species

Titles: Creator of Dungeon Laws; Creator; Guide of the Bloody Evolution; Legendary Craftsman; Master of Concentration; Reincarnated One.

Abilities: Absorb matter; Alter environment; Bestow knowledge; Break down components; Craftsmanship; Creation; Digging; Destroy creation; Dungeon laws; Enhancement; Equivalent exchange; Ether manipulation; Evolution; Interdimensional storage; Life bestowal; Life-energy harnessing; Mana absorption; Masterful mana manipulation; Modification of creations; Monster link; Telepathy; Trap building; Transfer dungeon.

Resistances: Magic (general); Mind control

CHAPTER TWENTY-FIVE

The bodies of the ogres and goblins dissolved into nothing as the dungeon claimed them as its own, breaking them down and absorbing the information without leaving a single trace of them behind. The creatures provided Smit with a pleasantly large amount of mana and the knowledge of how to create three different types of goblins in addition to the common ogres.

"Still... it's rather disgusting," Smit grunted as he received the information he needed to craft those creatures. He found them repulsive enough that even with extensive remodeling, they would probably never be called beautiful. As a matter of fact, the amount of enhancements and remodeling that would have to be used to make even a single goblin aesthetically pleasing was so large that Smit was completely sure the resulting creature would be an entirely different species.

"Now what sort of creature would that be..." Smit hummed to himself as images of pixy-like goblins with locks of brilliant hair and refined noses crossed his mind. Perhaps that would make for an interesting project one day. It had taken him a very long time to create the new species of two-headed spider, but how long would it take him to transform a species like a goblin? Days? Weeks? If so, the beatification of an ogre would at least be a few weeks wouldn't it?

Setting the thought aside for now, Smit opted to refrain from creating either ogres or goblins. Just the idea of having to create them made him feel like he had swallowed some sort of unpleasant ale that was far past its expiration date.

Focusing back on the real world, he studied his gains. He realized that he had absorbed a number of things besides the ogres and goblins, namely all equipment that they had brought with them. Loincloths, wooden clubs, low quality arrows and bows, and even a fire stone that a goblin had had on his person. How or why the goblin had a fire stone, Smit did not know, nor did he care. All the items were simply broken down and absorbed as material for him to use.

The amount of mana he had gained was significant. Each goblin had provided him with approximately seventy points of mana, while each ogre had fed him close to five hundred. It was clear to him that though the goblins were weaker than your average kobold, the ogres would have easily been able to fight five kobolds at a time. He was convinced that had he not had Pala or Echo ready to aid him, the number of resources needed to take down the ogres would have been at least three times what was spent.

"Speaking of which…" Smit turned his attention to the seven survivors of the assault, all of them exhausted. Pala, Echo, two bears, the alpha wolf, a kobold warrior, and a kobold mage. Less than a third of his original force. However, there seemed to be benefits even in this fiasco.

All of his seven creatures had significantly increased their levels of energy, making them stronger than before. As a matter of fact, two were ready to evolve, and Pala had leaped forward in his advancement significantly. He was on the verge of reaching the required energy to advance once more, so close that Smit might have been able to force the evolution, but he decided against it. Pala was a warrior through and through. He would prefer to earn his strength, and it would do him good to gather every ounce of experience that he could manage to get.

On the other hand, the alpha wolf and the kobold warrior, both of whom were survivors of the frenzy prior to the assault of the goblins, were both well past their evolutionary threshold.

"Now, the question is..." Smit muttered to himself as he started to channel mana towards his seven survivors, "should I evolve them now? Or should I hold off until the adventurers leave?"

After a second of weighing his options, Smit nodded to himself. He had plenty of mana, he could evolve them and still reset his dungeon composition. He would be a bit tight for time, but he had to risk it. With a group of adventurers that large just a few hours away from his home, he had to take every advantage he could.

"Let's start with you." Smit focused on the wolf, pouring his power over it, enveloping it in a cocoon of energy as he examined the wolf.

<<<>>>

Conditions met! [Common Mountain wolf (Alpha)] has met hidden conditions. Optional evolutions available.

<<<>>>

Smit blinked as he saw this, surprised by the window that had popped up. All previous evolutions had been automatic, following a natural pathway, so to speak. Never had he had this sort of thing happen, not even with Pala.

"Interesting..." Smit hummed to himself, focusing on the window and willing it to continue.

<<<>>>

Hidden condition: Leadership of separate species [Grizzly Bears], has led to the acquisition of skill [Natural Leader].

<<<>>>

<<<>>>

Hidden condition: Consume the flesh of a stronger being [Common Mountain Ogre] while protecting ally [Echo] has given rise to title [Selfless Defender of the Pack].

<<<>>>

<<<>>>

[Natural Leader] has given rise to evolutionary option [Great Mountain Wolf (Alpha)]. [Selfless Defender of the Pack] has given rise to evolutionary option [Sentinel Mountain Wolf (Alpha)]. Normal evolution [Superior Mountain Wolf (Alpha)].

<<<>>>

Smit curiously observed the options as he continued to feed his wolf mana, as he started to study the selection. The two additional options seemed like variants of the species, which usually were superior to the standard evolutions. This was common knowledge, and it was speculated that variants were randomly produced as mutations or perhaps due to external sources such as devouring mana stones that amplified their powers. Even Smit had hypothesized that different evolutions were possible based on their behavior and enhancements. However, it seemed that there was another possibility: Monsters could evolve differently based on achievements too, much like humans and other sentient species could obtain titles and skills based on their growth and achievements.

"Who would have known," Smit said with a chuckle. "Evolution is such a mysterious process. I should try to unravel its mysteries some time. But first things first. Let's see if there are any hints as to what the evolutions are beyond the names."

<<<>>>

[Superior Mountain Wolf (Alpha)] is a higher tier of wolf. They stand at twice the size of the mountain common wolf, and have higher intellect, speed, and agility to their prior form.

<<<>>>

<<<>>>
[Great Mountain Wolf (Alpha)] is a rare evolution of the [Common Mountain Wolf (Alpha)]. Their intellect is significantly increased compared to the normal evolution, and are capable of leading different species as well. These wolves have a somewhat higher speed and agility than the standard evolution, but have less strength.

<<<>>>

<<<>>>
[Sentinel Mountain Wolf (Alpha)] is a rare evolution of the [Common Mountain Wolf (Alpha)]. They are quite large, about two and a half times the size of the common mountain wolf, and have a thick hide. They have a higher defense and strength than the standard evolution; however, their agility is slightly lower.

<<<>>>

If Smit had eyes, they would have been bulging out in shock. Never had he had anything close to these definitions for his creatures. The great majority of them simply evolved on their own. He had close to no say on their evolution path and he would only find out about their abilities once the evolution had been completed. How or why he was able to see this information was beyond him, but he would hazard a guess that it was only possible due to the hidden conditions that his wolf had cleared. If that was the case, he wouldn't see this occur too much in the future, and therefore should take advantage of it.

"I see. Well, then let's go for that one," Smit said as he selected the [Sentinel Mountain Wolf (Alpha)] evolution.

<<<>>>
Warning! Evolving your wolf to this form will cause the title [Selfless Defender of the Pack] to be erased. Do you wish to continue?
<<<>>>

Nodding with satisfaction, Smit willed the evolution to begin. However, a moment later something violently tugged at his reserves of mana and anima. An alien force that he did not recognize intruded into his dungeon like lighting, and zapped the alpha wolf with... something. Whatever it was, it seemed to have dealt some sort of damage to the wolf, while simultaneously causing Smit to feed the wolf more mana and anima. The exhausted wolf let out a pitiful yelp as it writhed in agony.

"Hell!" Smit roared as he struggled to stabilize the wolf, but in an instant, it was over. Whatever that force had been, it had lasted but a second, and it had left Smit confused and on edge.

<<<>>>
Conditions met! [Common Mountain Wolf (Alpha)] has met hidden conditions. Optional evolution available.
<<<>>>

<<<>>>
Hidden condition: surviving from the brink of death by absorbing empowering essences has given rise to skill [Light of Healing].
<<<>>>

<<<>>>
Hidden condition: for being endlessly loyal to the entity [Smit] even at the edge of death when tested by holy powers, the title [Blessed Canine of Unwavering Loyalty] has been bestowed.
<<<>>>

<<<>>>

Alert! Special hidden conditions met! Multiple compatible hidden conditions detected. Synergy of [Blessed Canine of Unwavering Loyalty], [Light of Healing], [Natural Leader], and [Selfless Defender of the Pack] possible. Ultra-rare evolution [Saint Bear Wolf] available.

<<<>>>

"What in the name of Orfin's great hammer is happening?!" Smit finally shouted at no one. If he had had a body of flesh and blood, his heart would have been racing, his face would be flushed, and his eyes would have been wild with shock. Smit looked around his dungeon feverishly for a minute, expanding his consciousness without holding back as he searched for anything or anyone that might have caused this, but found nothing. Not even a single rock in his dungeon had been touched.

He took a few minutes to calm down, but eventually, Smit managed to regain his composure. Whatever that had been, it clearly was not around him or his dungeon anymore. The idea that something that had the ability to come and go in his dungeon undetected was terrifying, even more so when it had occurred with the speed of a bolt of lightning, leaving him no time to react. It was so surreal that he almost believed that he had imagined it all.

And he would have forced himself to believe he had imagined it, were it not for the window that was still present before him.

Ultra-rare evolution.

He stared at that for a minute, his mind twisting and turning as he tried to make heads or tails of what had just occurred. Whatever, or whoever, had messed with his wolf just now, had seemingly divine origins, and it appeared to have taken an interest in Smit. Whatever *it* had been, it had allowed his wolf to meet new hidden conditions and unlock an entirely new evolution. Even with over seven hundred years of knowledge, he could not recall ever meeting a creature called [Saint Bear Wolf], and that was saying something, considering that he'd often dealt with adventurers in the past.

"Now the question is," Smit said to no one, "is this a trap, or is this being trying to help me?"

Sighing after a moment of silence, Smit shook his head internally. It was abundantly clear that if that thing wanted him dead, it could have done it at any time. Of this, he had no doubt at all. Might as well accept the gift of an ultra-rare evolution and not ask any questions. He didn't have the time to question things anyway.

"Right. Saint Bear Wolf it is," Smit said as he willed his thoughts over to it, prompting another window to pop up.

<<<>>>

[Saint Bear Wolf] is an extremely rare evolution from the wolf category. They are creatures touched by the Light and are fiercely loyal. Intelligent, strong, and noble, these creatures are thought to be more rare than unicorns. Are you sure you want to evolve [Common Mountain Wolf (Alpha)] to [Saint Bear Wolf]? All skills and titles associated with synergy for this evolution will be erased.

<<<>>>

"Yeah, that should be fine," Smit said with a sigh as the window vanished from sight. He was getting tired of these windows. He couldn't recall ever getting bombarded with this many windows from the voice of the world before.

Without further ado, the wolf finally began to evolve before Smit's eyes. The wolf, while it had been large before, had tripled in size, making it as large as a grizzly bear. Its fur became long and fluffy, with two tones of color: silver and steel grey. Its jaw became a bit more square, and its shoulders became wider. Overall, the wolf looked like a cross between a wolf and a bear, as Smit expected. In fact, the creature seemed noble, but at the same time almost... cuddly. If you ignored the fact that it was large enough to stare a man in the eye even while standing on all fours and that it had teeth that were literally as long as the fingers of a human man and as thick as the fingers of a dwarf.

But Smit knew that underneath that gentle appearance lay a temple of muscle. It was as if the animal had first been crafted by the god of war-beasts and then the goddess of all things fluffy had covered its powerful figure with a misleadingly gentle and soft coat of fur, which was probably tough enough to resist the thrust of bronze stock or the smash of a wooden club.

Smit had no doubt in his mind that his creature was now physically stronger than the grizzly bears and probably second in intelligence to only Pala and Echo amongst his creations.

"Well now," Smit exclaimed, thoroughly impressed by the massive changes, "that's quite something."

The bear wolf slept soundly, like the dead, thoroughly exhausted despite his new form.

"Sigh. Well, that's one down. An expensive one it was, too," Smit commented, realizing that the evolution of his wolf took an impressive one thousand mana points and a hundred anima. Not one to get distracted easily, Smit moved on to the kobold warrior who had reached his evolutionary threshold. Smit looked at the female warrior and hesitated for a moment to begin the evolution. He really didn't have the time nor the patience for another round of endless pop-up windows and random, future-altering events. Nevertheless, he had to get it done.

Wrapping the kobold in his power, Smit allowed for the evolution to begin on its own. The minute that the evolution began, Smit readied himself mentally for any other surprises. He waited for a handful of seconds for something to occur, but he was only met with silence as the evolution continued.

Sighing with relief, Smit let the evolution run its course as he started to consciously repopulate his dungeon properly.

He still had lots of work to do.

As the sun started to approach its zenith, Ella and the other adventurers reached the entrance to the dungeon. The new adventurers let out a collective gasp when they saw the magnificent entrance. The temple-like structure of it all gave it a mystical aura that demanded attention.

Ella chuckled at the reaction, recalling that she and her team had responded the same way. She could hardly blame them; the entrance itself was impressive beyond doubt. She was willing to bet that she could come here every day for a year and she would not grow tired of admiring that masterpiece.

"Alright lads," Ella shouted, "enough gaping; the flies will start nesting in your mouth."

She practically heard them all click their mouths shut, and they nodded an apology at her. Most of them managed to regain their senses quickly and filed behind her and her team.

"My team and I will lead the way," Ella said loudly, "and you will follow. The first floor is fairly safe. However, do not forget the information you were given. For some of you, this will be your first dungeon dive and as such I will repeat what you already know: Don't be fooled. Though there usually isn't much of a difference between the inhabitants of the dungeon and the creatures found in the wilderness, there is a world of difference between being in a forest and being in a place that is littered with all sorts of traps."

"Lastly, how you decide to spend your time in the dungeon is up to you. However, know that the second floor is far more dangerous than the first. Enter at your own risk. Above all, do not be arrogant! That is all."

With that, Ella turned on her heel and led the way into the dungeon, quickly followed by the other adventurers.

<<<>>>

Status

Species: True Dungeon
Rank: 2
Name: Smit
Age: 3 months
Mana: 15,036
Anima: 429
Mana Reg.: 861 MP/h
Anima Reg.: 19.27 AP/day
Floors: 5
Inhabitants: 81 Species

Titles: Creator of Dungeon Laws; Creator; Guide of the Bloody Evolution; Legendary Craftsman; Master of Concentration; Reincarnated One.

Abilities: Absorb matter; Alter environment; Bestow knowledge; Break down components; Craftsmanship; Creation; Digging; Destroy creation; Dungeon laws; Enhancement; Equivalent exchange; Ether manipulation; Evolution; Interdimensional storage; Life bestowal; Life-energy harnessing; Mana absorption; Masterful mana manipulation; Modification of creations; Monster link; Telepathy; Trap building; Transfer dungeon.

Resistances: Magic (general); Mind control

<<<>>>

CHAPTER TWENTY-SIX

I could hardly believe my eyes when I came up to the entrance of the dungeon. The patterns, the workmanship, the blend of colors, and even the form of the entire thing was flawless, as if the stone itself had grown into the shape of a massive porch that led into the dungeon. The sight of it couldn't help but baffle any onlookers who got close enough, as there was nothing that would hint at the fact that this was made by mortal hands. Instead, the very presence of it made me wonder if this architectural wonder was truly crafted by a dungeon instead of a masterpiece created at the hands a demigod of some sort.

The sweet moment of inspired awe was cut short much too soon by the leader of our little excursion here, high C rank adventurer lady Ella Graz, leader of Azure Arrow. Born of a lesser noble family as the third daughter, lady Ella Graz took the path of the adventurer with her father's blessing. According to rumors, she was a prodigy with the sword, and well versed in the art of wielding dual weapons.

We marched across the small clearing to the porch-like structure, and made our way up the steps. I have to admit, the ancient set of eyes carved at the entrance were so realistic that I thought that the mountain itself was alive for a moment.

Once inside, I was confused. I did not know what I expected, but the empty and cavernous first room was certainly not on the list. If I had to describe it, the first room felt beautifully ancient, as if it had been carved by the elements over eons of existence. However, there was a slight odd quality to it, a strange beauty that seemed too well designed to be natural. The rock certainly seemed smooth and uneven enough to appear natural, but the paths that lead away from the first room all seemed too perfectly straight and too uniform in their dimensions to be natural. And as if that wasn't enough of a clue that this place wasn't a normal cave, the fact that there were statues hidden away in the halls also made it obvious.

"Well, this is different," someone behind me said in a muffled, but reverent voice.

"Hmph," a second adventurer said, with disdain clear in her voice. "It's just a cave with monsters. Let's go."

I turned my head to look over at the second speaker, and I found that it was Anastasy, my team leader.

"I don't know about that," I replied to her. "The reports had an awful lot of warnings."

"You actually read the entire thing?" She looked at me as if I had told her I was categorizing chickens.

"Why are you so surprised?" I retorted. "The guild master told us to."

I was answered by a loud snort from my left. Cecil, our auburn-haired huntress smirked widely. "Yeah, but I skimmed over it. No one actually reads a thirty-page report, Beth."

I felt my cheeks heat up as I heard her say that. In my heart, I knew that her words were utter nonsense, for who would dedicate themselves to writing thirty pages' worth of material to help someone without reason? Moreover, this was done four times, considering that each new team got a copy.

However, the disdain that I was receiving from my comrades was doing everything but reaffirming this belief. I squirmed internally under the semi-mocking gaze of my two teammates before turning towards my last bastion of comfort. "Dee! Back me up here!"

Dee turned to look at us with that disinterested gaze she usually has upon her face, unless she is reading one of her books. Her bountiful chest wobbles slightly as she walks, but her robes do an admirable job of containing the majority of the motion. "With what?"

"You read the report, too, right?"

"Yeah... most of it anyway," she said with a nod. "I forgot the last ten pages because I wanted to reread the third chapter of the ice grimoire, but..."

I sighed with relief at her words. At least she read the majority of it and didn't just skim over it lazily like my other teammates.

"See? Dee read most of it too," I said with a satisfied smile, completely ignoring the fact that I was the only one that read *all* of it. Then again, the latter half of the report was arguably the most important part, as it contained a lot of detail about the structure of the actual dungeon and its quirks, whereas the first half contained a lot of information on individual beings identified in the dungeon. It was all well and good to know that there were snakes that could strangle you, but it's even better to know *where* those snakes were found as well, and if there were traps around.

"Yeah, yeah. Whatever, Ms. Paladin," Anastasy said dismissively as she stepped forward nonchalantly, swaying her hips with a confident strut. "I leave it to you if we need any of that *crucial* knowledge, Beth. Now let's get on to exploring this juiced up cave. If all goes well we could move up to D rank adventurers before end of the week."

She gave us a cheeky grin and pulled out her dual short swords from their scabbards. "Onwards, ladies! Let us show these other adventurers what we are made of!"

I chuckled slightly at her behavior, trying to push the mild sinking feeling of despair to the back of my mind. Her speech would have been a lot more inspirational if we weren't the last team to enter the dungeon, but I didn't point that out to her or I would surely have been made fun of again.

Sighing, I paused and shook my head with determination. It wasn't the time to get distracted. I needed to get to work, and to do that, I required absolute focus.

Looking ahead with resolve, I join my team leader at the front, diving head first into the adventure.

AFTER A FEW HOURS of observing the adventurers, I was already feeling conflicted about their presence. On the one hand, the strength of the adventurers seemed to be somewhat below my estimate, which was nothing but good news for my critters. On the other hand, the new adventurers' skills were all over the place, ranging from just shy of complete ignorance to moderately prepared. This wide range in their skill level caused me to realize that the majority of them were highly inexperienced in dungeon dives. In all likelihood, about half of the newcomers were E ranks, just one step above the average villager with a pitchfork, which are roughly considered to be F rank.

As a matter of fact, I was almost convinced that any adventurer group other than Azure Arrow would have been unable to pass the second floor without suffering casualties. Due to this unforeseen lack of experience on their part, I was surprisingly safer than I'd thought at first. Just watching over some of the clearly less capable groups was enough to understand this. In the span of two hours, I witnessed five people fall into common pit traps on the first floor.

Everywhere I looked, I found faults in their approach to my dungeon. A man with a great sword attempted an overhead strike to a measly dungeon rat, only to strike his sword against the ceiling of the corridor, fouling his attack. Later, I witnessed a fire mage using a simple spell that sustained a small torrent of fire from the hands of the spell caster. Though the spell was successfully executed, the fire burnt a lot of moss and the fur of many mice, which created thick clouds of smoke. Naturally, this ended up backfiring on the mage and her party due to the narrow hallways. Of course, filling a tunnel with smoke caused them to retreat quickly as they coughed nonstop and their eyes grew red and filled with tears. Furthermore, several of the adventurer brats got bitten by rats and snakes and lost their composure from such shallow wounds. Hell, a few even managed to get cornered against a wall by their own team accidentally, as random spells and arrows flew through narrow corridors!

To sum it up, I came to the conclusion that three quarters of the new adventurers were absolute greenhorns with low intelligence and foresight. It was frustrating to watch them flail around like a bunch of confused monkeys that didn't know the difference between the hilt of their sword and the face of one of the snakes slithering around on the first floor. The only practical redeeming feature of some of these adventurers was that they seemed to be able to hold their own against basic dungeon mice and lesser snakes.

"Some of these don't even deserve the scraps of iron that they are wearing," I grunted, shaking my head internally at the poor equipment. Clearly these adventurers bought cheaper goods, probably from apprentice blacksmiths by the looks of their bronze and iron weapons.

By the end of the day, several adventurers had fallen into pit traps, been bitten by snakes and rats, and one female adventurer died when she slipped on the blood of one her own kills, causing her to tumble down into a hidden pit trap head first, smashing her skull against the hard, uneven ground below. She died instantly. I am unsure as to whether it was from a broken neck or a smashed skull, but her teammates descended to retrieve her before I could absorb her. Truly a pitiful end for an adventurer, but at least it was quick and painless.

Mentally shrugging at the first adventurer fatality in my dungeon, I noted that the amount of mana and anima gathered by the adventurer's death was comparable to that of the bandit boss I had consumed so many weeks ago now.

"Hmm... Speaking of which, don't I have another method of gathering some of these resources?" I muttered to myself, realizing that I have a number of skills at my disposal.

I skimmed over the list of twenty-five skills that I possessed, pausing at the ones I was looking for.

<<<>>>

Ether Manipulation: The ability to manipulate the Ether itself. To guide and touch the Ether, the energy that binds creations and transcends the material.

<<<>>>

<<<>>>

Life-energy Harnessing: The ability to attract, collect, and manipulate the energy essence of life. Simply by existing, anima and mana will be attracted towards the owner of this skill.

<<<>>>

<<<>>>

Mana Absorption: The ability to draw out mana from a source, actively pulling it towards oneself and making it your own.

<<<>>>

These three abilities had been present since the inception of my rebirth, and had been extremely useful for my cultivation. However, two thoughts crossed my mind after watching that adventurer die.

Firstly, I realized that I had never tried to *actively* draw out either mana or anima from another living being. Was it possible to draw these out from my spelunking guests? Secondly, what exactly was Ether and how do I use it? To my knowledge, Ether was at best a vague hypothesis that was more often regarded as a myth. Even with my extensive life, the most detailed explanation of Ether I'd heard was simply defined as "The essence that fills the void without existing, the boundary between the immaterial and the material."

At any rate, by the time night was approaching, the adventurers all started to vacate my dungeon, most of them looking more than a little worn, sporting several injuries, the majority of which were simple wounds that would heal with time or with some medicine. The worst injury of all was received when a cocky male warrior with leather armor thought it would be a good idea to throw several of my dirt golems at a snake. As punishment for wrecking my creations without having any need to do so, I instructed several snakes to drop on him from the ceiling to attack him. The adventurer got off easy thanks to his teammates, receiving only a few bites from the non-poisonous snakes on his face and a crushed hand as one of the young constricting snakes grabbed hold of it and squeezed it.

I did enjoy watching him running around like a headless chicken while the snakes obscured his vision, though. Never have I heard a man shriek with such a high-pitched voice before.

"Father," Pala's voice called out to me, "the adventurersss today did not go beyond the first level. Why?"

I turned my attention to him briefly, and nodded my head at him. I paused for a second and cursed internally as I realized I didn't have a head, so the action was meaningless. I would have to look into getting myself a body sometime in the future. Though being able to oversee everything as a dungeon core was useful, the lack of mobility was thoroughly irritating sometimes.

"They were greenhorns," I said bluntly. "Also, watch your pronunciation. You are stretching the s's by accident again."

"Sorry, Father," Pala said with an apologetic grin. "What happened to the last ones? The ones that reached the second level a while back?."

"They were busy helping the new brats," I replied. "The Adventurers Guild has finally started to move into the village, you know? They brought with them a few promising youths to the dungeon to have them train. However, it's clear that some of these brats are still fledglings that think they are better than the rest just because they can swing a piece of iron with some minimal amount of skill. If I had to guess, the guild master asked Azure Arrow to keep an eye on them for a few days. Or perhaps they feel the need to care for their juniors at least for a while? Either way, I predict that they won't be seriously diving into the dungeon for another day or two."

"Ah... I see."

His tone of voice caught my attention, making me look at my son closely. Pala was looking down at the floor at a slight angle, his tail twitching behind him, while his hand fidgeted with his spear. Smirking internally, I asked my question. "Disappointed?"

"What?!" Pala's head snapped up to look at me, his eyes wide. "Father, that's not, I-!"

"Calm down," I said with a chuckle. "It's normal. You are craving another battle, aren't you?"

There was a pause as Pala seemed to struggle with some internal conflict, before he nodded his head meekly. It's odd to see a tall bipedal, somewhat humanoid lizard nod meekly, but as a sentient creature, it's inevitable that he should have a variety of emotions.

"I thought as much," I said with a hum. "You are a warrior through and through. You have made it your goal to defeat that man in one-on-one combat, haven't you?"

He silently nodded after a pause, and opened his mouth to speak, but I interrupted him before he had a chance.

"Do not worry, son. I understand that you do not wish to say that you want people to invade our home. You merely relish the challenge. There is no harm in that. Challenging yourself is the only way to truly grow. It is why I give you and Echo special training, rather than letting you simply hunt smaller, weaker prey. Now, off with you, go tend to your duties. I have some things I must do."

Pala stared at me silently for a moment as he processed everything before he bowed to me slowly and with reverence and left my core room to do his training.

I hummed to myself in thought for a moment, and started to check off my list of things to do. Since the adventurers were of lower skill than expected, I lost significantly fewer creatures than I had expected to. Additionally, my dungeon didn't seem to be in any immediate danger. However, that was not to say that all was well. I was still in a rather vulnerable state due to the amount of mana and anima I had to spend to repopulate my dungeon. Should any other unfortunate event, such as a second goblin horde, occur, I would be left with a critically low amount of resources. Hell, if all those adventurers had decided to rush in and kill everything in sight, I would also have been in trouble.

Considering all of that, the only logical conclusion I was left with was to use my time wisely. I had a little time to set things into order, so I should do that.

I started with unfinished business. Namely, my two newly evolved creatures. I sent them both a mental command to come to my room and they both hastened to heed my call.

The first to arrive was the Saint Bear Wolf. He truly lived up to his name, looking like the perfect cross between a bear and a wolf. As he stepped into my chamber I examined him with care. The noble attitude was still present until the moment he saw me, at which point he went from a regal beast to a happy, faithful canine with a massive tail that wagged back and forth excitedly. I estimated that he must be just over a meter in height at his shoulder and, by the looks of it, he probably weighed close to three hundred kilograms.

He came bounding towards me with a big grin on his face and I realized that he was going to barrel right against my core at this rate.

"Stop!" I barked at it, and the large creature opened its eyes wide as it skidded to a stop right before my levitating core. Looking at the creature up close, its four, three-inch-long fangs were quite prominent. I had no doubt that this guy would be a terrifying enemy to have running at you if you had a look at those bared fangs.

"Sit," I ordered, sending the message transferred mentally to reinforce its meaning, and the large creature complied immediately, dropping onto his rump. "Good."

"Let's have a look at you," I muttered out loud as I examined him, pulling up his status window.

Status

Name: [None]
Age: 2 Months
Species: Saint Bear Wolf
Level: 1
Master: Smit
Monster Rank: ???

Abilities: Alpha of the pack; Guardian; Heal; Magic (Light, Nature); Mighty howl; Regeneration; Tough body

A beast created by the true dungeon Smit. Due to its unwavering loyalty and being touched by holiness, this creature has evolved into an extremely rare variant.

<<<>>>

I hummed as I looked this over. I couldn't help but wonder why the display window was different from my own, or from Echo's which I saw so long ago. Perhaps it had something to do with the type of entity? Or had my abilities changed because I ranked up? Or perhaps there are some unknown laws I have yet to discover.

Moreover, the "level" part of the status seemed to be out of place. Surely, this mighty beast was far more powerful than Echo in the beginning stages of my dungeon transformation. Such were my thoughts, until an idea struck me. A quick inspection was all that was needed, and the check of several critters around my dungeon proved that many of them were several levels higher than this beast, including relatively harmless creatures like dungeon mice. This confirmed that the level of a creature is not related to its strength relative to other species.

I carried out a second inspection, this time across ten different members of the dungeon and the only thing that I could notice that differed between them was how close they felt to leveling up. This then brought about a simple conclusion: The "level" of my creatures was simply how close they were to the evolutionary threshold. Once they evolved, the level would reset to one. I needed to confirm this, so I decided to keep an eye on the critters who were most likely to evolve soon, especially Pala, who I felt was very close to reaching that threshold. He was currently sitting at level ninety-nine, and so I hypothesized that once he reached his next level he would be able to evolve.

It would be very convenient to have a metric to track their evolutionary progress rather than just doing it by feeling alone, so I hoped that my hypothesis was correct.

"Now then, what to do with—"

I sensed a kobold had finally run into the room, and stopped before me, bowing her head in respect. Her raspy voice followed the bow, "I greet the great one."

"Ah yes. There you are," I replied simply without looking at her. "Hold on for a minute."

"Yesss!" she hissed, and stood as still as a rock.

Focusing back on the massive ball of murder and fluff, I mulled things over. This guy was supposed to be clearly brighter than the other wolves, but the lack of concrete communication was rather unfortunate. Despite that, I could feel that this new creature of mine was no pushover, and I dare say it would have been able to take on a hind-bear even now. It would have been a total waste to not make full use of him.

"Well," I grunted, "I suppose there is only one option. I suppose you are taking a name this time."

The moment I said that, I could feel the mood of the Saint Bear Wolf shift dramatically, going from content to shocked, to proud, to humbled in the blink of an eye. He bowed his head, and for the first time since he came in, his tail stood still.

<<<>>>

Warning! You are about to name [Saint Bear Wolf]. Only one named position available. Are you sure you wish to proceed?

<<<>>>

I quickly agreed to the message, causing it to blur out of existence.

"I hearby grant you the name Arturus!" I proclaimed with an unrestrained mental wave that touched every being in the dungeon. "Let it be known that you have been named by me."

<<<>>>

[Saint Bear Wolf] has been named [Arturus]. Naming process commencing.

<<<>>>

And just like that, I felt a stream composed of both mana and anima leave me once more to envelope my creation.

Light embraced Arturus as he absorbed the power bestowed to him, his form changing in response to it. He grew another ten centimeters in height and nearly twenty in length. His claws and fangs changed to a pearly white color, and his eyes now seemed to be made of molten gold. Lastly, the fur around the back of his neck and shoulders grew out somewhat, giving him the appearance of having a mane. It made his appearance truly regal.

"A thousand thanks, Father." A rumbling voice rang through the core room as Arturus spoke, taking me slightly by surprise. I had not expected the naming to allow him to speak as well. "I will be forever at your side."

"I have faith in you," I replied, while my mind wondered how comfortable it would be to stroke that mane of fur. Yet another reason to create myself a body.

"I am honored," Arturus said as he stood up on all fours and bowed his head, bending his forelegs so that his chest touched the ground while his hind legs remained standing, creating a position that was recognizable as a deep bow of some sort.

I sent him a mental nod, letting him know that I acknowledged his words, before focusing on the kobold.

"So, a high kobold..." I said with a hum as I looked her over. "Interesting."

At a glance, one could tell she was not your standard kobold. Her form was less hunched over, and her height was nearly the same as Pala's. Her thighs seemed thicker, her hands were more humanoid, and her snout was less pronounced. Her face managed to look more delicate. She even had grown small pointed ears and somehow managed to look more... feminine. That last one threw me off for a moment there, as I had never considered that a kobold could look feminine at all. At most, the females seemed to have softer features and were a bit shorter, but they were not something I would have labeled as *feminine*.

"How did the tests go?" I asked her. Even though I had watched her through the entire process, I still wanted her perspective.

"I thinksss that I am faster. Can move my fingers better. Fewer injuries now, too. Other kobolds seem lesss smart."

I nodded internally at her words. She certainly seemed to be handling her spear better and there were marked improvements in her fights compared to other kobold warriors. It was interesting to hear that she found the other kobolds less intelligent, so her intelligence had received a boost too. All in all, a nice little evolution that would increase the dexterity, agility, and intelligence, as well as the toughness of the scales of his kobolds moderately.

"Good work. Return to your training."

I watched her go for a moment, wondering what sort of evolutions might follow in the future. I remembered thinking that it would have been nice if high kobolds gained sufficient dexterity to craft things.

"Enough of that," I said to myself. "Evolutions are done. Next."

With the evolutions out of the way, the next items on the list were simple. Since the first floor repopulated automatically, I did not have to worry about that. As of now, my current list of things to do was rather short.

1. Cultivate and get stronger
2. Figure out what god or goddess interfered
3. Expand the dungeon
4. Create a body for myself
5. Evolve and strengthen my critters as much as possible
6. Find out about Ether
7. Prove the levels theory I have

Considering that I had no way to figure out number two as of yet, and that points three and four were dependent on my rank, I decided to go for the first item on the list.

It was time to cultivate.

IN THE DARK of the night a man with a cane made his way through the alleys of the city undetected. His figure was hunched over, and he had an unsteady gait. His breathing caused small whizzing noises that would have made most people wonder whether the man suffered from some sort of illness.

Eventually, the man made his way into a rundown shack at the outskirts of the city, near the defensive walls that surrounded the population of the capital. Inside, the shack consisted of just one room and one large table with many chairs. All the spots were occupied by hooded figures of many shapes and heights.

"You are all here. Good," the man spoke as he looked up at everyone, his face covered with a simple black mask. "I have brought some rather valuable news. I am sure your masters will be pleased."

"Hurry, scoundrel. We have neither time nor use for dragged out speeches," a feminine voice rang like a bell, interrupting the man.

"Patience! I won't hold you long," the man rasped out. "First, the price of this information. I-"

"Impudent whelp!" a man boomed out. "You have already been paid! You dare demand more?!"

"My lord," The man rasped out, "I guarantee that this request would be nothing but a benefit to you all. I simply wish that you crush Lord Lerron!"

Silence stretched out for a moment, before the loud-voice man let out a growling "Fine."

"This humble servant is thankful," the man said with a bow.

"Hasef! Get on with it!" a third voice barked, and the man hastened to proceed.

"But of course! I got this information from the palace itself. A brand-new dungeon has been discovered in the north and it is apparently so precious that the king himself has taken interest in seeing it protected. Moreover, the dungeon is predicted to be quite a resource in the future, enough to warrant building a city around it. It would seem that the region where the dungeon is located does not yet have a ruler. Hence, the king is going to create some sort of event to decide who will rule over the dungeon city in the future."

A silence stretched as Hasef finished his speech, and several figures looked at each other, while others bowed their heads in thought.

"Excellent," a soft voice said behind Hasef. An instant later he felt a flare of heat on his back, and his lungs seemed to fill with hot water.

No... not water, Hasef thought in panic as his mind began to haze. *My own... blood...*

A dainty hand caught him as his legs buckled, and deposited him gently on the ground. A pretty face under the hood smiled softly at him, while the owner of said face held a bloody knife in her free hand.

"Thanks for the information, Hasef," she whispered.

And then he closed his eyes as darkness took him.

<<<>>>
Status

Species: True Dungeon
Rank: 2
Name: Smit
Age: 3 months
Mana: 17,036
Anima: 389
Mana Reg.: 861 MP/h
Anima Reg.: 19.27 AP/day
Floors: 5
Inhabitants: 81 Species
Titles: Creator of Dungeon Laws; Creator; Guide of the

Bloody Evolution; Legendary Craftsman; Master of Concentration; Reincarnated One.

Abilities: Absorb matter; Alter environment; Bestow knowledge; Break down components; Craftsmanship; Creation; Digging; Destroy creation; Dungeon laws; Enhancement; Equivalent exchange; Ether manipulation; Evolution; Interdimensional storage; Life bestowal; Life-energy harnessing; Mana absorption; Masterful mana manipulation; Modification of creations; Monster link; Telepathy; Trap building; Transfer dungeon.

Resistances: Magic (general); Mind control

CHAPTER TWENTY-SEVEN

A small fine box clicked open and a pall of fire erupted from its depths, searing her eyes. A loud noise numbed the ears, leaving them ringing with a high-pitched sound that penetrated deep into her skull. Scorching flames leaped at her face, voraciously trying to consume her flesh. She let out a strangled scream, and a gust of sizzling air burned her throat even as the force of the explosion propelled her off her feet. Then, the painful ordeal ended as her back slammed against the nearby sewer wall, cracking her bones in the process.

Her heart beat erratically and blood spilt from the wounds of her arms, which seemed to have been shredded by the explosion. A metal bracelet broke from her ankle, crumbling into dust as a wave of vitality seemed to wash over her body. She drew in a shuddering breath and felt the grip of death grow weaker. Her wounds started to mend slowly, regenerating and reconstructing. Her eyes were the worst of it, painfully melting down and reforming in their sockets as new nerves grew all at once, feeling raw from their sudden construction.

But it wasn't perfect.

The damage was too extensive for the artifact to repair wholly.

She could feel a pain in her back that announced that her spine and ribs were probably cracked, and a brief look at her hands showed her the scarred new skin that enveloped her fingers, two of which had healed crookedly. She took another shuddering breath, and reached up with her hands to feel her face. She didn't have to look in a mirror to discern the damage she had received. Her face had burn scars all across, as if it had healed naturally from a terrible accident.

She sat still for a moment in the gloom, shivering and twitching for a time. She could not tell if it had been an hour or a minute, but a loud noise awakened her from her state of mind. A loud wail that came from her throat as she processed all the information at once. A second scream tore through the sewer just moments later, but this time it was a roar of rage and grief.

"LERRON!"

Drawing a deep, gasping breath, the woman pulled away from Hasef, her mind disconnecting from his head as she opened her eyes wide. Her eyes darted around the shack like a nervous twitch, before fixating themselves on a hooded figure.

"So?" a short, hooded man inquired roughly. "Out with it, Ayana."

"He had legitimate reason to betray Lerron," she said bluntly. "It was not a trick from the rich Lord. Lerron tried to be rid of him by setting a trap. Unfortunately for Lerron, it seems Hasef never fully trusted him either... or perhaps Hasef was more paranoid than we gave him credit for. Either way, it does not seem that this is a trap from Lerron, nor does it seem to be false information. This man truly did get this information from the royal court."

"Curious how he managed to overhear so much from the king and his trusted allies," a second figure commented from the shadows with a deep voice. "The castle is nigh impenetrable without a siege, and the king is no fool."

"Nevertheless, if you have confirmed the information to be real..." a feminine voice joined the discussion. The voice belonged to a rather short, hooded creature with a very prominent hourglass figure. "I have no complaints if the Witch of the Mist herself checked him.

A fourth young voice chimed in, this one from a thin womanly figure. "A shame for such a reputable thief of knowledge to die like this."

A grunt escaped the short man, as he dismissed any expressions of pity. "Do not be a fool. There is more to this than just plugging a potential leak of information. Lord Lerron is many things, but he is not a fool. He probably sent someone to check for a corpse and he is clearly not going to find one. Odds are five to one that he will send someone to try to find this poor sod, and that might lead them straight to us. And it might not just be a random group of mercenaries tracking him. Lord Lerron might manipulate a number of people, perhaps even the local knights policing the area, to help him find Hasef. That would be guaranteed to cause trouble for us. Putting down this broken dog was the safest bet."

"Even if Lerron doesn't send someone," the short woman said, "a crippled spy is worth little and a crippled spy running from his previous employer is worth even less. Who would trust a spy who betrayed his last employer, regardless of the reason? He would have had a pathetic existence if he managed to survive the hunt that is sure to be coming his way. We did him a favor."

"Enough of that," the owner of the deep voice said, his voice rumbling as he made a dismissive motion with his hand. "My master wanted him dead, anyway. Had the witch not suggested this ...mind diving method to ascertain the truth in his words, I would have killed him the minute he stepped out of this shack."

"How cold of you," the thin woman chuckled, her voice chiming like a bell. "I wonder, who could your master be?"

"None of your concern," the man said sharply. "Unless you want your neck wrung like a chicken's."

"How scary," the woman said in a singsong voice, betraying none of her emotions. "Don't worry my dear, I am more interested in who could have hired the Witch of the Mist for a meeting such as this. This seems so outside of your usual activities, Lady Witch."

"Just a favor I owed," she said with a hum as she looked over Hasef's corpse. She pulled her knife out from its sheath again, seeming to consider doing something with it as she looked over Hasef surgically. "Don't worry about his body, by the way. I'll take care of it."

Her words sent a small shiver through the other figures, who decided it would be best to keep silent.

"Then this matter is settled," the short woman said abruptly. "Gentlemen. Ladies."

Before anyone could say a thing, she leaped though a tattered window as gracefully as a gazelle.

There was a general murmur of agreement as the rest of the other hooded figures silently made their own way out. One faded into the shadows, another took the front door, and a third went out the backdoor, leaving the witch and the corpse alone in the building.

Humming to herself, the witch smiled with her pretty freckled face, her mouth stretching far wider than should have been possible. "Now then, what to do with you."

IN THE FIRST week of the greenhorn adventurers diving into his dungeon, Smit managed to find out a number of things. First, the loot system seemed to be working adequately. The adventurers seemed rather surprised about it, at first, and he was sure that they reported their findings to their superiors with haste. Smit wouldn't admit it, but he internally chuckled when the adventurers witnessed some of his fallen snakes dissolve into light, leaving behind some fangs for them to pick up. Of course, this only happened because the corpses of the snakes had been left unmolested for a period of time. Had they been quicker about it, they might have been able to skin snakes and pulled out its fangs, earning them more for their troubles.

At any rate, Smit fully expected his dungeon to be receiving even more adventurers in the future with this new ability of his, considering that now the adventurers could continuously earn materials without having to sit down and skin every creature. This would be particularly useful for parties that had no one with dismantling skills or abilities.

Smit had also managed to carry out a few of his experiments thanks to the large volume of fledgling adventurers with interesting results. His ability [Mana Absorption] was capable of drawing out some amount of mana from the adventurers. However, the rate at which it drew out the mana was rather low. In comparison, he could draw out significantly more mana from his own creations, which he could essentially drain until they were mana starved.

Additionally, he could even draw a bit of anima from his adventuring guests with [Life-energy Harnessing], but the amount drawn was even less than the mana. However, when compared to his own reserves, the amount of anima he managed to gather was considerably more significant.

The one mystery that remained, however, was Ether. Every time he activated his ability [Ether Manipulation], he vaguely sensed something around him, touching everything, yet not quite existing in the same way that magic or regular matter did. It was a phantom feeling, like the thinnest of veils stretching across everything, and beyond that veil he could sense that there was something he could reach. What that was, however, was a mystery to him.

He knew he would have to experiment more to attain any significant results. As such, he simply set the matter aside for the moment.

The most significant discovery came in the gratifying form of levels. As he suspected, the level of a creature indicated how close they were to evolving. This gave Smit a more accurate way of estimating when a creature would be able to evolve, rather than relying on that odd sensation that served as a vague indicator of when the creatures were ready.

All in all, the week had been very productive for Smit, allowing him to learn more about himself and the adventurers that visited his dungeon on a daily basis. Fortunately, there were no more accidental deaths during the week. That Anastasy woman that died accidentally on the first day had apparently made an impact on the other adventurers, and they seemed to be far more cautious since. However, this meant that none of the new teams had dared to attempt the second floor yet, making his first floor considerably crowded. This had forced Smit to seriously consider expanding the first floor of his dungeon to accommodate the number of adventurers he was expecting in the future.

"Well then... what's this?" Smit's senses detected the members of Azure Arrow working their way into the depths of the dungeon, heading up to the second floor. The team of five had clearly adapted to the first floor by now, cutting their way through it without much trouble.

Hmm... Seems like they decided that the whelps are ready to hold their own, Smit thought to himself as they reached the last room of the first floor, where he had placed a pack of wolves to defend the entrance to the second floor. Unfortunately for the wolves, Azure Arrow was perfectly capable of cutting them down with blades and hammer. The fight lasted no more than five minutes from start to finish.

Smit followed the adventurers to the second floor, feeling satisfaction as the adventurers once more admired his handiwork. The staircase that led from the first to the second floor was a masterpiece in its own right, but the ambiance he had created by simply leaving the stairs in a spiral with a hollow center and no railing gave the staircase a little of a mysterious aura. But now he had even improved upon that!

Since his acquisition of elemental spirits, he had sprinkled some on the tunnel of the staircase, letting a few spirits of each element float around gently in that space and shine with their tiny lights. It looked like stardust, and it gave the area a whole new level of beauty.

He was quite sure that the little elf practically forgot to breathe when she entered the staircase, which was amusing but understandable. Elves had a high affinity with nature; thus for her to be in a room with such gentle spirits dozing about must have added to the beauty of the place. Or perhaps she was entirely taken aback by the presence of the calm little spirits in a place that she associated with danger and death. Either way, whatever the reason had been, she was looking around with wide doe eyes, taking it all in like a child who had never seen a parade.

Once they descended the length of the stairs, he observed them prepare to run into the reception hall of the second floor. Clearly they had put a lot of thought into how to get through, as the spell caster put several buffs on the entire party. They even had different attires from what he recalled them having last time, with the exception of James. Though the attires of most everyone seemed to be light, the leather was clearly different, made of a sturdier material and tanned specially to gain a certain level of hardness.

Even that Ziggurd fellow had a vest of thick leather over his robes, which was rather uncommon for a mage, but it gave Smit a rough idea of what they were planning to do. It was a simple but effective plan. They were just going to rush it and take the traps as they came.

Chuckling, Smit grinned to himself as he saw through their plan. It wasn't a bad idea, truth be told, but it was far from elegant. Perhaps there was a reason tied to this method of theirs. Or perhaps they simply had no other ideas. The latter thought made Smit sigh. If that was the reason, then their strategical skills were lacking and things would be dangerous for them past the second floor.

But such is life, Smit thought to himself with a hum.

"Father." He turned his attention away from the preparing adventurers to watch Echo come into his room.

"Echo, how are you, my dear?" he replied.

"I am well, Father. I have finished my training for now and wished to talk."

"You know, I can hear and see everything in my dungeon," Smit reminded her. "You don't necessarily have to come to this room to talk to me."

"That's true," Echo replied. "But this feels... different. It feels right to come to speak with you, Father."

He wanted to ask her what she meant by that, but simply let it slide. It was of no concern to him in the end, as it didn't truly cause any harm or inconvenience. Perhaps Echo was simply adjusting to her life as a monster entirely, and felt the need to see him face to face.

"I see. What do you wish to talk about?"

"Well," Echo began, her words slowing down as she tried to articulate her thoughts. "I um... Hmm..."

She paused and seemed to collect her thoughts, seemingly unsure about how to proceed. This was obvious to Smit, who simply waited silently for her to continue talking. There was no particular rush anyway. Even if the adventurers managed to rush the reception hall, that surprise should be ready for them now. Even if they killed it, he would be able to re-summon it at full power now.

Eventually, Echo seemed to organize her thoughts properly.

"I want to know about... you."

If Smit had had a face, he would have stared at her blankly for a moment.

"Me?" He replied. "What is it about me that you wish to know?"

"Father, I want to learn more about you. I feel it in my soul, you are much more than any of us knows. Pala agrees, and even Arturus has commented on it. We wish to know."

"Even Arturus, huh..." Smit muttered to himself. How interesting. That oversized dog was more talkative than he expected.

Echo looked up expectantly, her eyes looking at the floating dungeon core before her with great expectations. "It doesn't even have to be much, Father! Just a bit is fine."

"Well then... I suppose I could," Smit replied, uncertain as to what would interest Echo so much about his past. Perhaps he could chalk it up to his creations being simply curious about their creators and leave it at that.

Echo's face lit up like he hadn't seen ever before, which made him do a double take. Who knew that she could look so sweet when she smiled like that?

"Well, let's start wi—" Smit began, but he was promptly interrupted by Echo's hurried words.

"Wait, Father, wait!" She said frantically. "I believe Pala and Arturus would like to hear too!"

"Hmm... I suppose it would be easier to say it once rather than three times," Smit said with a nod. "Go ahead and get them."

No more words needed to be said before Echo bolted out the door, making Smit blink. She could have easily tried contacting them mentally, but perhaps she was too excited to think of that. The thought made him chuckle. Imagine that, Echo too excited to think. Well, maybe this was better for him. It would give him a chance to organize his own thoughts too.

Perhaps even make a little song out of it? Smit considered. *It wouldn't be difficult to do it on the run... but perhaps a little structure was in order. Hmmm... Syllables. That would be the guideline.*

Satisfied with his decision, Smit began to form lyrics in his head, trying to sum up his life in a short song, which was a challenge considering his age. Not one to back down from a challenge, Smit decided to tweak his song a bit. Rather than his entire life, perhaps a short summary until his "death" would suffice.

ELLA AND HER team had managed to rush across the entire set of traps, with James taking the lead as he redirected or absorbed the majority of the damage with his great shield. Truthfully, the plan was crude but effective, as it allowed the rest of the party to follow in his wake and only have to worry about delayed traps or traps that had a wider range of effect.

With this tactic, they cut down the amount of time needed to cross the room significantly, making it across in about five minutes, despite the numerous close calls, and a few arrows embedded in the thick leather armor. These arrows however, had not managed to pierce the flesh of the adventurers, thanks to the armor and the defensive buffs, courtesy of Ziggurd.

"Well, it worked," Ella said whilst panting, doubling over slightly as she caught her breath.

"That was bloody terrifying," Adder said as he let himself drop to the floor, resting his back against a wall. "I swear that exploding pillar nearly took off my head with those fragments."

"I would worry more about the ones that spew fire. Leather won't do much against those flames," Mei pitched in, taking a swig from her water skin.

"Thankfully our—" Ziggurd began to speak, but was interrupted by a humming sound that resonated through the entire dungeon, yet it was little more than a whisper.

"Do you think it's...?" Adder asked, not even finishing his sentence. Fortunately, he didn't need to, for everyone understood what he meant.

"I think so," Mei said in a hushed tone.

"We better move," Ella said sharply. "We have no idea if its songs have an effect on the dungeon or the monsters. I don't want to be caught flat footed by a mob of kobolds. Let's move."

A dissatisfied groan escaped Adder as he stood up, but no one else complained. They knew she was right of course. A golden rule for dungeon diving was to always be wary of the unknown. And a singing dungeon was *definitely* a huge unknown.

"Ready?" Ella asked a few seconds later, and received confirmation from her team via a general murmur of agreement. "Let's go."

Steeling themselves, the group marched onwards with weapons at the ready. As they approached the exit of the stony hallway, they reached the wide pond room where they remembered facing off the kobolds. Nodding at her team, the entire group leaped into the room, staying just past the entrance, weapons raised and ready.

Instantly a small army of eyes locked onto them. They had run into about thirty kobolds, some of which were clearly warrior variants, and others shamans. Though the numbers of the warriors and shamans were small, only accounting for a third of the total, Azure Arrow knew better than to take it easy on them. With a soft chant, Ziggurd created a platform of earth that rose just a few feet off the ground beneath him and Mei, giving them a superior view of the soon-to-be field of battle. An arrow shot from a bow and blood flourished from the eye of a kobold shaman.

An instant later, chaos ensued as kobolds crashed against the adventurers in a flurry of blows and hisses. In a dance of steel and magic, the two sides collided with fervor. Azure Arrow aggressively tried to mow down the kobolds, attempting to cut the kobolds down before the music could trigger something. The kobolds fought bravely, tenaciously striking back even when an arm was cut off or a knife was impaled in their bellies.

If Ella had been forced to voice her thoughts, she would have admitted that she was disturbed by the kobolds, at least to a degree. Never had she seen a creature willingly lose an arm to stop a hand, nor had she seen a dying creature grab hold of her weapon to slow down her movements after she had stabbed their gut. Nevertheless, she and her team worked their way to victory, hacking, slashing, and piercing through flesh and bone.

Without wolves or Pala, the kobolds were far less of a threat, even despite their numbers. James and Ziggurd were particularly pivotal in the fight. One was like an immovable tower of steel, effortlessly sweeping any who would stand before him with his mighty hammer. The other focused exclusively on erecting barriers around his allies, denying the shaman kobolds the ability to deal too much damage to his allies while his teammates took care of the damage dealing. With Ziggurd effectively shutting down the damage from the shamans, the kobolds lost a significant portion of their firepower, forcing them to rush the adventurers.

But just as the last of the kobolds fell, there came a sound.

Though the sound of rippling water was soft, almost inaudible at first, as small waves started to rise from the pond, it heralded the entrance of a much larger creature. From the center of the pond, a long writhing tentacle-like thing stretched out. Mossy green in color, it looked like a thick pillar made of strange, luscious tangled vines. The pillar seemed to convulse and writhe, unfurling into a dozen tentacle-like appendages. The tentacles swayed back and forth slowly, turning this way and that, as if searching for something.

"What in the *balls* is that?!" Adder exclaimed loudly, staring at the new creature.

Instantly, the tentacles stopped moving and swiveled to point their tips towards him, giving the impression that they "saw" him.

"I don't think it liked that!" Ziggurd stated as he started to ready his magic.

The vines shot towards the adventurers like giant green snakes, barely giving Adder and James time to dodge. Ella ran towards them as more tentacles followed after them and let out a strong shout. Her rapier followed her shout and sliced off one of the tentacles, making the creature recoil from her touch for a moment.

"It's a Drowned Vine!" Mei shouted at her teammates as her eyes widened in surprise. That thing was definitely a lot bigger than it should be. "Don't let it catch you, or it will drag you underwater!"

"How do we—!" Adder screamed at her as he threw himself to the side to avoid a barrage of tentacle strikes, managing to slice the underside of one of those tentacles with his knife. "How do we kill it?!"

"Bleed it!" Mei replied as she prepared another arrow and let it loose at the tentacles. It soared through the air and lodged itself in the main body of the vine, making it tremble slightly before it resumed its attack. "Its sap is particularly combustible!"

"Setting it on fire it is!" Ella shouted back as she moved slightly to the side as a tentacle shot past her, cutting itself open along her extended blade. "James, back up and protect Ziggurd and Mei! Your hammer is useless here!"

No sooner had she shouted her commands, the stump of the tentacle she had just cut swung at her from below, smacking her head to the side. She staggered back, and swung again at the tentacle even as she tried to regain her balance, even as a second vine shot towards her leg, successfully grabbing her ankle despite her attempt to dodge it. Yelping, she was yanked to the side by the vine around her foot, and was only rescued by a timely knife from Adder that sliced through half of the vine, allowing her to tear her foot free as the sap splattered everywhere. Not being able to spare the time to look at her teammate, Ella barked at him loudly again. "Move, James!"

Grunting, James beat a hasty retreat with his heavy metal armor back towards Mei and Ziggurd. He understood that he was currently not equipped appropriately to fight an enemy such as this, especially when he was currently the slowest out of the team, thanks to his heavy equipment. The best he could do was provide some protection for the back line and stay out of the way of Adder and Ella. As if the plant monster could sense their intentions, it shot its vines towards James with a vengeance, trying to get a hold on him.

"It's sensitive to sound too!" Mei added quickly, but it was too late. The loud stomps from running and the clanging of the metal armor had drawn the attention of the creature. Ten tentacles shot towards James, snaking through empty air, attracted to him like iron to a magnet.

"Say that earlier!" Adder shouted back at her as he leapt aside as a particularly thick mass of vines swung down at him like a club. He would have continued to complain and shout, but unfortunately the vine had more than enough appendages to spare, some of which were attracted to his loud voice. They launched themselves at his body like whips, and unfortunately for him, his knives couldn't defend him from all of them. Two tentacle-like vines smashed into his gut, knocking him back.

Meantime, James was still trying to get to his position, unable to spare a moment to go help Ella or Adder with those tentacles chasing after him. In a split second of inspiration, James threw his shield and hammer off to the side, letting them clatter noisily on the hard ground. Several tentacles peeled off from the main group, wrapping themselves around the metallic objects and dragging them towards the pond.

The two thickest tentacles still followed him without veering off, hell bent on grabbing the large man. A tentacle wrapped around one of his arms, pulling back with force, slowing him down. A second one latched onto him at the waist, effectively stopping the giant of a man. Unlike Adder and Ella, who had been prepared to cut and avoid the tentacles, James didn't have the option to cut them down. At this time, James was painfully aware that the moment more tentacles latched onto him, it would only be a matter of time before he was the first victim to drown.

"Get. It. Off." James growled between clenched teeth as he strained to move forward, the muscles across his entire body bulging and straining to fight the powerful tentacles that threatened to drag him down to the depths of the pond. Even the veins on his neck seemed to throb under the exertion of the force he had to apply to keep himself from being dragged away.

"Hold on!" Mei shouted from a small distance away, still standing on her platform with Ziggurd. She loaded two arrows on her bow at once, and let them fly at the tentacles, piercing both. She did this twice more in quick succession, causing the tentacles to quiver and writhe, but they refused to let James go. If anything, they seemed to pull harder as they started to actually drag him back slowly now.

"Zig!" Ella shouted as she rushed towards James. "Ready up a fire spell! You can't miss! Adder and I will try to give you the best shot! Adder, use everything you got! Bleed it!"

Adder groaned as he heard Ella's words, but did not argue. Or rather he didn't have time for that as he rolled out of the way of another vine trying to snatch him up. Deciding to trust Ella, Adder ignored the painful sensation in his belly as he rushed in. Loosening up his knives, he breathed in as he started to throw at the enemy every last throwing knife he had available, slicing into every tentacle that stretched out towards his team mates. He did not bother to be silent at all as he tried to draw the attention of the vine. "Over here, you oversized octopus plant! Come here!"

For her part, Ella didn't wait for confirmation from Ziggurd and instead focused on gathering her spirit and focus for a special attack. She concentrated heavily, and the edge of her sword seemed to glow slightly, a silver streak of light as thin as a wire where her qi gathered. With a heave, she wound up a slash, her hands high over her head. A powerful chop sliced through the air and the tentacles were cut off cleanly, letting James collapse forward at the sudden release. The tentacles writhed in pain and retracted towards the main body, oozing their thick sap from the punctures and cuts it received.

"Ella! Some help here!" Adder shouted as he jumped and dodged like a dancer. He had clearly gotten the attention of the vine, and now more than a dozen vines shot at him from multiple angles. He was only managing to dodge thanks to Mei, whose arrows were slowing the tentacles down. "I can't hold them back much longer!

Ella ran to his aid, leaving James to go protect Mei and Ziggurd so that she could help Adder. She had seen Ziggurd's focused face for a moment, his brow starting to give off a wet shine as sweat started to come from the pores of his face. Satisfied, she leapt into the fray, and together with Adder, cut and sliced as much as they could, spilling the sap of the plant. Within minutes, they were exhausted, but by then the plant had been riddled with wounds and yet it stood strong.

A bead of sweat spilled into Adder's eye, making him flinch and close his eyes for a second, and next thing he knew, a vine had taken hold of his wrist, and yanked him painfully up in the air. Yelping, He tried to stab the tentacle with his knife, but the stubborn plant was clearly agitated, swinging him around dangerously and denying him the chance to land a good hit.

"Take aim Ziggurd!" Ella shouted as she jumped closer to Adder, and threw her short sword with every ounce of her strength towards the tentacle. The sword spun, and cut through the tentacle. Adder felt weightless all of sudden, and from below him he felt a pair of strong, but rather thin, arms catch him. Ella had launched herself to catch him. They tumbled to the ground together, scraped, dirty, bruised, but safe.

"Now!" Ella shouted as she rolled forward, away from the tentacles with Adder.

"[Fireball]!" Ziggurd shouted, finally releasing the spell he had so carefully aimed at the most damaged area of the Drowned Vine. A ball of fire the size of a human head launched itself from his staff towards the wounded mass of tentacles from the creature, which were covered in oily sap. The flames struck and the mass of tentacles caught on fire instantly as an explosion rocked the creature. The air vibrated and hot air struck everyone present, leaving their ears ringing and lungs feeling hot while the creature started writhing in obvious pain. The sap continued to burn at an alarming rate, and the fire spread into it. The creature thrashed about for a minute, wildly shuddering and swinging at empty air as it burned from the inside out. After a minute, it trembled and collapsed into the water with a loud splash.

That, however, was not the end of the effects of the explosion. Burning bits of the plant scattered, and lit on fire a few small puddles of the sap around the room. Unfortunately, Adder, who still had the severed ends of the tentacle-like vines around his body, was also hit by the fiery residue. The tentacles lit up as if they had been waiting to set themselves on fire, becoming engulfed in flames in seconds. Screaming in shock and horror, Adder scrambled on the ground wildly as the fire started to burn his outfit and sear his flesh.

"Adder!" Ella screamed, completely taken by surprise by the sudden turn of events. Ziggurd instantly tried to gather his mana again, but the hot air had dried his throat, which along with the exhaustion of using a fire spell that had drained him of most of his reserves of mana, made him unable to even start casting his magic at the moment. Panicking, Adder's eyes caught sight of the pond, and he launched himself into the water without a second thought.

As he sank into the clear pond water, steam was released from his body as the flames died out, and the cool water soothed him as he finally felt the pain start to subside. Only then did he open his eyes, and thus beheld the full size of the burnt vine. It was a mass of blackened greenery, coiled up and rooted to the floor of the pond. And not far from it, what seemed to be a treasure chest, ready for the taking.

Surprised, Adder released a breath that he had not realized he had held in. His air escaped, and he quickly scrambled up to the surface. Finding purchase, he stood out of the edge of the pond and breathed in relief. "I hate that plant," he finally said after taking a handful of deep breaths. "I hope that there is a hell for plants, because it definitely deserves to live there."

Everyone was too tired to do anything else but to exhale a sigh of relief. It was a terrifying moment for them, considering that just a split second before Adder had been set on fire, they had thought themselves victorious. They had been lucky to not have been lit on fire like Adder had, in truth.

"That..." Adder said after a moment of silence, watching the blackened tentacles below the water cautiously. "Was terrifying. You never said anything about the sap being explosive too, Mei."

"It shouldn't be." She sighed as she sat down heavily against a wall. "That thing was just... not normal. It was very aggressive too."

"Tell me about it," Adder replied as he collapsed on the ground, looking over his dirtied body. "That thing's grip is no joke. It hit like a truck."

"You weren't the one it got," James grumbled as he rubbed his arm. He was quite thankful for his armor, even if it had made a lot of noise. If he hadn't been wearing it, he might have had his ribs cracked by those tentacles.

"That's what you get for being loud," Adder chuckled, earning him a dirty look from James. "Besides, you didn't get set on fire."

"And you should learn to keep your trap shut in front of noise-detecting plants," James retorted.

"Enough of that," Ella intervened. "We had no way of knowing this was going to be here. It's clearly the new boss of this floor. Come, let's retrieve your weapons, James. We can decide what to do after that."

"Oh right." Adder said as he recalled what he had just seen. "There is a chest in the pond too. The Drowned Vine must have been guarding it."

Blinking in surprise, the rest of his team turned to look at him. Shrugging, he nodded his head towards the pond. "No idea what's inside it though. I didn't exactly have time to check," he added.

"A chest?" Ella asked in disbelief as James found and retrieved his hammer. "James, come here, help Adder pull this out."

Excitement filled the adventurers, and they eagerly rushed towards Adder. But then the humming began again, causing the adventurers to freeze. This time, it wasn't just humming. This time there was a voice in the air. An old, male voice that seemed to have a certain aura of... *something*. Something intangible that could not be ignored.

> *I walked the depths of the greatest mountains*
> *And dug their hearts from their core*
> *For my forge to create molten fountains*
> *I bled their veins for their ore*
> *I forged the greatest swords, axes known*
> *Wrapped their hilts in fire and gold*
> *I carved the greatest bows from dragon bone*
> *Imbued with thunder and cold*
> *Kings for my creations would swiftly kill*
> *Seeking greatness for their own*
> *Their praises and greed the most bitter pill*
> *Vexed, I left the kings for stone*
> *I traveled the world and found a new home*
> *A place to craft and create*
> *Away from the lands where mere mortals roam*
> *Away from kings and their fate*
> *Decades streaked past me like birds in flight*
> *And Death tore my soul from its host*
> *I was just a shadow cast in twilight*
> *Where life was only a ghost*

The song ended gently, with a tone that was neither sad nor desperate, just peaceful in its own haunting way. But somehow, it held the promise that this was not the end of it all. It took them a moment to digest these... lyrics that they had not expected to hear, but in the end, someone broke the silence.

"Forget the giant killer weed," Adder exclaimed. "The hell was *that*?!"

No one offered an answer. They could not even begin to fathom what this could have meant.

Not yet.

Status

Species: True Dungeon
Rank: 2
Name: Smit
Age: 3 months
Mana: 89,336
Anima: 504
Mana Reg.: 861 MP/h
Anima Reg.: 19.27 AP/day
Floors: 5
Inhabitants: 81 Species

Titles: Creator of Dungeon Laws; Creator; Guide of the Bloody Evolution; Legendary Craftsman; Master of Concentration; Reincarnated One.

Abilities: Absorb matter; Alter environment; Bestow knowledge; Break down components; Craftsmanship; Creation; Digging; Destroy creation; Dungeon Laws; Enhancement; Equivalent exchange; Ether manipulation; Evolution; Interdimensional Storage; Life bestowal; Life-energy harnessing; Mana absorption; Masterful mana manipulation; Modification of creations; Monster Link; Telepathy; Trap building; Transfer dungeon.

Resistances: Magic (general); Mind control

<<<>>>

THE END
Dungeon Heart: The Singing Mountain

DAVID SANCHEZ-PONTON

DUNGEON

HALLS OF STONE

HEART

THE ADVENTURE CONTINUES...

...in *Dungeon Heart: Halls of Stone*.

Adventurers are coming, and they will do anything to steal the dungeon's power...

Since awakening to his new life, Smit has hardly had a moment of rest. Goblins, ogres, and adventurers all seem to be attracted to him like flies to honey. Smit and his monstrous children only wanted to live out their days in peace, but now that his existence has been revealed to humanity, all eyes have fallen on the Dungeon of Origins.

Every noble in the kingdom has hired a team of adventurers to secure Smit's core, guaranteeing both a victory against their political rivals and their rule over him. This time, he cannot run away from the encroaching greedy and power-hungry nobles and ambitious men – his new family depends on him. Time is running out to save his dungeon. Can Smit grow his power fast enough, or will he and his children be enslaved forever?

CHARACTER LIST

Dungeon

Smit: The main character, the Dungeon Heart

Echo: Smit's first creation. Originally a dungeon core who lost to Smit's soul in a battle of dominance and became wholly subservient to him. She currently has been bound to the form of a golem.

Pala: The second named creation after Echo. Pala is the kobold chief, leading the rest of the kobolds of Smit's dungeon. Currently the most capable of Smit's creations when it comes to defending the dungeon, capable of going toe to toe with a high C rank adventurer.

Adventurers: Members of Azure Arrow

Ella Graz: Leader of the party, C+ rank adventurer. Ella is a strict woman with a low tolerance for nonsense. Her weapon of choice is the rapier, and she typically uses a short sword or long knife as a side arm. Though her red hair, green eyes, and rather slim appearance are attractive, her technique is topnotch amongst her peers of the same rank.

James Rhine: Party tank and defender, C+ rank adventurer. James is a giant of a man compared to most other humans, standing at 210 cm, which combined with his muscular body make him an imposing figure. He is rather calm but his strength is by far the greatest in the team. His preferred weapons are his war hammer and his tower shield, and he can be found wearing his full plate armor.

Mei Blatt: Ranger and sniper, C+ rank adventurer. Mei is a short and adorable half-elf that is quick and silent. Her detection skills are the result of hard work along with her half-elf heritage, which allows her to have a heightened awareness of her environment. Her preferred weapons are the bow and arrow, though she always keeps a hunting knife handy.

Adder Ru: Rogue, C+ rank adventurer. Adder is sarcastic and at times obnoxious, but the dexterity that he displays with his knives makes him one of the most versatile members of the team, allowing him to attack at short or mid-range with accuracy, or to hold his own at close quarters. He is not the most tactful fellow around, but his ability to discern traps and disarm them is well worth a bit of rudeness.

Ziggurd Am'id: Healer and magic user, C+ rank adventurer. Ziggurd is a polite and disciplined fellow that specializes in the use of light magic and water magic. He has large reserves of mana even amongst other C+ ranked adventurers, though his spells sometimes require longer chants to be carried out. He can often be found carrying a staff to help direct his magic.

Miscellaneous

Alester: Right hand to the king, acting as his representative or advisor depending on the occasion. He is on friendly terms with both king Vas and Ikfes. He is an intellectual man with a love for art.

Badack: Leader of a gang of highwaymen and thugs. He and his party became the first sentient victims of Smit's dungeon.

Princess Dianna Crown: The eldest daughter of King Vas and queen Shana. A genius in the art of the sword, Dianna takes after her father with her unruly red hair and toned body. A beauty in her own right, with long legs and athletic figure, she has captured the hearts of many men without even intending to. She has honed her skills with the sword to an unbelievable extent for a mere 18-year-old youth, giving rise to her nickname the Red Lioness.

Princess Emma Crown: Youngest daughter of King Vas and Queen Shana. A prodigy in magic, she was blessed from birth with talent in magic, especially fire and earth magics. Despite being only 16 years old, her beauty is considerable, taking after her mother with her deep black hair, and her thin but attractive figure, she has been nicknamed the Fairy of the Kingdom.

Gat: Talented hunter of the Nam village. Despite being rather young, barely eighteen years of age, he has a talent for hunting and tracking. He was the one to alert the village of the presence of Smit.

Ikfes Massan: Guild master of the kingdom. Previously an S rank adventurer. Friend with Alester and king Vas.

Queen Shana Crown: The wise and beautiful wife of King Vas. She is an enchantress and a scholar, with a sharp and inquisitive mind. Her skin is a healthy bronze color, her curly black hair is long enough to reach her waist, and her face seems to be almost elfish. She is highly dedicated to her husband and children, and is always there to guide and support them.

King Vas Crown: Also known as the "Red Lion" of duels. He is a well-known duelist of high skill, and a good commander. His broad, strong frame and strong facial features give him a fearsome yet dignified appearance. He is a passionate man with a high sense of duty.

BOOKS AND REVIEWS

If you loved *Dungeon Heart: The Singing Mountain* and would like stay in the loop about the latest book releases, deals, and giveaways, be sure to subscribe to the Shadow Alley Press Mailing List.

www.ShadowAlleyPress.com

Sign up now and get a free copy of our bestselling anthology, Viridian Gate Online: Side Quests! Your email address will never be shared and you can unsubscribe at any time.

Word-of-mouth and book reviews are beyond helpful for the success of any writer, so please consider leaving a rating or a short, honest review on Amazon—just a couple of lines about your overall reading experience. Thank you in advance!

You can also connect with us on our Facebook Page where we do even more giveaways: facebook.com/shadowalleypress

BOOKS BY SHADOW ALLEY PRESS

Shadow Alley Press

ENTER THE SHADOW ALLEY LIBRARY to take a peek at all of our amazing Gamelit, Fantasy, and Science Fiction books! Viridian Gate Online, Rogue Dungeon, Snake's Life, Dungeon Heart, Path of the Thunderbird, School of Swords and Serpents, the FiveFold Universe, and so many more... Your next favorite book is waiting for you inside!

ACKNOWLEDGMENTS

I would like to thank my family and friends, who supported my hobby of writing that led to this book. I would also like to thank my fans from Royal Road who encouraged me to keep writing, and put up with endless spelling errors on my part. In particular, I would like to thank Anne van Dalfsen, who stuck with me through months of writing in Royal Road, and helped edit and digitalize the initial drafts for some of my work. I also cannot forget Shan, who put up with endless bursts of random ideas and discussions about my book, and also helped inspire some of the characters.

I'd also like to thank Brian Oles, who scouted me and introduced me to Shadow Alley, and Jake Goodrich, who helped me manage my story all the way. Without these two, this book may never have been published. Last but not least, thank you to Shadow Alley Press, as they are an amazing team that helped in a hundred different ways. Thank you all for your help. This was only possible thanks to you.

ABOUT THE AUTHOR

David Sanchez-Ponton is a geologist, hydrologist, and author who resides in Canada. A man of many hobbies and a master of none, David has been a long-time fan of fantasy, science fiction, cultivation, and rebirth stories. After earning his Master's degree in hydrology in the Netherlands during the 2020 pandemic, he teamed up with Shadow Alley Press to release his first book, *Dungeon Heart: The Singing Mountain*. The influence of hundreds of different stories and a thousand chaotic thoughts can be felt in his writing, blended together in that tortuous maze of insanity that he calls a brain, to produce surprisingly coherent stories.

Lightning Source UK Ltd.
Milton Keynes UK
UKHW012121070223
416656UK00008B/135